RISE

MICHAEL THE KORYTA

DARK

HODDER &
STOUGHTON

First published in Great Britain in 2016 by Hodder & Stoughton
An Hachette UK company

1

Copyright © Michael Koryta 2016

A CIP catalogue record for this title is available from the British Library

Hardback ISBN 978 1 473 61457 4
Trade Paperback ISBN 978 1 473 61458 1
Ebook ISBN 978 1 473 61456 7

Printed and bound by CPI Group (UK) Ltd, Croydon, CR0 4YY

Hodder & Stoughton policy is to use papers that are natural, renewable and recyclable products and made from wood grown in sustainable forests. The logging and manufacturing processes are expected to conform to the environmental regulations of the country of origin.

Hodder & Stoughton Ltd
Carmelite House
50 Victoria Embankment
London EC4Y 0DZ

www.hodder.co.uk

RISE
THE
DARK

For Michael and Rita Hefron, who introduced me to Montana and always encouraged my writing, and for my father, who kept the lights on, literally and figuratively. Sorry about this one, Dad.

Our virtues and our failings are inseparable, like force and matter. When they separate, man is no more.

—Nikola Tesla

The mind of every assassin runs on a narrow-gauge track. But there are no loners. No man lives in a void. His every act is conditioned by his time and his society.

—William Manchester,
The Death of a President

Part One

ECHOES

I

The snow had been falling for three days above six thousand feet, but it had been gentle and the lines stayed up. At this point in the season, after a long Montana winter that showed no signs of breaking, Sabrina Baldwin considered that a gift.

Then, on the fourth day, the wind rose.

And the lights blinked.

They were both awake, listening to that howling, shrieking wind. When the omnipresent hum of electrical appliances in the house vanished and the glow of the alarm clock went with it only to return a few seconds later, they both said, "One," in unison, and laughed.

It was a lesson she'd learned in their first home in Billings, watching the lights take two hard blinks during a storm, Jay explaining that the system would respond to trouble by opening and closing circuits, automatically testing the significance of the fault before shutting things down altogether. You'd get maybe one blink, maybe two, but never three. Not on that system, at least.

In their new home in Red Lodge, the glow and hum of an electrified existence went off once more, then came back on.

"Two," they said.

Everything was as it should be—the alarm clock blinked, waiting to be reset, but the power stayed on and the furnace came back to life. Sabrina slid her hands over Jay's chest and arms. For five fleeting seconds, it seemed the system had healed itself, that all would be well, and no one would need to travel out into the storm.

Then the electricity went out again, and they both groaned. The problems of the world outside had just moved inside, announcing themselves through the staggered blinks like knocks on the door.

"The phone will ring now," Jay said. "Damn it."

Sabrina shifted her chest onto his and kissed his throat. "Then let's not waste time."

They didn't. The phone rang before they were finished, but they ignored it. She would remember that moment with odd clarity for the rest of her life—the unique silence of the house in the power outage, the cold howling wind working outside, the warmth of her husband's neck as she pressed her face against it, each of them so lost in the other that even the shrill sound of the phone caused no interruption.

The phone rang again when they were done, and he swore under his breath, kissed her, and then slipped out from under the covers, leaving her alone and still breathless in their bed.

A new bed, new sheets, new everything. She was grateful for the simplicity of Jay's scent, the only thing that was not new, not different. They'd moved to Red Lodge only two months ago, and while everyone told her she'd appreciate its beauty, she still found the mountains menacing rather than enticing.

When winter finally yielded to spring, her view of the place would improve. She had to believe that. Right now, all she knew was that they'd managed to move somewhere that made Billings seem like a big city, and that wasn't an easy feat.

She could hear his side of the conversation, providing a strange blend of breaking news and the customary—storms, lines down, substations, circuits. Even the bad pun was familiar: *We sure don't want the hospital to lose patience.*

A joke that he'd told, and his father had told, and his grandfather. It gave her a sense of the situation, though. The outages were bad enough that the hospital was running on backup generators. This meant he'd be gone for a while. In weather like this, the repairs were rarely quick fixes. Not in Montana.

She followed him downstairs and brewed coffee while he explained what was going on, his eyes far away. She knew he was thinking of the map and the grid, trying to orient the issues before he rolled out. One of his greatest concerns lately was that he wasn't familiar enough with the regional grid. In Billings, he'd known every substation, every step-down transformer, probably every insulator.

"It'll be a long day," he said. He pulled on his insulated boots while sitting in the kitchen that still felt foreign enough to Sabrina that she often reached for the wrong drawer or opened the wrong cupboard. It was a lovely home, though, with a gorgeous view of the mountains. Or at least, it would be gorgeous in the summer. The windows that Jay loved so much because they looked out at the breathtaking Beartooth Mountains were facing the wrong direction as far as Sabrina was concerned. The worst of the storms blew down out of those mountains, and here they could see them coming. She wished the kitchen windows faced east, catching the sunrise instead of the oncoming storms.

She was so sick of the storms.

Jay, meanwhile, was looking out the windows right now, and damned if he wasn't smiling. The peaks were invisible, cloaked with low-lying clouds, and the wind rattled a snow-and-ice mixture off the glass.

"Enjoy that snow while you've got it," she said. "This may be the last one of the season."

"Brett told me that last year they closed the pass in mid-June for fourteen inches."

"Tremendous."

She struggled to keep her tone light, to use the good-natured kind of sarcasm, not the biting kind. They'd moved here for her, after all. Had left Billings because Jay was willing to give up the job he loved for her peace of mind. Out there, he'd been a member of a barehanding crew, an elite high-voltage repair team that worked on live lines up in the flash zone, perching like birds on wires pulsing with deadly current. In November, they'd learned just how deadly.

Sabrina had met Jay through her brother, Tim. They'd been coworkers, although that term wasn't strong enough. They were more like Special Ops team members than colleagues. Every call-out was a mission where death waited. The bonds were different in that kind of work, ran deeper, and her always-protective older brother voiced nothing but approval of Jay. She'd met Jay at a barbecue, had their first date a week later, and were married a year after that. Someone put tiny high-voltage poles next to the bride and groom on their wedding cake, and they assumed that was the extent of the prank. It wasn't. The miniature lines actually carried a low-voltage current that Tim energized just as Jay went to cut the cake. Jay had jumped nearly a foot in the air, and the rest of the crew fell to the floor laughing.

For several years, that was how it went. Tim and Jay were closer than most brothers. Then came November. A routine call-out. Tim on the line making a simple repair, confident that it wasn't energized. What he didn't know was that less than a mile away, someone was firing up a massive gas generator, unwilling to wait on the repairs. The generator, improperly installed, a home-wired job, created a back feed. For an instant, as Tim held the wire in his hands, the harmless line went live again.

He'd died at the top of the pole. Jay had climbed up to bring his body down.

Three weeks after the funeral, Jay told Sabrina he was done with the barehanding work. There was a foreman's job open in Red Lodge, and taking it meant he'd stay on the ground, always, and she would never have to think of him climbing a pole again, never have to worry about the job claiming her husband as well as her brother.

"Love you," he said, rising from the table.

She kissed him one last time. "Love you too."

He went into the garage and she heard his truck start and then she pulled open the front door and stood in the howling wind so she could wave good-bye. He tapped the horn twice, the Road Runner good-bye—*beep-beep*—and was gone. She shut the door feeling both annoyed and guilty, as she always did when he went out in weather like this, torn between the fear of what waited out there for him and the knowledge that she should be proud of the work he did.

She *was* proud too. She really was. This winter had been worse than most, that was all. The pain of losing Tim compounded by the tumult of moving—those things were to blame for her discontent, not Red Lodge. The snow would melt and summer would come. The coffee shop she'd owned in Billings wouldn't have lasted anyhow. The landlord had been ready to sell, Sabrina hadn't found a good replacement location, and so summer in Billings had loomed ominously. Now summer was promising; she'd already found good real estate for a new location, and she had the peace of knowing that, whatever happened out there today, her husband would stay on the ground.

Red Lodge was a fresh start.

He called the first time at noon. She was outside shoveling the walk, out of breath when she answered.

"We lost a sixty-nine kV line just off the highway," he reported.

That translated to 69 kilovolts, which meant 69,000 volts. A standard home ran on 110 or 220 volts.

"The work is going fast so far, though, and the forecasts are good," Jay said.

She'd seen that. An Alberta clipper was blowing down out of Canada, drying out the air. The snow had tapered off and the roads were passable. At least up to Red Lodge, they were passable. Beyond, as the highway snaked toward eleven thousand feet, the pass had been closed for six months and would be for another two.

"Maybe there's a chance of a normal dinner," she said.

"Maybe." His voice held optimism.

A few hours later, it didn't.

The call at five was shorter than the first, and he was distressed.

"Definitely going to be a late one."

"Really?" She was surprised, because the storm had died off around one, and their power was back on.

"Never seen anything like it. Somebody's cutting trees so they fall into the lines. We're getting faults farther and farther up into the mountains, and they're *cut* trees, every time. Chain saws and some asshole on a snowmobile having himself a hell of a time, dropping trees onto the lines, keeping just out in front of us like some kid playing tag. We put one up, he cuts one down."

"Are the police there?"

"Haven't seen them yet. I'd tell you I'm almost done, but right now, I don't have any idea. They're fresh cuts; I could still see the sawdust in the snow on the last one. It's the damnedest thing…they've got a pattern, pulling us farther out of town. Whoever's doing it is probably watching me send my crew up on the poles and having a laugh."

Fatigue was often a factor in deaths on the lines, and the idea of Jay's team, men like her brother, climbing pole after pole in a snow-storm, gradually wearing down, all because of someone's vandalism was infuriating.

"I've got to go," he said. "Hopefully this asshole's chain saw is about out of gas. Actually, I hope his snowmobile is. I'd like to meet this guy."

She wished him luck, hung up, and, sweaty and tired, went upstairs to take a shower. At the top of the steps, she turned and looked back at the mountains, wondering where in them he was. They were already dark.

What's the point? she thought. Mindless behavior, drunk boys with powerful toys. But dangerous.

She wanted it to be mindless, at least. But as the water heated up and the room filled with steam and she stepped into the shower, she found that Jay's words were unsettling her more than the actual facts. It was how he'd described the fallen trees as *pulling us farther out of town.*

When she came out of the bathroom wearing nothing but a nightgown, a cloud of steam traveling through the door with her, she understood in an immediate, primal way exactly why it had disturbed her.

There was a man sitting on her bed wearing snowmobile clothes, goggles hanging around his neck and a pistol in his hand.

Sabrina didn't scream, just reacted without thinking, recognition at warp speed—*Threat is in the bedroom, phone is in the bedroom, escape is through the bedroom, so retreat is the only option*—and she stumbled backward and slid the door shut. It was a pocket door, most of the interior doors in their new home were, and when they'd viewed the house she'd told the real estate agent how much she liked them. Now she hated them, because the pocket door had no real lock, just a flimsy latch that her frantic hands couldn't maneuver, and she could hear the sound of the man leaving the bed and approaching. She barely got her hands out of the way before he kicked the door, and the lock turned into a twisted shard of metal as the door blew off its track and the frame splintered. A large, gloved hand reached in and grasped the edge of the door and shoved it backward and now Sabrina was out of options. Everything that could save her was beyond him, and she wouldn't get beyond him. He was so large that he filled the door frame, and even though his clothing was unusually bulky, she could tell that he was massive beneath it. He had dark, emotionless eyes and his hair was shaved down to stubble against his thick skull.

"Who are you?" she said. It was the only question that mattered to her in that moment. His identity, not his intention, because the gun announced his intention.

"My name is Garland Webb." His voice was deep, and the words came slow and echoed in the tiled room. "I am very tired. I had to make a long journey in a short time for you."

"What do you want?"

"We harnessed air for this," he said, as if that answered her question. "That's all we need. People think they need so much more. People are wrong."

Then he lifted the pistol and shot her.

There was a soft pop and hiss and then a stab of pain in her stomach. She screamed, finally, screamed high and loud and long and he let her do it, never moving from the doorway. He just lowered the pistol and watched with a half smile as she fell back against the wall, and her hands moved to her stomach, searching for the wound, the source of the pain. Her fingers brushed something strange, soft and almost friendly to the touch, and she looked down and saw the arrow sticking out of her belly just below her ribs. No, not an arrow. Too small. It had a metal shaft and a plastic tube that faded to small, angled pieces of soft, plastic-like feathers. A dart.

She felt warmth unfolding through her body and thought, *Something was in that and now it's in me, oh my God, what was in there?* and she tried to pull it free from her stomach. It didn't come loose, just stretched her skin and increased the pain and drew the first visible blood. The thin blue fabric of her nightgown kept her from seeing the point of the dart clearly, but she could feel what it was—there was a barb on the end, just like a fishhook, something to anchor it in her flesh.

"Air," the big man with the dead eyes said again, sounding immensely pleased, and the unfolding warmth within Sabrina reached her brain, and her vision swam and there was a buzzing crescendo in her ears like the inside of a hornet's nest. She looked up from the dart, trying to find the man, trying to ask why.

She slid down the wall and fell against the toilet, unconscious, with the question still on her lips.

2

The man who'd been accused of murdering Markus Novak's wife was in prison for the sexual assault of another woman when a talented young public defender won his freedom by pointing out a series of legal errors that had robbed Garland Webb of his right to a fair trial.

Mark wasn't present for the judge's ruling. He was on a fishing charter out of Key West with his mentor and former employer, Jeff London. The fishing trip was London's idea. Whatever happened in the appeal, he said, did not affect the case Mark was trying to build. Whether Garland Webb was in prison or out of prison, he still hadn't been convicted of Lauren's murder. That was the next step.

It all made good sense, but Mark knew the real reason that he'd been invited out on a boat in the Gulf of Mexico while Garland Webb learned his fate: He'd had a few too many conversations with Jeff on the topic and made a few too many promises. The promises involved bullets in Garland's head, and Jeff believed them.

Upon winning appeal and earning his release, Garland Webb met one last time with his attorney, a young gun named John Graham who considered the case his most significant victory to date. The prosecutor had made a series of egregious errors en route to conviction, so Graham had always felt good about his legal argument, but you never could be sure of a win when the original conviction involved a heinous crime. At that point you needed more than the law on your side, you needed to be able to *sell* it, and John Graham had put all of his considerable powers of persuasion into the case. He also felt good about the appellate victory for the simple reason that it was *right*. His client had not been granted a fair trial, and John Graham believed deeply in the purity of the process.

All the same...

He was troubled by Garland Webb.

In their final meeting, John offered his best attempt at a warm smile and extended his hand to his client. "Sometimes, the system works," he said. "How does it feel to be a free man, Garland?"

Webb regarded him with eyes so expressionless they seemed opaque. He was six four and weighed 230 pounds, and when he accepted the handshake, John felt a sick chill at the power in his grip.

"I guess you're not the celebrating sort," he said, because Garland still hadn't uttered a word. "Do you have everything you need? There's a release-assistance program that will—"

"I have everything I need."

"All right. I'm sure it will be a relief to walk out of here."

"Just back to business," Garland Webb said.

"What's that?"

"It's time for me to get back to business. No more diversions."

"Right," John said, though he had no idea what Webb meant, and he was uncomfortable with what he *might* mean.

Webb fixed the flat-eyed stare on him and said, "I have a purpose, understand? This detour was unfortunate, but it did not remove my purpose."

"Right," John repeated. "I'm just supposed to let you know that if you need assistance finding a job or locating a—"

"I'm going back to the same job," Webb said.

John fell silent. He'd spent several months on this case and he knew damn well that Garland Webb had been unemployed at the time of his arrest.

"Where will you be working?" he asked, and Garland Webb smiled. It was little more than a twitch of the lip, but it was more emotion than he'd displayed when the judge had announced the verdict in his favor.

"I've got opportunities," he said. "Don't you worry about that."

"Great," John said, and suddenly he was eager to get out of the room and away from this man. "Stay out of trouble, Garland."

"You too, John."

John Graham left before Garland did, although he'd initially intended to stay with him through the process all the way up to the point of escorting him out of the prison. That no longer felt right. In fact, winning the freedom of Garland Webb suddenly didn't feel like much of a victory at all.

On the day Webb collected his belongings and walked to a bus station, before he left, he bribed a guard to send a message to another inmate at Coleman. The message got through, and the inmate requested a phone call. Seven miles off the southernmost shore of the United States, Markus Novak's cell rang.

They'd been having a good day of it, but in the afternoon the fishing had slowed; the Gulf of Mexico began churning with high swells, and Jeff London turned a shade of green that matched the water.

"Bad sandwich," he said, and Mark smiled and nodded.

"Bad sandwich, eh?"

"I don't get seasick."

"Of course not."

When Jeff put his head in his hands, Mark laughed and set his rod down and moved to the bow, where he stood and stared at the horizon line, the endless expanse of water broken only by whitecapped waves. All of his memories of the sea were good, because all of them involved Lauren. Sometimes, though, when the light and the wind were right, the sea reminded him of other endless places. Expansive plains of the West; windblown wheat instead of water; storm-blasted buttes.

Not so many of those memories were good.

He'd been watching the water for a while when he heard the ring, a soft chime, and the charter captain, who was lounging with his feet up and a cigar in his mouth, said, "That's yours, bud."

Mark found the phone in his jacket pocket, and he remained relaxed, warm and comfortable and with his mind on this boat and this day, until he saw the caller ID: COLEMAN CORRECTIONAL.

For an instant he just stared, but then he realized he was about to lose the call to voice mail, so he hit Accept and put the phone to his ear.

He knew the voice on the other end. It was a man he'd spoken to many times, a snitch who'd contacted Mark for legal help, which Mark provided in exchange for a tip on who killed his wife. The police didn't believe the story; the snitch held to it.

"He sent me a note, Novak. For you. For both of us. Here's what it says: 'Please tell Mr. Novak that his efforts were a disappointment, and every threat was only so much wasted breath. I'd hoped for more. Let him know that I'll think of him outside this prison just as I thought of him inside it, and, more important, that I'll think of her. The way she felt at the end. I'll treasure that moment. It's a shame he wasn't there for it. She was so beautiful at the end.'"

The man on the phone had once beaten someone to death with an aluminum baseball bat, but his voice wavered as he read the last words. When he was done, he waited, and Mark didn't speak. The silence built as the boat rose and fell on the waves, and finally the other man said, "I thought you'd want to know."

"Yes," Mark said. "I want to know. It is important that I know." His voice was hollow, and Jeff London lifted his head with a concerned expression. "Is that all he had to say?"

"That's all. He's made some threats to me, you know that, but ain't shit happened, so maybe he's all talk. Maybe about...about this too, you know? Just one of them that likes to claim shit to make themselves feel hard. I've known them before."

"You told me you didn't think he was that kind," Mark said. "You said you knew better. You said he was telling the truth."

A pause; then: "I remember what I said."

"Anything changed your opinion?"

"No."

"All right. Thanks for the call. I'll send money to your commissary account."

"Don't need to, not for this. I just thought…well, you needed to hear it."

"I'll send money," Mark repeated, and then he hung up. Jeff was staring at him, and the charter captain was making a show of working with his tackle, his back to them.

"That was about Webb?" Jeff said.

Mark nodded. He found the horizon line again but couldn't focus on it.

"He's taunting me. He killed her, he knows that I know it, and he's a free man. He wanted to let me know that he'll be thinking of me, and her. From outside of a cell now."

"It's a dumb play. He'll go back to prison."

"Yeah?" Mark turned to him. "Where is he?"

"Don't let this take you back to the dark side, brother. You've got to build a case, and you've got to—"

"Someone has to settle the score for her."

Jeff's face darkened. "There are lots of tombstones standing over men who made proclamations like that."

"I don't want a tombstone. When I'm gone, you take the ashes wherever you'd like. Just make sure there's a strong wind blowing. I want to have a chance to travel."

"That's a bad joke."

"It's not a joke at all," Mark said. "I hope you remember the request should the need ever arise." He looked at the charter captain. "You mind bringing us in a couple hours early?"

The captain looked from Mark to Jeff and shook his head when no objection was raised. "It's your nickel, bud."

"Thanks," Mark said. "We had a good run this morning. Sorry to cut it short. That's just how it goes sometimes."

Jeff's voice was soft and sad when he said, "He won't be in Cassadaga, Markus. You know that. He won't go back there."

"He could."

Jeff shook his head. "You're just feeding the darkness if you do that. Think about Lauren. What she believed, what she worked for! What she would want."

"You're asking me to consider what she would have wanted in her life. She's dead, Jeff. Who's to say what she wants now? In those last seconds of her life, maybe she formed some different opinions."

3

The sun had barely been up when Jay left on the first call-out, but it had set and risen again by the time he made it home and found a stranger at his kitchen table.

Jay was so exhausted, so bone-tired, and the man was so relaxed, sitting with one leg crossed over the other and a polite smile, that Jay felt no threat. Just surprise, and only a modicum of that. He was confused by the stranger's presence but unbothered by it because of the way he sat so calmly, with a cup of coffee, still steaming, close at hand. It was one of Jay's mugs, and his perception was that his wife must have brewed the coffee. Everything that Jay didn't understand about his visitor, Sabrina must know.

"How's it going?" Jay said to the stranger as he shed his jacket and set to work unlacing his boots.

"Long day?" the stranger asked, genial and compassionate. He was a lean man with a narrow, pale face and long hair tied back in a tight topknot against his skull.

"A day so long it started yesterday," Jay said, liking the stranger well enough. He walked past him, out of the kitchen and into the living room, and called for his wife.

"Sabrina isn't home," the stranger said. He took a drink of the coffee. He didn't bother turning to face Jay.

"Pardon?" Jay's next thought was that the man must be a neighbor unknown to him, because Sabrina hadn't gone far—her car was in the garage. Sabrina was the more outgoing of the two of them, and she tended to the neighbors with an interest Jay had never been able to muster. His initial concern in Red Lodge had been getting to know the power grid, not the neighbors.

"She's not in the house, is what I mean," the stranger said.

Jay was standing in the living room, looking back at the man in the kitchen. The stranger set the coffee down, lifted a cell phone that was resting on the table, and beckoned to Jay.

"Come here. I'll show you."

Jay walked up beside him obediently. He wasn't sure if the man had a message on the phone or if he intended to call Sabrina, wasn't sure of anything but that the situation, however odd, was absent of menace.

Then he saw the phone's display.

At first he thought the image on the screen was a still photo. For a few frozen, shocked seconds, he was convinced of it. Then his wife moved, and shackles rattled across her body, and he understood that it was a video.

"She's unhurt, as you see," the stranger said in an unfazed voice. "A bit groggy now, but physically unharmed. She'll remain in that condition as long as you desire. Everything in Sabrina's future belongs to your choices, Mr. Baldwin."

On the screen, Sabrina shifted again. She was wearing a pale blue nightgown that Jay had given her two Christmases ago and there was a handcuff on her wrist that was fastened to long links of a chain that trailed offscreen. Jay was numbly aware of the floor beneath her—unvarnished boards, clean and showing no blood. He was looking for blood already. As Jay stood in his kitchen and watched, Sabrina glanced down at her wrist and cocked her head from side to side, as if she didn't understand the meaning of the handcuff and was trying to make sense of it.

Jay started to shout something then. A question, a threat. Maybe just a scream. He didn't know, exactly, because when he turned from the phone's display and gave the stranger in his house his full attention for the first time, he saw that the man now had a short-barreled revolver in his right hand that was pointing at Jay's belly. The genial expression was gone, and his eyes were empty.

"Her future belongs to your choices," he repeated.

Jay tried to focus on the man in front of him, on the tangible threat, but his mind was still on that image of Sabrina. He stood and trembled in silence, like a frightened dog.

"Let's not waste time," the stranger said. "You have many questions, I know. You'll have answers soon. But I can't give them here. We'll need to relocate. You'll drive. It's not so far. We can talk on the way."

"Why?" Jay said. Just one word, but one that carried the weight of all his terror.

"You've been selected, Mr. Baldwin. Consider it an honor. You're about to be part of something historic."

The stranger held the gun close to Jay's skull as Jay put his boots back on. While his head was bowed, Jay let his eyes drift to the stranger's feet, and he saw something there that bothered him.

He was wearing what looked like everyday construction boots, built for hard work, but they had unusually thick rubber soles, and none of the eyes or grommets were metal. Everything was leather or rubber. It was the kind of boot you wore when you worked around high-voltage equipment and knew that any trace of metal could kill you.

4

On the day he visited Cassadaga to see the place where his wife had died, Mark began by taking the same run she had made on the last morning of her life.

Lauren's route through St. Petersburg's bay front took him down Fifth Avenue and past Straub Park, facing Tampa Bay. There he angled left and ran alongside the seawall as it curved toward the bridge between Old Northeast and Snell Isle. At the bridge he stopped running and then walked back, letting his breathing settle. Once, during an early run here, he'd seen a shadow in the water and loudly announced the presence of a shark. It was actually a dolphin. Lauren, born and bred on the Gulf Coast, a scuba diver from the age most kids learn to ride bikes, laughed so hard that she couldn't breathe. Mark thought of that moment often—Lauren in running shorts and tank top, soaked with sweat, looking fit and impossibly young, doubled over and gasping with laughter she didn't have the air for, her ponytail bobbing as if to count off the wheezes of her silent laughs.

"I know you're from the mountains," she'd said when she could finally speak, "but I have never heard anyone yell 'Shark!' like that in my life. Outside of the movie *Jaws,* that is. It tells me things about you, babe—you see Flipper and you scream 'Shark!' That tells me things."

He told her that he hadn't *screamed* anything, he'd just *announced* what he thought he'd seen. Announced it a little loudly, maybe, for clarity's sake. That only made her laugh harder. She'd ended up on her butt on the sidewalk, arms wrapped around her knees and tears in her eyes, fighting for air.

Following today's run he stopped for a cup of coffee at Kahwa, the little coffee shop on his building's ground floor, then went upstairs, entered his condo, and walked out onto the deck. There he sipped the coffee, shook a single cigarette loose from a pack of American Spirits, and lit it. This was the last part of the routine, and the one he liked least. He had hated his wife's cigarette habit. It was the only consistent fight they ever had—he told her it was selfish to those who loved her because it could take her from them young.

Funny, the things you could be so strident about. So convicted of.

When she died and left a pack behind, he couldn't bring himself to throw them out. He smoked them instead, like a Catholic lighting candles for the dead. Then he bought another pack, continuing the one-a-day ritual. There in the morning on the deck, in the smell of sweat and cigarettes, he could close his eyes and, for an instant, feel as if she were at his side.

Today he stubbed out the cigarette early and headed for the shower. He had a drive to make, and he'd been waiting too long on it already.

Lauren's car had been returned to Mark nine weeks after she was buried. The title was in both of their names, so he was the rightful owner and the police couldn't claim it was a crime scene any longer. No evidence was in the car.

Their condo building in St. Petersburg had been designed to feel spacious despite the constraints of reality, and the garage featured an admirable attempt to fit two cars into a single parking space. Hydraulic lifts hoisted one vehicle in the air so another could be parked below it. A seamless system—provided that you and your spouse worked in strict military shifts or were indifferent to which car you drove. Lauren was not indifferent. She loved the Infiniti, its look, speed, and handling. It was her car. Mark's old Jeep—filled with empty coffee cups and notepads and the gym clothes he inevitably forgot to bring up and put in the laundry—was not an acceptable substitute. When she wanted to go somewhere, she was going to go in her own car.

He parked on the street. Problem solved.

Neither of them ever used the lift, but when the police returned the car to Mark, he put it up there. Lauren's pearl-white Infiniti coupe had been sitting on the top of the lift, untouched, for nearly two years when he turned the key that operated the hydraulics. The system hummed and groaned and then lowered the car slowly, like pall-bearers easing a casket into the ground. The tires were low, and the battery was dead. He used a portable generator to air up the tires, pulled his Jeep in the garage long enough to jump the battery, and then got behind the wheel, closed the door, and waited for the pro-found wash of memories.

He wanted to be able to smell her, feel her, taste her. He had a mil-lion memories of the car, and Lauren was in all of them, and he felt as if the vehicle should have held on to some of her. Instead, all he smelled was warm dust and all he felt was heat blasting from the air vents. It had been a warm day when she'd died but a cold one when he'd driven the car back onto the lift.

After he had listened to the engine purr for a few seconds, he backed out of the garage and drove toward Cassadaga.

Mark had never known anyone who was more emphatically op-posed to capital punishment than his wife. For many years, as they lived and worked together, Mark had shared her beliefs. He preached them, and he practiced them. When Lauren was killed, he continued to do so—publicly.

He wasn't sure exactly when he parted with them in his soul.

Maybe her funeral. Maybe when he saw the crime scene photo-graphs. Maybe the very moment the sheriff's deputy arrived to tell him the news.

It was hard to be sure of a thing like that.

The thing he was sure of now? The game was over. It had ended with Garland Webb's parting words. And it was time to be honest— he'd never really believed in it like Lauren did. He'd wanted to, and maybe even convinced himself that he did, because it was the ideology of the woman he loved. He often assured her of his understanding of the world: No man should kill another, no matter the circumstances, no matter the sins. He'd meant it then, and he thought that was important—he'd meant the words when he'd said them.

Back then, he had a wife he was deeply in love with, a job that fulfilled him, and no reason to wish death on anyone.

Things change.

In the three months that had passed since Mark resigned from Innocence Incorporated, the death penalty–defense firm where he'd worked as an investigator and where Lauren had worked as an attorney, he'd been focused on only two things: regaining his health after injuries he'd suffered during a brutal case in Indiana, and replacing the rumors about Garland Webb with hard evidence.

He'd come along a lot better with the first task than the second. He felt as good physically as he had in a long time. As for Webb's guilt, Mark had succeeded only in producing evidence that he *could* have been in Cassadaga, Florida, on the day that Lauren was killed there.

Evidence of any kind in Lauren's murder had been hard to come by. She'd been working a case that—on the surface—didn't appear to threaten anyone who lived within five hundred miles of Cassadaga, and her final notes supported that. There was no fresh information, no new names, nothing unexplained save for a three-word phrase she'd scrawled in the notebook that she'd left in the passenger seat of her car. Those words, *rise the dark,* had intrigued detectives initially, but nobody, Mark included, had ever been able to make any sense of them. As for Garland Webb, who'd allegedly claimed her killing, all Mark had was possibility. He didn't yet have any proof that Webb had been there when Lauren pulled her car to the side of a lonely country road, stepped out, and began to walk along a trail lined with tall oaks and thick stands of bamboo. She was shot twice in the head sometime after that. The person who found her could say only that the car's hood was still warm. The coroner said that Lauren was too. Dead, but still warm.

Whatever happened, happened fast.

Nobody knew why she'd stepped out of the car. A threat, maybe. Trust, perhaps. That's how close the police were to ascertaining the truth of her murder: somewhere between trust and threat.

The last indisputable fact of Lauren's life was where it had ended.

Mark had stayed away from that place for a long time. Too long.

5

While never allowing himself to see the actual spot, limiting his exposure to her death scene to the study of photographs and maps because he believed to see it would be too powerful, too devastating, Mark felt like he knew it well. Felt like he could give guided tours, in fact, of the strange little town that he'd never seen.

Turn your heads to the right, ladies and gentlemen, and you'll see the Colby Memorial Temple. In New York in 1888, a Spiritualist named George Colby claimed he had been given a directive from a spirit guide named Seneca: Colby was to move south and start his own Spiritualist colony. So it had been decreed. Colby moved.

He settled in Volusia County, Florida. And the colony lasted. More than a hundred years later, the residents of the Cassadaga camp maintain the Spiritualist faith, and most are registered mediums...

There he would begin to struggle, because there he would be confronted with all that he hated about the place. His mother had been a con artist in the West, and pretending to have access to the dead was one of her go-to moves for extra dollars. The idea of an entire group endorsing such behavior, of a town filled with "registered" mediums, seers of the past and future, repulsed him.

He parked in front of the Cassadaga Hotel, a Spanish-looking stone structure where people could make appointments with many of the area's mediums, including the woman who was the last known person to see his wife alive and who had once rented a room to a man named Garland Webb.

The hotel operated as sort of a central dispatch for the mediums. Some worked in the hotel, covering hours in shifts, while others met clients in their homes. The psychic Lauren had come to see was named Dixie Witte, and Lauren had gone to the hotel first, so that was how Mark approached it.

He had a gun on under a light soft-shell jacket. He usually carried a nine-millimeter, but today he had a .38-caliber revolver. That was the caliber of gun that had killed Lauren, and Mark wanted to return the favor accurately. He also had a small digital recorder in one pocket and a tactical flashlight in the other.

Once he was inside the hotel, though, the idea of needing any of these things seemed laughable. It was an open, charming place with a wine bar and a coffee shop. A sign indicated that appointments with mediums could be made inside the gift shop, which was tended by a woman in her fifties dressed in a swirl of loose fabric, everything flowing and brightly patterned and billowing around her. She told him cheerfully that of course she could set up an appointment with Dixie. Bracelets with heavy stones adorned her left wrist; he saw she wore rings on every finger when she dialed the phone. The little gift shop sold the kind of cheap trinkets that did not seem likely to promote anyone's belief in the legitimacy of the camp, making it feel more like a tourist trap than a place of heightened communication. He listened to the woman's side of the conversation, and then she put the phone to her chest and said, "Are there any special issues you'd like to discuss? She'll spend some time channeling the proper energy if she knows what to be open for."

Mark nodded as if that made perfect sense, thought about it for a moment, and then said, "Tenants."

The cheerful woman frowned. "Tenants?"

"Yes. I have some questions about tenants."

"Can you specify an emotional connection you have to this question about tenants?"

"Rage."

Her eyes narrowed and she seemed about to ask him something, but she held off, lifted the phone again, and said, "Mr. Novak has questions about...um, tenants, and he has issues with anger." She listened for a few seconds, then said, "Good," and hung up.

"Dixie will see you this evening at seven."

"That's great."

She took out a map and drew a circle and a square on it. "The square is us, and you're headed to the circle. It's easy to find, but there are two houses on the property. You'll want forty-nine A, not forty-nine B."

Garland Webb had rented 49B once. Fortunately for Garland, Dixie Witte didn't like record-keeping, and she dealt in cash. She'd never been able to recall whether he was present on the day in question. She also hadn't volunteered his existence as a tenant until after the prison snitch turned up with his report.

"I'm sure I'll find the right place," Mark said. "I assume the neighbors all have an uncanny sense of direction."

It was his first slip, the sarcasm bubbling forth already when he'd promised himself to contain it, promised himself that he would take them seriously, as Lauren had. Five minutes in town, and he was losing his footing.

"This is a place of healing, Mr. Novak," the woman said. "It's not the place you think it is, which I can see in your eyes. You have much scorn for us. That's fine, but it won't help you. If you wish to open yourself to possibility here, you'll be rewarded."

"I've seen some of this town's rewards," Mark said.

"If that were true, you wouldn't be a skeptic. But the reading will help, whether you're open or closed to it. A skeptic walks out of a reading with doubt intact, but also with echoes."

"I'll keep that in mind," Mark said, and then he left the gift shop and walked through the hotel lobby and back into the humid day, glad to be out of the place. The breezes were gone and the sky was a flat gray and when a truck passed by, the dust it lifted fell swiftly back to earth.

The woman in the hotel had felt too familiar to him, had stirred old angers. She was the sort who peddled bullshit statements that people could easily mold to fit their own situations. The crime of it, Mark thought, was that those people believed they'd been granted insight, not a fortune cookie. Mark's mother had been good enough at that. Her favorite role was Snow Creek Maiden of the Nez Perce, a white woman passing herself off as an American Indian because so many white people believed that Indians were more spiritually in tune, never sensing the inherent racism there. She would dye her hair and skin and don traditional garb. The tourists would look into her eyes—they were blue but shielded with dark contacts—and nod with amazement because whatever generality she tossed at them connected with something in their pasts. They made the connections themselves, but they credited her for it. And paid for the joke.

It was this experience that had left Mark with scorn for the people who practiced their games in a place like this, and it was that scorn that led his wife to take an assignment that had been headed for his desk and claim it as her own. The interview with Dixie Witte had been Mark's job. Lauren didn't think he'd be able to approach it with sincerity, thought that he was biased against anyone who claimed psychic gifts, and so she'd interceded and come to Cassadaga herself.

Never left.

Thunder, long and loud, chased Mark as he walked away from the hotel and through the camp. The air was thick with humidity and scented with jasmine and honeysuckle. There was only one paved street, the road that ran through the center of the camp, and the rest of the homes were built off narrow lanes of crushed stone and hard-packed earth. The lanes were framed by tall oaks that were cobwebbed with Spanish moss.

It was a strange little place. Some of the homes were neat and well kept, recently restored in a few cases, and others looked like they'd been built by someone using the wrong end of the hammer. Mark walked by a man who was doing clean and jerks with a barbell and a pair of forty-five-pound plates in the middle of his front yard. He was shirtless and had a thick mat of black hair across his chest and stomach, shining with sweat, and he called out the reps in a grunting voice as he powered the weights up. Who needs a gym when you've got a front yard? Or a shirt when you could grow your own? Ten feet to his side, chickens clucked and scratched their way around a coop that had been made out of an old truck's camper shell. The local power-lifter seemed to be of the waste-not, want-not mind-set.

Each street sign included a bold white 911 inside a green circle. Mark had never seen anything like it. The idea probably had something to do with giving emergency services a firm address on roads that had previously been unmarked or unnamed, but the effect was disconcerting, seeming to cry out that a disaster waited down each winding lane.

Mr. Novak? I'm afraid I have some difficult news to share. It's about your wife.

The deputy who'd come for him that night, who'd found Mark waiting at the Siesta Key beach house where he and Lauren were supposed to have a romantic weekend escape, had never heard of Cassadaga. That night, Mark had heard of it only from his wife.

Since then, he'd spent much of his time in the place, in mind if not in body.

Mr. Novak? I'm afraid I have some difficult news to share. It's about your wife.

The day after their engagement, Lauren's father had invited Mark over for a beer, just the two of them. Mark was expecting the typical "Now, you take good care of my baby girl" speech, and while he received a version of it, he wasn't prepared for the depth of pain in the other man's eyes. It was the first time he'd understood the fear that lived like a heartbeat within a parent. A good parent, at least.

"Having a child," Lauren's father had said, "is to spend your life swimming with sharks. You think I'm joking, but it's only because you don't know yet. You haven't seen one grow up and walk off into the world, and when you do, you'll think about all the things that could be waiting out there; you'll think of car accidents and cancer and kidnappings and all the other horrors in a way you didn't before you had a child. You always knew they were out there, but you didn't *care* in the same way. Then you have a daughter, and…well, then you see the sharks. They'll start circling in your mind, and they'll never leave. You'll just pray they keep circling forever. You understand what I'm saying?"

"I'm not a shark," Mark had said, and then he'd smiled, because he had no children and so he didn't understand what the water here was like. Lauren's father hadn't returned the smile. He'd searched Mark's eyes for a long time before he nodded. They drank their beers and talked football, boats, and movies, everything lighthearted and casual, but Mark was uneasy the rest of the night, because what he'd seen in the other man's eyes was something he'd never known himself. It had been many years since he'd last wondered who his own father was, but that night he did. He wondered whether that man had ever thought of the sharks. Even once.

More thunder. A stillness to the western edge of town, as if the trees were lying low, trying not to attract the attention of the oncoming bullying clouds.

Though Mark hadn't been in the town before, he knew exactly how to find Dixie Witte's home. He'd spent plenty of time looking at it on maps. The second story of the house leaned away from the foundation like a drunk trying to balance on one leg; the front-porch windows were cracked or had plastic where glass belonged; the ferns in the yard had grown so high they were nearly to the roof of a rusted-out Ford Taurus. The undergrowth was thick, so Mark couldn't tell for sure, but he would have laid a high-dollar bet that the car no longer had wheels. Might not even have an engine. A shed beside the house had a caved-in roof, and the blue plastic tarp that had been pulled across the hole was bowed with trapped rainwater. It was the sort of place that made you think you might catch a viral disease if you stood downwind of it.

Mark had lived in a lot of shitholes in his childhood, and in a truck for a time, but even his mother wouldn't have considered moving into this house.

This was where Garland Webb had lived for a two-month period before he moved on to Daytona Beach and was finally arrested for sexual assault.

There was a truck in the drive. A red Dodge lifted high on an after-market suspension with knobby terrain tires that were probably worth as much as the house. The truck was freshly washed and the red paint shone even in the gloom. Mark had met a few people who cared more about their trucks than their homes. It usually didn't suggest good things. He walked around the main house, and a guesthouse at the rear of the property came into view. A small but well-kept little home painted blue with clean white trim. It was an incongruous pairing— the large home gone to hell, the small one lovingly maintained. The flowering bushes that bordered it were neatly clipped, and a stepladder stood beside an orange tree just in front of the house. A barefoot blond boy in overalls, no shirt underneath, was picking oranges. He couldn't have been much more than seven years old, and he wobbled precariously as he reached for one.

"Careful," Mark said, stepping to brace the ladder.

The boy plucked the orange free, set it in a basket that was balanced on the top step of the ladder, and turned to Mark. He was incredibly pale for Florida, with bright blue eyes.

"Hiya."

"Hiya. Don't lose your balance up there."

"Don't lose your balance down there."

Mark grinned. "Fair enough. Is Dixie around?"

The boy shrugged. "She hasn't paid me yet. When I'm done she'll pay me. Fifty cents if I do the whole tree."

"You need to adjust for inflation, kid. You're getting taken."

Another shrug.

Mark said, "You know most people in this town?"

"I know everybody."

"You had the look of a connected man. Ever hear of a guy named Garland?"

"Nope."

"What about a Mr. Webb? That mean anything to you?"

The boy shook his head. "They come and they go, though."

"Who does?"

"People in the big house." The boy pointed at the decrepit structure behind Mark. "They don't stay long, and they don't talk much."

"What kind of people are they, would you say?"

"People like you."

"Like me? What's that mean?"

"Angry people," the boy said, and Mark's grin wavered. The clouds were shifting fast, and Mark was in shadow now, but the boy was in sunlight, his white skin bright beneath the grimy overalls. Only his bare feet, covered in dust, were dulled.

"I'm not angry," Mark said.

Another shrug. "Don't matter to me."

"Okay. But I'm not angry, and you don't need to worry about me."

"I'm not worried about you at all. If you were bad, Walter would tell me."

Mark raised an eyebrow. "Walter?"

"He's the man who used to own this house."

Now Mark's interest was genuine, because all he'd been told was that the home had belonged to Dixie Witte's family for generations, and if anyone had dealt with Garland Webb, it would have been her.

"Someone else owned this place? This man, Walter, he sold it to Dixie?"

The boy shook his head. "Nah. He's been dead almost since forever. He built the house way back during the Depression. But then he was murdered. The story I heard, someone cut off his hands. Put them in a cigar box. You ever seen something like that?"

Mark felt sick. Who in the hell was raising this kid, telling him that? What was the matter with the people in this town?

"Don't listen to those stories," he said. "Kids shouldn't hear things like that."

"It's just what happened," the boy said, indifferent. "But Walter likes you. He's been walking with you ever since the gate. And Walter don't leave the porch much."

Mark had heard enough. He said, "Okay, kid. Thanks for the help. Don't believe all the stories you're told. And don't fall off that ladder."

"I never do."

Holy shit, what a freak show this place is, Mark thought, and he was ashamed of the graveyard prickle he felt along his spine, as if there were really something to fear, when he walked back through the overgrown yard and out to the street. It was just because the weirdness had come from a child, that was all. If it had been only the woman in the hotel and others like her, the ones who made money shilling for clairvoyants and selling spook stories, fine. But to hear it from a child was disturbing.

The story I heard, someone cut off his hands. Put them in a cigar box. You ever seen something like that?

Freak show. Lauren had been right—there was no chance that Mark could have come to this place and conducted an interview without telegraphing his scorn. Not then, and not now. He didn't need to hear the spirit talk; he needed to hear the facts. When did Garland Webb move in, when did he leave, what did he do in between, whom did he speak to, who came to visit? That was where the focus would remain with Dixie Witte. No visions necessary, thanks, just the truth—if she even knew how to tell that.

He'd reached the end of the dirt lane. He turned right on Kicklighter Road and headed south, toward the place where his wife had died.

6

Jay Baldwin drove east out of Red Lodge with a gun pressed to the back of his head. The stranger instructed Jay to take I-90 away from the mountains and back toward Billings. The man had his wrist balanced on the seat just beside the headrest, and Jay thought that eventually his hand would begin to ache and he'd lower the gun.

He didn't.

For a few miles, Jay attempted to talk to him. He asked what the man wanted, told him that they had more money than the house suggested—he and Sabrina were savers, always had been.

The stranger didn't speak.

Jay changed approaches then and went from offers to pleas. To outright begging. He said that his wife was the only thing that mattered to him in the world, talked about the kind of woman she was, strong and smart and, above all, forgiving. If she had any weakness, it was an excess of empathy, a desire to believe the best of everyone at all times, a tendency to forgive what should have been unforgivable. If she was released, she would forgive this man for these sins. So would Jay.

The stranger never answered.

They were thirty miles out of Red Lodge, the last traces of the mountain snow falling behind them, when Jay finally asked a question that broke the silence.

"What is your name?"

"Eli Pate." This came conversationally enough, said with the same cordial manner he'd demonstrated in the house. Jay thought that it was a pointless question, because of course the man would lie. Still, he wanted something to call him.

"Eli…whatever you want from me, it's—"

"Stay eastbound. Continue the conversation if you wish, but I have nothing to say. When I have something to say, you'll hear it."

For the remainder of the drive, there were no words exchanged beyond Eli's curt instructions. They crossed the plains and cut through the Northern Cheyenne Indian Reservation. It was wide-open country, the famous Montana sky hanging above them unbroken and endless. In a one-stoplight town called Lame Deer, Eli ordered Jay to turn north. They passed the reservation school, an institution named Chief Dull Knife College, and drove alongside a creek. From the time they'd set out, Jay had hoped he was being taken to the same place as his wife. The farther they'd gotten from his home and the deeper into the desolate land, the more he'd believed this would be the case. While he still didn't understand the purpose behind it all, he took some solace in the idea that they would be reunited, no matter how awful the circumstances.

It wasn't until he saw the plumes of bone-white smoke that he began to fear he was wrong about the reunion and to suspect for the first time why he'd been selected for the day's horrors. As they pulled into the small town of Chill River, Jay was praying that Eli would send him farther north, toward someplace unknown. The unknown suddenly sounded better than turning east.

"Right on Willow Avenue and head east," Eli Pate commanded him.

Jay understood now.

They followed Willow Avenue outside of town and soon the source of the smoke appeared on their right—four mammoth stacks protruding into the sky like spires, clouds foaming out of them. A sign in front cheerfully welcomed them to Chill River. TOMORROW'S TOWN . . . TODAY!

"Pull over for a moment."

Jay put the truck on the shoulder of the road.

"You have an idea what you're looking at, I assume?" Eli Pate said.

"Yes."

"Tell me."

"You already know."

Eli Pate shifted in the seat and used his right hand to produce his cell phone. He kept the gun to Jay's head with the left, then extended the phone so that they both could see the display. No video feed this time, just a still image. Sabrina, bleary-eyed and confused, looking at the shackle on her wrist as if she couldn't make sense of it. Jay had to remind himself how to breathe.

"Tell me," Eli Pate said again. His voice was very low.

"A generating station." The words croaked from Jay's constricted throat. He couldn't look away from the image of Sabrina. When Eli Pate pocketed the phone, Jay was torn between relief and sorrow. He didn't want to see his wife like that, but he also couldn't bear not to see her at all.

"What generating station?" Eli Pate said. "Give me some detail. I'm nothing but a rube, Jay. You're an expert."

Jay stared at the place where the smoke met the sky.

"The Chill River generation station," he said. "We're looking at a coal-fired power plant."

"Sounds impressive. Do you happen to know how much power it generates?"

"Peak output is more than two thousand megawatts."

"Is that a lot?"

"Second-largest coal-fired station west of the Mississippi." The gun was still against Jay's skull, but he'd stopped noticing the sensation. All of his physical attention was now on those stacks and the snaking high-voltage lines that led away from the power plant. All of his mental attention was on the way his wife looked in that picture.

"Quantify that for me, Jay. How many people are fed by this operation?"

"Nearly a million."

"That seems hard to believe, considering how far out in the sticks we are."

"The power goes two hundred and fifty miles west of here. There it's distributed into different grids, different transmission systems. All the way to the West Coast." His words came in a monotone, his mind on Sabrina. Where did this man have her? The frame of the camera was too tight to indicate anything about her location. Only her condition.

"Fascinating stuff," Eli Pate said. "One more question: How does it move to those different grids?"

"Through the five-hundred-kV transmission lines."

"And how many of those lines are required to move all that electricity from here?"

Jay didn't want to tell the truth, but the man already knew it, so there was no point in lying. "Two," he said.

Eli Pate whistled between his teeth. "Goodness. How oddly vulnerable, don't you think? Imagine if the public knew! Why, the fear it would conjure...that would be something to behold. I've been told something about you, and please correct me if I'm wrong—did you once work on those lines? Before the move to Red Lodge?"

"Yes."

"Dangerous work. There's a technique, I understand, called barehanding. It requires very brave men, very specialized training, very sophisticated equipment. Helicopters, even, and sometimes high rope work. That's you, correct?"

Jay didn't speak. Eli tapped the gun lightly on his skull. "Do you know why you're here now, my friend?"

"No."

"Sure you do. But I'll humor you, because you've humored me. You're here, Jay, to shut this show down. You're here to turn off the lights."

7

In the last minutes of her life, Lauren had driven out of Cassadaga on Kicklighter Road, headed away from the interstate. That intrigued and confused the homicide detectives. No one was aware of any destination she might have had other than Siesta Key, where Mark waited for her with steaks on the grill as the sun settled behind the Gulf of Mexico. That route called for her to take I-4 West, crossing central Florida the same way she'd come, and I-4 was north of Cassadaga. She'd headed south instead, but she hadn't made it far before she pulled off the road. The investigators theorized that she'd stopped to get her bearings, realizing she'd made a mistake and not wanting to continue in the wrong direction down the wrong road.

The investigators didn't know Lauren, though. This was a woman who, when Mark had asked her if she knew what state was west of Montana, had looked at him suspiciously, as if it were a trick question, and said, "Well, am I standing up in it or lying down?" He had great fun with that one, but it was a bizarre illustration of the way she considered maps: one-dimensionally; the only directions that mattered to her were right, left, and straight. Tell her to drive northwest and you'd get a blank stare in response. She'd graduated summa cum laude from the University of Florida and aced the bar exam, but she had no interest in compasses.

All of this was part of the explanation for how she'd ended up driving southbound out of Cassadaga, according to the police. But again, you had to *know* her. One of the reasons Lauren was so bad with directions was that she'd always relied on technology as a crutch. Her Infiniti was equipped with a navigation system that she used constantly. If she was walking, she used the GPS on her phone. She'd do this even in St. Pete, let alone in a rural location she'd never been to before. A review of the GPS proved that she'd entered the address of the Cassadaga Hotel. When she'd headed south on Kicklighter, driving away from an unfamiliar town on an unfamiliar road, she'd had no guidance from the GPS, no programmed destination.

But she'd had a purpose. What was it?

Mark kept walking, passed an empty park beside a small lake, and then an opening appeared in the dense trees to his right. A path leading away from the road and into the woods.

His throat thickened and he felt pressure behind his eyes and heard a sound that seemed to come from inside his skull, a sound like a rubber band popping, stretched to its limits and about to snap. It was strange, disturbing. He blinked and rubbed his temples and the sensation faded and vanished. He stood there for a long time and looked at the road and the trees as if they would produce something, as if the dust would rise and swirl and materialize into a figure, someone with answers.

Not even the air moved, though.

It took him fifty paces to reach the spot. Her body had been found in a ditch just off the trail. The bamboo grew thick and tall around it, creating a jungle feel, a place of children's nightmares, of dares to pass through alone at midnight. Up ahead, the trail curved to the right and opened up, and the world seemed brighter and welcoming and just out of reach.

The rain was falling steadily now, a silent soaking, the thunder gone. He looked at the dark water in the ditch for a long time, and he felt as if there was some gesture he should make, some words he should say. Nothing came, though. He turned from the ditch and walked back the way he'd come.

Directly across the road was a lake with a shelter house built at the end of a pier. He walked down the pier until he was beneath the roof and out of the rain. The lake's surface was pebbled by raindrops, and trees bordered it in all directions. Close to the bank, thick layers of algae covered the water, giving it a swamplike look. Trash floated among the weeds, chip bags and plastic rings from six-packs and a stretched-out condom that looked like a sodden snakeskin. A beer can rode the water like a fisherman's bobber.

He was leaning on the railing with his back to the road when he heard the truck. First the engine, then the crunch of the oversize tires on the gravel. The red truck from Dixie Witte's property.

Next to the pier was a narrow ramp where you could put in a canoe or a johnboat. The lake wasn't big enough to call for anything larger. The driver brought the truck all the way down the ramp until the front tires stood in at least a foot of water, although that didn't even come up to the center of the hubcaps.

Mark didn't turn away from the lake. The water was so dark it looked like a pool of oil. You couldn't track the stems of the cattails for more than an inch beneath the surface. It was water that whispered of barely submerged alligators and slant-eyed cottonmouths curled around stumps, of rattling dredging chains, of men with badges and sunglasses working flat-bottomed boats, searching for bodies. In the rain, the lake's surface looked like hammered metal.

When Mark finally turned to the truck, the driver rolled down the passenger window so he could see Mark clearly. Or, based on his stare and body language, so Mark could see him clearly. A big bastard with a wide jaw and a close-trimmed beard and a sleeveless shirt that facilitated the opportunity to appreciate his muscles and his tattoos. He sat there with his arm looped around the steering wheel, his triceps flexing and popping against his skin, the truck's exhaust system growling like a tiger in a circus cage.

"Everything all right, bud?" he said.

"Just fine."

"You want to tell me why you were walking around my property? Neighbor said you seemed mighty interested in my shit."

Instead of answering, Mark watched the beer can bobbing among the green weeds and tried to match his breaths to it. He used to do the same thing with Lauren during sleepless nights. Match his breaths to hers until they were one. Sleep usually came fast for him then, but he never cared if it did. That was a good and peaceful feeling.

When the muscled-up man cut the engine, the loss of the big truck's motor turned the lake quiet, the only sound the soft drumming of the rain on the metal roof of the shelter. It was falling slower now, and the air wasn't stirring.

The driver's door opened and then banged shut and there were twin splashes as his feet landed in the water, as if he hadn't remembered how far into the lake he'd driven. Mark might have laughed about that, but as the big man rounded the back of the truck, he reached into the bed and grabbed a piece of rebar. It was about three feet long and had to weigh fifteen pounds. Swung with force, it would break a man's leg.

Let's not go this way, Mark thought, because he had worked so hard for so many years to bury this part of himself, to not be one of those grown men who fought like children for children's reasons, almost all of them boiling down to egos in the end, and usually fueled by liquor. There had been a time when he believed he'd succeeded, that the lessons instilled by his uncles had been overridden by willpower and wisdom.

But then Lauren had died and occasionally the darkness would rise, and rise with a smile, because a taste for fighting was like a taste for whiskey—once you developed it, you didn't rid yourself of it. Only controlled it.

The big man advanced, holding the rebar with strength and familiarity. Mark moved his hands from the dock railing, reached inside his jacket, and drew the .38.

The muscle-bound man came to a stop about two paces out on the pier, the rebar held in both hands and hovering in the air behind his right shoulder like he was a player in the on-deck circle taking practice cuts with a weighted bat.

"Right," Mark said. "You're already thinking maybe you should have been a touch more patient, aren't you?"

He lowered the rebar. The free end banged off the pier. Mark could feel the shudder of impact through his feet.

"This seems stupid to you now, doesn't it?" Mark said. "You're thinking that it would be dumb to die just because you got all butt-hurt over someone walking around your yard and looking at your house. You're right. But now that you've come this far, let's talk. What's your name?"

"Get fucked."

"Your parents weren't any more fond of you than I am, then. No surprise. Let's try another one. How long have you lived in that house?"

This time he showed his middle finger.

"Does that mean one year?" Mark said.

"You're lucky you were carrying today. Luckier that I wasn't. Next time—"

"You will be," Mark finished for him. "Sure. I believe it too. But the thing is? I wasn't *lucky* to be carrying. I was prepared. Not every-one who's passed through here in the past has been."

The big man seemed confused by that message, but he didn't have much room in his head for anything beyond hate right then.

"You really get that upset about me looking your house over?" Mark said. "Because to a rational mind, this seems like an overreac-tion."

"I don't know who in the hell you are. But I don't want you on my property."

"Duly noted. And my name is Markus Novak."

The big man smiled, and Mark's blood seemed to slow in his veins.

"That name amuses you?"

"You're a little late," the man said. "I wasn't here when she got popped, bud, but I've heard the stories."

When she got popped. Mark's mouth had gone dry and each breath felt hot and dusty. The man was gathering confidence, pleased that he'd rattled Mark.

"That gun makes you feel pretty tough. Lucky you had it."

"We've been over this," Mark said as he started toward him through the gentle rain, and the part of him that did not want the fight was gone now, vanishing with the man's smile as he'd said *when she got popped,* and the decision-making that came from above Mark's shoulders had been subverted by the old memories that filled his blood and bones like a genetic code, a promise.

"It's not luck," he said. "My uncles taught me about guns. They had some hard-and-fast rules. One of them, well, it's not particularly unique. Lots of people have the same rule. If you ever go so far as to draw the gun, you damn well better be ready to use it. You ever heard that one?"

The big man didn't answer. His eyes were on Mark's hand, and he was taking comfort in the fact that Mark's index finger wasn't near the trigger, and his thumb wasn't near the hammer.

"It's a good rule," Mark said, and then he swung the barrel of the .38 into the center of the big man's face.

Blood was flowing by the time he fell. He caught himself on the railing, went down on one knee, and the rebar dropped and rolled across the dock. He reached for it, but this time Mark did pull the hammer back.

"Technically, I just kept the rule," he said. "We can let this count, or you can push for more."

The big man sucked air in through his teeth as blood ran down his lips and splashed shining and red over the dock boards.

"You shouldn't have smiled when you spoke of my wife," Mark said. "That was a very bad decision. I'm going to give you the chance to make some better ones now. What's your name?"

"Pate." The word came from the back of his throat. He was fighting the pain hard, and fighting it well, and Mark knew it would be prudent to remember that.

"Full name."

"Myron Pate."

"Okay, Myron. How long have you lived in that gem up the road?"

He hawked blood into his mouth and spit it at Mark's shoes. Mark pushed the muzzle of the gun hard against his forehead and drove his skull back until his chin was tilted up and Mark could see his eyes.

"How long?"

"Nine months."

"If that's a lie, I'm going to learn it fast."

"Nine months."

"Who was there before you?"

"Dunno."

"Don't believe you."

He shrugged.

"Garland Webb," Mark said.

"Don't know him."

"I'm going to find out if that's the truth."

He shrugged again. Mark couldn't see a lie in his face, couldn't see anything but hate, but there was a problem with a man like Myron occupying a house previously rented by Garland Webb and coming on so strong with Mark now, ready to swing a piece of rebar at him for wandering the property. Coincidences happen, yes, but causation happens more often.

Myron Pate spit more blood. There were tears in his eyes now, but it wasn't because he was scared. He was hurting. Myron was going to need doctors, and depending on what he said to them, Mark could end the day in jail. His gut told him that Myron wasn't the type who was real interested in calling the police.

Mark stepped farther from him and used his foot to roll the rebar off the dock and into the water. It landed with a gulping sound, as if the lake were eager for it. He walked down the pier and around to the red truck, used his phone to take a picture of the license plate, then opened the driver's door and removed the keys from the ignition. He carried them back and stood by the water's edge and watched Myron struggle to his feet. He needed to use both hands and the railing to make it.

"I thought about shooting those stupid tires out," Mark said. "But they probably cost you three months' pay, and I'm in a generous mood. You can take two key points from today, Myron. One is that it is very unwise to take pleasure in someone else's pain. Show some

44

respect for the dead if you don't want to join them. The second is that if you know Garland Webb, you can tell him I'm coming."

He holstered the .38, jingled Myron's keys as if calling a dog for a car ride, and then tossed them out into the shallows of the lake.

"While you're getting those," he said, "pick up the chip bags, the beer can, and the used rubber. This is a beautiful place, Myron, but somebody's letting it go to hell."

8

Awareness flickered in Sabrina's mind like matches in a deep, dark valley. Snapped to life, then snuffed out. She knew that she should have wanted more of them, that the light was the part of the world she needed, the part to which she belonged, but as the matches multiplied and their glows lingered, she was more afraid of them than the dark.

This is not my home. I do not know where I am. I was taken from my home. I am alone. Where am I, and why am I alone? What happened?

Snap and burn, snap and burn. Eventually the match glows began to blend together and flame came with it and then light and for the first time Sabrina felt the weight on her wrist and looked at it with uncomprehending eyes.

There was a metal bracelet on her wrist. No. Not a bracelet. There was a word for it, and the word was scary. The word was terrible, the word was—

Handcuff.

It was in that moment of recognition that she slipped fully out of the dark fog and into understanding, and her fear poured forth like blood filling an open wound.

She cried out then. Said the only word that came to mind: *Help.* She cried it again and again, and her mouth was dry and her tongue felt strange, hard to maneuver, but the effort of shouting and the intensity of her fear were scrubbing the haze from her brain and she saw more of her surroundings, or at least understood more of them.

She was on a cold wooden floor, and the chain of the handcuff on her right wrist ran to an anchor bolt in the log wall, where the other cuff was clipped, holding her fast. The room was dim and though she could make out shapes, it was hard to get a sense of the place beyond the floor, the wall, and the chain between them. She turned her attention to herself then and saw her bare legs and felt the light fabric over them and understood that she was wearing her nightgown. She'd gotten out of the shower and put on her nightgown and she'd been ready to go to bed early, expecting to fall asleep alone, knowing that Jay might be many hours at work yet because the power was out in a lot of places and there was no telling how quickly he'd get it back on.

And then?

The large man. An intruder. He'd spoken to her. Said something about air, though she couldn't remember exactly what, just that it had been strange. She didn't have any clear memory of him, just knew that he'd been there, that there had been an intruder and she had been afraid. The lack of clarity in the situation told her that this should be a dream.

But it wasn't. The cold floor was real, and the prickling flesh of her bare legs under the nightgown was real, and, more than anything, the biting weight of that handcuff was real.

She pulled at the cuff, using her free hand to get a grip on the links of chain that led to the wall. She tugged with all her might, rotated so that she could use her feet to push against the wall, and all she achieved for her efforts was pain.

She was curled against the wall and crying softly when there was the sound of a lock working and then a door opened and light spilled into the room. It fell across the floor to Sabrina like an extended hand.

A figure stepped in and blocked the light.

"You may make all the noise you wish, but it won't change your circumstances, and I would prefer not to hear it." His voice was emotionless. She couldn't see his face because the light was behind him.

She didn't think he was the same man who had been in her home. He wasn't large enough and his voice wasn't deep enough. At first this seemed good, but then she realized what it meant—there were two of them. At least two.

"It seems bad now," he said. "That was expected. That was under-stood. But you'll begin to feel new things in this place soon, Sabrina. I promise that you will. You'll begin to feel a sense of purpose stronger than any you've ever known. You'll realize that you are a part of something larger than yourself, and it will please you. If you allow it to, it will please you."

He paused, and behind him another figure shifted. Oh Lord, there were more of them.

"It's a lonely predicament right now," he said. "Don't worry. You won't be alone for long. We'll have more guests soon, and I will expect you to demonstrate some leadership. You are, after all, the firstborn. Do you understand that?"

Sabrina didn't speak.

"Consider it," the faceless man said. "Consider that your old life was nothing but a womb, and a harsh, cold one at that. But now you've escaped it. Here you are, alive and well, your life preserved. This isn't a bad place, Sabrina. Great things are being kept alive here, and soon they will flourish. This place is an incubator. That's how you should think of it. As an incubator of the heart. Open your spirit and you'll know the truth. You'll know."

He turned and left. All she could see of him was that he was of av-erage height and whip-thin build with long hair tied back and pulled tight against his skull. His hands seemed unusually large for his size. He took three steps forward into the square of white light, and she thought she saw pines beyond him, and then he turned to the left and faded from view and was replaced by another figure, this one stepping in from the right and pulling the door shut. Sabrina was as-tonished to see this new one was a woman. Petite, with dark hair in a long braid and tanned skin. An attractive woman, probably in her fifties.

The woman said, "Baby girl, you'll be just fine," in a voice as tender as a mother speaking to her newborn. She knelt down, reached out, and brushed Sabrina's hair away from her face.

"You'll be just fine," she said again. So kind.

"Help me," Sabrina said. Her voice broke. "Please help me. Please let me go. I don't know what you—"

"Shhh." The woman put her fingers against Sabrina's lips, softly. Her face was weathered but still pretty, and once it had surely been beautiful. "You'll need to be quiet here, or the voices won't find you. You'll need to learn to put away all of that mental clutter. The fear and all the rest. Just listen. Now I'm going to get you some food and water and we're going to make you more comfortable. When the tribes arrive, you'll need your strength."

She moved gracefully away, and Sabrina stared after her in horror and confusion. The man she'd expected, somehow. From the moment the handcuff became clear, the instant she'd understood even that much about her situation, she'd known that there would be a man.

She had not counted on the woman.

When the tribes arrive, you'll need your strength.

The tribes? Sabrina worked saliva into her dry mouth and forced a swallow. She was dehydrated, and the crying hadn't helped. Her eyes adjusting, she could see the woman moving about in the far corner. She heard the splashing of water, the rustling of plastic bags. Hopelessly, she looked back at the bolt in the log where the handcuff was anchored, but now something else caught her eye—farther down the log, maybe two feet, there was another bolt. Beyond that, another still.

We'll have more guests soon.

9

Jay Baldwin sat at the kitchen table alone, no gun to his head. If he wanted a gun, in fact, he had only to go upstairs and take the nine-millimeter from his nightstand drawer.

The gun wasn't going to produce Sabrina, though.

The police might. But calling the police was no longer the easy fix it would have been once. Before Eli Pate had dropped Jay off, he'd shown him an image on his phone: a map with a blinking red dot.

"That's your truck," Pate had said calmly, and then he'd offered Jay a small plastic square. "And this one is you. Now, I understand that this seems intrusive, but obviously you and I are a long way from developing trust. In the absence of trust, I have to monitor. You understand that, don't you, Jay? It's like any parent-child relationship."

Jay took the small piece of plastic and ran his thumb over it and thought of how easy it would be to break, or microwave, or flush down a toilet. There were a million ways to destroy the signal this thing was putting out.

"There is no chance that battery will stop functioning," Eli Pate said. "And you will not know when I will arrive. But when I do, you'd better have that with you. Just keep it in your pocket, Jay. But I'll state this once, and very clearly: If I go to the place where the signal tells me you are, and you aren't there? Well, I have your wife. And I'm not a kind man."

They were the last words he offered. There was no overt threat, no guarantee of harm, but there didn't have to be one. He had said all he needed to.

Jay had today off due to the extended stretch of repair work, and he wished that he didn't. He'd rather be moving than sitting here alone. As he sat, he thought of every phone call he could make, of every type of law enforcement that he'd ever heard of, every agency that might come to Sabrina's rescue.

He never reached for the phone. He turned the plastic chip over and over in his hands and went through every conceivable option, but he never reached for the phone.

I'm not a kind man.

No, Pate was not. And he wasn't a bluffing man, Jay thought. The problem, then, was not all that different from Jay's daily tasks. There were some simple but critical constants in high-voltage work, the most important being that before you attempted a fix, you had to understand where the power came from and how it was controlled.

Power source: Eli Pate.

System control: Jay's tracking device.

He would stay at home today, he would not call for help, he would be at work on time tomorrow, and Eli Pate's computers would see all of that. They would also see something else, something natural enough for a man in his position—they would see Jay spend a full hour pacing his living room. Over and over he walked the same route, reminding himself of the power source (Pate) and the system control (electronic tracking device), mimicking the routine of a sleep-starved, terrified man anguishing over the right choice to make for his wife's safety. It was not hard to do. When Sabrina wasn't occupying his mind, the specter of those massive transmission towers with their nearly a million volts and the ghost of his brother-in-law slipped right in. It had been a closed-casket funeral. The electricity cooked you in your own blood, leaving nothing but a blackened, shriveled shell behind, featureless and horrifying.

It was easy to pace and worry. Very easy.

He did not go upstairs, and he did not go outside. Just paced and hoped that Pate's computers were recording it all. When Jay arrived at work the next morning, with no police called, no attempts made to destroy his tracking device, Pate would understand that when Jay was nervous, he paced the lower level of his house.

It was critical that Pate understood this.

10

When Mark returned to Cassadaga, the red truck was gone from the lake, and it wasn't parked outside of Dixie's house either.

Mark had spent the hours between his encounter with Myron and his appointment with Dixie Witte in DeLand, the nearest town of any size. It was only a fifteen-minute drive away but so unlike Cassadaga it could have been fifteen hundred miles. He was surprised by the relief he'd felt at the sight of things he usually hated about Florida, the strip malls and car lots and harsh lights. After only a few hours in Cassadaga, he found all of it reassuring, a reminder that contemporary society existed, that there were places where you wouldn't come across barefoot boys picking oranges and talking casually about the dead.

You ever seen something like that?

He drank a few beers in DeLand and tried to prepare himself to take Dixie Witte seriously, to grant her the patience and respect that Lauren hadn't believed he was capable of showing to someone who claimed psychic abilities.

You've got to let her be herself, Mark thought. *Do not challenge her or dismiss her. Not at the start, at least. Just get her talking.*

When he returned to Cassadaga it was past dusk, and the lack of streetlights enhanced that sense of driving out of one era and into another. He passed Dixie's house, noted the continued absence of the red truck, and then checked the park by the lake, which also remained empty. He left the Infiniti there, not wanting to make it easy for Myron to find him if he came back loaded up on painkillers or meth or whatever the hell made a guy like him tick. When he was sure that nobody had followed him or was watching, he got out of the car and began the walk back to the property once owned by a man who'd had his hands severed and placed in a cigar box.

The streets were empty and the moon hung in a perfect crescent and you could see a good number of stars for inland Florida, but he'd never seen stars in his life the way he'd seen them growing up amid the high peaks and open plains. Once on a dive boat on open water, there'd been something close, perhaps. Lauren had been with him then. That was in the Saba National Marine Park. He still carried her dive permit from that trip with him, putting it in his pocket every day, a talisman.

The afternoon rain had been swept away by a steady western wind and though the sun was down the temperature continued to rise. The moist streets steamed. The main house, Myron's den, was dark, but there were lights on inside the guesthouse where Dixie waited. When Mark stepped inside the fence, the wind seemed to die. He looked around and saw fronds moving in all directions, and overhead, a clump of Spanish moss that looked like a dead woman's hair waved steadily, buffeted by a breeze that he could no longer feel. The air around him was as still as a tomb and he could hear again that odd sound that seemed to come from inside his own skull, the dull popping of a rubber band.

He shook his head, readjusted, and that was when he saw his dead wife on the porch of the main house.

For a moment, a long and fine moment, he was certain that it was Lauren. She was standing in a pool of moonlight that silhouetted her lean frame and behind her, banyan leaves threw shadows that climbed into the starlit sky. She wore jeans and a black sleeveless top, and her blond hair just reached her shoulders. The visual cues were close, yes, but they were also generic. The catch-your-breath quality was in *presence*. There was just something about the way she stood, about the quarter tilt of her head as she looked at him, that said *Lauren*.

Then she stepped forward, off the porch and down into the yard, and the motion broke loose the bizarre sensation in his mind and he understood that this was a living woman and not a specter. She was holding something in her hands that looked like a bucket. "Who's there?" she said, and her voice was not even close to Lauren's. Mark shouldn't have needed that confirmation, but for some reason, in this place, he did.

"Markus Novak. I'm here to see Dixie."

"I'm Dixie. And you're early, Markus."

He didn't respond, couldn't. She walked toward him with confidence, and suddenly, foolishly, he wanted to have his gun in hand. When she got close enough that he could see her face clearly, it was obvious that she didn't look *that* much like Lauren. Her features were more delicate, almost fragile, and her lips were fuller, at odds with the bone structure, mismatched. There was a dimple in her chin, and her ears were lined with piercings, small silver hoops that ran from bottom to top. Up close, nobody would confuse them. But from a distance...he was still rattled from that moment in the moonlight.

"I didn't expect you so soon," she said. She was holding a metal bucket filled with ice and four glistening bottles of Dixie beer.

Mark nodded at them and said, "Brand loyalty, I see."

"What? Oh. Dixie. Right. No, that's just my preference. I was going to go for a walk. Shall we walk and talk? I prefer to conduct readings in the house, but you're not here for a reading. You're here for her."

"Her?"

"Your wife," Dixie Witte said simply. "Did you think I wouldn't recognize your name? Honestly, I've wondered what took you so long. I'm afraid that she has too."

Mark couldn't think of anything to say to that, because there was an element of it that seemed like the truth.

"Let's walk," Dixie said after a pause. "We aren't going far, but the energy is better. I'll need good energy for this talk. You understand," she said, handing him the bucket. "Here. Carry this, please."

She headed down the street with a confident sway of her slim hips.

She kept her stride fast enough to stay a full step ahead of Mark as he followed, holding the metal bucket, which sloshed water from the melted ice over his hands and numbed his fingers. Everything was still and silent and the lush smells of the oranges and rhododendrons were everywhere. In front of the moon, the scudding remnants of the storm clouds broke, re-formed, and then separated again like wet cotton.

They passed beside a still lake, not unlike the one into which Mark had thrown Myron Pate's keys earlier, but Dixie didn't stop or slow. They looped away from the park, went up the road toward the Cassadaga Hotel, and then they left the pavement and walked into a small garden.

"Medicine Wheel," she said.

Mark froze. Every muscle tensed; every nerve hummed. He could hardly breathe.

"What did you say?"

"That's what this park is called." She sat on the low back of a small stone bench, her feet resting on the seat.

Mark looked around the dark park and tried to find his natural voice, one that didn't betray the eerie spark he'd felt. "Officially?"

"What do you mean, officially? That's its name; I didn't make it up. There's a plaque that says it." She shrugged. "What's it matter to you?"

What did it matter to him? He looked at her and thought about a flat mountain summit in the Bighorn range in Wyoming where rocks were laid out in twenty-eight piles that matched the lunar cycle, rocks that had been there for hundreds of years, their origin unknown but still lined up perfectly with the sunrise of the summer solstice. Rocks that were sacred to tribal nations from all over the West and where people still came daily to honor their own mix of gods, leaving behind feathers and brightly colored cloths and bits of bone and even the hair of the dead. His mother had been arrested there when she'd shown up and tried her Nez Perce spirit-guide act.

That had been one of the more lasting shames in a childhood full of them, but it was also one of the most vivid, because he'd experienced something in that spot. Something not understood, only felt. He had felt, standing on that windy peak and watching people speak in unknown tongues and worship in ways he didn't comprehend, that he was a part of something beyond himself.

And then the rangers came for his mother, and they brought handcuffs. He would never forget the eyes of the grieving couple she'd been working with.

Now, twenty-five years later and three thousand miles away, he shook his head and said, "It's a strange name, that's all," and advanced to the bench where Dixie Witte was sitting. Something metal glittered in her hand and for an instant Mark thought, *Knife,* before he realized it was a bottle opener. She beckoned with her free hand, and he set the bucket down in the grass and passed her a sweating bottle of beer. She popped the cap and handed it to him and then he gave her another, which she opened and kept. She looked at him with a sad smile.

"I knew you'd come," she said. "It was a matter of time, that's all. You weren't ready before, were you? You had to get ready. In another place, maybe."

"Something like that. I didn't see the point, early on. The police were interviewing you plenty, and I read all of their transcripts."

"The police asked the wrong questions."

"Oh? What should they have asked?"

She didn't answer right away. She drank some of the beer and then said, "Sit."

"I'm good."

"No. You're putting a shadow on the road. Sit down."

Why the shadow mattered, he had no idea, but he sat. He took the actual bench, so that Dixie was sitting above him, perched up by his right shoulder. He didn't like that; he liked to be able to see her, to have the best vantage point and the freest movement possible. That was a consistent desire for Mark. Some would call it obsessive-compulsive, but he called it practical. Wild Bill Hickok didn't get shot until he broke his own rule and sat with his back to the door.

Dixie Witte said, "Your wife had death all around her that afternoon."

Mark didn't speak, didn't move.

"You, um...you were able to see this," he finally said, thinking of a hypnotist he'd known in Indiana and trying to be accepting of things he knew better than to believe. To be tolerant of them, at least. That wasn't so much to ask, but still, his own wife hadn't thought he was capable of it on the day she'd made her drive to this place.

"Yes," Dixie said. "Death arrived with her. It was very close. Unnerving, because I'd felt that before, but always in situations when it was anticipated. Home visits, usually, dealing with the terminally ill. Those things. But your wife, she was so vibrant. Her body was strong, her spirit was clean. Illness was not present."

Mark had nothing to offer to that.

"I was relieved that she didn't ask for a reading," Dixie said. "Because I knew what I'd have to tell her. Then she told me the purpose of her visit, and I made a mistake. I've regretted it every day since. I mean that. Not one day has passed that I have not thought of her with regret."

"You and me both," Mark said. "I understand my regrets, Dixie. What are yours?"

"I let her leave without a warning."

"What would you have said? What would the warning have been?"

"That death was close. Perhaps she would have laughed and gone on her way. I don't know. But if I'd said it? Perhaps even if she didn't take me seriously, it would have lingered in her mind just enough. The words linger, and sometimes, the words affect choices. And so I think of her, and I wonder, would she have had her guard up? Would it have mattered?"

"Yes," he said. His voice was scarcely audible.

Dixie looked pained. "She had that quality. Skeptical but not aggressively so. That was something you shared, of course. You both wanted to believe in challenging things, but you kept that desire secret."

"I just need facts, Dixie. Not mysticism."

"You're not going to succeed with that attitude, and you already *know* that. If what you've experienced recently hasn't taught you that, what will?"

There was a tight tingle at the back of Mark's skull, and he had a sudden vision of an accused murderer, Ridley Barnes, vanishing into dark cave waters, and he heard an echo of a hypnotist's voice, revenants of the last case he'd worked, an experience that had taught him more than he'd wished to learn. He gave a small shake of his head, and Dixie watched him knowingly.

"You don't care for coincidence, do you?" she said.

"No."

"But you don't believe in fate either."

"No."

"Do you realize there are no other options?"

"Sure there are."

She shook her head. "It's either coincidence or fate, Markus. You're going to have to decide."

"I don't think my wife was fated to die here. I think someone made a choice to kill her."

"Of course. But there's one element in the mix that you *do* believe in already. At your core."

"And what might that be?"

"Purpose," she said. "You believe in purpose. You believe that it all fits, that opposing forces will find balance, and that your role in all of it matters."

She put her left hand over the top of his right. Her eyes had the tender but firm expression of a good mother assuring her child that there were no monsters, and it was time to trust the dark and get some rest.

She said, "You are correct, Markus. Your role in all of it matters. It will matter—and it already did."

Her touch put an electric heat through him that he wanted to deny, but he didn't move his hand away. She was leaning forward, a posture that pressed her breasts high against her tank top.

"The answers you need won't come from me," she said. "You've got to believe that. But I can still provide them."

"How does that work?" Mark said. His voice sounded the way steel wool felt.

"They'll come from your wife," she said. Then she squeezed his hand tighter. "I'll need to let her enter me, do you see? Once she makes contact...I become the conduit. And you'll have all that you want then."

She leaned closer, her chest nearly touching his face. "You don't want to believe in that, I know. It's not your way. But you'll have to. I can't tell you anything about Garland Webb. I can't tell you anything about what happened. But Lauren can. Of course she can."

Mark was silent. She rubbed her thumb lightly over the back of his hand, and when she spoke again, her voice had the same caressing feel.

"I'm a channel, Markus. A conduit for energy. When we return to the house, the rest will be your choice, not mine. If you want the truth, you'll need to let me open myself for Lauren. And once I have...you'll need to believe that she's within me. Will you be able to do that?"

"I'll try."

She nodded and squeezed his hand again. "That's all that you can do. So let's try together, shall we? We'll go back to the house, and we'll find your wife."

She released his hand and climbed down from the bench, and he rose and followed her back through the moonlit streets.

11

The big house was dark and there was light in the windows of the guesthouse behind it, where Mark expected to go, but Dixie led him up the porch of the old home.

"I thought this was Myron's," he said. "Your tenant. The man in the big truck."

She frowned. "My tenant lives there." She pointed to the guesthouse. She used a key to turn the ancient lock, then pushed the door open and smiled reassuringly at Mark.

"You'll need to accept the darkness."

"What?"

"It helps. Trust me on this. We can have candlelight, but nothing more. Not if you want to hear from your wife. From Lauren."

The way she said the name was musical, and it hurt him. *I take thee, Lauren…*

She hooked one index finger through his belt loop and tugged him forward. "Don't be scared, now."

In truth, he *was* a little scared. Everything, from the sound of the lock ratcheting back to the smell of the place, age-old dust and mildew, was unappealing, but there was more to it too. Sparks of concern, flickers at the edge of his consciousness like orbs.

Bad energy.

Mark told himself that the sources of that energy were pretty damn clear—when you blended Myron Pate and Garland Webb and this strange town, how could the house feel anything *but* bad?

That was to intellectualize it, though, and as Mark stepped inside that house with Dixie Witte, there was nothing intellectual or rational about the negative charge he felt; it was pure emotion, something primal, something that would have told his ancient ancestors, *You need to run now*.

Just in front of them a staircase led to the second floor, a window at the landing illuminating them. To the left a living room stretched out and blended into a dining room. Dixie hadn't turned on any lights and the furniture stood around them in shadows. Then she slipped away from him and in seconds was on the landing halfway up the stairs.

"Markus?"

"Yeah," he said. "Coming."

The stairs creaked. The wood felt soft, yielding. Dixie Witte waited on the landing, and Mark was glad, because there she looked nothing like Lauren. Then she took another step away, into the darkness, and in silhouette she could have passed for his wife once more.

Were you here, Lauren? Were you ever inside this house?

He dearly hoped not. He knew that she hadn't been killed here, but all the same, he prayed she had never been inside. It was that kind of place.

From the landing, he noticed what he thought at first were odd shadows on the walls. Then he realized they were actually paintings, and when he leaned close enough, he saw that the pictures had been painted directly onto the wall. The ancient plaster was the only canvas.

The paintings were strange symbols. Mark couldn't make them out very well in the dark, but they seemed heavy on circles and triangles. Masonic symbols? He leaned closer to the wall, trying to identify the shapes. Not Masonic symbols, or at least not any he'd seen before. The triangles blended into a circle with what appeared to be a spiral at the center. In the uneven moonlight, the spiral drew the eye and made Mark feel suddenly dizzy. He put a hand against the plaster to steady himself.

Dixie Witte came back down the steps, took his belt loop again, and let her body press against his. When she spoke, she reached up so that her lips were next to his ear.

"She's close to us now, Markus. I can feel her. It's so special. I can't explain just how special it is. But if you can trust, if you can open yourself to the energy…you'll feel her too. Are you able to trust?"

"I'll try."

"Don't try, just believe. Soon my energy will cease, and hers will replace it. You'll know when it happens. You'll feel her within me."

The house felt too hot, with none of the fresh breezes scented with oranges to cool him here. He wondered if she'd paid the boy, the strange boy who spoke of the dead. *Fifty cents if I do the whole tree,* he'd said. *Someone cut off his hands. Put them in a cigar box,* he'd said. *You ever seen something like that?*

There was sweat on Mark's forehead and he was breathing hard, as if the stairs had been a laborious climb. Dixie moved her hand to his forehead and wiped off the beads of perspiration gently. Her hand felt cool and wonderful. He didn't want her to step away. If anything, he wanted her to come closer, press tighter.

You'll feel her within me.

What he felt was sick. Disoriented and dizzy. Were there no fans in this damn house, no open windows? It was like a tomb.

"Trust," Dixie Witte breathed in his ear. "You've got to trust." Then she stepped away again, heading up the next flight of stairs. "She'll have the answers for you. She knows if it was Garland Webb. She knows, Markus. She's the only one who does."

He climbed after her, sweating freely now. At the top of the stairs Dixie turned toward a room that was on the side of the house facing away from the moonlight, which left it in total darkness. Mark followed her in and his sense of claustrophobia rose to new heights. The room was small but it was also blacked out, with thick curtains over the windows, and smells of sage and other incense hung heavy in the air. Cloying and unpleasant, nothing like those cool orange-scented breezes in the yard. He thought of the strange boy again and wondered if he should ask about him. She would know who he was, who had told him that story about the man named Walter with the severed hands. Maybe it had been Dixie. She certainly seemed right for the part. Or maybe one of the people who'd passed through, the angry people. *They come and they go,* the boy had said.

"We'll try to make contact with her now," Dixie said. "With Lauren." She stepped close to him and then, in a strange and sudden motion, she slid down to her knees and took his hands, gripping them tightly, bowing before him. "Close your eyes and trust. You're resisting. You're not open yet. Just trust."

He could barely make out her shape. The room was that dark. Cave dark, he would have said once, before he got a lesson in what cave dark really was. She held his hands and swayed in silence, and he tried to find the part of himself that felt scorn for this, the part of himself that should be laughing at the whole act, but he couldn't. That part was gone now, in this place. She was compelling. And disturbing. The most disturbing thing since that boy...

They come and they go.

The boy had pointed at the big house when he said it. Not the guesthouse. He had pointed indisputably at the old house, the one where angry people came and went.

Dixie Witte had begun to hum, a low and eerie sound, and her fingers were sliding over his hands, tracing the lines on his palms.

"Lauren," she whispered. "Lauren, join us."

Mark didn't like hearing the sound of his wife's name from her. He wanted to tell her to stop saying it. But Lauren had given this woman respect; that was what had brought her here in the first place. Unlike Mark, who for two years had settled for the transcripts of police interviews, and now he had to—

Too young.

The thought came to his mind unbidden, a blitzing image, the opening page of one of the police transcripts. They'd asked Dixie to state her name and age. She'd said she was fifty-two.

Mark stepped back fast, releasing the woman's hands and fumbling in his jacket. She got as far as "Markus, you've got to relax—" before he withdrew the tactical light from his pocket and hit the thumb switch.

These days they gave the label *tactical* to everything from socks to polo shirts, but with the Surefire light, it was more than an adjective—the light was a weapon in its own right. The thumb trigger flooded five hundred lumens directly into Dixie Witte's eyes, approximately ten times more light than human night vision is prepared to handle, and the overload both blinds and freezes. She lifted her hands and swore at Mark in a harsh voice that bore no similarity to her Tennessee Williams–heroine tone.

"Who are you?" Mark said. "Who in the hell are you? You're not Dixie, and you're not in the right house, so—"

He stopped talking abruptly, the woman's identity suddenly unimportant. The flashlight had caught a glint of metal and drawn his eye to an old table just behind her shoulder. Knives glittered from every inch of it. A dozen, at least, and no standard blades in the mix. There were fat, curved bolo machete blades, hard-angled *tanto* tips like small samurai swords, an ancient knife with a stone cutting edge and a bone handle. Ancient, but honed. Any of them would kill you, and cruelly. They were not knives designed for simplicity. They were designed for pain.

"What was the plan?" Mark said. His voice was hoarse. It took an effort to look away from the knives and back to the blond woman who'd promised to find his wife's energy. A moment ago she'd looked weak and under attack, on her knees and temporarily blinded. Now she lowered her hands and smiled with empty contempt.

"You shouldn't have come here," she said. "But it wasn't up to you, was it? I bet that's even what you tell people. I bet you've said that already. If you haven't, you will soon. You'll explain how you ended up in this room. Do you know what word you're going to use? *Called.* That's what you'll say. You felt called here. You might blame the dead bitch, but when you're alone with your thoughts, you'll know that's not true. She's the smallest part of it. And you'll be sure of that by the end."

Mark had once gotten a murder confession from a man who'd calmly and precisely explained how he'd gone about killing a husband and wife in their own living room following five days of careful hunting and planning. He said he'd done it because he'd understood that the gods—plural; he was clear on that too—wanted him to carry lessons of respect into the world. For many years, Mark had thought he was the most chilling specimen of what could appear on this earth disguised as a member of humanity.

That was before he'd met this woman.

The flashlight trembled just the faintest bit in his hand, but because of the play of light in the dark room, the shaking was obvious, and her smile widened, a leering, rictus grin.

"What do you know about my wife?" Mark said.

"More than you, which is to say that I understand she's inconsequential. When you accept that, you'll be better off, but it won't really matter." She shrugged. "Your mind isn't strong enough to matter to us."

"Who is *us*? You and Myron? You and Garland Webb?"

"I have many brothers," she said.

"Is Garland Webb a brother to you?"

"I don't know that name."

"He shared your house."

"He never shared *my* house." She rose from the floor and reached for one of the knives, grabbed the one with the bone handle. By the time she lifted it, Mark had cleared the .38 from its holster and had the muzzle pointed at her.

"Wrong weapon," he said.

She didn't answer, just backed out of the bedroom with the knife held at shoulder level. Then she headed for the stairs, and Mark was left with only a few options, none of them good: try to stop her and invite the opening of his arteries in the process, shoot her in her own home, or let her go.

He let her go.

When the front door banged shut behind her and he was alone in the house, Mark moved to the wall, sagged against it, and looked at the table of knives. He wondered how close he'd come, how many minutes—or seconds—he'd had left when he'd drawn the light.

65

And whether he'd been the first Novak to cross this threshold.

As silence descended around him and sweat dripped from his forehead, he pushed off the wall and gathered himself. He didn't know how long she'd be gone or how many people she'd bring with her when she returned, but right now he was alone in a house that might have evidence relating to Lauren's death, and he wasn't about to waste that chance.

12

At first Sabrina thought the voices were a trick of her mind, because they were usually faint, whispered echoes, and in the brief period she'd had light, she'd become convinced that she had seen the entirety of the cabin.

Eventually, she realized that there was a second level above her, and that was where he was. The sound had confused her because there were no interior stairs, no evidence of a second story. Access had to come from outside.

Her first reaction to this realization was added fear, because now she knew that even when she thought she was alone, she wasn't.

In time, though, she decided that it was a good thing. The more she understood about her situation, the better her chances of escape. All the things she could not see were potential threats. Having a greater sense of the layout was a help. When she ran, she would need to know as much as possible.

So far her escape plan had only its first step: obtain the woman's assistance. Sabrina thought that she could get that. In the time the woman had remained in the cabin, preparing food for Sabrina in the small kitchen, she had been both tender and obviously uncomfortable. She'd kept her eyes away from the handcuff and the chain, and Sabrina was certain that they bothered her. When she'd brought food to Sabrina—oatmeal with brown sugar—she'd actually tried to feed her with the spoon, like a loving mother, before Sabrina simply used her free hand to do it herself. The woman had made a soft cooing sound and stroked Sabrina's hair sympathetically. At first Sabrina had recoiled from the touch, feeling only madness in it, but then she realized the concern was real. However powerful the madness was, it had not evaporated the human concern, the empathy. It was there, and real, and it could be used. How easily it could be used, Sabrina wasn't sure.

In this, as well, Sabrina found comfort. This woman wasn't chained and shackled, but she was still dominated. Controlled. And somewhere in her, Sabrina believed—*had* to believe—there would be resistance to this. Resentment.

Please God, let that be true.

She understood that trying to make one of her captors into an ally was hardly a first-class plan, but she was chained to the wall with only three feet of movement; it was the best she had.

She needed her captor's concern, and the bathroom. She was considering the latter, and not just because of the rising pressure in her bladder. The cabin was too neat and they went to too much effort to provide a bizarre illusion of comfort for her to believe that they intended her to sit in her own mess. At some point, the handcuff was coming off that bolt in the wall. She was almost sure of it.

She had to be sure of it. Because if it wasn't true...

She cried again then, softly but desperately, her body aching. Leaned against the log wall and sobbed herself dry, and when it was done, she told herself that it was the last time.

Until the woman returned, at least. The woman who was weaker than the man, and certainly weaker than Sabrina. Anyone who could be controlled by this man without chains and handcuffs was far weaker than Sabrina. She would use emotion as a weapon, because she believed the woman would respond to it. The tools she had now were limited, and so it was critical to identify them and sharpen them.

Her mind was clearer now, whatever narcotic she'd been drugged with cleansed from her veins, and she had begun to make mental lists—the things that she knew about her situation, a short list, and the things that her captors did not know.

It was in this second list that she was starting to find more strength. Things they did not know about Sabrina Baldwin:

She had been orphaned at twelve, her parents killed by a jackknif-ing semi on an iced-over Michigan interstate; she and Tim, closer than most siblings because of the tragedy, had gone through three different foster homes. Before she turned eighteen she'd earned a partial athletic scholarship to the University of Montana for track, where she won conference titles. Before she'd turned twenty-five, she had started her own business, and had paid off every loan within two years. When she buried her brother, the only family she had left, she'd moved to a new town and faced new challenges and none of that had broken her yet. What her captors saw—a helpless woman in a nightgown, frightened and cowering—was not what they actually had.

Sabrina Baldwin was a lot of things, and frightened was sure as shit one of them right now, but helpless and cowering never had been and never would be.

These were the things she had to remember.

She continued to build onto the list as the minutes—hours? It was impossible to know—passed by, and though she did not move from the wall and could not, she began to feel less anchored to it. Some kidnapping victims escaped. She had seen the stories; everyone had. It was possible. She just had to remember that it was possible.

When the woman returned, she was alone, entering through the front door that seemed to provide the only access to the lower portion of the cabin. Sabrina had slept in fits and starts until the pressure in her bladder built to such a constant ache that she could sleep no longer. She'd been about to give up and succumb to her body's demands when the locks turned.

"Dear? Are you awake? Are you all right?"

"I'm awake. I need the bathroom." Sabrina's voice cracked and rasped. It had been hours since she'd spoken, and the crying bouts had left her dried out. The request *I need the bathroom* felt childlike and weak, and she hated herself for it.

"Of course! Of course, dear."

Remember that she can be manipulated, Sabrina told herself. She shouldn't fear showing weakness around this woman; she should strive for that. It was clear that the woman could be manipulated—her very existence in this place, her acceptance of it, announced her coercion. You could sell this woman a lie.

A flashlight came on, and Sabrina squinted against the harshness of it. The woman was carrying a bag, and inside the bag were Sabrina's own clothes, apparently stolen from the house along with her.

"For your comfort," the woman said. "I'm sorry it took so long. I didn't know where they put them."

There was a metallic jingling and then a key ring appeared in the light and the woman set to work unfastening Sabrina's handcuff from her wrist. She carried herself like a concierge rather than a kidnapper. She gave Sabrina her clothes, then went into the little kitchen and turned her back politely to allow Sabrina to change in privacy. The feeling of slipping into jeans and a sweatshirt was remarkable; they felt more like armor than clothes, made her feel so much less vulnerable than she had in the thin nightgown.

And the only thing between her and freedom was the door, and the woman had the keys for it.

You could run, Sabrina thought. She could knock this woman aside and run. She was stronger than her, and far, far faster.

"Ready for the bathroom?" The woman walked for the door, keys in hand. Sabrina stared at her, astonished at how easy she was making it.

Just run. You posted a sub-six-minute mile for five years straight. Just run!

Then the door was open and the woman shone her light outdoors, and Sabrina understood much more.

The cabin stood in the center of a fenced enclosure, like a shelter in a zoo's pen. The wooden fences had to be fifteen feet tall, maybe twenty. The corner posts were constructed from telephone poles.

"This way, dear. This way."

Using the flashlight, the woman guided her away from the cabin and down a short path to an outhouse. Traces of snow lined the path, and Sabrina was shivering, her breath fogging the air. They were up high, but they weren't in the Beartooths, because there would be much more snow there. How many miles had they covered before she'd regained consciousness? Were they even in Montana?

The woman opened the door and smiled awkwardly.

"I have to wait, of course, but you'll have privacy."

Sabrina stepped into the outhouse, pulled the door shut, and fumbled her way onto the seat. When she'd relieved herself, she rose again and tried to stretch in the dark, cramped quarters to get as loose as possible.

It's just a fence. Fences can be climbed.

The truth was, it had looked easy to climb. It was constructed with plywood panels nailed against a frame of two-by-fours, cheap and easy work, and the frame was on the inside, providing handholds and foot braces all the way to the top. She couldn't afford to wait in hopes of a better opportunity. This might be the *only* opportunity.

"Are you okay?" The voice came from just outside the door.

"Yes," Sabrina said, massaging her hamstrings, bouncing up and down on her toes, telling herself she was just getting ready for a run, that was all it would be, just a short run and a climb and then go, go, *go!* "I'm fine."

When the woman opened the outhouse door, she was smiling—right up until Sabrina punched her.

It was a wild blow, catching the woman on the side of her face, just below her left eye. She stumbled backward and cried out and then Sabrina charged her like a linebacker, lowering her head and leading with her right shoulder. The woman fell easily, just as Sabrina had hoped; she went down hard and landed with a grunt of pain and then Sabrina was past her and alone, nothing between her and freedom but that fence.

They didn't think I would try! How could they think I wouldn't try?

She was running now, giddy to the point of dizziness with fear and adrenaline, expecting some disaster, expecting the man from her house to rise up again, that strange dart gun in hand or, worse, a real one, but nobody came. It was just her and the open ground and she covered it easily, her stride fast and smooth, and she was half laughing and half crying as she neared the fence, the adrenaline so intense that there was a high hum in her ears, so strong it was something she could almost *feel* as she reached for one of those two-by-four braces that supported the fence and was about to provide her easy escape over the top.

She didn't register the impact, didn't register even any pain, just surprise. There was a reason they called it an electric *shock*. One minute she was running free and strong and the next she was down on her ass and her right arm felt like it was missing and the rest of her tingled as if spiders were swarming over her flesh. She looked from the ground to the fence in bewilderment, dazed, and finally she understood that the hum in her ears hadn't been imagined and realized why the woman had freed her from the handcuff with such casual confidence.

The fence was electrified.

Powerfully electrified.

From pole to pole, strands of exposed copper wire ran along the wooden braces, and the voltage passing through was so strong that the hum was audible. Each brace carried a wire. It would take a pole vaulter to clear this fence without contacting the electrical current.

Get up, she thought stupidly, *get up and try another place. You can't just sit here.*

She heard a sound behind her then and turned to see the woman approaching. Not running, just walking with a steady stride, all the kindness gone from her face. When she reached Sabrina, she knelt beside her.

"You got buzzed pretty good, didn't you?"

Sabrina didn't answer. The woman turned the flashlight away from the fence and panned it to the right, and Sabrina saw the cabin clearly for the first time—two stories, with only one door to the lower level and a set of exterior stairs on each side of the house leading to the second floor. All around the fence were tall pines, and just behind it a cluster of dead trees that hadn't been cut. Then the flashlight beam stopped moving, and Sabrina gasped.

They weren't trees. They were telephone poles, ten of them, at least, and what looked like old transformers had been mounted high on them, though no wires were strung.

"What are...you...doing here?" Sabrina croaked as the pain from the shock began to pulse through her arm, the surprise gone and only the agony left. *"What do you want?"*

"It's not what we *want*, dear, it's what we *need*. All of us. It has to be done."

"What does?"

"Awakening. Every society needs one. It's undeniable, one of the firm truths we have. Eli will explain this to you. He'll tell you what the mountains have told him. I know that it will be hard at first, but please, please listen. Open your mind, open your heart. Here's what you need to remember, Sabrina—the mountains have been here since before any of us were even imagined. Now, you tell me: Would they lie?"

Sabrina couldn't formulate a response, and the woman smiled again, her eyes glittering in the flashlight glow.

"Exactly, dear. Exactly. The mountains wouldn't lie. They couldn't! And we should be very grateful that Eli can hear them. Are you ready to go back to the cabin? Have you satisfied yourself with your little experiment?"

There was no point in resisting. She couldn't climb the fence, so she'd have to figure out how to disable it. She was thinking about this when the woman said, "And, oh yes, dear, there's one other thing— you're not allowed to hit me. That's against the rules."

She swung the flashlight and hit Sabrina full in the face.

As Sabrina howled in pain and blood poured from her nose, the woman regarded her with the sympathetic eyes, the caretaker eyes.

"Let's not have a problem like this again," she said. "It's bad for everyone, isn't it? But as Eli always says, rules need to be enforced or they aren't rules at all. It's a matter of energy, dear. Whatever you put out will be returned to you. It will pay to remember that while you're here."

I 3

By the time Mark had worked his way through the house, he was talking softly to himself. It was more a prayer than anything else. *Please tell me she was never here. Please tell me she was never in this place.*

The idea of Lauren gunned down in that dark thicket of bamboo beside the ditch had always felt more than horrific enough.

That was before he'd seen the house.

Between the ground floor, the stairwell, and the upstairs bedrooms, he counted sixty-seven paintings on the walls and chalk drawings on the floors, all some variation of a spiral theme. Each one pulled him in like a hypnotic eye. Beyond the spiral imagery, there was only one constant to the artwork: the center of each spiral was black. Even in the chalk drawings, black paint had been used in the center.

What mattered the most to him, though, was in the bedroom at the far end of the upstairs hall. There, words had been painted among the drawings. Each drawing was carefully, artistically done, clean and precise. The words were not. They were lettered unevenly, growing larger and bolder, conveying a sort of mania, and while Mark didn't understand their meaning, the words were familiar.

Rise the Dark the DARK will RISE RiSE the DARK RiSE rise will RISE the DARK

The only unexplained words in the notebook that Lauren had left on the passenger seat of her car before she'd stepped out of it on her way to death. As Mark had told the detectives, that was the first time he'd seen the phrase.

And the last, until now.

The house was so stifling that he felt dizzy when he moved too fast, but as he read those words he felt a chill. Every time. And he returned to them often. As he searched the rest of the house, he kept interrupting his progress to go back to that room and stare at the wall in the glow of the flashlight.

Did you see this, baby? Were you here?

He had to order himself away from that wall, force his attention elsewhere, and elsewhere the hypnotic-eye drawings loomed in every corner, like funhouse mirrors.

Sweat was dripping down his face and along his spine, but now it felt like the clammy sweat of sickness. He went to wipe his face with his jacket and realized he'd taken it off and wasn't carrying it any longer. At one point he'd been holding it. Where had he put it? He couldn't remember. He wiped his forehead with the back of his hand instead, and the flashlight beam bobbed crazily around the walls, catching first one spiral drawing and then the next.

No. Not spirals. You're using the wrong word.

That was true. There was a term for the shape in those drawings, and it wasn't *spiral*. It was—

Vortex.

He heard the word in his own head but it seemed to be spoken in someone else's voice. It was a sensation he'd had before in a place he didn't want to remember—endless caverns of damp, dark stone—on a day when he'd been certain he'd never see daylight again. See any kind of light. The voices down there had saved him, though. Maybe. He tried not to think of them often.

They're gathering here for something. But what?

The house provided no answers. Nor did it provide much in the way of tangible evidence of who its occupants were. There were no computers or phones, though there were power cords and chargers; no mail, none of the standard artifacts of modern human existence. The closest thing Mark found was a bookshelf filled with texts that had clearly been read often, and recently. Most of them were books about energy and psychic phenomena, but there was also an investment in the works of Nikola Tesla and Thomas Edison. Mark combed through every closet and every drawer and found not a single piece of paper with a name or even a clue as to the identity of the blond woman. Perhaps Dixie Witte—the real Dixie Witte, the one in the guesthouse awaiting him now—would be able to answer that simply enough, but Mark didn't want to leave the property until he was convinced he'd seen all there was. Once he walked out, he didn't think he'd be coming back without a subpoena...and, truthfully, he hoped he'd never be back at all. There was something sick about the place.

Rise the Dark the DARK will RISE RiSE the DARK RiSE rise will RISE the DARK

They were words of madness, and yet he stood looking at them again as if he were intending to solve a riddle. He played the light over each wildly painted letter, trying to think of what the phrase might be from. A poem, a song? The look of the word *rise* reminded him of something, and eventually he got it—the Manson Family. They'd painted the word in blood at the home of their victims. The Tate house. No, not Tate. The second house. The LaBiancas. Husband and wife, butchered in their own home. *Rise.* The Manson girls had been in that house before. They'd broken in and moved things around, let the dog out, just generally left a sense of intrusion, invasion. Creepy-crawling, they'd called in. That house was where the police had found the words *helter skelter* too. Had inspiration from that bloody summer of 1969 found its way to Cassadaga? The Manson Family, with their pretty young girls with changed names, new identities.

I have many brothers, the blond woman had said.

They come and they go, the boy had told him about the people in the house.

He moved away from the wall, panning the light from left to right across the room to illuminate those odd drawings, and felt dizzy again.

Rise the dark. The dark rise.

Again he heard a voice in his head that was not his own. A male voice, but not one he knew, saying: *Too long in here, Markus. Too long. Time to go.*

He pulled away from the wall with an effort, went down the stairs, and noted numbly that his jacket was on the floor in the living room. He gathered that up and was about to head for the front door and escape when he realized that he hadn't checked the kitchen. He'd been about to when he'd had one of those strange urges to go back upstairs and revisit the bizarre painted words. As bad as he wanted out, he couldn't go yet. He had to finish the job. See everything there was to see.

There wasn't much in the kitchen, but a door there led to a cellar. He hadn't expected to find a cellar, because houses of that age in Florida usually didn't have basements. They were built over crawl spaces most often, prepared for tropical rains and flooding. The house at 49B, though, didn't have a Florida look. It had been built by a Northerner for a Northerner. As soon as Mark opened the door that led downstairs, the air told him why the basement had been a bad idea. The trapped smell of a thousand floods leaked out, a sickeningly sweet mustiness.

The cellar ceiling was so low that there was no way he could stand up, and he had to go down the bottom steps in an awkward crouch. The confinement, paired with the smell of damp stone, brought back memories of Indiana caves, and he wanted none of those.

The space was cluttered, stacked with what seemed to be random pieces of machinery, like a salvage yard. It took him a moment to realize what they were—generators. They were all in pieces, disassembled and scattered. Some were so ancient that it was little surprise he hadn't recognized them at first. The presence of the generators wasn't so strange—in a place where hurricane season was serious business, you saw a lot of them—but so many in scattered pieces just added another layer of frenzy to the house. It looked as if someone had been frantically trying to assemble one as time was running short.

There was a special delusion going on in the home, that was clear, but Mark had no sense of exactly *what* the people who lived here believed.

Beyond the generator was a workbench, and when Mark moved his light to its surface he saw more metal, but this was different from the generators, clean and gleaming. New.

He approached it with caution. There were angled pieces of steel on each end of a central piece that looked like a grate or maybe a drain cover, with ribbed bars and gaps between. The angled sections were hinged. He reached out with his flashlight and tapped the center of the object, and the bench seemed to explode.

The flashlight was torn from his hand and he felt something snap at his finger like a wolf's teeth and then the flashlight was on the floor, rolling, its beam painting crazy patterns of the generator shadows, and Mark couldn't see the workbench anymore and didn't have a damn clue what had happened. It had felt like an explosion, but there was no fuel, and no debris. His heart was thundering and he'd reached for his gun as if he needed to return fire.

He knelt and found the light and turned it back to the bench, and finally he understood—it was a trap. A literal trap, with a spring-loaded central piece that banged those angled jaws home. If he'd tapped on it with his fist instead of the flashlight, he'd have a broken hand.

He turned from the device and back toward the stairs and that was when he saw the dead woman.

She was jammed beneath the short flight of steps, her body pressed into a crevice barely large enough to contain it. He'd walked right over her when he'd entered. Her eyes were open, glittering in the light, bright, but not as bright as the blood that saturated the front of her white dress. Her throat had been slashed, and not long ago—the blood wasn't entirely dry.

Mark said, "God, no," as if he could deny the reality.

Slow drips of blood plinked down from the gash in her throat and joined the horrific pool below.

This, Mark thought dully, *would be the real Dixie Witte.*

When he'd arrived, the blond woman had seemed startled, legitimately bothered by the fact that he was early for his appointment. Had she emerged from the cellar just a few minutes earlier? Had she smashed the remains of a human life under the steps like so much discarded junk and then gone up and put beer on ice?

What if you'd been on time? What was supposed to be in the beer? Was that walk to Medicine Wheel Park actually part of the plan, or was she filling time?

The dead woman's eyes were fixed on his, and they were the only part of her that seemed to hold a trace of life. He had the disquieting sense that she wished to tell him something, or wished for him to tell her something.

Did you hold hope, even as you died? Did you watch your own blood fill your hands and, even as you understood that it was too much, too fast, still think that there was a chance?

I'm glad they shot Lauren, he thought, because he'd read the autopsy reports, read the expert opinions stating that she wouldn't have known pain. But who in the hell could say that, really? The living could only guess at how it had gone for the dead. There was no such thing as an expert opinion when it came to death.

He was standing there staring at the corpse when he heard a low, distant rumble like far-off thunder. For a moment he thought that was exactly what it was, the coming of another storm, but the sound remained.

Not thunder.

Myron's truck.

Shaken back into motion, he straightened and promptly slammed his head into the low ceiling, a teeth-snapping crack; he swore and dipped low again, back into a crouch, and drew his gun. There was a small window in the cellar, right at ground level, that let a small amount of light in. When he went to it, though, the pane was so filthy that it didn't allow a clear look anywhere, and even if it had, the window faced the backyard. The sound of the truck was coming from the front.

He turned from the window. The only path of exit was up those steps, right over the dead woman.

He crossed the basement in an awkward crouch, trying to keep his eyes on the door but not look at the woman, which was impossible. He'd just reached the base of the steps when he heard the front door open.

He had no idea where his Dixie Witte impostor had gone after she left the house or whether she knew that he'd remained so long. What he did know was that the man who had called himself Myron Pate had probably not been kidding when he promised that the next time he saw Mark, he'd be armed. If Mark stepped out of the cellar now, he'd need to be ready to step out shooting.

Two voices became audible, one deeper, one softer. Floorboards creaked overhead as heavy footsteps pounded through the ancient house. Mark looked at the dead woman just a few feet from him and a part of him felt as if giving himself up to an exchange of gunfire would be better than waiting down here with her any longer. He could smell the blood now; it seemed to be all he could smell, and he wondered how he'd missed it before. He stepped back, turning his face from her.

The sounds above grew louder—too loud, thumps of furniture and banging against the walls, and the front door opened and closed and opened and closed again. How many people were they bringing? It sounded like an invasion. Mark blinked sweat out of his eyes, his shoulder beginning to ache from holding the firing position, his gun aimed at the only door they could come through.

The corpse lay before it like a promise of his fate.

Upstairs, the front door banged open again and Mark heard a male voice say, "Take this," and he realized what all the traffic up there was: there weren't more people entering—they were packing up.

You've flushed them out, he thought. *They're emptying the house, and doing it in a hurry.*

A female voice: "He said to shut it down, and he meant it."

Then a new sound, splashing, and Mark was painfully slow in understanding it. He had been listening to it for several seconds, confused, when his nose told him what his ears hadn't—gasoline.

Footsteps pounded into the kitchen for the first time, and he tensed his finger on the trigger, but the door didn't open. The gasoline sloshed against the door and then the footsteps were gone and all that remained was a slow, steady drip at the top of the stairs. The fuel leaked down the steps and trickled onto the dead woman, joining her blood. Mark stared in horrified fascination as a single drop of gasoline landed directly on her open eye, splashing off the cornea but triggering no blink.

The thundering sound of the truck engine's starting jerked his attention away. They were ready to leave, and that was both good and bad, because he knew what was coming once they were gone.

Almost immediately there was a *whoosh* of ignition, and the closed door at the top of the cellar stairs was outlined in a thin orange line.

The house was burning on top of him.

He went up the stairs, crossing over her body. Then he pulled the door open and almost fell back down the stairs in the face of the wave of flames that met him. The kitchen was aglow with fire; flames climbed the walls. Somewhere in the living room, what was left of the gas can exploded, and the blaze that followed it had a flash of blue trapped in the orange and red.

Mark slammed the door against the heat, and the cellar returned to blackness, but there was heavy smoke already, and he knew time was short.

He left the stairs and stumbled to the window. It had an iron lock, rusted shut. He hammered on it with the butt of the .38 but made no progress, and the smoke was thickening already, so he gave up on the lock and bashed the butt of the gun into the center of the glass. The old pane fractured but didn't give, and he swore and smashed it again and this time it broke and he put his hand through the window and over the glass, razoring his thumb open. He balled his jacket in his fist and used that to clear the remains of the glass, then he put his right foot on the old generator nearby, the massive hunk of rusting steel, and stepped up high enough to reach through the small window and get a grip on the exterior wall.

It was tight, but he'd wormed through tighter spaces in caves in Indiana, and with the fire crackling just behind him, motivation was not an issue. He dragged himself through, leaving thin ribbons of flesh behind as he swept over remnant teeth of glass, and he was on his belly in the grass, gasping for air, when he saw a figure just ahead. He fumbled to get his gun upright and had nearly pulled the trigger when he recognized the boy from the orange tree, illuminated by the flames. He was offering a hand.

Mark accepted it and the boy helped him to his feet and they stumbled away together as a window blew out somewhere upstairs and the fire roared through the old house.

"It wasn't me," Mark said.

"I know." The boy released him and stepped aside, regarding the burning home with curiosity but no evident fear. "I saw them. I didn't know you were inside, though. I saw them with the gas cans."

A siren rose over the sound of the flames and they both turned toward it. No emergency lights were visible yet, just the sound. The flames cast flickering orange glows over the palm leaves but out beyond the village was dark.

"I think they hurt Dixie," the boy said.

"Yes," Mark said. "They hurt her." He rubbed his eyes as if to remove the image of the woman's body jammed indifferently under the cellar stairs. "Do you know who they are?"

The boy shook his head. "No, but they said the name you asked about before. The strange one."

"Garland?"

"That's it. They're going to him now."

"Where?"

"They didn't say a place. And they said another name too. Eli."

Eli. It meant nothing to Mark. He said, "Do they work for Garland, is that it? Is he in charge?"

"No. The one named Eli is in charge."

"How can you be sure?"

"I just am. I know things, sometimes. Everyone here does. One day I'll be better at it than I am now. But I know some things already. Eli is the worst one." The boy was backing up as the flames grew taller and hotter. "He's very bad."

Mark had trouble imagining anyone worse than Garland Webb, but he nodded and said, "Okay. Thank you for telling me. And wait, please. I need something from you. Please, it's important." He fumbled in his pocket with a bloody hand. "Son, I need you to take something for me and keep it until I'm back. Can you do that? It's very important. It will help me find them and stop them from hurting anyone else."

He extended his cell phone with its photographs of the red truck's license plate from earlier in the afternoon. He didn't want to have it on him when the police came, didn't want to have to explain any of the photos. He needed a head start. The boy regarded it suspiciously.

"Why don't you give it to the police?"

"Because I need to find those people before the police do."

The boy looked into Mark's eyes for a second and then turned his chin slightly, his gaze drifting up and over Mark's shoulder.

"I shouldn't do it, but Walter says it's fine."

A few short hours ago Mark would have told the boy to stop telling his tales about ghosts. Now he said, "Listen to Walter, son. It sounds like he knows something about what happens when bad people stay out of prison."

By the time the police arrived, the boy had pocketed the phone and was standing in the shadows just outside the circle of firelight, where a crowd of onlookers had gathered.

"Is there anyone inside?" an officer asked.

"Yes. But you're not going to be able to help her now," Mark said, and then he glanced back for the boy, but he was gone.

Part Two

THE HIGH COUNTRY

14

Doug Oriel, known in Cassadaga as Myron Pate, had driven through the night and Janell slept as Florida fell behind them and they carved into the Georgia pinewoods. She had dreamed often and well in Cassadaga. Sometimes, they were memories of the Netherlands, her first days with Eli. Other times, visions of the dark world and the horrified faces of the foolish people who feared it. In the truck, though, she struggled to find deep enough sleep for dreams at all, and when they came, they were more like flashes of recent memory, Novak behind his circle of light, shining it into her eyes.

Their first stop was well north of Atlanta, an obscure spot on the map that would have been forgotten completely if not for the interstate that ran through it. Doug pulled into a gas station beside a pump, shut the engine off, and looked at her.

"It's your role," he said. "I can call him, but he will say that—"

"No. I'll call. I'm senior."

Usually this grated on him, but today he was relieved. This was the very reason he hadn't been granted leadership. He was a weapon, nothing more. An operator. Without her guidance, useless.

"If he needs to hear from me, I'll back up your story."

"Just pump the gas," she said, and got out of the truck.

In the backseat was a black bag designed to hold a laptop computer, innocuous-looking, invisible. She unzipped it and selected one of the forty cell phones inside, then powered it up for the first time. The gas was pumping, but she could see Doug watching her, and she walked away from the truck and into the shadows at the far end of the parking lot. Then she dialed the first of three carefully memorized numbers. Each one asked for a new number, rerouting her, rerouting her, and rerouting her again. Then, finally, a ring.

Her throat was tight and her skin prickled. When he spoke, she thought she would not be able to answer. It was that wonderful to hear his voice again. For months, their only communication had been short e-mail messages.

"It's me," she said. "We are in motion."

"But Novak is alive?"

"I believe so."

"You *believe* so?"

"It is my understanding he escaped the house unharmed."

"Then this is not a question of belief. This is a fact."

"Yes." The fact that she had failed.

"What does he understand?"

"Nothing."

"That seems impossible."

"It's true. His interest is only in Garland."

"He can't see beyond that?"

"His whole world exists in that ditch where his wife died. It is all that he sees. I spent extra time with him to assess this. Now I wish I hadn't."

"It's important to know." He sighed. "But Garland taunted him. If he can possibly track Garland here, we will have to deal with him."

She was unaware of the taunt and wanted to know more about it, but he didn't like questioning or prolonged phone calls, so she stayed silent. For a time, so was he. Thinking, no doubt, about her failure. She could picture Novak in the darkness, his hands in hers, and the memory made her wince. She'd been so close. A few seconds faster, that was all she'd needed to be. She hadn't expected him to move so swiftly. Hadn't expected him to move at all. He'd obliged her every request to that point, so there had been no sense of a rush.

"The house was clean?" he asked at last.

"Completely."

Silence once more. She could hear wind from his side of the call and tried to picture his surroundings. She'd imagined them many times but never seen them. They'd been apart so long, Amsterdam seemed like another life.

"We will need to move faster," he said. "That's the only choice. I've already taken steps to expedite operations here. You will have to hurry to join us, and you must not be stopped."

"We won't be."

"It will be different energy for you now. Not as strong as it was there. You'll have to find it in yourself."

"Not a problem," she said, and truer words had never been spoken.

"So it begins," he said, and she wasn't fearful, but joyful.

It had been a long wait.

She powered the phone off, smashed it against the concrete wall until fragments of it scattered, and threw the remains into the trash. Doug was waiting nervously beside the truck, and she extended her hand for the keys.

"I'll drive now," she said. She couldn't keep the smile off her face.

It was not the way things were supposed to have begun, but they were in motion now, and that was all that mattered.

15

The jail reminded Mark of many he'd known in his youth.

It was a rural jail, and the deputy who'd arrested him shared a last name with his booking officer, suggesting that good-ol'-boy policing flourished in Volusia County. At least here, though, the good ol' boys were polite enough, if confused. In the jails of Montana and Wyoming, Mark had met plenty who weren't so polite. In those days, the officers also hadn't had cameras recording them, and they'd been drinking buddies with the prosecutors and the judges.

Tonight, the deputies didn't know what in the hell to do with him, so they'd put him in the drunk tank. He'd gotten one phone call and had used it to reach Jeff London, offering no details beyond his location. Then they'd locked him up and gone off to consider the situation and determine whether he was a murderer or an arsonist or both.

Mark passed the time sitting on a bunk beside the stainless-steel sink and water fountain that were mounted on the back of the toilet, a one-piece unit. If you desired a drink of water, you'd better hope there wasn't another drunk vomiting or shitting. Fortunately, Mark was alone and sober, and—all that really mattered, as he recalled the blond woman down on her knees before him in that dark room, her hands so close to the waiting knives—he was alive.

The police who eventually came for him weren't local. It wasn't the arresting deputy but a captain from DeLand, along with an agent from the Florida Department of Law Enforcement. They took his statement, recording all the while.

"He told you his name was Myron Pate, and she didn't give you a name?"

"Correct. She pretended she was Dixie Witte, but she didn't give a name. He said he was Myron Pate, but I think he lied."

"We think so too."

"Okay. Then I can't help you. The only person who would know is Dixie Witte, and I never spoke to her. I assumed it was her body that I found in that basement."

"You assumed right."

"It's a small town," Mark said. "Someone has to know who they were."

If the police had heard any names mentioned, they didn't care to share them. They returned to asking questions, and Mark answered them. Most of them. The captain from DeLand was most interested in why he hadn't fled the house when he'd had the chance.

"I was curious."

"Not curious enough to call the police, even though you thought you might have just escaped a murder attempt?"

Mark shrugged.

"A woman was killed in that house, Mr. Novak. You don't seem committed to helping us understand how that happened."

"A woman was killed in Cassadaga more than two years ago," Mark said. "It's why I was there. You now know everything I know about the woman who was killed tonight. We can talk through it again, but you've already heard it."

They wanted to talk through it again.

It was somewhere around four in the morning when Jeff London managed to rouse a judge from sleep and convince her that Mark's questioning had reached excessive lengths if he wasn't going to be booked.

Jeff met him outside the jail.

"Let's talk in the car," Mark said. "I've spent enough time here."

Jeff drove, and they talked.

"Unless they were better at bluffing than I think," Mark said, "the police don't know any more about who was renting that house from Dixie Witte than I do. Am I wrong?"

"No. From what I've been told—and this comes from the prosecutor here, a guy I've known for years—all they're sure of is that Dixie rented the place for cash, didn't keep records, and was a big believer in respecting privacy. The neighbors all agree on this. Most of them didn't like her tenants, and a couple of them saw the guy you know as Myron go into the house with the blond woman, both of them carrying gas cans, right before it went up. That's good news for you."

"Anyone mention a young boy? He was there."

"A boy? Not that I've heard of."

"He was the one who told me people in the house turned over often. And once you're inside, it is pretty clear that the various tenants think it's a special home," Mark said, remembering the wild words scrawled in paint.

"Tell me what happened," Jeff said, and Mark did. It was the same speech he'd given the police, with one addition.

"I have a license plate I need you to run. But first I need to find the kid who has my phone, assuming he kept it. I think he did, because he believes I've got the support of a dead man. It's like being a made guy in the Mafia, apparently. In Cassadaga, a dead man named Walter vouched for me."

Jeff stared at him. Mark shrugged. "It's a different kind of place."

"I'm familiar with that. What I want to know is why in the hell you chose not to give the evidence on your phone to the police."

Mark didn't speak. Jeff grimaced and said, "Don't go down this road. Please, do not go down this road."

"I need to find Garland Webb before the police do."

"There are other victims now. Not just Lauren. And other suspects. It's bigger than you, bigger than her."

"They know where he is," Mark said as if Jeff hadn't spoken. "And the police have had their shots."

"There's no coming back from the choice you're making."

"Would you drive me to the town, at least? If I can find the kid and get my phone, I'll figure out another way to get the license plate run. My PI license is still valid, even if I don't work for you."

Jeff's voice was sad and distant. "We'll get you the plate."

Mark hadn't expected him to agree to that. He said, "You're losing your faith in the system a little bit yourself, aren't you?"

"No, Markus. Not even a little bit."

"Then why help me?"

A mile passed in silence before Jeff said, "Because she died on my watch. Working for my company, on my case. The things you feel? I don't pretend to know them. It's not the same. But that doesn't mean I don't feel anything."

"It wasn't on your watch."

"Like hell. I could have stopped her if I'd wanted to. She pushed it, but I could have said no."

"She pushed it?"

Jeff nodded. He usually looked far younger than his years, but not now. "It was her idea. She didn't just ask to go. She *demanded,* almost. She wanted to see the town, she said. It was odd, and I shouldn't have allowed it. So, yeah, it was on my watch. Her interest in the town was strange, and I didn't listen to my instincts. She never belonged there, and yet I facilitated it."

"How she could put any kind of faith in the stuff they're selling in that town, Jeff, it just kills me. Because it's so *obviously* a con. And she was too smart to fall for a con. Too analytical, too by-the-book. She knew the psychic claims wouldn't be worth a damn in court, and all she cared about was building courtroom product. I didn't understand it the day she left, the last time we spoke, and I still don't. She *knew better.*"

He heard the anger in his own voice. So absurd, but so hard to avoid. The grief never left, but the anger came and went, just like the boy had said of the people at that evil house in Cassadaga. It came and it went, an outlandish, self-righteous rage: *How could you let yourself get killed, Lauren? Didn't you understand how much I loved you, needed you, how absolutely lost I am now and always will be without you?*

As if it had been selfish of her to die.

Jeff pinched his brow and held it for a few seconds. Then he said, "You're a good detective, and a better man. You might actually find Webb first. And when you do, you'll make the right choice. You don't believe that anymore, but I still do."

They didn't speak for the remainder of the drive.

16

Sabrina was fed oatmeal again. The woman who'd smashed Sabrina's nose with a flashlight only a few hours earlier now watched her eat with a smile.

"I need something to call you," Sabrina said.

"No, you don't."

"That's not true. You've already given me Eli's name. I know Garland's. And you told me that I need to learn to be happy here, and to listen. That's hard to do if I'm scared of you, and everything is more terrifying if you're all strangers. Don't you understand that?"

The woman hesitated, then said, "Violet."

"Violet. Any last name?"

"No, dear. Just Violet. Eli has a presentation for you. Are you able to go outside without the trouble we had last time?"

Sabrina's face ached and she could breathe comfortably only through her mouth. She had no desire to repeat the last time.

At least not until she had a plan for the fence.

"I'll be good," she said. "I know the rules now."

"I hope so."

Violet uncuffed her and they went to the door. Both interior and exterior locks required keys. When they stepped out into daylight, Sabrina got her first sense of the scope of her surroundings.

They were on a high plateau rimmed by mountains, peaks looming in all directions. The slopes fell away from every side of the cabin, and fir trees screened it from view. Beneath the tree line was a ring of boulders; some of them seemed natural to the terrain, but others were too carefully aligned, as if they'd been excavated and moved into place to form a perimeter fence. Far below, down a steep slope of loose sandstone and scree, a stream cut through a valley basin. Where the stream fell out of sight, tumbling down to a lower elevation, another tree line blocked visibility. Traces of old snow lingered, but nothing fresh, and most of it had melted. They were somewhere well south of Red Lodge, and maybe east. There were no roads that she could see, no homes, no cars.

They were entirely alone.

"Good morning," a voice from behind her said, and she turned to see the man named Eli, the first look she'd gotten at him in daylight. Average height, average build, with long hair tied back. There was absolutely nothing remarkable about him except for his eyes. They were inkwell dark, and forceful.

"Where is my husband?" Sabrina said.

He smiled. It was a smile that would have charmed anyone, she thought, or at least anyone he had not chained to a wall first.

"Your husband is fine and well. He's doing important work. You should be very proud of him."

A gust of wind rattled the fence. Eli faced it and breathed deeply, contented.

"Here's something you should consider," he said. "A quote that inspired me. Perhaps it will inspire you." He paused, and when he spoke again his voice was deeper, with a powerful timbre. Violet nodded at the sound.

"'For your people, the land was not alive,'" he said. "'It was something that was like a stage, where you could build things and make things happen. You were supposed to make the land bear fruit. That is what your God told you.... There were more of you, so your way won out. You took the land and you turned it into property. Now our mother is silent. But we still listen for her voice.

"'And here is what I wonder: If she sent diseases and harsh winters when she was angry with us, and we were good to her, what will she send when she speaks back to you?

"'You had better hope your God is right.'"

He stopped speaking and smiled.

"What do you think of that?"

"It's a powerful question."

"Isn't it?"

"It also sounds like it belongs to the Indians. And that isn't you."

The smile widened. "Ah, Sabrina, but you're wrong. We're too far gone in this world to worry about heritage, about ethnicity. There are only two relevant parties now—people and power. Who has power, and who deserves it."

"I guess you think that's for you to determine."

"Oh, I won't determine a thing, Sabrina. Your nation is laced with the fuses of fear. All I'm going to do is provide the match. I'm fascinated to see how it turns out." He looked out over the mountains again, took another deep breath, and whispered, "'You had better hope your God is right.'"

When he finally turned back to her, the smile was gone.

"I understand that last night you made a mistake that led to two injuries."

Sabrina waited.

"Are you familiar with the work of Nikola Tesla?" Eli Pate said.

The name was vaguely familiar. "Electrical genius," she said, and he seemed pleased until she added, "like Edison."

His eyes tightened immediately. "Tesla's understanding was far ahead of Edison's—ahead of the entirety of mankind—and it still took years for the money-obsessed pigs who ran the world to recognize it. And while the battle raged, Edison engaged in a campaign designed to destroy Tesla's reputation, to obscure the truth with lies, to promote his own ideas even though he knew they were inferior, and to line his pockets rather than help the world. Highlights of this campaign included the slaughter of innocent animals that he claimed were dying by the droves due to Tesla's alternating-current system. Our dear hero Thomas Alva Edison reached his zenith when he electrocuted an elephant in an attempt to discredit Tesla's system. This is true."

He glanced away then and Sabrina followed his eyes and saw, for the first time, a small cage near the fence. There were soft sounds coming from inside.

"Last night you were reckless, thankless, and dangerous. Two people were injured. I blame myself."

He walked to the cage.

"This man who is celebrated in every schoolroom in the nation once electrocuted animals in the interest of his own commerce. We have neglected to teach the children that lesson. His team made movies of these atrocities, designed to prove one thing and one thing only: that his baby, direct current, was safer than the alternating current of Tesla. But guess what, Sabrina. It was not safer. It was not better. It was in all ways inferior, and Edison, if we are to believe anything of his genius, should have understood this. I suspect he did, down in his bones, where whatever remained of his engineering instincts hid, concealed by the instincts of the business tycoon. I suspect that he had slipped past the point of being concerned with what was *right* and wandered into the territory of what was *righteous*. It was all about fury then, about ego. Do you understand the difference in this?"

It was clear he wanted an answer, so she said, "Yes."

He regarded her with disdain, shook his head, and then leaned down and fumbled with a latch on the cage. Three chickens emerged. A rooster and two hens, clucking and pecking; they approached Eli with immediate trust. He smiled at them and reached into his shirt pocket and withdrew some feed, which he shook out at his feet. The birds ate happily.

"Alternating current," he said, "is indeed a dangerous thing."

Sabrina said, "You don't need to do this."

"I'd hoped not. But you proved me wrong. I'm afraid you'll have to watch the effects of your choices, Sabrina."

He walked backward down the hill and toward the humming fence, spreading more feed. The birds scurried after him, using their wings for balance in their awkward runs. They swarmed over his boots and against his legs, and when he reached down and stroked one large hen, she showed no fear. Only trust. Sabrina tasted bile in the back of her throat and turned away.

"Sabrina? I'll need your attention. If you turn away, I'll have to find new methods of teaching. And I assure you that I will."

Reluctantly, she looked back at him. Satisfied, he sidestepped and tossed a final handful of food at the base of the fence, near the lowest of the humming copper wires.

The first bird, a bantam rooster, made contact almost immediately, and there was a blink-fast bang and a small cloud of feathers blew into the air and the smell of charred flesh followed behind it. The rooster, blown five feet back, lay motionless and steaming.

The remaining hens, spooked by the bang, made frantic attempts to flee. Eli kicked the first one, catching her sideways and driving her into the fence, where a squawk of fear died abruptly in a shower of sparks. The final bird, the large hen who had let Eli stroke her just seconds earlier, was faster. She escaped the kick, ducking her tail as she scurried off, peeling her head back and uttering a high, warbling sound of terror. She sensed Eli's pursuit and angled away with un-canny instincts and surprising speed, eluding him in a wobbling run up the hill and toward Sabrina. She was only a few feet from her when Pate finally caught her. He grabbed the hen by the neck and lifted it as she squawked and flapped, twisting in midair. One of her claws caught his forearm and opened a bright red gash, but he didn't react, just marched down the hill, turned, and slung the hen at the fence. She had time to flap her wings twice in a desperate attempt to regain control before she made contact.

It wasn't enough.

The once-fastest of the birds slid down the fence, sparking and smoking, to join her dead companions. He kicked the dead bird away from the fence, one blackened wing flapping against the white body, and then turned back.

"Violet, take Sabrina inside and secure her, please. Leave her enough mobility to pluck feathers, though. Sometimes sensory cues are necessary for a lesson to take hold."

Violet hurried down to collect the birds. She shoved the fastest hen, the last one to die, into Sabrina's hands. The body was still warm, and Sabrina could see that one eye had ruptured. Blood ran from the eye and over the beak. The smell of burned flesh and feathers was heavy.

Eli watched with a smile.

"Good news," he said. "You'll have a break from the oatmeal now."

17

Jeff dropped Mark off at his car, which was still in the park, unbothered.

"You should be driving west with me," Jeff said. "Go home, get some sleep, and we'll talk through this."

Mark nodded, but they both knew he had no intention of doing anything close to that. Jeff sighed and said, "You want help finding the kid?"

"No. I don't want you any more involved than you already are. I'm sorry."

"Just be careful. You'll make the right decisions at the right times. I still believe that, like I said. But on your way there...watch your ass, Markus."

"I will."

Jeff drove away and then Mark was alone in the park. Everything about the place felt right except for the smell. The flower-and-orange-tinged air had an undertone of smoke this morning.

He didn't know the boy's name or where he lived. It was just past dawn and if he began knocking on doors he was sure to cause a stir and have his friends from the DeLand police called back out. It seemed like a problem, and yet somehow he wasn't troubled by the task of finding the boy. He thought the boy would find him.

He was right.

It was no more than twenty minutes after Jeff left, and Mark had spent the time walking the streets of the camp, passing twice by the burned-out remains of 49B, glancing at it only briefly before moving on but feeling a bone-deep chill each time, remembering the blond woman's smile and the glitter of the knives in the flashlight glow. He was on his third pass when a voice came from behind him.

"They put you in handcuffs. Why was that?"

When he turned, the boy was standing beside the hedge Mark had just passed, looking as if he'd been there all the while.

Mark said, "They were afraid I was one of the bad people. Then they figured out I wasn't."

The boy nodded.

"Did you sleep at all?" Mark said.

"No. I was waiting. Did you sleep?"

"No." Mark looked from him to the houses nearby and said, "Son, who are your parents?"

The boy didn't answer. Instead, he reached in his pocket and withdrew Mark's cell phone. There was a bloodstain on the case.

"I kept it. Didn't tell anybody either."

"Thank you. That was brave, but it was the right thing."

The boy regarded him with flat eyes. "You fit in here. Not in the house where you went last night, but *here*. In the camp."

"No, I'm afraid I don't."

The boy looked disappointed in Mark. He handed the phone over, though, and then stepped back.

"You think I'll see Dixie again?" he asked.

"No," Mark said. "I'm very sorry. She was—"

"I know what happened. I watched them take her body away. But sometimes I see them again. Like with Walter. I wonder if she'll be like that."

"I hope not," Mark said.

"Then you don't understand what it's like. That's okay. Dixie always told me everyone had different learning speeds. You know what that means? We all figure it out, just at different times. I'm early, she said."

Mark pocketed the cell phone and took a step back, as if the child posed a threat.

"I don't know anything about that," he said. "All I can say is thank you. You helped me last night. Saved me."

"Not yet. You might still die. Maybe soon." He said it calmly and thoughtfully.

"I hope not."

"Me too. But it will be close, I think. If you go to the mountains, it will be close."

"Who said anything about mountains?" Mark asked. "Son, which one of them said anything about mountains?"

But the boy didn't answer. He just lifted his hand in a wave and ducked back through the hedge in a soft rustle of leaves, and then Mark was alone again on the strange street with the smell of smoke in the air.

18

Mark used Jeff London's username and password to run a reverse match of the license-plate number from the red truck with the registration through the BMV.

He knew by now that it wasn't going to produce anyone named Myron Pate, but he was still expecting to find a male name. Instead, the BMV records returned a corporation: Wardenclyffe Ventures, LLC.

It was a smart choice. Registering the car under a corporation prevented the immediate attachment of a human, and unless pains had been taken to associate the license plate with an arrest warrant, it would keep any officer who ran the plate from seeing a driver's record or conviction history. There was an address for the LLC, though, in Daytona, Florida, not far away, and every LLC needed a registered agent. The smoke screen was effective enough to deter cursory police attention but not much more. Mark went to the Florida secretary of state's page and found the registered agent of Wardenclyffe Ventures: a Janell Cole.

Armed with this, he returned to the BMV and found her driver's license. The image of her face was small on the phone's screen, but Mark didn't need a larger shot to recognize her: he'd seen her just hours before, smiling as she told him that his wife was inconsequential.

"Janell." He said the name aloud, thinking that it didn't match the person. He ran a few preliminary criminal-records searches but found nothing. Under the identity of Janell Cole, she was a model citizen. The only place he had to start was the address from the truck registration, and he didn't think it would take long for the police to get there through their own means.

He drove fast on his way to Daytona Beach.

Janell Cole had lived above a garage in the sort of place people referred to as an in-law apartment. Between the garage and the main house was a courtyard with a bubbling fountain, a koi pond, and a brightly colored flower garden shaded by tall palms. The garage and apartment were painted in vivid colors and had flower planters under the windows, and the place didn't fit with anything he understood about her. The polar opposite of the house in Cassadaga.

He climbed up the stairs and knocked. Nobody answered, but the blinds were angled to let some sunlight in. When he shaded his eyes and put his face to the glass, he could see that the place was empty, the carpets freshly cleaned and the walls gleaming with white paint, waiting on a new tenant.

"She moved."

Mark stepped back from the window and looked down into the courtyard. A too-tan woman in shorts and a sports bra stood below him, dripping sweat and breathing hard, fresh off a run.

"Janell moved?" he asked, to test which name his girl had been using during her stay here.

"Yes. What kind of detective are you?"

Mark didn't think he wore his profession like a fragrance, so either this woman belonged in Cassadaga herself, giving readings, or there had been other detectives looking for Janell Cole.

"The best kind," he said, walking down the steps. She smiled at that, which was good, suggesting she wanted to cooperate rather than protect her former tenant. "You don't seem surprised that a detective would be looking through the window of that apartment. Mind telling me why?"

"Because they've been here before." She took a deep breath, her torso filling with air, then released it in a long, slow hiss like a leaking balloon, bent at the waist, and began to stretch her hamstrings.

"Which ones have you spoken with?" he said.

"The woman, mostly." She straightened. "You don't work with her?"

"No. But I'm sure as hell interested in talking to her. Do you know her name?"

"I don't remember it, but I still have her card. Would you like that?"

He told her that he'd like that very much, then waited in the garden while the woman jogged around to the front of the main house and disappeared. When she returned she had a business card, and Mark took it and almost laughed.

"No shit," he said. "The Pinkertons?"

She gave him a puzzled look. "You know them?"

"They never sleep."

"What?"

"Never mind." It was sad that she had no knowledge of the most famous private detective agency in history. Mark had grown up on stories of the Pinkertons. His uncle Ronny had traveled with a stack of paperback novels, romanticized old pulp stories, mostly Westerns by George Ranger Johnson but also many featuring the daring Pinkerton detectives. Mark had read them countless times, although as a PI, he'd never encountered anyone who actually worked with them. He knew that the company had been bought out long ago by a security conglomerate, but it still retained the brand and, according to the business card, that distinctive watching-eye logo. The investigator was named Lynn Deschaine, and she was based out of Boca Raton, just north of Miami. He snapped a photo of the card and handed it back to his new acquaintance, who was now standing in a midair stretch as if she were about to take flight. She accepted the card and tucked it in her sports bra, resumed her pose, and inhaled so deeply Mark thought she was going to uproot the palm tree. Then she closed her eyes.

"So," he said, "what can you tell me about Janell?"

For a few seconds it seemed like she wasn't going to respond, but finally, eyes still shut, she said, "I didn't know her well. I will say I found her unusual. She didn't like the sun. Her skin was so pale you could see the veins. That's not healthy, you know."

Her own skin was cured enough to be ready for belts and boots.

"You talk to her much?" Mark asked.

She shook her head without affecting her balance. "No. I really can't say much else about her. Just like I told your partner. Or your predecessor. Whoever. She paid rent on time, she was quiet, and she left. When she left, she broke the lease, and I told her she couldn't have the deposit back. She was fine with that. I had the impression that her new job was rather urgent."

"What kind of job?"

"She's an engineer."

"An engineer?"

His shock was enough to finally disrupt her stretching routine. She blinked and looked at him. "Yes. That's what she told me, at least. What do you think she is?"

A murderer, Mark thought, but he said, "That's what I need to figure out."

"Oh. Well, I can't help beyond telling you that she paid rent in cash, which was her preference, not mine, that she paid promptly, and that she needed to spend some more time in the sun. That's really all I know, Mr. Pinkerton."

He liked that mistake so much he didn't correct it.

Lynn Deschaine didn't answer her office line, but he caught her on the cell. He identified himself as a fellow PI and told her he was working a case that had taken him to Daytona Beach and seemed to overlap with her work.

"Really sorry, Mr. Novak, but we don't share information on our cases. It's a confidential business. Good luck."

"Hang on," Mark said. "I'm not asking for you to fax over a dossier with Social Security numbers, Ms. Deschaine. If anything, I thought I could help *you*. I was told that you were—"

"I'm quite certain I don't need outside assistance on my cases."

These modern-day Pinkertons were real charmers.

"I'm sure you don't," Mark said. "So I won't bother to tip you off about some problems with President Lincoln's planned trip to the theater tonight."

There was a slight pause, and then she said, "That's both a silly remark and a historically inaccurate one. The Pinkertons were not providing security to President Lincoln on the night of his assassination."

Her curt tone hadn't changed, but Mark had the feeling that Lynn Deschaine, wherever she was, had smiled. He was almost certain.

"Fair enough," he said. "I'm sorry to bother you. Really just meant to offer some information in case you still had any interest in locating Janell Cole, but it sounds like you've got everything in hand, so I apologize for interrupting your day."

He hung up on her. It wasn't something he would have done in ninety-nine cases out of a hundred, but Lynn Deschaine felt like number one hundred. If she was half the PI that her bravado suggested, she'd be too curious not to call back. If she was even a *fraction* as combative as she seemed, she'd be too pissed off not to.

The phone rang in about thirty seconds. He answered.

"Markus Novak. I never sleep."

"Hilarious," she said, but there was neither humor nor anger in her voice. Just interest. "Tell me about Janell Cole."

"I thought you didn't need the—"

"I know what I said and I apologize. What do you know about Janell Cole?"

"I know where she's been staying for the past few months, I know some people she's associated with, including a man who just walked out of prison, and I know that the police aren't going to be far behind me, as she recently cut someone's throat and set a house on fire. Is that enough to interest you?"

He listened to her breathing. It took several seconds before she spoke.

"Where did this happen? And who did she kill?"

"No, no," Mark said. "It's going to be an exchange of information, Ms. Deschaine. Not a gift."

He expected her to balk. Instead, she said, "Are you in Daytona now?"

"Yes."

"I can make it in four hours. Maybe less, depending on traffic."

It was a long haul from Boca Raton to Daytona Beach, and her willingness to make the drive rather than continue to haggle with him on the phone told him just how intense her interest in Janell Cole was.

"I'll be here," Mark said. "But be prepared to trade intel, Ms. Deschaine. I'm not giving any away."

19

Jay and Sabrina had talked about having a baby. In the months just before Tim's death, they'd spoken of it often. Jay was perhaps more enthusiastic about the prospect than Sabrina had been. She saw the reality of it in a different way than he did. Time she needed to devote to her business would vanish with the ring of the phone and the report of an outage, Jay heading out the door and leaving her a single parent. Why rush into that? They had time. She'd said that over and over again, reminding him of their youth, of the expansive horizon ahead. Plenty of time.

That was before they went to the closed-casket funeral for her brother.

Time changed that day. Time changed in a hurry as she stood in the receiving line that was not so far removed from the receiving line of her wedding and accepted condolences instead of congratulations, a large photo of her grinning, adolescent-humored brother at her side. His remains just below.

She'd never seen the way he'd looked at the end. She'd asked, but Jay refused to speak of it. It didn't seem like the sort of thing you pushed. Not with someone who did the same work, certainly. However he had looked—and it had to be terrible, she knew that—it would have been more than a horror for Jay. It would have been a possible future.

They had stopped speaking of the baby then. A topic once omnipresent in their lives gone in a flash, just like the uncle the child would never know. There was the unspoken but absolutely shared knowledge of how easily it could have been Jay, Sabrina left a young widow and, if they'd had a baby, a single mother.

She wondered, in private moments, if that was the reality she'd considered the whole time, if the funeral she hadn't allowed herself to envision for fear of making it real was not her brother's but her husband's. And so her business and their youth became the most convenient reason, but not the real one. Single-parent nights were one thing, and she'd had no trouble voicing that concern. Single-parent life, though? To tell him of that would have been so much harder. *You'll make a mistake someday. Just like Tim. It will happen, and to pretend otherwise is selfish, Jay.*

But he'd come down from the lines, had taken that foreman's job in Red Lodge. Why hadn't they spoken of the child again then?

Time again, that was why. The endless supply of time. They had time to get settled in Red Lodge, they had time to put distance between themselves and the tragedy, time for everything.

Then a man with a pistol entered their home.

Time changed again.

She wondered, if she ever saw Jay again, what would be said about bringing a child into this world. A world that had sent her brother to an early grave and brought Garland Webb into their new home.

You're imagining he's still alive. What if you're all that's left? What if this is the end?

Her brother had been unmarried and childless. Plenty of time for him too. He'd been dead for six months. If Sabrina never left here, that was the end of it. Their parents had been only children, and they'd been dead before they reached forty. Their son had already joined them. Their daughter sat in shackles in the mountains.

She pulled feathers from the dead chickens and piled them beside her, not looking at the birds as she worked. Her fingertips were sore and raw. She suspected Eli hoped for more disgust from her, hoped to find her cowering in revulsion, maybe even vomiting from the smell of the charred flesh, from the fading warmth of the bodies.

Should have picked a dog, asshole, she thought as she jerked another feather free. *If you knew me even a little bit, you'd have done that to a dog. Then you might have gotten the reaction you wanted. But a chicken? Please.*

Eli wouldn't have a dog, though. Not up here where his particular brand of obedience was required. You had to earn obedience from a dog. From the chickens and Garland Webb and apparently from Violet, it came easier.

But there was more to Violet than he knew. Sabrina was sure of that. Violet's obedience with him, which was more disgusting to Sabrina than anything else she'd seen in this place, also seemed questionable. Ironically, this revelation had come in the moment she hit Sabrina in the face with the flashlight. In that instant, she'd been nothing like the demurring follower she appeared to be in Eli's presence, and she was not to be taken lightly. *He* took her lightly—dismissed her entirely, even—and Sabrina wondered about that. What was the great hold he had on her? How had it been achieved?

Violet was older than he was by a decade at least, maybe much more. She had a past without him, and Sabrina wondered what was in it. Who was in it. There were some things about the situation that made a perverse level of sense. Garland Webb and Eli, for example, were clearly predators, the type of people you knew were out there in the world but just never expected to cross paths with.

Violet was a different matter entirely.

There was a metallic clink as a key found the lock on the front door and then it opened and filled the room with daylight and Violet stood there with her strange smile, cheerful as a New England B and B hostess.

"I've got something to make you more comfortable," she said.

It was a sleeping pad, a Therm-a-Rest like people took on backpacking trips. It *was* surprisingly comfortable, and Sabrina adjusted herself onto it without breaking her pace on plucking duty, watching Violet instead of the birds.

"Why don't you see the truth of this?" Sabrina said.

The older woman blinked. "I'm sorry?"

"I've been kidnapped. I am chained to a wall. You know this is evil. I can tell that. I can tell it because *you* are *not* evil."

"Please, dear. Just be patient. If you'll just listen to Eli, you'll learn that—"

"Eli is insane," Sabrina said. "I already know it. Why don't you?"

"Dear…" Violet sighed and shook her head in the manner of someone dealing with an impossible rube. "It's so much larger than what you understand."

"It's evil," Sabrina repeated. "And you're not."

Violet dismissed her with a wave of her hand and turned to go. Sabrina didn't want that; she wanted to engage her, and so she asked a bizarre question, born of her own muddled thoughts.

"Do you have children?"

Violet stopped short. She didn't turn. "Why do you ask that?"

"I don't have any," Sabrina said, plucking another feather. Her right index finger was bleeding now. "I was never sure I wanted any. Some days, yes. Others…my God, things can go badly for children in this world. I was an orphan. Did you know that?"

"I did not." She still had not turned. But she hadn't left either.

"Sure was. So I know exactly how bad it can go. But my husband and I talked about it. If things had gone differently, I might have had a baby by now. Would you still be so comfortable with all this if that were true? If you knew a child had been left behind? Is there a point where you'd look at this and admit that it was evil? What if the chicken had been a child, Violet? What if that had been a baby reaching for that fence? Would you still admire Eli?"

"It wasn't a child."

"If it had been?"

"It wouldn't be. He's not what you think, dear. He's a pacifist to his core. We all are. No harm will come to you here unless you demand it."

"And what good will come of this?"

"So much more than you know." Violet turned, finally, and faced her. "The *world* will thank us when this is done. It's an awakening. A desperately needed awakening."

Sabrina stopped pulling feathers. She held one of the electrocuted birds in her hands and stared at the older woman and thought, *This is the difference. This is what makes her special.*

Violet believed. She and Eli said the same things, and in fact he said more of them, but Sabrina felt it was an act with him, a grandiose stage play. When Violet spoke, she *believed,* and the difference was palpable.

"What if he's lying?" Sabrina said.

"He isn't lying, dear. He isn't even speaking. He just listens. The earth speaks, and he listens."

"Indulge me," Sabrina said. "Imagine, for one moment, that he is actually a brutal man. Nothing like the pacifist you believe in. What then?"

Violet left the cabin and closed the door behind her. Sabrina stared after her for a few seconds and then resumed plucking feathers. It occurred to her that Violet had never answered the question about children.

20

Jay's goal for the day—the most immediate goal, at least—was simply to get through it without attracting attention or questions. He thought the truth was as visible on his face as a sunburn, but he survived the morning without drawing so much as a raised eyebrow.

Then came lunch.

They were running switchgear tests at a substation for one of the company's electrical engineers, a good guy from Ohio who seemed to know the system better than most men knew their own families, and Jay had always liked him, or at least liked him as much as a lineman could like an engineer. That changed at the deli, when the engineer said, "Something wrong with your food, Jay?"

Everyone looked at him. They were all nearly done with their sandwiches, and Jay's was untouched. He'd tried one of the potato chips and barely got it down. When their eyes went to him, all of them scrutinizing his face, he felt a flush of panic.

"You just gotta observe everything, don't you, Pete?" he said. "I've had the shits, that's all. I was hoping not to have to announce it, but I guess you've got to run diagnostics even during the lunch hour. Frigging engineers."

That got a small laugh and they turned away again, probably more worried about whether he was contagious than whether he was hiding a secret, but still he felt like he'd made a fatal mistake.

He tried to follow the conversation, people arguing about football now, most of the group Broncos fans, Pete a Cleveland Browns fan, which required heckling, and Jay did his best to grin and chuckle in the appropriate places. His mind was far from the restaurant, though. It was back in Billings, in a darkened bedroom with Sabrina.

They'd been married three months when the power went out in their apartment, and he'd started for the phone automatically, intending to call the control center to see if he was needed. She'd pulled him back to bed, her lips against his ear as she reminded him that he was off that day, and someone else could fix this one.

They'd made love in the darkness with a warm summer breeze blowing through the cracked window, and afterward, spent and breathless, he'd been close to sleep when she spoke.

"So what happens to make it do that?"

"It seems like you understand exactly what happens to make it—"

She'd laughed and smacked his chest. "The *outage,* smart-ass. There's no storm tonight. Why'd the lights go out?"

"Could be a lot of things." He was groggy, drifting blissfully toward sleep, but she was awake and alert.

"Like what? The storms I get. Or equipment failure. But sometimes it's neither. What triggers those?"

He'd propped himself up on one elbow and searched for her face in the black room.

"Squirrel suicide bombers."

"I'm being serious."

"So am I. Now, it may be a tree limb blowing into the lines, but limbs are easy to find. A dead squirrel is tougher. They'll get down into the switchgear and chew." He reached out and pinched the base of her throat lightly, tickled up her neck, giving a ridiculous impression of a rodent's biting sound. Her skin was warm and damp with sweat.

"If that's all it takes, I'm amazed the lights don't go out daily. One squirrel in the wrong place can shut off the lights? One tree limb?"

"Well, it depends on the circumstances. The system tries to heal itself." He put his index finger on her shoulder. "If your limb falls into the lines here, and it gets blown over to here..." He traced the finger to her other shoulder, beading her sweat on his fingertip. "Then the lights might take one hard blink. That's a transient fault. Brief contact, brief disruption. The system senses that there's voltage leaving the lines and going to ground somehow, and the system is scared of voltage going to ground. It has an automatic recloser that will test this, open that circuit up and see if there's still a ground path for the voltage. If it's a limb that fell and made brief contact, the ground path will be gone, and the lights will stay on. But..." He traced his finger back to her left shoulder. "Let's say the limb stays tangled in the lines. Or the squirrel suicide bomber gets into some switchgear." He tickled her left shoulder again, and she laughed. "Then the fault is still there, and the recloser will cycle just once more. You'll get two hard blinks, and the next time it's going dark for good. Three strikes and it's out. Because by then, the system will have decided that the problem is dangerous. It kills the current to prevent larger problems. That's when yours truly gets sent into the mix."

"You really think it's a squirrel that did this?"

He shrugged. "No idea. Clear day like this, equipment failure is possible. Suppose an insulator breaks and two lines touch. If two energized lines touch, say good night for a while. The system does *not* like that."

He traced his finger lower, down her shoulder, between her breasts, down. He could barely make out her face in the dim room, but the outage had brought a special silence with it, like a snowfall, and their home felt safe and sacred.

"Not all bad," he said. "People find ways to pass the time without electricity."

"Sometimes," she agreed, guiding his hand, "a little darkness is not a bad thing."

"Jay? *Jay?*"

The voice shook him back into the present, and he looked up and saw that he was the focus of the table's attention again. It wasn't Pete calling to him now but Brett, one of his own crew, who was looking at him with concern.

"You okay, boss? You're kind of pale."

"Yeah," Jay said, "I'm okay. Just...just fighting through this. I hope it's not catching."

He got unsteadily to his feet, picked up his untouched sandwich, crossed the room, and threw it into the trash.

21

Eli heard the growl of the ATV's engine before it came into view, and he moved quickly to a high vantage point and turned his binoculars on the steep, rock-strewn, and forested slopes that led to the cabin. The path to the cabin was difficult to traverse, by design; only a skilled ATV rider would even attempt the final pitch. When he saw the driver of the Polaris begin to make the ascent without hesitation, he knew his visitor.

"Who is it?" Violet said nervously, extending a hand for the binoculars, but he stepped aside.

"I'll deal with it. Stay here. Tend to our guests. No disturbances."

"But who is—"

"Violet. Do you think I haven't anticipated this? Do you think the spirits haven't already informed me of this? Do you actually believe in your heart that the mountains have allowed me to be *surprised* by this?"

"Of course not," she murmured.

"Then please do as I say."

He left her and went out the door and down the exterior stairs, moving with long strides, knowing that he had to cover the ground to meet Shields before he became visible. As much control as Eli had over Violet, he knew that she still had a weakness for Scott Shields. Perhaps something more than a weakness.

He punched a code into the keypad that worked the electrified fence, shoved through the gate, and clamped it shut behind him. He was standing in the middle of the trail when Shields arrived, standing in such a position that Shields had to cut the wheel abruptly to avoid running Eli down. On the precarious slope it was a dangerous maneuver, and for a blissful moment Eli thought he might roll the thing down the mountain. Shields was too experienced, though, and he cut the wheels back and hit the throttle when most men would have let off it, allowing him to spin up and over one of the high boulders and find flat ground above.

"What in the hell are you doing!" he shouted as he cut the engine.

"You're capable enough with the machine," Eli said. "And I'm anxious to speak with you. There's much to discuss."

"I should damn well say there's much to discuss," Shields snapped. "I haven't heard from you in weeks. I'd like to know what you're accomplishing on my land."

Eli nodded. "Let's speak, but not here. I need to return to town anyhow. We'll have a beer together, like the old days."

Scott's eyes had drifted from Eli up to the fence. From this angle, the tops of the utility poles were just visible.

"What in the hell are those?"

"They'll provide backup power as needed."

Scott gaped. "You're using *power lines* to run generators into the lodge? That's the craziest thing I've—"

Eli said, "I'm not flush for time. I'm headed to town, and you can accompany me or you can stay here."

For a terrible moment, Eli thought he would demand to stay, and then things would become messy in a hurry. Instead, though, he jerked his head at his ATV and said, "Get on. I got plenty of questions. And when we come back, I want a look around this place."

They bounced down the trail, the creek glittering beneath them and the Bighorn Mountains that abutted the property clear and beautiful in the morning sun. They rode on twelve hundred remote and rugged acres that were protected by miles of national forest; there was no access road, and the site was deeply concealed in the difficult terrain, as perfect a spot as Eli could possibly have hoped for but one that he would never have been able to afford. Enter Scott Shields. The land was his, purchased with settlement money from a lawsuit that had occurred three years earlier, when Shields had crashed a plane in the Alaska bush and his wife had been killed. Shields had sued the manufacturer, who had just "rehabilitated" the aircraft prior to the engine stall, and they settled for what was no doubt peanuts on the company's books but a windfall in rural Wyoming. Shields had purchased a property described as a ranch in the listing, though the land was worthless for cattle—steep, wooded, and rugged. His vision, though, was a hunting lodge with private guiding. Elk were plentiful, some moose as well, and the stream was filled with trout. The challenge was in access, but Shields had visions of using that to his advantage by bringing his clients in on horseback, enhancing the wilderness experience. It was a ridiculous use of a spectacular property. For Eli, however, the site was ideal. And so Eli had begun to work with Shields, which required working through Violet, the only woman Shields trusted. He believed she could bring him messages from his dead wife. These were the things Eli had to indulge in order to fulfill his own mission.

Violet had provided unexpected gifts. While he personally regarded her as a foolish woman who would believe a lie with eagerness and regard the truth with sorrow if not outright denial, others found her an expert navigator of the human spirit. As such, she was an ideal recruiter for Eli. The things that mattered to her—connections between earth and people, bridges between cultures, experiences of psychic phenomena—were all perfect for the candidates Eli sought. In many instances, they trusted Violet before they trusted Eli.

Shields had left his truck, a white Silverado splashed with mud, parked on the forest road, but rather than hike the two miles up, he'd used the ATV. Eli climbed off and watched as Shields got a pair of folding ramps out of the bed and used them to drive the ATV up into the truck. Eli had to turn away so his contempt wasn't evident. Here was a man so dependent on technology that he was literally driving one vehicle into another.

While Shields worked with his ramps, Eli squinted at the high slopes. Nothing of his camp was visible to the naked eye. The tops of

the utility poles blended with the dead lodgepole pines. Without a helicopter, one was unlikely to stumble across the site.

"We'll go to my place first," Shields announced when he had the
ATV secured. "I'm not interested in running you into town until I've
gotten my answers, Eli. The work I hired you to do up there doesn't
seem to be getting done."

Eli didn't realize he was smiling until Scott Shields said, "Something funny about this to you?"

"No," Eli said. "Not at all. I was just remembering something."

He was remembering that Shields currently lived in a massive
Winnebago and considering that the man had loaded one vehicle onto
another to drive to another still. What was next for him? A tractor-
trailer for the Winnebago? A ship for the tractor-trailer?

*At what point will you have enough large machines to feel confident
about the size of your pecker, Scotty?*

They drove down the forest road to the paved county road and
then went west toward Lovell and continued west, toward Byron.
The drive was excruciating, pulling Eli farther and farther away from
the work he could not afford to delay.

They headed into a blighted countryside along another forest road,
this one leading to the Shoshone River, where Shields paid for the
privilege of parking his motor home. He claimed it was for the fishing, but Eli knew it was because the location was remote but still
easy enough for the bikers to reach. Shields had a drug habit that
had started with painkillers after his plane crash and progressed from
there, and he was on a regular route for the dealers that growled
through northern Wyoming, working the oil fields.

As if finally comfortable now that they'd arrived, Shields began
talking even before he opened the driver's door.

"That property is a *hunting camp*. You said you'd get it powered
for me cheap, using your windmills and whatever the hell, but we've
missed every hunting season this year and now I'm not even hearing
from you."

Eli took a deep breath and turned away briefly, reminding himself of why this had to be tolerated, why the burden had to be borne. Then, just as Eli turned back to Scott Shields with a calm face and a ready explanation, he paused.

Things were different now. Markus Novak, down in Cassadaga like a thorn in a wolf's paw, required acceleration. But…if the timetable was sped up, why did he need Scott?

Scott said, "I asked you a question, Pate. Give me an answer."

Eli turned from him again and gazed down the lonely road to Byron. At some point, someone would come looking for Scott Shields. But how soon? Scott, paranoid sort that he was, did not maintain much contact with the outside world.

It will take some time. A few days, at least. What is the bigger problem for you, a walking and talking Scott Shields or a corpse?

"Scott," Eli said, "I'm on the brink of a crisis decision. Please understand that."

"*You're* on the brink? Son of a bitch, you're bringing these packs of idiots onto my property without giving me so much as a word of notice? I don't give a damn about your troubles, I'm concerned with preventing my own."

"You don't give a damn about my troubles. Is that so?"

"Better believe it. We had an arrangement."

"I remember. One stipulation was privacy. Have you told anyone else where I am?"

"Of course not. I know you're lying low."

"I'm just curious what my exposure here is."

Scott's eyes widened. His big chest filled. "Curious about *your* exposure? It's *my* property! I've got the risk!"

"And I intend to eliminate that for you."

That mollified him just slightly. "How are you going to do that?"

"Before coming to see me, who did you speak to? Maybe have a beer with, do some bitching about the problems I'm creating for you up there, running behind schedule?"

"Not a soul. I came up to see you and find out what the hell was going on."

"No other contact, then. You haven't spoken to, say, Lawrence Novak?"

"Larry? Hell, no. I told you, he thinks I'm back in Alaska. What does he have to do with it?"

"Not a thing, evidently, which is excellent to hear. Now, Scott. About your risks…the way I understand it is that, so long as the property remains in your ownership, you're worried about every activity that occurs there."

"Damn right I am! You already knew this. That was the—"

"You don't own the land," Eli said. "You only rent it."

Scott pulled back as if Eli had slapped him. "What kind of drugs are you on? I *own* that land. Go down to the damn courthouse and look at the deed."

"The deed is not the point. We're all renters here. Of earth, of our time. We don't own either of those things. Understand?"

"You're a lunatic. My only concern is—"

Eli lifted a soothing hand. "I can assure you—absolutely *assure* you—that all of your worldly concerns have reached their terminus."

Scott Shields cocked his head and gave Eli a confused stare with the barest glimmer of suspicion. Then he spoke again and got as far as "You mind putting that in English, you crazy son of a—" before Eli drew a tiny .22-caliber Ruger from his jacket pocket and shot him directly in his right eye.

Scott reeled back; his feet tangled, and he fell. Eli closed on him without hesitation, a pouncing cat, pressed the pistol directly to Scott's left eye, and fired again. The little gun barely kicked, but Scott's face spit blood back at Eli. He wiped it away and remained there, kneeling over the man, until he was sure that he was dead.

"Well," Eli said, "we approach warp speed, it seems."

Passersby here would be rare, and the RV was unlikely to give them pause, but a body lying in front of it would. Eli fished through Scott's pockets until he found his keys, and then he unlocked the oversize motor home and stepped inside. There was a back bedroom with closed window blinds and a door that screened the room from every other window. It would do. There were far better hiding places in any direction in this rugged land, but Eli was short on time, and Shields was a large man, certain to be difficult to maneuver.

He left the motor home, returned to Shields, and grasped the collar of the dead man's jacket. He dragged Shields inside and all the way to the bedroom, and then he heaved him up onto the bed. Shields's head flopped onto the pillow and his body fell naturally into a sleeping posture. The peacefulness of it bothered Eli. He took the gun out and fired two more bullets, one into each eye again. With the existing wounds, the small .22 shells worked like drill bits, boring cleaner tunnels.

Better. Those who found him should be able to grasp the problem that had led to Scott Shields shuffling off this mortal coil: his eyes were useless, for he had no capacity to understand what they offered him. By any definition that truly mattered, Scott had never been able to see things for what they were.

"Thanks for the land," Eli told the corpse, and then he left the bedroom, checked himself in the bathroom mirror, washed the blood speckles off his skin and clothing, and returned to Scott's truck. The pickup would be valuable; the ATV even more so. Eli hated the ghastly clatter of the vehicles and the smell of the exhaust, but sometimes, you had to make your deals with the devil.

22

Mark met Lynn Deschaine at a bar overlooking the Halifax River, a stretch of Intracoastal Waterway that was more like a lagoon than a river, separating the mainland from the barrier islands.

He sipped a beer, the cold bottle numbing the bandaged cut on his thumb, and watched a wood stork shift from one dock pylon to another, studying the water, and he waited on the Pinkerton to arrive. He thought of his uncle, wished he had a number for him, just so he could call and tell him that, because Larry would have loved it. Ronny would have loved it even more, but he'd been dead for years. Now it was just Larry, if he was even alive. That thought made him deeply sad. He'd walked away from his past for smart reasons, but he missed them all the same. His uncles, in particular, had been good men to him, if not to the rest of the world. And they'd cared for his mother.

Lynn Deschaine called from her cell phone while she stood in the shadowed interior of the bar, and Mark raised a hand to indicate where he was sitting. She was tall, only a few inches shorter than Mark, with hair so dark it shimmered in the light like oil. Her features betrayed some of the French look of her name, with high cheekbones, a delicate jaw, and eyes that seemed to be in on a joke that the rest of the world hadn't gotten yet. They weren't eyes that matched her phone style. Except for that one time he'd felt certain that she had smiled.

After she shook his hand, she said, "If you don't mind my asking… what happened to you, Mr. Novak? You look a little worse for the wear."

His face, neck, and arms were lined with scratches, and his hand was wrapped in gauze.

"Had a little trouble getting out of a house last night."

"Why was that?"

"Your friend Janell had set it on fire."

She stared at him.

Mark passed her a cocktail napkin that he'd been writing on while he waited.

"Refresh yourself," he said.

She looked at the napkin and what he'd printed on it.

Pinkerton Agency Code of Ethics, 1850

1. Accept no bribes
2. Never compromise with criminals
3. Partner with local law enforcement agencies
4. Refuse divorce cases or cases that initiate scandals
5. Turn down reward money
6. Never raise fees without the client's pre-knowledge
7. Keep clients apprised on an ongoing basis

"That came from Allan himself," Mark said. "The big boss."

She lifted the napkin and held it up with two fingers of her left hand. He noted there was no wedding band. It had been a long time since Mark had noted that about anyone. He felt strangely ashamed by it.

"I truly don't understand this," Lynn said.

"Ethics?"

"No. Your amusement with my agency."

Mark shrugged. "As a student of the profession, I feel like this is a really special opportunity for me."

"I'm sure that it is."

He leaned forward and took the napkin, set it down in front of her, and tapped it with his index finger. "These still hold true, right? The company never disavowed them?"

"Mr. Novak, if we could communicate like adults for just a minute here, I'd like to know what—"

"I think they're still governing rules," he continued. "In which case, I'm in luck. While I'm not local law enforcement exactly, I am working on a case *with* them. I can provide you with the name of a police officer in DeLand who will confirm that, but it will mean I'll tell him about Janell before I tell you."

"Let's not rush," she said.

Interesting.

They were silent for a moment, and then she broke it, saying, "You want an exchange of information. I can't do that. Client confidentiality."

"I don't need to know who your client is. I just need to know who Janell is."

She hesitated, trapping the tip of her tongue between her teeth as she took a deep breath. "A basic profile of what I know about her, that's all?"

"That's all."

"And in exchange…"

"I'll tell you where she has been staying for the past few months, what vehicle she's traveling in, and the name of at least one associate. As for the house, well, as I said, it was burning the last time I saw it. And the owner was dead. I think your friend Janell cut her throat."

"Let me call my client," she said.

"That's fine," Mark said, though he was disappointed. You could only push so hard when you weren't sure of your leverage. "I'll go inside to the bar and leave you in private. You want a drink?"

"Vodka tonic," she said, and she extended a credit card to him as she got her cell phone out. He waved it off but she reached out and caught his wrist.

"No, no. I'll pay for my own drink, thank you. If I could refer you to rule number one, Mr. Novak?"

She had her index finger on the cocktail napkin: *Accept no bribes.*

That was the first time Lynn Deschaine smiled at Mark. First time she touched him too. Sometimes you don't remember those things and later wish you did. Sometimes they stand out, almost as if you know from the start. Like someone whispers in your ear to take note. The last time Mark had experienced that feeling was on a dive boat on the Gulf of Mexico, and he'd been watching his future wife underwater, working her way slowly toward the surface.

Toward him.

Mark ordered another beer and Lynn's vodka tonic and stood in the cool shadows of the bar and waited while she talked on her phone. It wasn't a short conversation. He had time for another beer, and most of the ice had melted in her drink when she was finally done.

"Well?" he said, returning to the table and handing her the vodka tonic.

"I'm assuming you aren't willing to lead off the conversation by telling me how you located Janell," she said. "So you'll want me to open the dialogue."

"Correct. If I led, I'd have nothing left to bargain with. And you, Ms. Deschaine, strike me as a hard-bargain lady."

"Your intuition exceeds your sense of humor. And please start calling me Lynn."

"Lead the way then, Lynn."

"Janell Cole is thirty-six years old, originally from Pennsylvania. She's a graduate of Purdue University, where she earned a degree in electrical engineering."

"She really is an engineer."

"A very good one. She left her job fifteen months ago. She gave no indication as to why she was leaving."

"Where did she work?"

"Atlanta."

"I mean the company, not the location."

She hesitated. It was brief, but it was there. Then she said, "I believe it was a utility company," and took a long drink of her vodka.

Mark said, "That's your client."

She responded with total poise, unfazed. "I didn't mean to imply that, sorry. But I also asked you to respect the confidentiality of—"

He held up a hand. "I don't care about your client. But it might be easier on us both if you didn't have to dance around it either. You're too good not to know the name of her employer, Lynn. You won't share it, though, and that means you're trying to protect them, but I honestly don't give a damn."

She looked irritated, but he didn't think it was with him. It was with herself for allowing him to make the determination so easily.

"Independent detective one, Pinkerton zero," Mark said. "You hate that, don't you?"

She didn't bother to respond and chose to pick up where she'd left off. "After leaving her job, Janell moved from Atlanta to Daytona Beach. She had no known contacts or friends in the area. By the time I was asked to locate her, she'd left there too. I haven't had any success finding her. As for the vehicle you mentioned, I'm assuming it's a red Dodge truck? Purchased a year ago?"

"That's the one."

She nodded. "That's how you got the Daytona address. BMV records."

"Yes."

"Let me ask you a question," she said. "Do you know where she is *now*?"

Mark shook his head, and he could see the air go out of her.

"I know where she was last night. She just took off and left the house burning down behind her. That's what led me to knock on her door out here."

"So you're looking for her? You're not just interested in background. You'd also like to find her?"

"I'm doing more talking than you," he said. "That wasn't the deal. So tell me this: Do you know of any overlap between Janell and the criminal element? I've got to tell you, I didn't have her pegged for an EE. I was going to guess any paperwork she'd left behind was in vice reports, not diplomas."

"She has no criminal record. Not so much as a speeding ticket."

"I asked about connections."

She hesitated again. Mark sighed and set his beer down.

"Listen," he said, "I get it—"

"My first responsibility is to—"

"Stop." He leaned forward. "I'm going to go ahead and tell you what case *I'm* working. Why *I* want her. Then you can make a judgment call. Okay?"

"Okay."

"Here's my case," Mark said. "Lauren Novak. Homicide. Unsolved." She didn't say anything. She'd gone very still.

He pushed back from the table. "Spend some time on your phone, Lynn. Do some searches for Lauren, and for me. Then call your client back. When you've decided what level of cooperation you're willing to show, I'll be ready."

Mark left the deck and returned to the bar.

23

Lynn left Mark in the bar for maybe ten minutes, then she slipped in and took the stool beside him and said, "I'm sorry."

He nodded.

"That's an awful thing."

He nodded again. What the hell did you say? *Yes, they shot her in the head, it's an awful thing.*

"So your case is really—"

"Of personal interest," he finished for her. "Yeah. I don't have a client, Lynn. I've got nobody to protect. I just want to find the woman."

"You think she had something to do with your wife's murder."

"I think she knows the man who killed her. His name is Garland Webb. He walked out of prison and vanished. No contact with the parole office. I've got a witness to the, um, events of last night who says that Janell and the man she was with are on their way to meet Garland Webb. "

He didn't mention that the witness was a child who also believed Mark was attended by the ghost of a murdered man named Walter.

"Where did the *events of last night* take place?"

"Cassadaga. The house is one weird place. Someone's very fond of painting on the walls. Mostly vortex symbols, but some words. *Rise the dark, the dark will rise,* things like that."

Even in the dim light of the bar, Mark could see color drain from her face.

"Rise the dark?"

"That mean something to you?"

"Maybe."

"Bullshit, *maybe*. You just reacted more visibly to that phrase than you did to learning they'd killed somebody. Why?" He didn't want to admit his own interest in the phrase, not yet. He had to hold some cards back.

"Was there any reference to a place called Wardenclyffe?" she asked.

"No, but I saw it was her company name, and the vehicle is registered to the company. What does it mean?"

"It was the site of Nikola Tesla's financial ruin, a place out on Long Island that has been a popular home to conspiracy theories over the years. But the name means something else to these people. It's a place, a movement, something. Do you know anything about the man she's living with?"

"The only man I know is the one who helped her burn the house down. He is a big bastard with a short temper and, as of yesterday, a broken nose. That one is on me. Myron and I got off to a bad start."

"Myron. Do you know his last name?"

"I know what he told me, but it's a false name. He was going by Myron Pate."

Again her face showed recognition. Mark watched and remembered what the boy had said and played one of the last cards he had left.

"They're off to meet Garland and a man named Eli," he said.

"Eli Pate." She said it immediately, and he didn't question it. He'd heard no last name for Eli, and he'd assumed Myron's was an alias, but the way she connected the names suggested it wasn't a shot in the dark.

"They're going to see him? That's what you were told?"

"That's what I was told. Who is Eli Pate?"

She studied his face. "You really don't know?"

"My only interest is Garland Webb. Who is Pate?"

She slid off the stool and stood up. "I've got some pictures to show you. You might not recognize anyone other than Janell, but maybe we'll get lucky."

She took an iPad out of her bag and opened a photo album that was labeled with only a case-file number, no names, and began a slide show. Some photographs were facial close-ups that had clearly been pulled from driver's license photos, some were lifted from social media sites, but there were also others in which the subject had obviously been unaware of the camera. Surveillance shots.

The first five photographs were of the same woman, and Mark had no idea who she was. Janell Cole followed, looking nothing like the woman he'd last seen leering at him in the flashlight beam. Here, she was the picture of the perfect young professional. There was another unfamiliar man, and then the screen filled with a close-up image of Myron Pate's face.

"Stop. That's the guy she's traveling with."

"You're sure?"

"Positive. Who is he really?"

"His name is Doug Oriel."

"If you tell me he's another electrical engineer I'm really going to begin to lose respect for the profession."

"Not an engineer."

"Good."

"He's a demolitions specialist."

Mark paused. "Ex-military?"

"No. His background is in construction. He recently attended a school near Cleveland where he obtained certifications in blasting concrete, underwater blasting, vibration and air-blast control, and delayed-timing methods."

She rattled this list off like someone who'd prepped for a job-interview question. Myron, like Janell, had been on her mind a good deal.

"Did he work with your client company too?"

She shook her head. "We pulled surveillance photos that put them together. We aren't sure how they met."

She closed the cover on the tablet. For a while she watched the boat channel without seeming to see it and then she said, "How confident are you that they're really going to Eli?"

"Very," Mark said. It was true, though if he explained the boy to her she probably wouldn't agree. "Do you know where he is?"

"Only a possible town. He maintains a post office box, and there's been surveillance conducted there before, but without success. The box is still active, though. We're told he sporadically appears to gather mail."

"Who is he?"

She hesitated, and he said, "Lynn, come on. I just signed my soul over to you. I thought we were past this."

She nodded, almost to herself. "Okay," she said. "I'll give you the gist."

The gist took them about twenty minutes. The gist started with a power company in Georgia and ran to the FBI. The gist was the type of scare that some in the electrical industry and some in national security roles had been warning the nation of for decades.

The Pinkertons had been brought in by the Georgia power company after its prized young systems engineer Janell Cole quit her job and took some highly sensitive data with her. By the time the company realized it had been hacked, she'd left not just the building, but the city. Lynn had been tracking her ever since. "I'm in regular communication with Homeland Security and the FBI," she said, "but I don't think you need to be very astute to understand why the FBI is interested in a missing grid-systems engineer and a guy who specializes in industrial demolition."

"No," Mark said, "I don't think there's much of a reach there. But what's their affiliation? Is there a shared group, some sort of right-wing fringe deal, religious fanatics, environmental nuts, or..."

She shook her head. "No affiliation is clear yet."

"What's Eli Pate's role?"

"Online communication suggests he's a recruiter. We wondered if Janell would head his way at some point, but she didn't seem to be. Until now."

"Where is *his way*?"

"The post office box is in Lovell, Wyoming."

Mark set his beer down and stared at her. "Lovell?"

"You know the place? Did they talk about it?"

"They didn't talk about it, but yeah, I know the place." He felt queasy suddenly, the beer stirring in his stomach. Lovell, Wyoming, was not a coincidence kind of town. Anything was possible, he knew that, but it didn't feel right.

It's the Cassadaga effect. The freaks got in your head, and now you're superstitious, jumping to silly conclusions, having silly fears.

"How do you know the place?" Lynn asked.

"I lived there when I was a kid, but I lived a lot of places when I was a kid. It's not as odd as it seems, not when you've gone through as many small towns in your life as I have." He was saying this more for himself than for her. "There's nothing in Lovell to draw anyone, though, so what in the hell brought him there?"

"Probably the nothingness," Lynn said. "But if they're headed to him, that's his last known address."

Cassadaga had occupied pole position of the places Mark didn't want to see for a long time. Wyoming, though, was one of the places he'd already promised himself he would never see again. But if Garland Webb had headed west, then Mark would too.

"I can go and tell you what I find," he said.

"I don't want to ask anyone else to do my work," she said. "I'd like to go myself, if I can get the budget approved to fly into Wyoming."

"Are we doing this together, then? It's going to be odd if we're working on top of each other, overlapping questions and suspects."

"Working together is fine with me. It helps me. You've seen her recently, you've seen him, and you apparently know that part of the world."

"Yes, I know that part of the world." Mark's voice was empty, the words clipped. "And you don't get to Lovell by flying into Wyoming. You fly into Montana. Billings is the closest airport. Or you can start from Bozeman, but the drive to Lovell is longer."

Such familiar names, familiar places. He could picture them all easily. He didn't want to see them again.

He thought of the boy who'd told him that if he went to the mountains he might not survive. Only a few hours ago, there had been no mountains involved. Now here he was, discussing a return to them.

"If they're driving," he said, "we'll beat them to Wyoming."

"They'll be driving. They pay cash and they drive. They stay away from airports. So, yes, we'll be ahead of them."

"I wonder where they are now," Mark said, picturing the red truck headed northwest on the interstate, slicing through an oblivious nation, at least one murdered woman left in their wake already.

"I've been wondering that every day for months," Lynn said. "This is the first time I might have an idea."

24

On his way home, Jay passed a police car and had the overwhelming urge to pull a U-turn and chase after him, screaming for help.

But he couldn't. He understood the way it had to work now; he understood the power dynamics, and it required patience.

At home, he paced the lower level of the house, the tracking chip clutched in his hand, and waited for the hours of the night that belonged to emergency workers and insomniacs. Occasionally he stopped and stretched out on the couch, setting alarms each time to prevent sleep, but sleep never came.

Mostly, he thought of the things he had never said to Sabrina.

Things like the truth about why they were here. Why he'd led them to Red Lodge, to this house from which she'd been taken. Now that he was alone in the dark, still-foreign house, the things he *had* told her appalled him. They'd all sounded good at the time, sure. The move would keep him on the ground. That part was always honest. What he'd allowed her to believe in the silence that followed it, though, was unforgivable. In the silence, he'd allowed her to believe that the decision was for *her*. Never had he confessed to freezing on a climb. Never had he described her brother's face, the smoke that left his mouth like a final attempt at words, some last message that dissolved into the dark sky, unheard.

You're next, the smoke seemed to promise Jay then.

But he hadn't been next. Sabrina was next. And he'd led her here. Would Eli Pate have found him in Billings? Possibly. It didn't feel that way, though. It felt like the result of Jay's own deceit, his own secrets. He'd hidden the truth, had fled from the truth, and in so doing he'd guided them here.

What if you'd told her? Where would you go then? What if you'd just told the truth? Maybe you'd never have ended up in this place. You'd take another job. Work for her, work side by side with her, never let her out of your sight. All of this was possible if you'd just told the truth.

He rose and walked again. Paced in anguish. Every step recorded.

At four in the morning, with a few hours left before dawn and his movement patterns well established, he crawled on the floor, following the wall into the kitchen, then fumbled with the drawers until he found the duct tape. Then he crawled back through the dark living room to the entryway closet, where an all-time failure of a Christmas gift waited, a reason you had to stay away from late-night television advertising. The robotic vacuum cleaner, two feet in diameter and with the look of a large hockey puck, was useless when it came to cleaning floors, and Sabrina hated the sound of it as well as its inefficiency. Jay's intrigue in the gadget had earned it a place in the closet instead of the garbage can, but he had to admit it wasn't effective. All it did, Sabrina had pointed out, was circle the house in confused patterns, bouncing off the walls like a drunk man.

Or like an anxious man pacing away a sleepless night.

Jay taped the tracking chip to the top of the vacuum, turned it on, and released it. The device spun away. It bounced from wall to wall, and, just like Jay had, remained on the ground floor.

He had an hour, at least. He listened for a few minutes to make sure the device was running problem-free, and then he crawled to the front door and slipped out into the cold night.

25

Mark worked on Eli Pate late into the night, gathering intelligence on him before they flew out of Miami to try to find him. Lynn Deschaine already had plenty of knowledge about Pate, but that didn't keep Mark from digging and, maybe, truth be told, digging a little competitively. She had resources that he didn't, but he didn't want to have to rely on those resources to do his job. There was another cloud on the horizon with Lynn, and that was the collision of goals. She thought that they were both looking for Janell Cole and company, and that much was accurate. What Mark intended to do once he found them—found Garland, at least—was another matter.

He suppressed that and focused on Eli Pate. When they arrived in Billings, Mark wanted to know everything about him that he could.

Unfortunately, there wasn't much out there—except for the surprising discovery that he seemed to be operating under his own name. What that suggested—the fact that he kept his own name, and people like Doug Oriel renamed themselves to match it—was both interesting and alarming.

Eli Pate was forty-one, his Social Security number had been issued in Kentucky, and his address history painted the portrait of a nomad, with short stints in seventeen states. There was no record of Eli having a phone in the past three years. He also had no active driver's license. The last one Mark could find was more than a decade old, issued by the state of Idaho. In the photo, he looked whip-thin and mean, with brown hair that hung down around his shoulders and hostile eyes like flint chips. The last address on record in any of Mark's databases was the same one that Lynn had, a PO box in Lovell.

He didn't like seeing the name of the town. He knew it was the memories he connected to it that were to blame for that, but still, it troubled him. Lynn's recognition of the phrase *rise the dark* troubled him too. When Ridley Barnes had vanished in Indiana, wading off into the unknown depths of an elaborate cave system, he'd left Mark with a strange set of promises. One of them had lingered in Mark's mind ever since, Ridley's last words: *She doesn't want you yet.*

He'd meant the cave. Everyone knew that in Ridley's disturbed mind, the place had a personality, and Mark understood that. Still, he often found himself thinking about Lauren, some small, absurd part of him always wondering, *What do you mean, she doesn't want me yet, Ridley? What's left for me to do?*

That question had made sense, though. Mark was already focused on Lauren's unfinished business—Garland Webb. It was natural that he'd bridge Ridley's final, raving words to that mission. He could bridge *anything* to that mission. The other words had been easier to discard, because they'd had no such connection. In fact, Mark hadn't thought of them much at all until today.

When things go dark, Ridley had told Mark, *you're the one who will have to bring the light back.*

Madness, of course. Ridley had left his rational mind somewhere in that cave years earlier, and by the time he'd said that to Mark, he was also wounded and hypothermic. He'd had no idea what he was saying.

Still, his words rose in Mark's mind tonight.

It was deep into the night, and the flight to Billings, with a layover in Minneapolis, left at seven in the morning, but still Mark kept searching. Even after he'd taken a second Ambien and knew that he didn't have the focus for the work, he kept at it. At first he drifted into searches involving Eli's name and terms related to electricity and energy. Nothing. Then he tried Janell Cole and Doug Oriel, and eventually, half asleep, without any real consideration, he ran a search for recent news using the words *Wyoming* and *power grid.*

Most of the first-page results were related to efforts to bring enough power to the oil fields to keep up with the drilling needs, but there was one floater from the *Billings Gazette* with a two-day-old date.

Outages in Wyoming and Montana Result of Vandalism

According to the article, communities including Red Lodge and Laurel, Montana, and Lovell and Powell, Wyoming, had lost power for most of a day after someone had felled trees on the high-voltage lines in rural locations.

> Employees of the Beartooth Power Alliance who repaired the damage were left convinced that a crime had occurred.
>
> "I've never seen anything so intentionally malicious," lineman Jay Baldwin, 34, of Red Lodge said. "The location and manner in which those trees were brought down doesn't really leave any question about an accident. Someone intended to knock some lights out, and they did."

There was a picture of Baldwin accompanying the story; it showed a man standing beside a utility truck. He held a hard hat in one hand and a radio in the other and appeared weary but not worn-out. It was a compelling shot, really—he looked like the exact sort of man you wanted responding to emergencies.

Mark fixated on the picture, and when he blinked back to reality, he blamed the Ambien for the pointless level of scrutiny of a simple photograph. He closed the computer. It was time for bed—past time, in fact—and he'd be jet-lagged tomorrow after the flight to Montana.

The state's name chased the photo of the lineman through Mark's brain in a spiral of odd images as he drifted toward an unsettled sleep. That name had texture, somehow, rough and jagged and ready to wound: *Montana*. It got nothing but love from tourists, but tourists didn't understand it. You had to see it through four full seasons to know a damn thing about Montana.

Mark had seen it through plenty more than that.

The dreams that came for him were varied and vivid. He dreamed first of Ridley Barnes, more memory than dream, Ridley in the endless dark of Trapdoor Caverns, warning Mark that great responsibility and great pressure awaited him on the surface. Then Ridley was gone, replaced by an unfamiliar man with no hands standing in a moonlit stairwell with odd symbols painted on the walls behind him.

She held all the beauty of the world, the man said. *Her only mistake was her taste in men. The way she died wasn't her fault, you know.*

In the dream Mark said, *I know, it was mine,* because he thought the man was talking about Lauren. By the time he realized that the stranger wasn't, it was too late, because a wave struck the house, a tremendous splash of gray-green salt water like a hurricane's storm surge, and it swept up the stairs and drove the handless man away from Mark. They were in the water together and Mark thought that Lauren was too and maybe someone else, a woman he knew but couldn't name, but as the waves rose and fell, they all drifted farther apart until Mark couldn't see or hear the others anymore, and he was alone in an empty sea. The waves were towering and powerful but never drove Mark under. Instead he rode them through sleep and toward dawn, and though he'd lost track of the others in the water with him, he didn't feel any panic, because he knew they were merely out of sight and earshot, not truly gone. The storm was raging, but they were all in it together.

The water faded then, receded in the abrupt fashion of dreams, and mountains replaced the waves. High, menacing peaks.

The mountains just sat there, lonely and wind-whipped, impenetrable and unyielding. All the same, Mark was grateful for the alarm that shook him from sleep and forced the image from his mind. The hurricane dream had somehow been more peaceful than the mountain image, despite all of the crashing waves and the loud power of the storm.

In that dream, he had not been alone.

26

The phone began to ring when Jay was three blocks from the police station. Unknown number. He stared at it without answering, let it go to voice mail, and continued walking. Almost immediately, the phone chimed with a different tone—not a voice mail, but a text message.

GO BACK HOME, JAY.

He stood dumbly on the sidewalk, looking from the phone's screen to the empty streets around him. There was nobody in sight, no watchers. And yet...

The phone rang again. This time he answered.

"Jay, Jay, Jay." Eli Pate sighed like a disappointed parent. "You're not making wise choices. Certainly, you're not thinking of Sabrina. What a risk you just took! Imagine what could happen to her. Imagine what you could have just provoked. Why, Jay, I might have been incited to do terrible, horrible things. Just *think* about it! Can you picture those things? My God, what you have invited into her life!"

Jay said, "Please, don't." His voice broke.

"Please? Well, okay, since you said *please*." After a long pause, Pate spoke again, and the humor was gone from his voice. "Go home, Jay. I expected you to try once. I'd have been wrong about you if you hadn't. But I'll tell you this: I do not expect you to try again. Because now you know better. You'll go home and think about the things that might have happened, and you'll think about electricity in wires and wonder how on earth you could have made any decision other than to simply do as you've been asked. Go home. When you step inside, please wave to the camera."

The camera. He had a camera. Where in the hell was the camera?

Eli Pate began to laugh. "Lord, you really believed that would work, didn't you? A *vacuum,* Jay! That is *brilliant.*" His laugh, rich and carefree, boomed through the phone again. "Oh, that was beautiful. But I don't have the time to waste letting you try again, I'm afraid. You're going to need to understand that. Do you?"

"Yes."

"I'll believe you this time. But Jay? I can replace you. Can you replace her?"

The call disconnected.

Jay Baldwin lowered the phone, looked up the street toward the lights of the police station, and then turned and walked back to his dark house.

27

They were thirty thousand feet in the air somewhere over the Dakotas when Lynn Deschaine fell asleep with her head on Mark's shoulder.

She'd been dozing on and off for a while, and so it was likely that she'd slipped down in her seat a bit and was unaware of the contact.

He was very aware of it, though. He was frozen by it. He could smell her hair and feel her warm, slow breaths on his neck, and he didn't want to so much as blink for fear of waking her.

He also wanted to push her away.

As they flew through the cloud cover, Mark was both grateful for her presence at his side, the touch of her skin, and angry with himself for enjoying it. He realized there was no need for the latter—you can't cheat on the dead.

Explain that one to your heart, though. Anyone who'd ever had to try, Mark thought, would understand.

When the flight attendant came down the aisle to see if anyone needed fresh drinks, Mark made the slightest motion possible, a tiny shake of the head that came more from the eyes: *No, thanks, and please don't disturb her*. The attendant moved on in polite silence, and Lynn didn't wake, and her breaths came steady and slow against Mark's skin and his throat tightened and he closed his eyes and made himself think of his wife.

At some point, Lynn woke, realized her position, and moved away from Mark quickly. He felt her turn to him, no doubt prepared to apologize, but he kept his eyes closed so she'd think that he was asleep, and she didn't say anything. He was glad of that. His neck cooled as the memory of her touch faded.

He didn't open his eyes until they touched down, but he never slept.

There were only four gates at the Billings airport—A and B, 1 and 2. Mark was struck by how small it was and said so upon landing. Lynn looked at him with surprise.

"I thought you were from here? Sounded like quite the Montana expert."

"I've never been in the airport. I could tell you what the bus stations are like."

She tilted her head and studied him. "How exactly did you end up in Tampa?"

"It was a circuitous route," he said. "That's the best I can explain it. There was never a destination in mind."

That was the truth. He'd had destinations he wanted to avoid, however, and they'd just arrived in one.

As they left the airport and crossed to the rental-car parking lot, Mark felt his breath catch a little. The Billings airport was built on a plateau above the city, and while the mountains were far off in the hazy distance, the big sky was right there on top of you. The Montana sky felt older than time and endless as space itself.

It was a humbling sky.

They took I-90 across the Yellowstone River and out of Billings, followed it to Hardin, and then angled south through the Crow Indian Reservation and toward Wyoming. He saw Lynn rubbing her face just above her eyes.

"Headache?"

"Yes. Strange."

"Not really. Elevation change. You came from sea level, and we are going to hit ten thousand feet. Let's stop for some aspirin."

They stopped at a gas station in Crow Agency. Then they drove out of the town, and she was quiet as she watched it go by. He understood why. To drive through the places where the natives had been when the white settlers found them and then to drive through the places those settlers had left for those natives seemed to demand shame. Or should have.

"You should hear the music at a powwow," Mark said, and she looked at him with confusion.

"The chants and drums. It's powerful. Really powerful. I've never heard anything else like that, where the sound brings the past into the present. There's a place called the Medicine Wheel that *feels* like that, though. Feels the way the music sounds."

He was talking too fast and felt foolish for bringing it up. He wasn't making any sense, and he was telling her things he'd never shared with anyone. It was all the fault of this place, the sensory memory of the return.

"Who introduced you to the music?" Lynn asked.

"My mother, I guess, but I'd hate to give her the credit."

He hoped his tone indicated that the subject was done, and it seemed to, because Lynn didn't press him.

They continued south into Wyoming, and in Ranchester they broke off the interstate and headed west, into the mountains. At least thirty minutes passed in silence and Mark was lost in thought when Lynn said, "What are you smiling about?"

He hadn't realized that he was. "Lot of memories, that's all."

"Let a girl in on the fun."

He glanced at her, saw that she was smiling, and went along with it, though he knew better.

"We drove a stolen car out of Sheridan on this highway once, me and my two uncles," he said. "One of my uncles was convinced that it was a legitimate thing to do because the guy he'd boosted it from owed him more in poker debts than the car was worth. But what he didn't know about the car was that the gas gauge was broken. This road gets up as high as ten thousand feet, basically two miles in the air, and we were right near the top when the car died. The argument my uncles had there on the side of the road was one for the ages. Then, once we got to walking, they turned philosophical and carried on for a few miles about how much easier things were in the days of the horse thieves, because at least you could tell what you were getting. It was harder stealing cars, because unless you were a damn mechanic, you might get screwed. I always liked that logic. Sucks to steal a car that's a lemon, you know?"

When he looked back over at her, she had wide eyes, but there was no indictment to them. Just that faint amusement.

"A circuitous route to Tampa," she said. "You weren't kidding."

He nodded and drove on as the rode wound in sharp switchbacks and climbed steadily—seven thousand feet, eight thousand, nine. The Bighorn Mountains closed around them, still snowcapped on the peaks, weeks from wildflower season. At Baldy Pass they crested ninety-five hundred feet, Mark's ears popping as they drove just below the clouds, more like flying low than driving a car. Melted snow was all around them now, bleeding out in the sun in the places of trapped shadows where it had been able to survive so long. A voice inside Mark's head that was not his own said, *Welcome home,* and it wasn't kind. It was a mocking voice.

And a knowing one.

The post office box in Lovell was all they had for Eli Pate, but lounging around the post office waiting for him to show up was hardly the most effective way to go about finding him. Still, they started there, asking the girl behind the counter if she knew Pate. Mark thought he saw a ripple in her face, like the name had a sour taste.

"Well, sure. There are less than two hundred boxes in use here. I know everybody who uses them regular, but I'm not allowed to speak about it." She was looking Lynn's business card over. "What's he done?"

"Nothing. We just need to talk to him."

"Sure. But I'm just not, you know, allowed to tell you. It's a federal crime. If I was to tell you that Mr. Pate comes in here once every two weeks, usually on Tuesday, and he didn't come last week, that would be a federal crime."

Lynn smiled at her. "Then we won't ask you to do that."

Today was Monday.

"Be careful with him," the girl said, and Lynn's smile faded.

"Pardon?"

The girl pocketed Lynn's card and glanced out the window at the street. It was empty and they were alone. She seemed to take comfort in that.

"I would've remembered him even if he came in only the once," she said. "He has these real intense eyes, real dark eyes, and they're just, like, so...so *focused*. And I was running the paperwork for the box and all of a sudden he reached his hands out and I almost jumped, you know? But he didn't actually touch me. He just kept them out, like this."

She was holding both hands flat, palms toward her breasts, hovering about six inches away from her body.

"The way you'd put your hands out in front of a vent if you wanted to know whether the furnace was running," she said. "Like he was testing me for heat. He did that, and he smiled, and he said, *You're very weak*. And I don't even remember what I said exactly, told him he'd have to stop being weird or that he had to leave or whatever, but before I got much out he put his hands back in his pockets and said that it was a good thing. Then he acted normal the rest of the time, just filled out his papers and thanked me and left and he's never been anything but polite since then, but still...I remember it, you know? Fucking weirdo." She had a distant expression when she added, "And I'm *not* weak."

Mark was interested that what had lodged deepest in her mind seemed to be Eli Pate's assessment of her, not his actions.

"You ever tell anybody about that, or ask about him or anything?" Lynn said.

"No. But like I said...be careful with him."

They left the post office and walked back to the rented Tahoe.

"Your first claim in the West, and you've already hit gold," Mark said. "If he shows up tomorrow, that'd be a gift."

"It would be a lot of waiting if he doesn't, though. Hopefully, we'll find him first. Next date is with the sheriff."

"Befriend the local law," Mark said. "You're really sticking to that 1850s approach."

"Hardly. I think he runs with troubled people, and in a small town, the local law is indeed likely to know him."

"If he's been in trouble, he hasn't served any time. Not under that name."

"You've checked?"

"I checked on a lot of things." He told her about his searches the previous night and concluded with the vandalism near Red Lodge and Laurel. "Probably unrelated, but from a timing standpoint, it bothered me."

"Show me those places on this map."

The map she had didn't show any highways or roads. For a moment, Mark thought that the interconnecting lines across it were railroad routes, but then he realized it was a map of the national electric grid. It was too large in scale for him to locate such a small town easily, but there was one point that was close.

"That's too far west," he said. "But not by so many miles."

"That's the Chill River generation station," she said. "I'd like to talk to their security people, see if they've had any issues, threats. Maybe show some photos."

"What else do you know about this guy?" Mark said. "You've taken the time to familiarize yourself with power stations, but you don't know anything about Pate?"

"He's just a name tied up with Janell Cole. He's not my focus. She is."

Mark said, "I wrote the high-voltage lineman's name down and found an address in Red Lodge. The quote in the newspaper was short, but he was pretty emphatic that it was vandalism. We might want to check on him, see what he saw."

A guarded silence, then, "Yes. We might. Sheriff's office first, though."

"You're the boss. It's not a bad place to start. They'll know we're in town fast enough, anyway, so we might as well lead the contact."

Lynn looked down the street. "Where is the sheriff?"

"In Powell."

"Another town?"

Mark nodded. "You've got to wait for the law around here, Lynn. The small towns, you're kind of counted on to police yourselves, for better or worse."

"There are a lot of empty miles out here," she said. "Do you know how to get to the sheriff's office or should I use the GPS?"

"I'm familiar with the route," Mark said. Numerous family members had spent time there. Unless they'd moved the jail, Mark could get there without a map.

28

The sheriff's deputy who spoke to them in Powell said he'd never heard of Eli Pate, Janell Cole, or Doug Oriel. Mark and Lynn showed him the photos and got slow shakes of the head.

"None of my local lovelies," he said. He was a small man and his gun belt looked oversize on him, but he was gray-haired and weathered and had probably seen everything Powell had to offer several times over by now. "That doesn't mean you won't find him somewhere between here and Sheridan, of course."

"He's not in your frequent-flier program, though," Mark said.

The deputy grinned. "Definitely not, and we got plenty in platinum class."

"You heard anything about the vandalism of the electrical lines around here?" Mark asked. "Chain saws and trees, is my understanding."

He nodded. "Mine too. But this department isn't involved. Montana grabbed that one." He pointed at the picture of Eli Pate. "He's part of that mess?"

"Can't say for sure," Lynn answered, "but we're curious, at least."

As she was thanking him for his help and giving him a card, Mark looked at the booking counter, where a deputy was leaning back in a chair working through a can of Pringles and a bottle of Dr Pepper. Mark knew better than to ask, but damned if he could stop himself.

"You ever heard of anyone named Novak?" he asked the gray-haired deputy when Lynn was finished.

When he'd introduced himself earlier, he'd just said Markus, no last name, and let Lynn take the lead. Now the deputy studied him with fresh interest.

"Which one?"

Mark shrugged. "Any."

"Haven't seen them in a year, maybe two, but they'll be around, and you'd be wise to start with the jails if you want to find them. Some of them are in our—what did you call it? Frequent-flier program. The ones who aren't dead or disappeared, they'll mooch a few meals off the county in due time, I'm sure."

He'd said nothing wrong, nothing that Mark wouldn't have said himself, and so he shouldn't have felt his blood begin to boil and the skin around his eyes and mouth go tight.

"What do they have to do with it?" the deputy asked.

Mark shook his head. Lynn was watching closely.

"I knew a couple of them," Mark said. "That's all."

"Sorry to hear it. Which ones?"

Mark felt like there was something ticking in his chest. He looked to the side of the old cop's face when he said, "Larry, Ronny, and Violet, mostly."

"Shit, you knew the brew crew!" The deputy was jovial and smiling. Mark's body felt very still, and he could feel the ridges of his teeth on the sides of his tongue. The deputy kept going, oblivious. "There aren't many jails around here those three didn't drink themselves into. Last I knew of Larry, he was in trouble for running a hunting-guide service without an outfitter's license."

Mark nodded numbly. He was aware that he'd made a mistake in asking and now he just wanted out, but the deputy spoke again.

"You're likely too young to remember Violet the way she used to be, but back in her day, we didn't mind bringing her in at all," he said, and he winked at Mark. Conspiratorial, man-to-man. "She had an ass like a…a…" He glanced at Lynn and stuttered to a stop. "Sorry. She was a bit of a looker, but what a train wreck of a human being."

The ticking in Mark's chest had moved into his brain and he knew from experience that it would not pause there long before it found his hands, and so he turned and walked away from them without a word. He passed through the doors and out onto the street, where a chill wind blew down out of the mountains. The sun was high and bright but with that wind blowing, it was hard to feel much warmth. It could stay that way right into the summer here. You could shiver your way through a sunburn in this country.

Mark felt a hand on his arm and looked back to see Lynn Deschaine staring at him with concern. "What was that about? Why were you asking about your family?"

"That was a mistake. I don't know why I did it. Just curious, I guess. Time passes and you wonder if anybody remembers you. I guess they do."

He walked back to the Tahoe with Lynn trailing behind, and he kept his hands in his pockets and the fingers of his right hand wrapped around the plastic disk from the Saba National Marine Park. He'd been there with Lauren on an endless blue sea where the sun shone warm on his skin. There was a wind over the Saba, too, but that wind didn't chill the sun. He remembered that day regularly, called the visual up often. Sometimes it felt harder, though. Sometimes it felt very far away.

They drove northwest out of Powell and chased the Clark Fork of the Yellowstone out of Wyoming and into Montana. The water was running high and fast. Any place that had white water would be a screamer right now. It was too early in the season for the rafting guides to be out, but they would be soon enough.

Mark was driving in silence, feeling the fatigue from no sleep accumulating with the miles. Lynn must have been thinking the same thing, because she said, "I feel like we should have knocked on a lot more doors than this by now."

"That's the problem out here. You've got to commit to several hours on the road just to get from one door to the next."

"You think the lineman is going to be able to tell us anything?"

"Hell, I don't know. Your client will want to hear what he has to say, though." Mark's voice sounded curt, and he didn't mean for it to. His mind was back on the deputy in Powell, the sly smile that had creased his good-ol'-boy face. Once upon a time, somebody would have knocked that smile into a bloody line. Once upon a time, that somebody might have been Mark.

No more, though. No more. Mark had killed that man in a place not far from here, up in the Beartooth Mountains, and later he'd buried him in a warm southern sea. That man was gone for good.

"Did you know Violet?" Lynn asked. Her voice was quiet. Gentle. She was looking at Mark, but he didn't take his eyes off the road.

"She was my mother."

"I'm so sorry."

"I got that response a lot growing up."

"No, I mean I'm sorry that you had to listen to that guy—"

"He was fine," Mark said. "He remembers things just right, I'm sure. A little different perspective from mine, but that doesn't make him wrong. I shouldn't have asked." He paused and a few miles fell behind them in silence and then he said, "It's just a bit of a brain-bender, being back here, you know? I still know all the roads, all the mountains, all the towns. It's just as it should be. But I don't want it to be. I want it to be so damned different that I don't even have to think about the way it was."

"I'm sorry," she said again.

Mark nodded and drove on toward Red Lodge. Through one corner of the windshield, he saw the Beartooths taking shape, jagged granite towers that looked like they intended to take a bite out of the clouds. They were very much like the lonesome peaks he'd seen in his dreams.

29

They were out of the flatlands and into countryside that had begun to fill with rolling hills, the mountains still many hours ahead, when the police flashers went on behind the truck.

Janell had driven for most of the day, the cruise control locked exactly four miles per hour above the speed limit, fast enough to blend in but not fast enough to invite police attention so she would know immediately that any police interest concerned the identity of the truck, not its speed. They'd switched positions just an hour earlier, though, so she said, "How fast were you going?"

"Maybe ten over, max."

Just enough to leave the situation in doubt. She watched the mirror and saw the driver's door of the cruiser open and an officer get out. Older and overweight, with a mustache. He hadn't spent any time on his radio or with his computer, and that was encouraging. He also kept his head down as he approached, and that was even better, because if he knew anything about the people inside this truck, he would have had his eyes up and his hand close to his gun.

"Speeding," she said. "You idiot. You risked us for an extra five miles an hour."

"I'll talk him down."

"You're a probation violator. When he runs your license, he'll see that."

"He won't run the license."

"If he runs the plate we're in trouble. And everybody runs the plate."

They'd stolen a plate off a similar make and model truck in Georgia, but the VIN wouldn't match if checked. The longer the stop went, the worse things would become. The cop was at the door, rapping on the window with his knuckles. Doug put the window down and said, "Taillights out again? They've been giving me hell."

"There's no trouble with your taillights, pal, and you know it. What's with the fast-and-furious routine here? Speeding, driving all over the damn roadway."

All over the roadway was a lie; Doug's driving had been fine, just fast. But they were on a lonely stretch of highway in a shitkicker town in the middle of nowhere and they had a vehicle with a Florida license. They were good for a stop, and good for the county's coffers.

"He's only driving fast because I told him to," she said.

The deputy lowered his head so he could see past Doug and over to the passenger seat.

"Why would you tell him to drive reckless, miss?"

"Because I'm about to be sick. I've been sick three times in the past eighty miles. Food poisoning."

"Is that so?" He studied her. His mustache was unevenly trimmed and his breathing was heavy, as if the walk from the car had winded him. Only one vehicle had passed since he'd turned the lights on. It was a lonely stretch of road.

"I'm about to be sick again," she said.

"I'm sorry to hear it. But I'm still going to need the gentleman's driver's license and registration."

"No warning?" Doug said. "It would sure be nice if we could—"

"License and registration," the officer repeated firmly. His name tag glittered: M. Terrell.

"Just give it to him," she said. "I'm going to throw up."

When she opened the door, Terrell barked at her to stay in the vehicle, but she ignored him and lurched out of the seat and hurried several feet away, off the shoulder of the road and down the steep slope, and then she kept going, past the tree line, where she made a show of falling to her knees and retching. She could hear him instructing Doug to stay where he was, and then grass and leaves crunched beneath his boots as he made his way toward her. He wore heavy work boots, the kind her stepfather had worn. The first man she'd killed.

"Y'all been doing some drinking, maybe?"

She shook her head. She was on her hands and knees with a string of spit hanging from her mouth. She sucked air in noisy gasps, making sure her back rose and fell with the effort. He stopped just behind her, nothing visible of him but the work boots. She thought he probably liked the view just fine. She lowered her forehead to the ground, touched the cool earth with it, and closed her eyes.

"What's your name, miss?"

She said, "Abenaki." An old joke, one shared only with Eli, who was dealing with Violet, a woman who believed deeply in the spiritual power of American Indians. Eli would have laughed, hearing it under these circumstances. The deputy did not laugh.

"Ab-a-what?"

"Abenaki."

"That's some name."

"It's Indian."

"You don't look the part."

"Who are you to say whether I look like my own name?"

"Fair enough. I'm going to need you to stand up and come back to the road. You have to puke, you can do it over by the side of the truck where I can see you. We're not staying down here in the woods."

She nodded absently, her head brushing the dirt, her hair falling around her face. She moved a hand to her belly and groaned.

"You sure y'all haven't had a few too many?"

"None."

"Okay. We'll see about that. But let's get over to the truck, like I asked. You can sit outside of it, but you're going to sit where I can see you."

She lifted her head, wobbled, and then fell again. "Can you help me up? Please?"

He hesitated, then stepped forward. "Let's go." He reached down and took her left arm, the one that wasn't pressed to her stomach.

She leaned her weight into him as he lifted so that he had to choose whether to use both hands or move back and let her fall. He chose to use both hands, one on her left arm and one around her waist. That was when she pivoted toward him, drew the knife from her belt, and opened his throat with a single, smooth slice.

His eyes went wide and he tried to step away from her, reach for his gun, and reach for his throat all at the same time. She held on to his right hand, held tight, feeling his pulse in his palm as he gave up on the gun and settled for reaching for his throat with his left hand, as if he could seal the wound with pressure, stem the inevitable tide. He fell over as blood seeped between his fingers and his mouth worked but no words came. She moved closer to his side, still clutching his hand, and watched. Life left his hand first, and then his eyes. The shortest of delays, but still there. Life seeped from the limbs first, and lingered longest in the eyes.

She knew this well.

She wanted to stay with him but there was no time. She released his hand and studied the front of her shirt, which was splattered with blood. Then she looked up the slope at his cruiser. It was a new-model Dodge, and it would have an in-dash video system that started recording as soon as he activated the emergency lights. That was why she'd come so far into the trees. She doubted the video would show what had happened, but it would show the truck.

She didn't need long, though. She just needed to stay in motion. She got in the passenger seat and slammed the door, wiping the blade of the knife on her jeans.

"Drive."

Doug stared at her, wide-eyed.

"What did you do! He wasn't going to stop us, he was just going to give us a ticket, and now we're—"

"In a hurry," she said. "We were in a hurry before, and we are in a hurry now. Nothing has changed. It's all about forward momentum. We just need to keep it going forward. Either start driving or get out of the seat so I can."

He put the truck back in gear and then looked in the rearview mirror. It was still filled with the dancing colored lights of the police car.

"Forward momentum," she said again, and he lowered his eyes and pressed on the accelerator and pulled them off the shoulder and back onto the road. Ahead, the mountains loomed in shadow.

"I'd change roads fast," she said. "And I think we're going to need a new truck."

That was a shame, because she'd always loved the bloodred truck with the big tires and the throaty motor. All the same, it had to be done.

"Get off the highway. All of these hillbillies will have four-wheel drive. Look for a driveway that goes back into the trees. Someplace isolated."

He didn't answer. She leaned her head back and closed her eyes. The smell of blood was heavy in the cab of the truck, and if she concentrated, she could still feel the officer's pulse against her thumb.

30

BMV records told them that Jay Baldwin lived on Twenty-Second Street West in Red Lodge, the last street off Highway 212 before it began to climb into the Beartooths. The home was a nice A-frame with a garage below the decks and wide banks of windows facing the mountains.

Mark parked on the curb, and they had just gotten out of the Tahoe when the garage door went up. A man's boots and jeans became visible, and then the whole of him—Jay Baldwin, standing at the top of a short staircase, locking the interior door to the house. He had his back to them, and when he turned and saw them he jerked and moved a hand toward his heart like they'd given him a coronary.

"Mr. Baldwin?" Lynn said.

"Yes. What?" He hurried down the steps and out of the garage. "Who are you?"

"Private investigators," Lynn said.

He stopped walking. Stopped breathing, it seemed. He looked like they'd fired off a flash grenade in his face.

"There's nothing wrong," Lynn said. "Nothing about you, I mean." She offered him a card.

"Your name came up in an article about some vandalism on the high-voltage lines around here," Mark said. "We were hoping you could tell us a little about that."

"The lines?" He had frantic eyes. They bounced from Mark to Lynn and then out beyond, to the street. Most of the time, in fact, they were on the street.

"Yeah. In the paper, you were quoted as—"

"I don't know anything about that."

Mark raised his eyebrows. "Pardon? You don't know anything about the words you provided to the newspaper?"

"I know what I said. I just mean...look, we've got public relations people for this. I can't just..." He finally brought his eyes back to Mark. "Do you think you know who did it?"

"We might have some ideas. First, though, we need to know the situation. You said somebody had been cutting trees onto the lines. You called it, I believe, intentionally malicious."

"Right. So who do you think it was? What's his name?"

He shifted his weight from one leg to the other. A subtle movement, not as jittery as his eyes, but still restless. Something about him didn't feel right, and Mark realized what it was: Jay Baldwin in person did not convey the same impression as Jay Baldwin in the photo, the man who looked a little worn but plenty steady. The guy you'd want responding to your emergencies.

"Everything okay, Mr. Baldwin?" Mark said.

"Fine, yeah, but I can't deal with this. I just...it's not for me." Mark saw that he had something in his hand, something that for an instant looked like a twin of the dive permit Mark carried. A small plastic chip. He put it in his pocket before Mark could see it clearly. "Listen," he said, "I'd really like to know the specifics of your case."

"We can discuss all of that," Lynn said. "You mind if we come in for a couple minutes? We can tell you—"

"No!" He barked it at her, and she tilted her head back, startled.

"Okay. We can stay out here. But—"

"No," he repeated. "I'm not the guy who can discuss things like this. It's, you know, it's a, um...a policy. It's a corporate policy. You'll have to call the company."

He backed away from them but kept his head up, his eyes darting. The street was empty but you'd have thought there was a pack of feral dogs out there. He reached his truck, tried to put his key in the door lock, fumbled, and dropped the keys. When he moved to recover them, the white chip fell free and hit the garage floor and he swore at himself in a harsh whisper. He went for the chip before the keys, picked it up from the floor and inspected it as if he'd dropped a Rolex facedown onto gravel. He put it back in his pocket, but it was a different pocket this time. His breast pocket. He had to unzip his jacket to secure it.

Mark walked back out to the street and joined Lynn in the Tahoe as Jay Baldwin backed out of his garage and lowered the door. He pulled away without looking at them, driving too fast for the street. On 212, he turned left and headed northeast.

"Waste of time," Lynn said. "That guy isn't much of a talker, is he? I'm amazed he gave a quote to the newspaper."

"We scared him," Mark said.

"He was a little leery of us. Didn't even give me a chance to charm him."

"No," Mark said. "We *scared* him, Lynn. Really. He was afraid of us."

She gave him an odd look. "What do you mean?"

"Did you see the way he tried to unlock his truck with his key?"

"He dropped the key. He was flustered."

"When was the last time you saw someone unlock a modern vehicle by actually turning the key? That's a new truck, it has keyless entry, they all do. And he didn't need to do *anything*. The truck was unlocked. When he finally did get in, he just opened the door. He was just going through motions before, like he was stoned."

"Maybe he was."

Mark shook his head. "He thought we were coming for another reason."

Lynn already had her phone in her hand. "Is there any place in this state with a good cell signal? I've got a dossier on Pate from the office, but I can't download it. Can you find us someplace with Wi-Fi?"

"Sure." Mark started the Tahoe, drove out to 212, and turned toward town. The main street looked just as he remembered it. The flickering neon sign of the Red Lodge Café was even still there. When they'd had the money, his family ate breakfasts there. It was also the last place Mark had stopped for coffee before he'd left the state of Montana entirely, heading south. At the stoplight by the gas station,

Mark could see the taillights of Jay Baldwin's pickup as he headed out of town. He felt like he was missing something, that Jay had shown Mark something he should have understood but had failed to pick up on. He wondered what the plastic chip was and why Jay handled it the way Mark handled Lauren's old dive permit.

"He showed his hands," Mark said.

"What?"

"He made a point of it. Like a guy might do if he's hustling cards and he knows people are watching close. He made a point of showing his hands. Even when he didn't need to, like the bit with the truck keys. That was about showing his hands."

"Why would he think we cared?"

"Either somebody is watching our boy," Mark said, "or he thinks somebody is."

Jay's truck had vanished down the highway, and the reddening pines stood silent as the sun fell behind the Beartooths.

31

They found a motel in Red Lodge called Benjamin Beartooth's Last Chance Inn that promised Wi-Fi. The supposed last chance did not have anything to do with rooms, apparently—when they asked if there were two available, the clerk laughed and said they could have twenty if they wanted to pay for them. Mark's mind was still on Jay Baldwin as they walked to Lynn's room so she could set up her laptop and download the files her office had sent. She sat at the desk, clicking away, and he went to the window, looked out at the same street he'd traveled a hundred times in what now seemed like another lifetime, and wondered about the fear he'd seen in Baldwin. It was a particular kind of fear—fear of being caught.

But caught doing what?

Lynn said: "I thought you said Eli Pate had never done prison time."

"Correct."

"Incorrect."

Mark turned from the window in surprise. "I ran his name last night."

She had a small smile, one that was smug but not in an unattractive way. Pleased with herself, that was all. Still, he felt stupid, a step behind.

"What did I miss?"

"Amsterdam," she said.

"What?"

"We have an office there."

"Of course you do."

The smile widened and filled her eyes. "Pinkerton Global," she said. "Isn't this what you were having so much fun with, giving me shit over my firm?"

"I gave you only respect. If anything, it was envy disguised as respect."

"Yeah, right."

"Just tell me what the hell I missed."

She pushed back from the desk so Mark could come close enough to see the screen. He bent down and looked at the dossier her office had sent.

In 1998, a youthful Eli Pate had been arrested in Rotterdam on charges of conspiring against the state, which led to four years in prison in the Netherlands before his eventual extradition back to the United States. He'd been in the Netherlands on a student visa, studying petroleum engineering and history.

"What exactly does *conspiring against the state* mean?"

"Keep reading."

There was a short abstract detailing the charges. According to the Dutch authorities, Eli Pate had been involved in a plan to blow up sixteen ships in the Waalhaven harbor of the Port of Rotterdam, Europe's largest port. Although he was aligned with members of a self-described environmental watch group, all parties agreed that he was not himself a member. Rather, he'd attempted to recruit them to *his* cause. Affidavits claimed that Pate's express goal was to "make a statement" about the shipping industry, which was responsible for more air pollutants than all the cars in the world, he explained. Due to the fact that nobody had made any real progress with the plan— news of it was leaked to Dutch intelligence agencies before Pate had secured any recruits, let alone explosives—the prosecution didn't garner as much attention as it might have. Following his prison stay, he was sent back to America, leaving behind an unfinished degree and a two-hundred-page thesis on the energy theories of Nikola Tesla.

"I wonder what that thesis reads like," Mark said.

"I can ask our Amsterdam office to put together a file."

"You really like saying that, don't you? *Our Amsterdam office.*"

She grinned at him. She had a hell of a smile. Mark hadn't seen much of it because she was all business most of the time, and he felt the same—this wasn't a pleasure trip. He felt the same, at least, until he saw that smile. When the smile reached her eyes and they took on that beautiful dark light, he wanted to forget why they were there. He wanted to forget about Eli Pate and Janell Cole and even Garland Webb.

He wanted to forget about his wife.

"What?" Lynn said. Her smile was gone and she looked concerned.

"Sorry. Mind wandering."

"Low blood sugar."

"I don't think that's it."

"Well, it sure is for me. We haven't eaten all day. You're the local guide. Surely you can find a decent meal in this town for us?"

"There's a Mexican-and-pizza restaurant called Bogart's that isn't bad."

She raised an eyebrow. "A *Mexican-and-pizza* restaurant called Bogart's?"

Mark shrugged. "It's Montana. We don't need to make sense to the tourists."

We. He'd said it easily, no hesitation, as if he belonged to the place. You can't go home again, or so the saying goes. *Bullshit,* Mark thought. *You just take it with you.*

They walked down the street to Bogart's, a brick building with a sign featuring Bogie's face, and Lynn said, "You weren't kidding. It's really about him. Why?"

"I honestly have no idea. But the food was good once. It maybe still is."

They went in and sat at the bar and Mark looked at the beer taps and saw that they had Moose Drool. He ordered one.

"Moose Drool," Lynn said. "You actually wish to consume this. You're even willing to pay for it, I gather. Unless the bartering system is employed here? Do I need to find some pelts and beads?"

"It's a damned good beer. Now, my uncles drank Rainier, mostly. They didn't have much interest in craft beer. Rainier they called fuel. 'Markus, run in the gas station and grab us a case of fuel for the road.'"

The Moose Drool tasted the way he'd remembered, a brown ale with a smooth finish. Lynn ordered the same, took a drink, and gave a small nod indicating that it was at least palatable.

"How'd you end up with the Pinkertons, anyhow?" Mark said.

"Swung and missed on the FBI. Came out of law school and wanted to get into the Bureau but they didn't take me. I didn't blame them, really, I was straight out of school and didn't have any other experience. I thought I'd beef up the résumé with private-sector work. I ended up just liking the private-sector work."

"You enjoy it?"

"I enjoy it. It's hell on relationships, though. I travel a lot, and I can't talk about why I'm traveling. All the things that men expect women to tolerate, they don't do a very good job of tolerating themselves." She held up a hand. "Sorry."

"No need to be. It sounded like the truth."

She nodded. "So I like the job. Enough that I didn't try to get into the Bureau again. I've been treated well, I've been promoted fast, I've gotten good cases. I didn't love the Boca Raton assignment, but it was a step forward. Just not my scene."

"Where are you from?"

"New Hampshire, originally. My first assignment was in Cleveland. You'd think it'd be hard to miss Cleveland, but I do. I miss the seasons. Florida, it's hot or less hot, you know? You don't feel the turnover. Spring comes, and it's nice, but..."

"You don't feel like you've earned it."

She smiled and pointed at him. "That is *exactly* the problem. If you don't have to work to get through winter, what difference does spring make?"

They ate and drank and talked about the intel report on Pate. Drank more. As the beer went down Mark began to feel looser about the town, that cold dread of arriving here going a little warmer, and then he was telling Lynn stories about his uncles. The good stories, the ones that always got laughs. They got plenty from her. He loved hearing that laugh. He didn't tell her any of the bad stories, or the sad ones. He didn't tell her any about his mother. Lynn didn't ask either. She'd heard all she needed to from the deputy in Powell, probably. Mark was grateful that she was content to leave it there. Lauren always had been too.

"You said Ronny is dead," Lynn said after he'd told a particular classic about Larry getting arrested for public intox. Larry had been cuffed and was being guided to the patrol car by a cop when Ronny walked leisurely across the street wearing a ski mask and carrying a shotgun, which, as one might expect, got the attention of the cop. Both activities were perfectly legal in Montana; it was an open-carry state, and although wearing a ski mask in July when it was damn near ninety degrees outside was strange, there wasn't anything criminal about it. While Ronny was explaining his fears of sunburn and skin cancer to the officer, Larry simply walked away from the patrol car, still wearing his handcuffs. Mark cut the chain later that night with a hacksaw, which made life easier for Larry but not exactly problem-free.

Eventually Mark's mother showed up and picked the lock. She was a Houdini with locks.

He left that part of the story out.

"Ronny is dead, yes," he said. "Cancer took him young."

"And Larry?"

"You heard the deputy today. Sounds like he's in Sheridan."

"But you don't speak to him? Or…"

Mark shook his head and ordered a fresh beer. Lynn watched in silence.

"I don't have communication with any of them." He took a drink. "The act got old, Lynn. It just got old."

That was as much as he could tell her. He couldn't tell her what he was already feeling, and fearing—that he was home. That without

Lauren and without his job, Florida had become foreign to him. That the smell of snow in the air on a day filled with sun and dry winds felt natural and comfortable, and that Mark suspected he could come back to this place very easily, come back and stay, but that the man who stayed here wouldn't be much like the man who'd lived in Florida.

"Let's get out of here," he said. "I've wasted enough of our time on old bullshit stories. We've got work to do, and tomorrow we'll need to be up early."

He was in bed but not asleep when she knocked. He got up and pulled on his jeans and a shirt but left it unbuttoned as he opened the door. She was standing there holding a six-pack of Rainier in one hand. She was wearing just a white tank top over jeans and it was too cold for that and the goose bumps stood out on her tanned skin.

"I thought you might need some fuel," she said. Her gaze was steady on his at first, but after a moment, she looked away. "Sometimes I make bad guesses. If this is one of them, I apologize."

"You're not wrong," he said. His voice was hoarse. He pushed the door wide and she stepped inside and set the beer on the little table by the window and started to free two cans from the plastic rings. She was awkward with the cans, knocked one onto its side. When she opened them, she closed her eyes at the snap and sigh of the released pressure. Then she kept her eyes closed and shook her head.

"I should go back to my own room."

Please, don't do that, Mark thought, but he said, "Why?"

"Because this stopped feeling professional to me sometime tonight, and I do not like it when I stop feeling professional. Because I am here to do a job."

"We both are."

She nodded and opened her eyes, looked at him with a gaze that showed the first traces of vulnerability he'd seen in her.

"You're not what I thought," she said. "Who I thought."

"What does that mean?"

Instead of answering, she said, "I'm not wrong, am I? Not that you'd tell me if I was. It's up to me to decide whether to trust you."

Mark said, "Lynn? I don't know what you think of me. What you trust or don't. I've not lied to you, and I won't."

Still she was silent.

"If you think you should go," he said, "then you need to go."

She took a deep breath. "No harm in having a beer."

"What harm are you worried about?"

She ignored the question, reaching back down for the beers as he stepped toward her. When she turned to hand him one, he was standing close, and for just a moment she paused, just long enough for a heart to skip a beat, and then he took the beer cans out of her hands and set them back on the table. She reached up and looped her arms around his neck. Her expression was both earnest and wary.

"A mistake?" she said.

"I usually am."

They stood like that for a second, and then Mark leaned down and kissed her. Her lips were warm and soft and tasted faintly of beer, but that was good, that was right, that was Montana again. Home. The girls Mark remembered from here were not Lauren, and that was good.

Lynn slipped her hands inside his unbuttoned shirt and ran her palms over his stomach and up to his chest and drove an electric thrill into him that left him short of breath. He broke the kiss as she pushed the shirt off his shoulders and let it fall to the floor. She kept running her hands over his torso, but she was studying it too.

"What happened to you? You're all cut up."

"I crawled through a broken window."

Lynn touched a band of scar tissue that ran across his stomach and up toward his shoulder, thick as a snake.

"That one is not fresh."

"No."

"How'd you get that?"

"A rope."

"A *rope?*"

"I was a rafting guide for a while. I went over once and got tangled up."

"Ouch." She lowered her face to the scar and kissed it, then traced its length with the tip of her tongue. Though the feeling was sensual and wonderful, Mark pulled her back up. She started to speak but he kissed her, hard, before she could. He didn't want to hear any more questions, because he didn't want to tell her how many times his wife had kissed that scar. The body remembers whether the mind wants to or not.

Right now, he didn't want to remember anything.

They moved to the bed in an awkward walk, laughing as they bumped into it and fell onto the mattress. Mark slipped his hand under her shirt and felt that beautiful dip in the small of her back, something that is entirely the province of women and is unfailingly sexy. She sat up and pulled her shirt off and then pulled his head to her breasts as she worked the button on his jeans with her free hand. They shed the rest of their clothes gracelessly, and then she closed her hand around him and guided him into her. She leaned back and made a soft sound, and if Mark could have frozen time right there, it would have been all right.

When she began to move, though, that was all right too.

They finished in a breathless hurry that first time, but they hadn't even spoken yet, were just lying side by side, breathing hard, when she felt him begin to stiffen against her thigh again and she gave a low laugh.

"Well, now," she said. "Right back at it, I see."

Right back at it. This time was slower, and longer, and better. When they finished, the sheets were damp with sweat and they were both out of breath and she lay on top of him with her head on his chest and one leg hooked around his, and he thought of the way she'd fallen asleep against him on the plane and how he'd wanted her never to wake up and shift away.

And then he thought of Lauren. Inevitably. He could picture her and smell her and taste her, Lauren, who'd been dead for nearly two years, and whatever had been warm within him went cold and small.

You couldn't cheat on the dead. But, Lord, you could certainly feel like you had. The heart and the mind do not always align.

Mark lay there stroking Lynn's hair and feeling like a first-rate heel, in violation of both the memory of his dead wife and Lynn, because she deserved better, she deserved Mark's mind to be empty of all thoughts that weren't about her.

Then, as her breathing went deep and slow and she edged toward sleep, he thought that was an ignorant notion. He didn't know who else was in Lynn's mind, but he knew that it would be foolish—and arrogant—to believe that it had been just him. Everyone carries the past with them. It shifts and re-forms and adds layers, but it never leaves.

But now she slept easily, adjusting so that her arm and one leg were wrapped around him and her head was nestled against his shoulder. Mark realized that his Ambien was out of reach, and he didn't want to disturb her, though he knew he'd have to at some point if he wanted to sleep. He hadn't slept without the pills in two years. Right then, though, he was comfortable. Right then, he was as comfortable as he'd been in a long time. He thought he'd give it a while, and so he listened to her breathing and found himself matching his own breaths to hers.

Stop that, damn it. Those are the wrong breaths from the wrong woman.

But the right woman didn't breathe anymore.

Soon he was asleep.

32

They'd stuck to the back roads after Janell killed the deputy. Sirens became audible not long after they left, but those had screamed north on the highway while Doug drove west on a narrow, winding lane. She tried not to look at the clock. This was going to cost them precious hours, and she'd waited on the reunion with Eli for so long that she could hardly bear the delay, wanted to keep speeding toward him.

She couldn't bring danger with her, though.

Several times Doug slowed and suggested cars to take. She dismissed each of them, but she saw what he was looking for—an empty car and a dark house. That was troubling. His resolve was weakening.

"You're only picking out houses that are dark," she said. "Tell me why."

"It should be obvious."

"Evidently not. Explain."

"Speed!" he snapped. "Get a new car, one without all the police in five states looking for it, and get the fuck out of here."

"Hmm." She pursed her lips. "So you want to gain two things: time and distance."

"No shit."

"Can you find the flaw in your solution, or do I need to point it out?"

He didn't answer. She nodded. "Time and distance are joined for us, obviously. The more time we gain, the more distance. Now, you're attempting to gain time by rushing. It's the exact philosophy that created the problem with the deputy back there."

"You *killed* him. That created the problem!"

"No. You were speeding, in a foolish attempt to gain distance and time. This is the underlying problem. You're bringing the same approach to the current situation. If we steal a car from someone who isn't home, how much time did we buy?"

"More than we've got now."

"That's not an answer."

"Well, we wouldn't know. Depends how long until they got home and called it in."

"Exactly. So maybe we gained a day, maybe twenty minutes. The unknown isn't desirable." She'd lost the sensation of Deputy Terrell's pulse under her thumb, but the odor of his blood lingered.

Doug started to speak, to object, but she cut him off.

"Slow down. I want to look at this one."

There was a steep gravel driveway angling away to the right, climbing a wooded hill. Through the trees, the lights of a house gleamed. It was high on a forested ridge and would barely have been visible if not for those lights.

"Turn in here."

"Somebody's home."

"I'm not disputing that. Just make the turn."

He wasn't happy about it, but he pulled into the drive and they crunched over the gravel. Halfway up, dogs began to bark and howl. Lots of dogs.

"Terrible choice," he said. "Listen to all that."

"Anyone who can hear them now has heard them before."

A vehicle came into view, parked in front of a shed, a small house beyond, kennels just past that. A half a dozen dogs, floppy-eared hounds of some sort, stood with their paws on the fence, howling. The vehicle was a giant SUV, a Tahoe or a Yukon, covered with dust, the tailgate a hideous array of bumper stickers pledging allegiance to dogs, guns, and God.

"Promising," she said.

"How in the hell you figure? That thing will be even easier to spot than this frigging truck."

"This feels like the home of a lonely soul. All those dogs."

Doug hadn't even cut the engine before the front door of the house opened and a man in a flannel shirt appeared on the porch, peering out at them.

"Shit. See what we got now?"

"Exactly what we need," she said, climbing out of the truck.

The man on the porch looked to be about sixty, tall but with stooped shoulders and thinning white hair.

"Can I help you?" he called.

"I hope so! We've lost our dog. I thought he might have headed toward the sound of your pack here."

"What kind of dog?"

"Beagle. A fat, dumb old beagle." She laughed when she said it, and the man on the porch laughed with her.

"He light out after a rabbit?"

"Most likely." She was close to the porch steps now, walking quickly. "You haven't seen him? He was running through the woods right there."

She pointed to the west, and he turned to squint speculatively into the trees when she came up the porch steps and drew her knife. He kept studying the woods.

"Usually my own would take to barking if they heard another dog," he said, "so I'd figure he must have headed in the other direction, or he might have crossed the road on you and doubled back. I'll help you look if you give me a minute to—"

When he turned, he saw the blood on her shirt. He started to voice a question, but then he noticed the blade and stood with mouth agape, the question forgotten.

"Walk inside, please," she said. Behind her, Doug finally got out of the truck. The man's eyes went to him. He didn't move toward the door.

She said, "The choices you make in the next few seconds are important. I'll ask you again to walk inside the house."

He went to it, with her just a step behind. Inside, the place lived up to the promise of its exterior. From the dirty dishes stacked in the sink to the jackets and boots in the corner and even to the smell, there was no indication that anyone lived here except for him and the dogs.

There was an Adirondack chair in front of a cold fireplace. "Sit there," she said. Doug had appeared behind her, gun in hand, and he closed the door and set to work on the blinds. The white-haired man watched him with far more apprehension than he'd shown her, seeming to view Doug as the primary threat. The bull-moose approach of males, always deferring first to gender, then to size. Likewise, the gun scared him more than the knife when what mattered was not the weapon but the willingness to use it.

"Sit," she repeated, and he finally followed her instruction, talking while he moved.

"Only cash I've got is in my wallet on the counter. Every gun is in the cabinet. It's locked, but the key's tucked on top. Take what you want."

"We will," she assured him. "But first we need to talk."

The natural incline of the Adirondack chair forced him to lean back and look up at her, the height difference reversed, the power differential self-evident. She stepped forward, slipped her left foot through the gap between the arm of the chair and the seat, then her right, and settled onto his lap. He flinched and made a small whining sound, like a whipped dog. She smiled. Reached up with her left hand, which was still streaked with rust-colored dried blood, and stroked his cheek. His jaw trembled beneath her hand. She ran her fingers through his thin, wispy hair until she found enough for a solid handhold and tightened her fist. She pulled the hair at his scalp, forcing his head back. She kept her eyes on his while she brought the blade up to his throat and, with a precise hand, trimmed a few whiskers away from his Adam's apple. He made the whining sound again and there was a sudden wet warmth beneath her thigh as his bladder released.

"I think you're ready to be honest, aren't you?" she said, releasing her tight hold on his hair and stroking his head, the blade still resting against his Adam's apple.

He wanted to nod but the knife at his throat prevented that, so he had to speak. He gasped out the word "Yes" as tears formed in his eyes.

"What's your name?"

"Gregory. Gregory Ardachu."

"Okay, Greg. Does anyone else live with you? Or is it just you and the dogs?" Still stroking his head.

"Just me."

"Good. You see, time is a concern to us. Replacing the unknown with a known. If we were to take your truck, for example, we would want to know how long we could drive it safely. Do you understand?"

Again he tried to nod, and this time he actually moved enough to press against the blade and open a thin red line on his own throat. He was that desperate to please. This was exactly what Eli understood so well—a man properly motivated by fear would do damn near anything, even if it amounted to a self-inflicted wound.

Doug was still and silent behind her. The white-haired man kept flicking glances in his direction. He was conditioned to fear a large man with a large gun, even while a small woman with a small knife was directly in front of him. Such was the way of his world. But that was a terrible mistake.

"The next question is critical," Janell said. "Honesty will make all the difference."

She paused, studying his face. He was breathing in quick little jerks that made his lips twitch. She could feel his racing pulse under her legs.

"If we were to tie you up and leave you here," she said, "healthy and unharmed, how long would it be until you were found? You need to be *very* sure this answer is true."

It took him a few seconds to steady himself enough to answer. "Two days," he gasped. "In two days...friend coming for his dog. I've been...training the dog."

"Two days! That's wonderful. Did you hear that, Doug? Do you understand how much better this is, to replace the unknown with the known?"

"It's great," Doug said. His impatience—or was it fear?—was evident in his voice. "Get his keys and we'll tie him up and we'll go."

"Does that sound good?" she asked the white-haired man. "We'll borrow the truck, and you'll wait here? It's not ideal for you, but..." She shrugged. "Consider the alternatives."

"Kitchen counter." The words jerked out between his hitching breaths. "Keys on counter."

Doug moved into the kitchen, and there was a metallic jingle. "Got 'em."

Janell hadn't looked away from those watery, terrified eyes.

"So all we have to do now is tie him."

"Yeah."

"There's a problem with that."

"What?"

"I don't have any rope," she said, and then she drew the blade through his throat.

33

Mark registered the weight and warmth of Lynn's body just before he woke, and for an instant he felt like he was surfacing from a long, terrible nightmare and that the woman pressed against him was his wife, the bad dream finally over.

Then he opened his eyes and saw the dimly lit motel room and reality returned just as he heard his wife say, *Get out*.

The words were crystal clear, the voice unmistakable, undeniable, as real as the motel room he was in, and he sat up with a jerk and looked around.

Empty, of course.

But still...

Get out.

It's what she would have said, *should* have said. He was in bed with another woman. What in the hell else would Lauren have said to that? She'd have been more likely to shoot him than speak to him in that circumstance, but if she'd paused for any words...

Get out.

He had the fleeting thought that the imagined voice hadn't been angry, just urgent. No rage, not even a reprimand, but a clear command.

The mind played cruel tricks.

Or maybe it was the heart.

He shifted away from Lynn, and she murmured what might have been an objection but then fell back asleep before giving full voice to it. If she'd spoken clearly and asked him to stay, he would have. But now he was awake and she was asleep and he felt like an intruder in the bed.

He slipped out from under the covers, dressed quietly, then walked to the table, took one of the warming Rainiers, and stepped outside. Without the sun there to even put up a fight, the frigid mountain air had won out, and he could see his breath. He sat on the sidewalk and drank the beer and told himself that he'd done nothing wrong.

He wondered how long it would be before he really felt that way.

With Lynn, maybe not so long. Maybe not so long as he'd believed.

He wasn't sure whether to get back into bed with her or get in the car and drive away, put distance between them, remove possibility. It wasn't the sort of thing someone should be torn over, but he was.

What do you really want, Markus? What are you hiding? Deep down in the darkest corner of the well, what do you want?

"Leave me alone," he whispered, and he wasn't talking to Lynn. He was talking to Lauren. If she couldn't come back, why wouldn't she just fucking leave? Didn't she understand how damn cruel it was to stalk him like a shadow, invisible to the rest of the world but weighing on every choice he made?

Lord, if only you could cleanse your heart. Wouldn't that be the way to live.

He got to his feet, stood in the cold wind and said, "I'm sorry," and this time he wasn't sure which one of them he was talking to. Both, maybe.

He looked at the closed door to the motel room, where Lynn lay waiting for him—or not; how was he to know whether she truly wanted him there?—and then he started to walk. There wasn't any purpose to it, but the odd dream-waking sensation that Lauren was with him had been so disturbing that he needed to clear his head before he went back inside. He'd dreamed of her before, of course, but this time had been so different because there was no visual, just the voice, and he was sure he'd been fully awake when he heard it.

It reminded him of the caves again, and that was bad. On the list of memories Mark wanted to forget, his last exchange with his wife and his hypothermia-induced hallucinations in the cold caverns beneath Indiana's frozen ground jockeyed for first place.

He put his hand in his pocket while he walked and found the dive permit that he always carried, the Lauren talisman, and he thought again of Jay Baldwin, of his bizarre behavior. Walking as he was, with no destination, Mark thought Jay's house seemed as good a place to go as any.

It was only a few blocks away, and Mark had no trouble finding it because it was the only house in town with the lights on.

He checked his watch. Two in the morning. The expansive glass made Jay's silhouette visible, and Mark could see him standing at the window, looking out at the dark mountains like a lonely sentry.

Leave the man alone, Markus, he thought, but still he walked on toward the house. Baldwin spotted him when he was coming up the drive; the reaction was evident, a stiffening followed by a rapid move away from the windows, and then the door was open and Jay's voice called out, "Who's there?"

"Another guy who can't sleep," Mark said. "Just like you, it seems." He kept on walking, and Jay Baldwin turned and looked over his shoulder nervously, as if there was someone else in the house with him, and then he stepped out into the cold and pulled the door shut and hurried down the driveway.

"Get out of here," he said. "Damn it, get away from here."

Even as he spoke, he was looking over his shoulder, at the house, and he had his hand on Mark's arm now, pushing him back. The resistance was strange—he wasn't trying to force Mark straight down the driveway to the street, he was guiding him at an angle across the pavement and into the yard. The snow was slick underfoot, and Mark struggled to keep his balance. The whole while, Jay Baldwin had his eyes on the house, though. He stopped abruptly just outside the branches of a white-barked pine in the side yard, then pivoted to look at the road, into the darkness behind the tree, and back to the house. It was as if he was triangulating their position somehow, trying to locate a precise spot.

"What are you doing, coming here in the middle of the night?"

For the first time he looked at Mark, apparently content that whatever danger he'd perceived from the house was no longer a factor. Just over Mark's head, a snow-laden branch waved in the breeze, the long needles making faint, cold contact with his scalp.

"I didn't expect you'd be awake," Mark said. "Let alone standing guard. What's going on with you?"

"Get the hell out of here before I call the police."

The pine needles swept back and forth over Mark's scalp, spreading its chill to him, stray snowflakes falling on his neck.

"Call them."

Jay Baldwin was silent.

Mark reached for his cell phone. "I'll do it myself, then."

Jay stepped forward and caught his arm. His grip was strong. With his face close to Mark's, he said, "Don't do that," and his eyes were fierce.

"Okay. Let go of my arm, I'll put the phone down, and we'll talk."

"We're not going to talk."

"Then I'm making the call."

A tear leaked out of the corner of Jay Baldwin's left eye. "You don't understand what you're doing. Please just go. *Please.*"

The wind picked up and the pine boughs struck Mark's head harder, and he did the natural thing and tried to step sideways, clearing himself out from under. Jay grabbed his arm again, and this time his grip was painful.

"Don't step over there."

Mark looked at him and then back at the house. "Are there cameras on you?"

No answer.

"You had a little plastic chip in your hand earlier," Mark said, and Jay released Mark's arm and stepped back fast, as if the statement had burned him. He opened his mouth but he didn't speak, and Mark felt strangely close to him right then. He put the cell phone back in his pocket and took out the old dive permit and held it up.

"This belonged to my wife. She was murdered. I don't give a shit about your power lines, Jay. I'm looking for someone with information about my wife's murder, and that person might intersect with your issues. That's my interest. I'm shooting straight with you. Why don't you try to do the same?"

Mark was wholly unprepared for Jay Baldwin's response. He slid down onto the pavement like something melting, fell on his ass, and began to cry without making a sound. The tears dripped down his cheeks and he stared past Mark at the empty street and he said, "Please, God, please, don't do this to me."

"Mr. Baldwin...what's going on? Tell me, and I can help."

He shook his head. His eyes had no point of focus. Whatever he was seeing was out beyond the visible. He said, "What would you do to get your wife back?"

"Anything."

Jay nodded and drew a breath that shook in his lungs like dust blown down a dry street. "And if you had the chance to go back and save her? If you could have made a deal to keep from losing her? What would you have been willing to do?"

"Same answer. Anything. Whatever was asked."

Jay blinked the tears out of his eyes and focused on Mark's face.

"Okay," he whispered. "Then leave me alone. Because, brother? I've still got a chance. If you leave me alone, I've got a chance. But you've got to leave, and fast."

Mark knew without question that if he pressed Jay right then, he'd break. But instead, he said, "You really believe this? That whatever you've got in front of you right now changes for the better if I walk away?"

Jay nodded.

Mark turned and walked back down the empty street.

34

He went back to the motel, shaken, ready to wake Lynn so he could tell her what had happened. Then he opened the motel door and stepped inside and saw that she was gone.

The sheets were thrown back on the bed, and the imprint of her body remained. He wondered if she'd been annoyed to wake and find that he'd left, if she'd taken that to mean something he hadn't intended.

You see, Lynn, I heard my dead wife's voice, and she didn't love the look of the situation, so I decided to take a walk...

He left the room and went back outside. Her own room was next door, still dark, as if she'd just changed beds and gone back to sleep alone, a silent suggestion for him to do the same, and he felt guilty for leaving now, for being gone so long.

When he was close enough, he saw a faint blue light on in the room—a computer monitor. She was awake, and working. He knocked and waited.

When there was no answer, he knocked again, louder, and said, "Lynn?"

Still nothing. He sidestepped from the door to the window, shielded his eyes, and looked inside. She wasn't in front of the computer, and the bed seemed undisturbed.

He stepped back and looked at his own room as if he might have missed her in there. The bathroom? No. The room had been empty. That one, and this one. And the Tahoe was still parked in front of his door.

"No," he said aloud, his voice calm and reasonable. No, she couldn't be missing. He'd just left her. The small town was silent and safe.

Like Cassadaga?

He tested the door handle. Locked. The motel wasn't of the key-card-and-dead-bolt variety, though. It was old-school, thumb lock and chain. Mark's mother could have gone through it in three seconds.

It took him about twenty. On the fourth try he shimmed the lock with a credit card and stepped into the room and saw that the laptop wasn't all she'd left behind.

Her purse was on the table, her computer bag on the floor below. On the nightstand was the folder with the printouts of photos of Eli Pate and Janell Cole that she'd shown the deputy and the post office clerk.

She went looking for you. That has to be it. She saw you were gone and went looking for you.

That was hard to believe, though. Mark had just walked the length of the town's main street. If she'd been looking for him, he was hard to miss. And why wouldn't she have taken the car?

He went to the desk and looked at the open computer. The screen was still lit because the laptop was open and plugged in. As long as there was a constant power feed, the computer didn't need to conserve battery. There was even music playing, though the headphones were plugged in and so the sound was soft. The music would have helped to keep the computer from entering sleep mode. Between the wall plug and the running application, the computer thought she was still there.

He walked around the desk so he could see the screen clearly, thinking it might tell him something, give some evidence of whether she'd returned here after leaving his room, and then he stopped moving and his breath caught.

There was a photograph on the monitor—she'd been churning through an album of surveillance photos, and while this was one he hadn't seen, he knew it all the same.

He was looking at his mother's face for the first time in nearly two decades.

35

She was only in her midfifties now, and she didn't look even that old. She could have passed for his sister instead of his mother. In his mind, he'd advanced the image and turned her into an old woman. In reality, time had treated her well. She wore long sleeves, so you couldn't even see the tracks on her arms.

Mark sat down and looked at the computer and shook his head. He wanted to say no, to deny the image's very existence, as he had when he saw Dixie Witte's body under those basement steps. His mother could not be involved with this. The family he had left behind all those years ago, they could not have anything to do with the death of his wife, a woman they'd never known, never seen.

There was no way.

But the photo, just like Dixie Witte's unblinking eyes, stared him down.

After sitting in numb silence for several moments, he scrolled down. Below the photograph was a text summary from an unnamed investigator.

Real name is Violet Robin Novak, but currently uses only first, Violet, and provides no surname. Tells people that surnames have no purpose. It appears that she met Eli Pate in Cody, Wyoming. She does not own a home or vehicle and has no driver's license. Her only known family in the area is a brother, Lawrence, and when she sees him she does so without Pate. Only other known family is a son, not local, and there does not seem to be contact between them: Markus R. Novak, of St. Petersburg, Florida, age thirty-three, father un-known. There is no indication that Markus Novak has been in Montana or Wyoming in the past decade.

Violet Novak was living in a motor home owned by Scott Shields, fifty-two, of Cody, Wyoming, when she met Eli Pate. Witnesses suggest that Violet Novak ended a romantic relationship with Shields after meeting Pate. What income she has is derived from providing what she calls "spiritual counseling" and giving palm readings. There are some in the area who are loyal cus-tomers, and they were distressed when she left Cody.

Friends paint a picture of Novak's beliefs as being very ripe for Eli Pate's exploitation. Although she is ap-parently of Germanic descent, she insists that she is of Nez Perce ancestry, though when pressed she will back down the claim to "spiritual ancestry." She is an intense supporter of virtually any environmental cause, though she does not appear to put much effort into the study of these issues. A blanket supporter, easily swayed. Sim-ilarly, she is vocally opposed to many industrial efforts in the West but does not exhibit a great deal of under-standing of the efforts she opposes. In these ways, she seems a perfect target for Pate, and with her existing beliefs and practices as well as her local contacts, she may be beneficial to his recruiting efforts. Her previous existence was already essentially "off the grid" through circumstance if not choice, so converting her on this front will not be difficult for him.

She was last sighted with Pate in Lovell, though their current location remains unknown. Her brother claimed no knowledge of Wardenclyffe and said he had not seen Violet in over a year, but she visited him just last week at his current residence (see supplemental), when the at-tached photographs were taken. She was alone for the visit, which lasted slightly over an hour, and drove there in a truck registered to Scott Shields. Visual contact with her was lost on Highway 301 near Belfry, when it appeared likely that she became aware of surveillance.

Both criminal records and acquaintance interviews suggest that while she has demonstrated little respect for the law or concern over legal consequences, she has always been a nonviolent offender and displays a general dislike of violence.

Further intelligence efforts on Markus Novak have shown no indication that he's lying to you re contact with his mother. He's a tough trace, very consistent in recent years but an absolute mess before that. In the past eight years he's had two addresses; in the eight prior, he had twenty-three at a minimum. Most of those were in the West or Pacific Northwest. His criminal history is undistinguished, mostly misdemeanor charges stemming from fights or alcohol incidents. After he left the West, the only story of note, besides his wife's murder, is his recent activity in Garrison, Indiana, with which you're already acquainted. He appears to have reached a point of stability once in Florida, and there's no evidence of efforts, successful or unsuccessful, to contact Violet. There is also no evidence of association or overlap with Pate, Cole, or Oriel until his arrival in Cassadaga. His ignorance of the phrase *rise the dark* appears genuine based on his interviews with police investigators in his wife's homicide. With all that said, you should still consider him high risk.

He tried to open Lynn's e-mail, but it was password-protected. He searched for other files, tried them, found the same problem. The only thing he could access was the file she'd left open before she came to see him. The last thing she'd read before she made a decision about him.

Consider him high risk.

He couldn't locate the supplemental report referenced with the picture, but he didn't need to. The surveillance photo was enough. It had been shot with a long-range lens, and his mother occupied most of the frame, either because the photographer had cared about nothing else or because he'd been trying to conceal her location, but if it was the latter, he would have needed a much tighter focus. When you were shooting pictures of a woman in a town with a population of fewer than two hundred, you had to be damn sure to hide all landmarks. In the picture, over her shoulder was a single sign that told Mark all he needed to know. It was a white square with the letters *M* and *S* painted on it, the *S* falling away from the *M*. There were no words, but he didn't need them, not with that sign. It was Miner's Saloon in Cooke City. Sixty miles away from where Mark sat, just over the Beartooths. Cooke City and Silver Gate had been frequent retreats for his family, both because his uncles loved the area and because the only police presence was second-day sheriff's service from Gardiner. When things heated up, Mark's family ended up in Cooke City more often than not.

He could not bring himself to believe that this was connected to anything. Not to Janell Cole, not to Garland Webb, not to Lauren. It couldn't be.

Further intelligence efforts on Markus Novak have shown no indication that he's lying to you re contact with his mother.

Mark drew a breath in through his teeth and looked at the window. The sidewalks were empty, the town dark and silent. Somewhere not far from this place, maybe just over the pass and in Cooke City, his mother waited. He'd kept his wife from any contact with her. Always.

This is a lie. All of it. Some sort of trick, Garland Webb's work. Because the man in that report is not the man who lost his wife in Cassadaga. Not anymore.

Get out, his dead wife's voice had whispered, and he had left, and now Lynn was gone and his mother remained.

His hand trembled a little as he withdrew his cell phone and called Jeff London.

Jeff's groggy first words were "Please tell me you're not in another jail."

Not jail. Worse. Mark said, "Jeff, I need a big favor, and I need it fast."

"That always seems to be the way."

"I'm going to have to relay this information to Montana police in a hurry."

Jeff's tone changed instantly. "What happened?"

"I came here with another investigator whose case involved people associated with Garland Webb. She's gone. I think she was taken. I need to speak to somebody who knows what she was working on. I think she lied to me, or at least withheld details. She's with the Pinkerton office in Boca Raton. You have a contact with them?"

"Yes. A guy named William Oliver. High on the food chain."

"Get him for me. The higher up, the better. His investigator's name is Lynn Deschaine. D-e-s-c-h-a-i-n-e. He needs to know she's missing, and he needs to help me with the police."

"I'll call back in five minutes."

It took him fifteen and they passed like an hour. Mark tried to determine how long he'd been out of sight of the motel. Thirty minutes? Forty-five? The walk to Jay's, the conversation, then back. That was all.

In that time, she'd vanished.

The phone finally rang. "Will he help?" Mark asked without preamble.

"He can't."

"Bullshit, Jeff, this isn't about confidential client information. I think his investigator has been kidnapped!"

"She's not his investigator. Nobody by the name of Lynn Deschaine works for the agency or ever has," Jeff said. "Nobody named Deschaine, period."

Mark didn't say anything. He sat there in front of Lynn's computer with the phone to his ear and couldn't speak, couldn't think. She was a Pinkerton. He'd called her from the card, they'd joked about her agency, she'd gotten information from their Amsterdam office.

Jeff said, "Did you see an ID for her? Any proof of her name?"

"Just a business card," Mark said, but then he shook his head. "No, wait. We boarded a plane together. I didn't look at her ID, but I saw the boarding pass. That's her name, Jeff. I know who she is."

"Well, they don't."

Mark rose from the chair and picked up her purse. Jeff was speaking on the other end of the line, asking a question, but it didn't register. Mark rifled through the bag, found the wallet, saw her driver's license. Lynn Deschaine, of Florida.

"I've got the right person," he began, but then he flipped past the license and fell silent.

There was another identification card in the mix, and it had been issued by the Department of Homeland Security.

36

They brought the new hostage in during the middle of the night. When the door opened, Sabrina awoke with a jerk and gasp. Then she heard rattling chains that were not her own. In the darkness the source wasn't visible, just those rattling chains, like one of Charles Dickens's ghosts.

A battery lantern clicked on and she saw them in the doorway: Eli Pate and Garland Webb and, between them, a handcuffed, dark-haired woman who looked like she was drunk, eyes open but unable to support herself.

Not drunk, though. Drugged. The woman was seeing exactly as much of the cabin as Sabrina had when they'd brought her in here— nothing.

Sabrina sat up on the air mattress and pulled herself back against the wall. Eli Pate set the lantern down by the door and it spread Garland Webb's massive shadow against the wall, a towering shape. He held the woman with ease when Eli released her, supporting her entire body weight with one hand.

Eli said, "Sorry to disturb your rest, but we have unanticipated company!"

His genteel tone was as steady as ever but Sabrina had the sense that it was taking more effort than usual for him to achieve it, that his actual mood was many shades darker and that the new woman was a problem, not part of the plan.

Garland dropped the woman without interest, like a bag of garbage, and then he unfastened one of the handcuffs and clipped it to a free bolt in the wall and snapped it shut. The dark-haired woman followed the motion with her eyes, but too slowly. She was looking at the bolt in the wall several seconds after she'd been chained to it.

Eli knelt and put two fingers under Sabrina's chin and turned her face to his.

"We're in the midst of an acceleration. Unanticipated and undesired, but, as they say, man plans and God laughs. Do you believe that?"

It was clear that he wanted an answer, so she said, "Yes."

"I do not. I believe all that man needs to do is listen. We've lost that ability. Most of us. Fortunately for you, Sabrina, you're in one of the few places on the planet where there is a man who both listens and hears." He paused. "It will move fast now, Sabrina. How reliable is your husband? How skilled?"

"What are you doing to Jay?"

"The only question that matters, Sabrina—how much does he love you?"

She didn't answer. Eli looked into her face for a long time and then nodded.

"I hope you've pleased him, Sabrina. I hope you've been the wife of his dreams. He needs that inspiration now."

The cabin door opened again. Violet, with a bottle of water in each hand. She looked questioningly at Eli and he nodded and stepped aside. Garland Webb had moved away, the obedient guard dog in the shadows, and Sabrina couldn't bring herself to look in his direction.

Violet crossed the room in the slanted lantern light and set two water bottles on the floor, pushed one to Sabrina, kept the other in her right hand. She used her left to force the new woman's head up. Violet tilted the bottle and splashed some water on her face, and the woman blinked and spluttered.

"Drink, dear. Drink."

But she didn't drink. Instead, she blinked, and recognition came into her eyes for the first time. Not just of the circumstances, but *real* recognition, and Sabrina, watching in astonishment, thought, *She knows Violet*.

Violet didn't seem to know her, though. She exhorted the woman once more to drink and had the bottle pressed gently to her lips when the woman spoke.

"Your son lied."

Violet lowered the water bottle, her face stone still and pale. "What did you say?"

"You talk to him," the new woman slurred, her words thick. "You talk to him. And he lies. He left me for them. For you. He knew you were coming. And he left."

"You're mistaken," Violet said. "I have no..."

Sabrina was waiting on her to say *son* or *family*, and she would have accepted either. To picture this woman as a mother was both difficult and disturbing. Violet fell silent, though, the sentence unfinished, and then the new woman spoke again.

"Markus."

Violet dropped the water bottle.

Eli Pate had been standing near the door, watching, but suddenly he was on them again, kneeling just in front of Sabrina but with all his attention on the new woman.

"You were with him? With Markus?"

Violet said, "Don't ask her that. She's confused. She's not—"

His stare silenced her. He turned from her back to the new woman and reached out and slapped her, a hard strike that triggered another blink and a refocusing of the eyes.

"You came here with Markus?"

"You know that," she mumbled.

"That is a lie," Violet said. Her usually distanced, daydreamer eyes were nightmare-focused now, staring down a monster.

Eli said, "Where is he?"

The new woman said, "With you."

The impenetrable calm he usually wore was obliterated now, his frustration clear. He looked like he wanted to hit her again but didn't. Instead, he turned to Violet.

"She believes it," he said. "You can see that. She's half out of her mind now, but she remembers him. Because he was the last one with her. We know she was not alone. Not during the day. It was him."

Violet shook her head. "I haven't spoken to him in years. You know that."

"And yet he's here," Eli said.

"Then he came for him." She pointed at Garland Webb.

For a long time, the cabin was silent as the three of them stood staring at one another in the dim light, completely ignoring the two women handcuffed to the wall beside them. When the silence was finally broken, it was by Eli.

"If he came for Garland," he said, "then he shall have him."

Violet said, "You promised me that no harm would come to him."

"Does this look like a place of harm to you?"

Violet looked at the two women chained to the wall, one with fresh blood trickling down from a split lip, and said, "Of course not."

37

Mark didn't even try to go to Jay Baldwin's door this time. He just returned to the same spot beside the white-barked pine, standing so close that the boughs touched his head, and waited. It took all of ten seconds for Jay to open the front door. When he reached Mark, he looked like he didn't know whether to punch him or cry.

Mark didn't give him a chance to do either. He just held up the photograph of Eli Pate.

"Is this the guy who has you so scared?"

He didn't answer, but his face said more than words could have.

Mark said, "You asked me what I would do if I had another chance with my wife. I'm here to give you the same chance, but it's going to have to be fast and you've got to talk to me. There are going to be a bunch of police in this town soon. I'm here to warn you of that and tell you that I haven't mentioned your name. In exchange, I need to know what in the hell the deal is here. I can't leave you alone. Not now. A woman is missing, and it's because of this guy, and you know *something* about it."

"You can't tell the police about me. You *can't.*"

"Then you've got to tell me why."

Jay's voice was softer when he said, "You were right. They've got cameras inside. I finally found where. Thanks for going back to this place and not the door."

"Who is watching you?" Mark said. "Is it Pate or somebody else?"

Jay took out his cell phone and fumbled with it and for a moment Mark thought he was making a call. Then he shoved it toward Mark. On the screen was a photograph of a woman with a disoriented, foggy gaze. She wore a blue nightgown and her hair was disheveled and there was a handcuff on her right wrist.

"That's my wife."

It took Mark a moment to find his voice, and when he did, it was ragged. He said, "I'm not taking any of your options off the table. I promise you that."

Jay Baldwin nodded without a word and put the phone back in his pocket.

"Let's talk fast," Jay said. "They'll notice if I'm outside too long. Trust me."

They stood in the cold dark while Jay Baldwin told Mark what he knew of Eli Pate, told the story of the night of the vandalism on the high-voltage lines and how he'd returned home to find Pate present and his wife missing. He told him of the ride to Chill River and the video of his wife in shackles. He wept while he told it.

"He sends pictures, and video clips. She's alive; she doesn't seem hurt. She's still alive. That's why I can't... I just can't risk doing anything. If you'd met him, if you'd seen that man's eyes or heard him talk, you'd know. You'd know."

Mark said, "The woman who was working with me is gone, Jay. We were together just a few hours ago, and then I left and came up here, and by the time I got back she was gone. She's a federal agent, by the way. Not a private detective. I didn't know that myself. But when I say there are going to be police all over this, we are talking big-league ball. You might have to cooperate. But right now I need to know how they knew we were in town. Did it come from you?"

He looked away, his cheeks wet with tears.

"Jay... I just need the answer."

"Yes." His voice was choked. "He calls, and he watches. He told me what would happen if I lied, and so I told him... I told him that you'd come by. I told him what you'd asked about. And what you were driving."

What they were driving. That was all it would have taken. Red

Lodge was a small town with only a few motels. They'd parked the Tahoe directly in front of their rooms.

"Lynn Deschaine didn't disappear tonight without his help," Mark said. "So he won't be surprised when the police hit town, and he won't be surprised if they find their way to you. I think he probably trusts you to say the right things."

"You're not going to tell them?" Jay's face was so desperate it hurt to look at him.

"I'm not going to close any doors for you, Jay, but I don't know that you're making the right choice either."

"It's the best I have," Jay whispered. "You think I haven't thought about it? It's all I think about, every minute, but the thing is...I believe him." He was wearing just a T-shirt and the night was cold, but his shiver had nothing to do with the weather. "When he says that I have only one choice? I believe him. If you'd ever met him, you would too."

"So you're going to do it. You're going to try to shut that place down."

"As long as I know he has Sabrina, I am going to do what he asks."

Mark did not condemn him for this. If someone had told Mark that he could have Lauren back if he blew up a power plant, his only response would have been *Where's the fuse?* There was absolutely no way Mark could blame Jay for his decision, but he also didn't think it would work. If Jay Baldwin was going to see his wife again, it wouldn't be because he'd followed Eli Pate's instructions. That wasn't Mark's call to make, though. He wasn't going to take the choice away from Jay either. He couldn't bear to.

"When are you supposed to do it?" he said.

"I don't know. Soon. That's all he told me."

"Okay. So you've got no timeline, and until then he watches your movements with the GPS chip and cameras, and he calls you to check in."

"Yes."

"Do you have any idea where he is?"

"I don't even know *who* he is. I just came home one day and he was here. It was like being picked by the devil." He'd taken to rubbing his hands together, the muscles in his forearms bunching. "Tell me something—do you think he's alone?"

"No."

That dismayed Jay. "You know anything about who's with him?"

"The man who killed my wife."

The wind gusted and tousled Jay's hair and flapped his T-shirt around him and he looked into Mark's eyes and then away, and for a moment Mark thought he was going to slide down to the pavement again as he had before. The more Jay had heard, the stronger he'd seemed—until Mark's last disclosure.

Mark said, "I'm leaving you to your choice, Jay. I don't know if the police will come for you or not. They know that the woman who was with me is missing, but I don't know if they have any idea that we came here. You were my idea, not hers."

"How did you know?"

"Because I've been you," Mark said. "A version of you, at least. When do you think Pate will call next?"

"I'm not sure. But he will. Maybe an hour. Maybe two."

"When he does, you tell him that I've gone to Lovell to find him. You don't know my name, but you do know that I'm in Lovell looking for him. You're going to tell that much of a lie for me. It's not so much to ask, and it'll help you. I think I've got a shot at him, Jay. A better one than most, probably."

"Where are you really going?"

Mark shook his head. "I'm letting you keep your secrets, Jay, because I understand your reasons. You gotta let me keep mine."

He left then and got into the Tahoe. Back in town, he could see the lights of a single police car. Jeff had made the call, at Mark's request, and now the locals were doing their preliminary work. It wouldn't be long until the Red Lodge police realized they were overmatched.

Lynn Deschaine, Special Agent, Department of Homeland Security.

No, it would not be long at all.

Mark pulled onto 212 and looked to the right, where the Beartooths loomed in the darkness. The quickest way to Cooke City was to follow 212 over the pass, but even though there wasn't a trace of snow in Red Lodge and the temperature had been in the sixties during the day, he knew that there was no chance the pass was open. Where it crested at nearly eleven thousand feet, there would be snow-pack as tall as three men. In a good year, they got it open by Memorial Day. Sometimes it was closer to July.

You could still get to Cooke City, though. The Chief Joseph highway was open. It took longer than 212, but you could get there.

Mark left Red Lodge and headed into the mountains in search of an uncle he hadn't seen in more than fifteen years.

38

The white-haired man with the hounds in the kennel hadn't even finished bleeding out before Doug began to fall apart. They were in the yard, and Janell was busy transferring their gear from the red truck to the GMC Yukon that reeked of wet dog fur. Working alone, because he was standing in the driveway, bitching.

"This was never part of it," he said as she shoved past him with another bag. "What happened with the cop—okay, maybe you needed to do it, or felt like you needed to. But inside that house? That was fucking *murder*."

"Guilty as charged." She slammed the bag into the tailgate. She'd added all of the dead man's weapons, which was not an insignificant arsenal. He had four shotguns, two rifles, three pistols, and plenty of ammunition for all of them. There'd been three hundred dollars in cash as well. Cash and guns were good—always useful, obviously, but she'd also thought they would appease Doug, the necessary spoils of the war he believed in.

It wasn't working. He hadn't even helped her search the house. He'd spent his time in the living room, standing in front of the corpse as if he didn't understand what had happened.

"We could've tied him up, just as you said. It wouldn't have changed anything. We'd still have had two days. The only difference now is you've made us a date with the electric chair. That's all you did."

She didn't bother to tell him that after she'd killed the deputy, that date had already been arranged. Instead, she tossed another bag into the Yukon, turned to face him, and tried to find a last reserve of patience. It was like sifting through sand in search of water.

"We've been working toward this moment for nine months," she said.

"Not *this* moment. *This* was never a moment I dreamed of!"

"Everyone else is in motion. Every…one…else. We're already running behind. The world will change in the next twenty-four hours, and where do you want to be when it happens?"

He stood with his jaw slack, breathing through his mouth. A car passed on the road below the house, the headlights throwing fast shafts of light through the trees, and though it drove on without slowing, it was a reminder that police might be patrolling nearby. They were wasting time, and meanwhile another band of followers was gathering with Eli, where she belonged.

"I suppose we can wait here," she said. "We can sit down and talk through all of this. Discuss what was planned and what was necessary. Argue the semantics of warfare. But I'd rather not be having a fucking philosophical debate when the police arrive."

He shook his head. His hands opened and closed at his sides— tightening into fists, relaxing, tightening. The only way he could express himself, through his hands. She had warned Eli of this. Doug Oriel was a physical titan, and a mental child.

"It's time to run," she said. "I'm going, with or without you. You want to head south while I go north, take the red truck and give it your best shot. You'll be in jail before noon, and I'll be operating as planned."

"Nothing is as planned."

The dogs had stopped barking and howling and now paced their fence lines uneasily. She was sure they had smelled their owner's death in the air and were curious about their own fates. How pathetic, that through smell alone they were farther along in understanding than Doug was.

She turned from him and jerked open the Yukon's driver-side door. "Last chance for a ride."

She had the engine running before he moved. Even then, he was hesitant—he looked all around him in a great, confused circle, as if searching for some other path, and finding none, he put his head down, walked to the Yukon, opened the passenger door, and climbed in beside her, his hands still clenching and unclenching. They were large hands, and she remembered the way the dead man who'd owned this car had looked at them and thought that it would be wise to watch them herself.

She backed out of the dead man's driveway and turned onto the country road, heading north.

"We'll get some distance between us and this place and then we'll make contact with Eli," she said.

Doug didn't answer. One of his knuckles popped as he tightened his right fist.

Janell drove on.

39

The road to Cooke City was filled with ghosts.

Mark was used to traveling with them, had become accustomed to that since Lauren was killed, but there were more of them now. He was in the Sunlight Basin, carving through country he'd once known so well, and the faces of men and women who had probably been dead for years rose smiling in his mind. Also in the mix, all too often, was Lynn Deschaine, her face just above his own in the dark, her body pressed tight to him, her racing heart pounding against his chest.

The Chief Joseph Scenic Byway links Cody, Wyoming, with the northeast gate of Yellowstone, just a few miles from Cooke City, Montana. It crosses through the Shoshone National Forest and the Absaroka Mountains. The Beartooth range looms to the north and the Absaroka range falls behind to the south and the Clark Fork of the Yellowstone River winds along through the low country—if a vertical mile up can be considered low country—and then the road begins to climb again, and seeing it in the daylight, many people would consider it the most beautiful drive in the West, at least if they hadn't driven the Beartooth Highway up and over the top.

Tonight, none of the grand country was visible beyond the reach of the headlights, and the road mocked Mark. He'd come here to settle the score for the family member who had been taken from him, but instead, he was driving the old roads in search of the family he'd left behind willingly, and he felt as if the mountains were laughing at him now. Even the route he had to take felt predestined, promised.

They never met, he thought. *Never spoke. There cannot be overlap, not between my mother and Lauren, between this place and that one.*

But already he knew the latter was false. Cassadaga, Florida, connected to Lovell, Wyoming. The place where Mark's future had died was bridged to the past he'd left behind. And if that connection was possible, why not more?

She went to Cassadaga on a case. Went for Dixie Witte. That was all. It had nothing to do with my past.

Somewhere, a missing Homeland Security agent might have disagreed.

It was still dark when he arrived in Cooke City, and the temperature was at least fifteen degrees colder than it had been in Red Lodge. The traces of snow that were visible on the peaks down there lay in drifts on the ground up here. He drove slowly into town and Miner's Saloon came into view, the sign that had been over his mother's shoulder in the surveillance photos sent to Lynn Deschaine.

He parked in front of the saloon and cut the engine and the headlights. He turned on the cell phone just for the hell of it and saw the expected—no trace of a signal. Mark was, for the moment, at least, very securely off the grid.

He stepped out of the car and into the bracing cold and walked down the road to see what had changed in the town.

The answer: not much. There were a few new buildings, but for the most part, things were the same. They had a fire station now. That was impressive. Mark wondered if they had any firefighters. The summer before Lauren was killed, a forest fire had done some serious damage just beyond the town, ravaging the base of Mount Republic and chewing through the forest along Pilot Creek. Arson, apparently. People died. He'd read about it and looked at the photographs, and that was one of the few times he'd discussed the place with Lauren at any length.

At the end of the town the road curled away toward Silver Gate, just two miles farther on, but he knew that it would be as silent as Cooke City. It was the dead season, after the snowmobiling and before the Yellowstone summer tourists. Anyone who'd seen Mark's uncle in the past few months was sound asleep, and the way to get cooperation wasn't by banging on doors in the middle of the night.

He stood at the edge of town feeling very small, powerless. Night in the mountains could do that to you, reminding you of your place in the world and laughing at any sense of self-importance. Tonight it was worse. Mark didn't feel just powerless; his entire understanding of the world had been ripped away from him.

His ignorance of the phrase rise the dark *appears genuine based on his interviews with police investigators in his wife's homicide.*

He walked to the car with his breath fogging the air, the stars brilliant against the blackness, and then he fell back on family tradition on his first night in Cooke City: he slept in the car and waited for the saloon to open.

40

Eli took Garland Webb down the mountain beneath a blanket of spectacular stars, but his ability to find comfort in the spectral illumination was ruined by the clatter of the ATV engine and the harshness of the headlight.

And the news of Markus Novak's presence in Montana.

At the base of the slope, where the stream cut through the valley and nothing could be seen of Wardenclyffe, he shut off the ghastly machine and stepped into the shallow remnants of the spring's last snow.

"Everything is rushed now," he said. "Because of you. You know she spoke the truth. She came here with Novak. Who knows how many will follow?"

Maintaining control and order of violent men was difficult, and Garland Webb was exhibit A—a critical player who had nearly been lost because he could not keep himself out of trouble. Garland was both a mechanical genius and a sexual predator. Eli needed the former, had no use for the latter. The problem was that you couldn't separate the two.

"You taunted him," Eli said. "That is why he came to Cassadaga, and from Cassadaga he got to Homeland Security somehow, and from there to here. Because of your taunt."

"He tried to have me killed. You would have done nothing, said nothing?"

"Not until greater goals had been achieved. Absolutely not."

Garland didn't respond. The sound of the stream was all that could be heard. In the moonlight, it was a quicksilver ribbon.

"You passed the test in Coleman," Eli said. "That was already done. You'd succeeded, but success was not enough for you."

The test in Coleman had been vital indeed. Eli had instructed Garland to take full ownership of the murder of Lauren Novak, to claim it to his cell mate as an attempted sex crime, a random victim. Eli wanted to bring police attention to Garland and see if that would result in the utterance of Eli's name, mention of Wardenclyffe, any of it. That much Garland understood. What he had not known was that Eli had another listener in the prison, and an execution planned if Garland didn't follow through.

But Garland had obeyed. He'd confessed to the killing—a low-risk confession, cell-block boasting, immediately denied to police—and Eli watched from afar and waited to see if Garland would implicate him. He did not. Instead, he drew the focus of authorities, and also Markus Novak. Eli had been satisfied with this, and so he allowed Garland to live and came to realize that he was perhaps more useful in prison, where he couldn't make any more mistakes, than on the outside.

Eli had not counted on his release.

"I followed your instruction," Garland said. "Every bit of it. I could have let her leave town. She might never have returned."

"With the questions she asked? She was going to return."

Garland shrugged, uncaring. Eli knew that Garland felt little interest in the fate of Lauren Novak. He hadn't when given the order, and he didn't now.

"You'll have to miss the council now," Eli said. "The timeline has changed."

Garland nodded.

"The traps are your responsibility," Eli said. "Activate the ones already installed. We have no time for the others."

He took out the keys to Scott Shields's pickup truck, which was parked at the far end of the forest road.

"When they're active, wait in the third warehouse until I've given you the word."

"All right."

"You might have visitors."

Garland tilted his head. "Who?"

"Novak."

"How will you arrange that?"

"There's only one link between him and this place," Eli said. "That's his uncle. If he chooses to take that route, I know where it will lead him, and I'll see that he is redirected. Right to you. You'll need to be ready."

Garland spun the keys on his massive index finger, a glittering whirl in the moonlight.

"I've been ready for Markus Novak for a long time," he said.

4 I

I t was just past dawn when a fist hammered on the window of the Tahoe and Mark jerked upright. A man in a short-sleeved Hawaiian shirt was peering in at him. He had a mug of coffee in his hand, steam rising off it. There was a glaze of frost on the windshield and over the hood. Mark opened the door and climbed out stiffly. The man in the Hawaiian shirt sipped his coffee and regarded him without much interest.

"Well, that's good, at least," he said.

"Huh?" Mark tried to stretch his neck, without much success.

"You're not dead. Sleeping drunks out front are the easy kind of trouble. Dead guys out front are a different thing. That would have been a ballbuster this early."

"Sorry," Mark said. "Came in late last night and didn't have a place to stay."

"I'd love to pretend that I give a shit, but I'm an honest man, so I can't. You're not going to be sleeping out front all day, okay? Bad for business. Now, if you were dead...that would have sold some drinks, actually. Huh. Maybe I miscalculated. Maybe it would have been better if you were dead."

It was cold enough that Mark was shivering, and this man was wearing shorts and sandals to complement the Hawaiian shirt. Springtime in Cooke City.

"I'll get out of your hair real fast if you can point me in the right direction," Mark said.

The man in the Hawaiian shirt lifted his hand and pointed down 212 toward Silver Gate. "That way. The other way, the road is closed. Those are the only directions we've got. Pretty damn simple."

He was headed for the door of the saloon when Mark said, "I'm looking for Larry Novak."

The man turned back, looked the Tahoe over, and nodded as if something made sense to him that hadn't before.

"Never heard of him."

"I'm not serving any papers."

"Oh. Well, in that case, I've never heard of him."

"You own a place in this town that pours whiskey. You've heard of him."

He drank his coffee and stared at Mark in silence.

"He's family," Mark said. "It's a family issue, and it's damn important."

That was so interesting to the man that he almost raised an eyebrow. Almost.

"Listen," Mark said, "I'm Larry Novak's nephew. I came all the way up from Florida to find him. I know damn well he's passed through here at some point in the past few months. If he's gone now, you can save yourself some trouble and say so. If you want some dollars for your help, that's fine. But I need to find—"

"I'm not taking any dollars to narc somebody out, bubba."

"You aren't narcing, you're helping him." Mark took out his wallet.

"I just said I'm not taking any money to—"

"I'm not giving you any." He handed over his driver's license. The man didn't take it, but he read the name, and there was a little light in his eyes. He looked up over the steam from the coffee.

"Markus."

"Yeah."

He rubbed his jaw and didn't say anything for a minute. He was staring up at Mount Republic when he said, "Tell me your dog's name."

"What?"

"You had a dog that got left here. Most people called him Town Dog. Larry didn't. What would he have called him?"

"Amigo." The dog had been Mark's best friend for a short time.

Then his mother got arrested and the dog was left behind in Cooke City. Mark swung at the cop that day, not because he was arresting his mother, but because he'd said that Child Protective Services wouldn't let Mark bring Amigo with him. When Mark met with the social workers, his only questions were about the legal recourses available to get Amigo back.

The man was still regarding him in silence, so Mark added, "We also had a raccoon named Pandora for a while. My mother saved it from the side of the road, and it bit Larry twice. He did not have fond feelings for Pandora."

The man in the Hawaiian shirt said, "Well, hell. I wouldn't point anybody else toward him, but that old bastard has been sitting at my bar talking about you and wondering where you are for as long as I've been in this town, and that's twelve years now. Unlike most people who ask after him, you he'll actually want to see."

"Where can I find him?"

"You know the Bannock Trail?"

Mark nodded. The Bannock Trail was a dirt-and-gravel road that ran parallel to 212 through Silver Gate, along the base of Mount Republic.

"He's up there in a cabin with a green tarp over most of the roof."

That sounded right.

42

In Silver Gate there was a wooden bridge that crossed over the Soda Butte Creek, a stream that fed the Lamar River a few miles farther down, inside Yellowstone. Mark had fished the Soda Butte with his uncle Ronny before a few state-run disasters with fish stocking, followed by fish killing, effectively ruined the stream. On the other side of the water, the pavement disappeared and the road went to packed dirt. This was the Bannock Trail. The modern highways through Yellowstone follow it pretty closely, but the Bannock was originally the path used by bison-hunting parties of the Nez Perce, Shoshone, Kalispel, and Flathead. He saw several cabins that were new to him, and some of them were pretty high-dollar.

The one with the green tarp over the roof was not one of those.

The cabin was set back far from the road, and he almost missed it because the tarp blended with the pines. That was why you went with green instead of blue—class.

He pulled in the drive and parked. The pines here were thick and the place was in the shadow of the mountains and so it was very dark. When a large part of the darkness moved beside him, Mark almost had a heart attack. He was fumbling for his gun when he realized what the massive shape was: a buffalo. A big bastard, too, taller than the Tahoe, with a matted hide that had bits of branches stuck to it. Only one of his massive eyes was visible, and it didn't look friendly.

Larry was guarded by a Cyclops.

Mark opened the door and stepped out slowly. People who were not cautious around buffalo were people who didn't know anything about buffalo. Every year a handful of tourists who expected the animals to be cute, harmless oafs were gored while trying to take photographs. Buffalo could be mean, and fast. This fellow didn't look like one of the low-key breeds, and the fact that he was roaming solo, far from the herds in the park, wasn't a good sign. Based on the baleful stare he was getting, Mark suspected this old boy had been ejected from the herd due to attitude issues.

Mark walked slowly toward the cabin and the buffalo watched as if he were considering chasing him, then he lowered his head and began to chew on one of the bushes. Apparently Mark wasn't worth the effort.

Mark went up the steps to the front porch, which was surprisingly solid considering the condition of the roof. The cabin looked like it had been there a hundred years and probably wasn't going to have much trouble lasting a hundred more. He knocked on the door and heard a slurred curse, then a rhetorical and profane question about the time. There were footsteps and the door opened and Mark's uncle looked at him without recognition.

He'd aged in the ways Mark's mother hadn't. His hair was a thick shock of white and his face was leathered and there were gin roses on his cheeks. He wasn't a tall man—a few inches shorter than Mark's six feet—but Mark knew that you underestimated his strength at your own peril. He was built like a sapling. Some of the muscle Mark remembered was gone, but not all of it. He was wearing long johns and a sleeveless undershirt, standing barefoot on the wooden floor.

Mark said, "How are you doing, Uncle?"

Larry blinked and his misty blue eyes sharpened their focus and then he said, "Good Lord in heaven. Markus?"

Mark nodded, and Larry came out and hugged him. Hard and without any hesitation. It jarred Mark, and he was slow returning the embrace. Then Larry stepped back and looked Mark up and down, assessing him against his memory.

"You look good, son."

"You too, Larry."

"Shit." He laughed and then said, "What in the hell are you doing here?"

"Looking for Mom."

The smile went away. "Sure. Figured you would one of these days. It ain't gonna be the reunion you want, though. Not if you got ideas of fixing things up."

"That's not my idea."

Larry waited.

"A few things have happened in my life since the last time I saw you," Mark said.

"I'd sure as hell hope so."

"I got married."

"That's great."

"My wife was murdered."

Larry winced, shifted his weight, and was casting about for something to say when Mark spoke again.

"Even I have trouble believing what I'm going to tell you," he said. He felt unsteady suddenly, wanted a chair. "So I don't know why in the hell you'd believe it. But there are people...there are some law enforcement people who seem to think that you and Mom might know something about who killed my wife, and why."

Larry's eyebrows arched and he leaned forward with his head cocked, as if he hadn't heard correctly. "That *we* might know something? Son, I didn't know you were married. I didn't know you were *alive*. When you left, that was that. And I didn't blame you, but anybody who says otherwise...shit, all I've done is wonder about you. And hope for you."

Mark nodded. "It happened in Florida, but it seems to be connected to a man up here. Somebody Mom knows."

Larry looked away, a contemplative sideways glance at nothing that Mark remembered well. He had a habit of looking to the side like that just before the shit hit the fan, like he was considering advice from an invisible man in his corner. His invisible man usually gave piss-poor advice.

"Don't say Pate."

The confirmation was like another blow, part of the combination that had been building in intensity since Lynn Deschaine had first mentioned the town of Lovell. All roads leading back.

"He's one of them," Mark said, "but the one I want most is Garland Webb."

"That one doesn't mean anything to me."

"He'll be with Pate," Mark said. "I'm almost sure of it. I came up here with another investigator who was looking for Pate, and—"

"What do you mean, another investigator? You're *police*?" Larry said it as if Mark had announced that he made his living testing razor blades on the ears of live bunnies.

"Private detective. I was, at least. The woman who came up here with me is missing, I suspect at Eli Pate's hand. I need to find him. Can you help?"

Larry worked his tongue under his lower lip. "You ever met a man and felt almost right away, down in your bones, like you'd be doing the world a favor if you popped him? That's Eli Pate. That's the boy you're looking for. And he won't be easy to find. He's down in a hole somewhere."

"What's he hiding from?"

"Not hiding. Waiting."

"On?"

"The end of the world."

Mark gave a slow nod. "One of those. A prepper, that kind of thing?"

"I wouldn't say that, exactly. He's his own breed. Get inside so I don't have to stand here in the cold." Larry stepped away and then added, sadly, "I wish it wasn't this that brought you to my doorstep, son. I wish to hell it wasn't this."

"Me too, Uncle."

43

Watching the new woman come slowly awake was a horrifying déjà vu; she mumbled to herself and tugged on the handcuff as if she didn't understand it, then drifted back to sleep, indifferent, and Sabrina remembered what it had felt like, dealing with the match fires of awareness in the dark valley of drugged sleep.

Worse, she remembered what waited on the other side. How this woman would handle her reality—when she was able to comprehend it—would affect Sabrina's own chances at survival.

She didn't speak when the woman first began to show clear thinking because she could hear the voices upstairs and she didn't want to draw the attention of whoever was up there. Each time the woman looked at her, Sabrina held one finger in front of her lips, urging silence. She didn't want to risk speaking until she was sure she was talking to someone who was responsive.

When the woman said, "How long have I been here?" in a whisper, it was obvious that the moment had arrived.

"Maybe five or six hours," Sabrina whispered back. "It's hard to keep track of time. I'm not sure how long I've been here. A few days, at least."

That news brought horror to the other woman's face, but Sabrina didn't say anything to soothe her. There was nothing *to* say. This was reality. She'd either accept it and fight alongside Sabrina or deny it and panic and risk them both.

She didn't look like a panicker, though. When she'd finally been able to make sense of the handcuff and assess her situation, she'd taken stock of her surroundings and then asked that one question, trying to reason things out, not simply react.

"Who are you?" Sabrina asked.

"My name is Lynn Deschaine."

"I'm Sabrina Baldwin."

The woman cocked her head. "Baldwin."

"You've heard my name before?"

"I met your husband. You're the reason…you're why he was so strange."

She had met *Jay?* This seemed incomprehensible, like someone bringing a message from the dead.

"Where was he?" Sabrina said. "How is he? Do they have him here or…" She heard her voice rising, took a breath, then whispered. "Where do they have him?"

"Nowhere," Lynn Deschaine said. Her dark hair had fallen over her face as she shifted, and she blew it away to clear her eyes. "He was at home. We interviewed him about the vandalism on the lines. Mark was right. Your husband *was* scared of us. Because of you. You were already gone, weren't you?"

Sabrina was listening, but her brain had stuck on *he was at home.* That news gave birth to tangled emotions—relief that he was safe, but also astonishment at the idea of him just being *at home* talking to people about vandalized power lines when she was up here, chained to a cabin wall.

As if sensing this, Lynn Deschaine said, "I think he's going through the motions to keep them happy and keep you safe."

Sabrina nodded numbly. Sure, that was it, he just wanted to keep her safe. But still, she felt betrayed.

"Do you know more about them?" Sabrina said. "About why we're here?"

Lynn seemed to choose her next words carefully.

"I don't know why we are *here,* if you mean the specific location, but I understand why they have us. I know why they have me, at least. I've been investigating him for years."

"Eli?"

"Yes."

"Who is he?"

This time, Lynn didn't hesitate. "If you gave Charles Manson the mind of Nikola Tesla," she said, "you would find yourself with Eli Pate. Or so he thinks."

Sabrina had a strange memory then. A clear recollection of the way the lights had blinked on the morning of her kidnapping, the outage that summoned Jay out of the house and into the storm. *Just like a knock,* she thought. *Like there was evil at the door, announcing its presence.* They'd blamed the storm then, but by midday she'd known it wasn't really the storm. She just hadn't known it was Eli Pate.

"How many do you think are up here?" Lynn asked.

"At least three. Maybe more. When they brought you in, you were talking about Violet's son. They seemed concerned about him. Who is he?"

Even in the shadows, she saw something change in Lynn Deschaine's face. "I don't even know anymore," she said. "I fell asleep feeling this horrible guilt because I hadn't told him the truth. I thought I knew more than he did, and that wasn't fair. But he knew more than I did. He knew exactly where I was headed."

"They don't seem to agree," Sabrina said.

"What do you mean?"

"You were incoherent when they brought you in. But the idea that you were with him seemed to...shock them, really. They never lose their composure, but they came close when they heard that."

For a time, there was silence. Then the quiet was shattered by the sounds of engines. Voices rose briefly, then faded away until the second engine started. Actually, the second and the third—two different pitches that merged into one sound.

"Not motorcycles," Lynn said thoughtfully. "Maybe a four-wheeler?"

"Yes," Sabrina said, and she was disappointed with herself for not recognizing the sounds first. "That's exactly what it is."

"And they're only arriving. They're not leaving."

They looked at each other in silence as they contemplated what that meant.

Thirty minutes later, another engine. Five minutes after that, another still. Then two more.

Sabrina and Lynn had stopped looking at each other.

44

Mark's uncles had spent some time on the rodeo circuit, though neither was much of a rider. Larry was a trick-rope artist, as good as any Mark ever saw, and he could shoot like he'd been born with a gun in his hand. All of the stunts in Westerns that people said couldn't be done in real life, Larry did in real life. He'd toss a quarter in the air and draw a revolver and put a hole through the center, shooting accurately by fanning the hammer, and even though he wasn't a lefty, he was better with his left hand than most marksmen were with their right. For a couple years he'd done sporadic stunt work for film and TV gigs. Then, as the popularity of the Western died and computer effects removed the need for any real human achievement, he was just an unemployed trick-shooter with a few stories about Hollywood starlets.

He drank on those stories for years, though. His brother began to call one of Larry's actress conquests the Annuity because of how consistently the tale paid out for him. Chivalrous.

By now enough years had passed that Larry would have had to wait for people to Google the names of the starlets he'd bedded before he began the stories, and even then, nobody would have bought him a drink just to listen, but he was still shooting. Matter of fact, he was giving lessons, and that was how he'd met Eli Pate. It wasn't trick stuff, and it wasn't pistols.

"Your mother told me she knew a guy who wanted to learn how to shoot a sniper rifle," he said as he and Mark sat in the small cabin and the early-morning light began to creep down from the peaks and fill the pines. Larry had started a fire in the ancient cast-iron woodstove and the small space quickly filled with heat.

"Now, usually when your mother says *I met this guy,* it's trouble from the get-go," he said, and then he caught himself and awkwardly added, "Sorry, Markus."

"Come on, Uncle. It's not like I don't have a sense of the woman."

Larry nodded ruefully and ran a hand over his unruly white hair as if to flatten it against his skull. He was sitting close to the stove, the fire poker still in one hand.

"So I never look forward to meeting the fellas, but, you know, I needed the money at that particular juncture. I'd hit a hard spell."

Larry had spent his life hitting hard spells like a bug hits a windshield.

"At the time I was working for an outfitter in Wyoming named Scott Shields. He'd bought a ranch just outside of the Bighorns, had plans to put in a bunkhouse, get a good cook, set it up right, you know? He'd made his money up in Alaska, guiding for bear and moose out on the peninsula, but he was a Wyoming kid and wanted to come back. I met him through your mother. They had a good situation all the way around."

"But it didn't last," Mark said.

Larry shook his head. "She was living with him down in Cody and I was working on this property, fixing up the cabins, and she brought Pate up, said he wanted shooting lessons. He had top-of-the-line equipment for a man who didn't know how to use it. At least five thousand in the rifle and scope. He wasn't much of a shot, but he asked all kinds of questions about range and impact. What he wanted to shoot at was metal."

"What do you mean?"

"The questions he had were about different rounds and their damage at point of impact. He had these things he wanted to use as targets, like big ceramic canisters. Looked like electrical equipment, insulators maybe. He didn't even want me to tell him how to shoot, he wanted me to do the shooting so he could see how these things blew up with different rounds at different distances. I said, 'Okay, let's set the bullshit aside, chief, and you tell me what you're really after.' And the weird bastard looks at me with this smile like a pedophile in an amusement park and says, 'I intend to remind people about the true nature of power.' That's exactly what he said, word for word. I remember it because it was strange and the look on his face when he said it chilled me to the bone."

Mark said, "He wants to shut the electrical grid down. I have no idea why."

"Here's the bullshit he's slinging, and it's bullshit your mother has bought: Spirits talk to him. Spirits of the mountains and of the old Indian chiefs. You know how much that pisses me off, listening to a white man claim that?"

"It's smart," Mark said. "It's exactly what Mom would want to hear."

"You got that right," Larry admitted. "The last time I saw your mother, she told me about how he'd go up into these caves in the Pryor Mountains and wait for the spirit voices to tell him…Markus? What's the matter?"

Mark hadn't moved, but his face must have changed plenty. "Nothing's the matter. I just had a bad experience with caves."

An understatement. He could see Ridley Barnes standing in water a few hundred feet underground. Ridley, whose corpse had never been found, saying, *She doesn't want you yet.* Saying, *When things go dark, you're the one who will have to bring the light back.*

"It doesn't make sense," Mark said.

"What doesn't?"

"You say it like Mom's buying the con. She's usually selling it."

"Give her points for both this time. She's still peddling the stories, but they're chapters in a bigger one now, and Pate writes that. She can draw in a different type for him. People who wouldn't trust him, or at least not trust him easily…they believe in Violet. Always have. You know how she does that."

"What's she getting out of it?"

Larry looked away and made a drinking motion with his hand and then a plunging motion with his thumb, and Mark felt a sick, impotent rage as he remembered the syringes he'd taken from his mother and the bottle she'd had in her hand on one of the last days he'd ever seen her, the day he'd gone out into a howling snowstorm and found her passed out in a drift, near death, her flesh tinted the blue of a pale winter sky.

"Of course."

"She got clean for a bit," Larry said, somehow always able to rise to his sister's defense. "She really did. After you left. That knocked her sideways, son. When you left, she got clean and dry and held on for a long time. But then…"

"Right," Mark said. "But then." He shook his head. "You mentioned the Pryor Mountains. You think Pate is up there?"

"No idea."

"Well, I'm going to need some ideas. I'm not the only one looking for him either. The police are too by now. But I need to get there first."

"Why?"

"Because I think the man who killed my wife is with him. She wrote three words in her notebook on the day she was killed that didn't make sense to anyone I knew. It makes sense to everyone around Eli Pate, though. *Rise the dark.* I suppose it's referring to the moment, this attack they're planning. The man who told his cell mate he killed Lauren is supposed to be up here with Pate. I just need a shot at him, Uncle."

Larry said, "You came up here to kill a man?" His voice steady. Unfazed.

"Yes."

"Then you should know this: After my first go-round with Pate, I went looking for your mother to get her the hell away from him. Scott Shields had left by then, gone back to Alaska, and she and Pate were living in a campground. Couple bikers, guy with an RV, a few tents. You said something about preppers earlier? That's what this group felt like, sure. And they protect him well."

He got to his feet and pulled his undershirt off and Mark hissed in a breath and nearly turned away. Larry's torso was wrapped with ribbons of scars, raised and red. Though the wounds had closed, the flesh would never look right again.

"That's from a whip," Larry said quietly. There was anger in his voice, but also shame. "They chained my hands to the tow hitch of an old Jeep and my feet to a cinder block and they whipped me like a dog. Why? Because they'd heard me telling your mother what I thought of Eli Pate. They told me that disrespect—that was the word they used, *disrespect*—wouldn't be tolerated."

Larry regarded his own wounds in silence for a few seconds, then said, "The most important lessons are the ones that leave scars, boy. That's what your grandfather used to say, whether we'd gotten a lip split in a fight or been thrown by a horse or whatever. The most important lessons leave scars."

He pulled his shirt back on.

"So that was the last time I saw Pate's crew. Saw your mother once more. She came up here looking for me, wanted to apologize, she said, but it was more warning than apology. She knew what it would mean if I went back at them, and she knew I had the inclination to try."

"Why?"

Larry looked at Mark as if he'd asked why he needed oxygen.

"They whipped me, Markus. Tied me down and whipped me. The hell do you mean, *why?*"

"Tell me where to find him," Mark said.

"You don't want to find him. It's not worth it."

"They shot my wife twice in the head and left her in a ditch," Mark said. "Don't tell me it's not worth it."

"You go after Pate, the same thing might happen to you."

"So be it. I'm not concerned about this being my last ride."

"And I'm not supposed to be concerned about it being *mine* either?"

"Just tell me how to find him. I don't need you to come along."

"Oh yes, you do. Because he isn't going to be easy to find, son! This boy is the type you need to flush out of the deep weeds."

"Tell me where to start, then. Who to ask."

"You're not going to find Pate by *asking*, Markus. And you're going to need me riding with you, or you'll be dead before you get started."

"Then ride with me. Please."

Larry let out a long breath and opened the stove door and poked at the dying fire. When the flames were licking upward again, he closed the door, set the poker aside, sat down, and said, "I would've liked to know you got married. That would have been a nice thing to hear. Anything from you would have been nice to hear."

"I'll give you all the apologies you want, but right now isn't the time."

"The hell it isn't! You just showed up at my door and asked for my help killing a man. Don't tell me what you've got time for and what you don't."

Mark didn't speak. Larry turned and looked out the window, up at the crown of Mount Republic, and made a soft sound with his tongue.

"And God made family," he said. Then he got to his feet.

"Tell you something, Markus—older you get, the more you realize the only things in this world that can *really* cause you pain are the people you love. I always did love you, son, and it's damn clear you loved your wife. No doubt about that. It would be easier on us both right now if we weren't so afflicted, right?"

Mark stayed silent. Larry nodded as if the silence were a good enough answer, then said, "I s'pose it's time for me to put my pants on, isn't it? We're burning daylight, and you're running a race against the police. Won't win that one sitting here by the fire, will we?"

"Thank you," Mark said. His voice was rough. "And I'm sorry."

His uncle stood looking out the grimy window at the mountain. "You know what I thought, the day those cocksuckers whipped me? I thought, *Lord, if only my brother were still alive.* Not that it would have put the numbers in my favor, but with Ronny, I didn't mind being outnumbered. Ronny's been in the ground a long time, though. I always miss him, but never more than I did that day. I needed a brother, and my brother was gone." He turned back to Mark and gave a cold, humorless smile. "I got a nephew, though. How 'bout that. Now the question is, how much of Ronny is in you, boy?"

Part Three

WARDENCLYFFE

45

The council fire had been planned for evening, but Eli's accelerated timeline forced him to move it to dawn, and for once he
saw a benefit. The sunrise was more powerful than the sunset in this
location; from the ridgetop, the earth seemed to be lit from within
for a few spectacular minutes, an ethereal glow that spoke of the ancient world. That would matter to the group he was assembling.
Any extra touch that enhanced their mission commitment was valuable, if not imperative. Eli's command was going to be tested during
this ceremony, and he would need to call upon the natural world for
power. While the gathering crowd had been pliable enough in initial talks, everything was different on the eve of action, and they
would arrive with at least some level of doubt. The group en route
was as close to battle-tested as any Eli could assemble, minus a few
key parts. He thought of the women in the cabin, of the empty
shackles that lined the walls, and the image was bittersweet. He had
counted on five more alongside Sabrina Baldwin, and Lynn
Deschaine had not been in that mix. But those people remained
available to him for the future, and in the future, a world of fear
would be easier to rule.

When darkness fell, chaos would reign, and the man who controlled the chaos? His ascent to leadership was natural order. Proof of
this was in the history books of every civilization.

Eli read voraciously about biological warfare and understood both
the potential and the challenge—you needed to determine how to
infect the first wave of carriers with the virus. A careful study of human nature, however, told you that every human on earth already
carried two viral qualities: fear and hope. Each was contagious and

could spread rapidly under the right conditions, but at first glance they seemed to be natural enemies.

False.

Fear and hope were fundamentally joined, inseparable. Anyone whose fear drove him to make predictions, to offer dire warnings, nursed a secret hope that these things would actually come to fruition. If you devoted much of your energy to, for example, a political campaign against a candidate you feared deeply and then that individual rose to power, would you not wish him to fail? Perhaps with spectacular consequences?

Eli believed that most people would. And for those he had found on the radical fringes, the ones itching to be mobilized for a cause, it was simply a matter of joining their fear and their hope. This is what he had nursed so long among so many. First he coaxed forth a prediction born of fear—*The Islamic terrorists are coming; The Christians will kill us; We'll die when they take our guns; We'll die because they won't take our guns*; the details of these fears were less interesting to Eli than what they could do, because all fears harbored potential for action. They harbored, he believed, a secret hope: *The doubters will finally see that I was right.* Any prophet wanted his prophecy fulfilled.

And so Eli coaxed them, encouraged them, nurtured them. Then he solicited the promise: *When it happens, we will act.*

When the western electrical grid went down, Eli was confident that at least seven groups of wildly different ideologies would be compelled to act, and he was hopeful about five more. Yesterday he began careful cloud-seeding of rumor, issuing predictions of a massive action from, depending on the message board or forum, ISIS, the U.S. government, the Tea Party, Greenpeace, the Ku Klux Klan, and Wall Street.

In return, he had his promises: If it happened, action would be taken, and—most critically—his varied cells promised that they would not be fooled by whatever narrative their opposition offered. Because *of course* they would offer an explanation, *of course* they would bury the truth in a lie. Eli had warned of this as well.

When a nation was attacked, the nation looked for an explanation, tried to understand what would incite anyone to take such action. It was an arrogant assumption that any strike against society implied an ideological cause, some bizarre attempt to *correct* society, rather than a clean and simple desire to watch it burn.

The group that would initiate the most significant terrorist strike ever made on North American infrastructure gathered on the ridge just before dawn. They shared only a few words of greeting, some no words at all. There was palpable tension. They had to be wondering how ready they really were. And, perhaps, wondering what they were doing there at all.

Eli shared none of their doubt. He'd been years in the planning of this operation, and in its study. If you could convince a band of people that the evil they were doing was not only justified but also the opposite of evil—a righteous act, a noble act—you could coax far more out of them than they would have ever dreamed. There was much to learn about humanity from watching a lynch mob.

The dozen he'd gathered here had been carefully culled from fringe environmental movements, castoffs drawn in by Violet's ludicrous appropriation of American Indian spirituality. In her bizarre ways, she was perhaps the most brilliant recruiter he'd found. He knew the secret of her success was her sincerity. She believed with a depth of passion, a true intensity, that few could match. When she spoke of the way the strike on the grid would provide a needed wake-up call for the nation, she *believed* it, and her words carried that.

There was no messenger so effective as a true believer.

She also preached nonviolent resistance. Eli had explained this dilemma to Garland and the two other guards he'd recruited, men who responded well to whispered assurances that only a select few were being trusted with the task of pulling triggers. None of them were present now. Eli didn't want any guns in sight.

As the sun made its first timid appearance on the horizon, a faint band of gray, Eli put his back to it and stood on the summit, looking down on the chosen twelve.

"We gather in darkness," Eli said, his voice the deep, textured thunder that he had practiced so long to achieve, "because we do not fear darkness. We know its necessity. And we also know this— those who would keep us in darkness have reached their day of accountability."

A few murmurs, a few nods. Eli held silence for several seconds, staring at them.

"Here is what we know," he said, voice lower now, cool as the mountain wind. "We know without question that those in power, be they government actors or titans of wealth and greed, have manipulated the very planet itself for their own agendas, their own gains. The greatest gift we're given, the source of our very existence, has not only been abused, it has been *claimed*. There are many who think that they have dominion over the planet.

"Make no mistake. They will attempt to identify us as evil. To label this band of people who believe they have certain rights, certain freedoms, as enemies of humanity. They will say this about people who believe that the *very earth itself has certain rights and certain freedoms!*"

He shouted the last words, expecting to hear support, excitement.

Instead, the group was quiet, and the energy in the air was weak. They were uncertain. Hesitant.

He studied them and thought about their hopes and their fears. He knew the language that would incite them—it was what had brought them here. And yet now they seemed strangely unmoved.

He looked toward Violet. He wanted this to be his own moment, and he deserved it to be, but he'd arrived in this place through a special understanding of manipulation. Each audience had its own trigger.

"Violet," he said. "I would like you to speak for the land."

For several seconds she was silent, and he was afraid he'd made a mistake. If she could not inspire, things might unravel swiftly. Just before he was about to speak again, she broke the silence.

She didn't speak. She chanted. An unknown tongue, but a musical one, an ancient half wail that belonged to this place, to the peoples she'd studied for so long.

The murmurs of approval grew louder, the energy from the group changing. Eli saw one woman reach out and squeeze the hand of the man she'd come with. Another man closed his eyes and bobbed his head as if in agreement with the wordless song.

The sun was tinting the edges of the earth now, the gray giving way to a thin band of pink, and it was magical. It was perfect.

Violet stopped the strange chant.

"The land speaks," she said softly. "The land speaks to those who care to hear. There are whispers from the high peaks, whispers within the deepest caves, the emptiest oceans. And for those who can hear, the tone has changed. The whispers are louder now, my friends; they are shouts. More than shouts, they are cries. The land is crying out, and do you know what it says?"

She paused, looked at every individual face, each of them beginning to take on a new clarity in the rising dawn light.

"It says that it will not be mocked."

The woman who had been clutching her companion's hand now dipped her head as if she were about to faint. Another man had made a fist so tight his knuckles bulged. He held it in front of him like a weapon, but his eyes were locked on Violet.

All of their eyes were.

For this, Eli thought, *tolerating her was worth it.*

The truth was, he couldn't summon his usual contemptuousness of her. He'd become suddenly uneasy. There was a unique magic to her voice, the depth of the believer. He wanted to interrupt her, to reclaim control of the moment, but he knew better and willed the impulse down.

"Someday," she said, "we will all be returned to the earth. This is the certainty of our existence, the only certainty. Ashes to ashes and dust to dust. Whether as ashes or dust, you will return to the earth. How do you wish to be greeted?"

No one spoke. Violet began to make a soft humming noise, rising and falling like a chant, and Eli knew that she had said all she intended to say. The baton was back in his hand.

"We will be challenged," he said. "We will be pursued. We will be hated. All of this is understood and accepted, because the time has come. Not the day of reckoning, but the day of reminding. Perhaps we are not all as lost as it often seems. Perhaps there is more hope out there than we have often believed. But the reminder must be issued. The populace *must* be shaken. And then, I hope, I *pray,* that we will all find the essential things we lost along the way."

He turned from them and faced the sunrise. The pink had deepened to crimson, and it lit him and cast his shadow large across the ground. He closed his eyes and breathed, deep inhalations and exhalations, seven of them, and then he spoke again without turning.

"The world awakens. She calls to us. Today is the day. If some of you choose to depart, you will not be stopped, nor will you be questioned or shamed. The task ahead is not for everyone. If anyone wishes to leave, now is the time, and go in silence."

No one moved. He counted seven more breaths.

"So we begin. I will ask you to speak now. Not to me, but to the land. This is a sacred place, and it is filled with listeners, I assure you. Speak to them now. Share the day's message."

They spoke nearly in unison but just enough ahead or behind each other to make the group sound larger than it was; their fourteen voices turned to forty. They spoke loudly, eagerly, and they spoke without fear. Eli closed his eyes with pleasure. Finally, it was here. Finally, they announced it to an unknowing world at the break of the western dawn.

"Rise the dark, rise the dark, rise the dark."

46

By the time Larry was ready to go, the sun was fully risen and the Soda Butte glittered like scattered diamonds in the white light. Larry surveyed the Tahoe and said, "Damn nice vehicle, and I'd like to take it, but how's your back trail?"

It was a good question. By now the police probably had the make, model, and plate number.

"I don't think anyone knows that I headed this way when I left Red Lodge, but the vehicle is a risk," Mark admitted.

"Kind of figured that. We'll take Blue, then."

"Blue?" Mark had a bad feeling. "You don't mean the Ford?"

"Hell yes, the Ford!"

"That truck was barely running twenty years ago, Uncle."

"I've made some improvements."

The improvements certainly weren't visual. The 1971 Ford Sport Custom pickup was behind the cabin, and the wheels seemed to be attached to the axles. That was the best that could be said for the truck.

"Get your shit," Larry said. Mark got his things out of the Tahoe and slipped his shoulder holster on. Larry watched without comment.

"Where are we headed?" Mark asked once he was in the truck, the passenger seat wheezing beneath him, and Larry cursing and pumping the gas as he tried to coax the engine to life. The exhaust let out a burst like a cannon shot and then settled down to a clatter that shook the dirt on the floorboards, but Larry smiled with pleasure, so evidently this was a good sign.

"Five Points Hot Springs."

"You think Pate is holed up in a resort?" Five Points was an old-time inn built around a natural hot springs. It catered to people who wanted a taste of the rugged West but without leaving fine dining behind.

"No, I don't. But I think Salvador Cantu will be. He's blowing his cash at the bar down there and trying to blow his load with a waitress."

"Who is Salvador Cantu?"

The truck went into motion, and it seemed that the lurch forward had been at least partially inspired by the engine.

"He runs meth out to the oil fields," Larry said. "He's been doing well lately. The Bakken's been better to the drug business than it has to the oil business. He also helped with the whip on the day that I mentioned."

His voice didn't change when he said that, but Mark's throat tightened.

They crossed the Soda Butte and turned onto 212 in Silver Gate. The Range Rider, an old boardinghouse and saloon, was just across the street. That had been Larry's favorite hell-raising spot in the old days. Mark wasn't looking at the town, though, but up at the once-wooded slopes of Republic Pass. The thick forest that faded out into the granite peaks was a grim gray burnout now, a testament to the pair of brothers who'd set it on fire three summers earlier. Blackwell, their names had been. Dangerous men.

Mark saw the giant buffalo that had been outside of Larry's cabin reappear alongside the road. "Is that your personal guard bison?" he asked.

"That's Jackson. He's a surly bastard. Chased some tourists into an outhouse last year and kept them there until he got bored." Larry smiled. "I'm partial to Jackson."

Outside of Silver Gate, Larry got the truck up as high as fifty, at which point the suspension system announced that was the limit. Mark was really beginning to wish they'd taken their chances with the Tahoe.

He wondered where Lynn Deschaine was and whether she knew there'd been a sunrise.

It was midmorning when they arrived at Five Points, and the old resort was quiet. Or at least it was quiet until they arrived. The blue Ford took care of that.

"Couple things we need to be clear on," Larry said when he killed the engine, leaving a backfire and a cloud of exhaust smoke as final warnings. He'd been quiet for most of the ride, and now his voice was low and contemplative. "You want to move in a hurry, as I understand it."

"I have to, yes."

Larry nodded. "Sal Cantu is not going to want to move in a hurry. Such conflicts are sometimes unavoidable." He sighed and worked a cigarette into his mouth. "He won't be staying in the main lodge. But they'll know him at the bar."

He was right on both counts. When they walked into the dimly lit bar, with the blue-water pools of the hot springs looking bright on the other side of glass doors, there were only employees inside, and maybe half a dozen people out in the water, young couples drinking brightly colored drinks in plastic cups. The bartender, a young guy, asked what he could do for them, and Larry said they were looking for Sal Cantu, and the bartender's face went from friendly to wary.

"He's not in the lodge, and he won't be again."

"Had some trouble with him?"

The kid picked up a dry glass and dried it again. "If you know him so well, then you'd know we had trouble with him."

"Sure. But I was told he'd be here, and I was—"

"Fishing camp. We just rent the cabins, we don't own them, and we don't have the authority to evict. That's up to the individual owners." He put the glass down and looked from Larry to Mark. "You two probably know the owner I'm talking about."

Mark surely didn't, but Larry just nodded. "Right. Okay, boss. We'll take two shots of Maker's and then get out of your hair."

It wasn't noon yet. Mark drank the whiskey with his uncle, though, and it sat sour and burning in his empty stomach as they walked back to the parking lot.

"Who owns that cabin at the fishing camp?" Mark asked.

"No idea, but it wasn't going to help me to say that. If Sal's been booted from the main lodge but they can't keep him out of one of the cabins, it belongs to somebody he supplies something to. Drugs or protection. Maybe both."

"Protection?"

"Sal's not a small boy. Or a nice one." Larry turned and gave Mark a hard look. He seemed like a starkly different man from the one who'd opened the door bleary-eyed and in his underwear just a few hours ago. A lot more like the man Mark remembered. The transformation told Mark plenty about how things were likely to go with Sal Cantu.

The fishing camp was on a dirt road that ran through pasture and down to a trout stream where there was a handful of limited-access, privately owned sites with small cabins that were rented out during peak season. Larry pulled the truck off the road, reached in his duffel bag, and got out a revolver with worn bluing, which he stuck in his belt. Then he brought out a length of paracord, put that in his back pocket, and grabbed what looked like a short piece of a belt. Mark knew it at once: a homemade blackjack. Larry had always carried one. He would cut inserts into a thick leather harness strap and load in pieces of lead shot. He referred to it as a slapjack because of the extra flex. He put that in his back pocket and said, "I'm an old man trying a young man's game today, Markus."

He didn't seem dismayed by that.

They walked up the road and came to the gated drive. The gate was locked and there was barbed-wire fencing on each side. Larry climbed the gate looking very much like the young man he'd said he wasn't, and Mark followed.

They hadn't even reached the cabins before a door to one of them opened and a Hispanic man as thick and solid as an oil drum stood before them.

"Private property," he said. "No fishing, no access, don't bother asking."

He was a couple inches shorter than Mark but at least eighty pounds heavier, with an oversize jaw traced by a thin beard. His hair was cut short, and you could see white lines of old scars across his skull. He'd been looking primarily at Mark, but when he let his attention shift to Larry, there was a blink of recognition.

"Shit," he said, "you really dumb enough to come back around looking for your sister, man? She's where she wants to be. Stay out of it."

Larry looked to the side. There was silence for a moment. Then he nodded. Cantu had followed his glance and he looked confused when Larry nodded at nothing. Mark wasn't confused—it was the old gesture, the appeal for guidance from a voice that rarely counseled peaceful action. He wasn't surprised when his uncle's right hand flashed out like a cat's paw and he cracked Salvador Cantu in the face with the slapjack.

He hit him flush on the cheekbone, and Cantu reeled back and fell into the cabin's front wall but didn't go down. Instead he pushed off it with a roar of pain and rage and came at Larry with one heavy fist balled up and raised as if to knock Larry's head right off his shoulders. Mark caught his wrist before he could come out of the clumsy windup, wrenched his arm down, and slammed him back into the wall. Cantu threw a left hand that was more of an awkward slap than a punch but one that still landed on the side of Mark's head, and his strength made even the clumsy punch a heavy one. Mark took a step back, just enough to clear space, and then brought his right fist up under Cantu's jaw so hard that the man's teeth cracked together. Cantu reached for him as he fell, trying to tackle him, but Mark slipped the grasp and Cantu fell to his knees, his big torso swaying. Mark drew his gun and put the muzzle of the .38 to the top of his head. Sal Cantu's breath came in hot gasps, and he looked at Mark with hate, a red mouse already swelling high on his cheekbone. Behind them, Larry chuckled.

"How 'bout that," he said. "You got some of your uncle Ronny in you after all, boy."

Then he hit Cantu again with the slapjack, two rapid smacks, one above each knee, in the thick muscles of the quads, and Cantu grunted with pain and fell flat on the porch, writhing on his belly. Mark glanced at Larry, who was circling Cantu like a wolf around fallen prey. Mark wanted to tell his uncle that it was good enough, that they didn't need to push it any further; Cantu was down and they had the guns and there was no need to hit him again. Mark hadn't been the one tied to a trailer hitch and whipped, though. Larry would decide when it was done.

Larry took off his baseball cap and ran his fingers through his long white hair. When he put the cap back on he spent a little extra time bending the grimy bill, and Mark could see that the busy hands were designed to keep his emotions in check, bleed out a little of the tension that filled him.

"I need you to be able to talk, so be grateful for that," Larry said. He kicked Cantu in the ass, hard. "Where's Pate?"

Sal Cantu looked like a trout left on the rocks, bug-eyed and fighting for breath, mouth open wide, a string of spit between his lips. Despite the pain he had to be feeling, though, there was a smile in his eyes, and the smile had risen at Pate's name.

"Speak," Larry said.

Cantu lifted his head. It took some effort. "You actually think your sister matters, Larry?" he said. "You really think her tired old cooze means a damn thing?"

When Mark hit him, he did it so fast and so hard that even Larry said, "Shit!" Mark backhanded Cantu across the face with his .38, driving his head sideways, and then caught him again for a forehand, using the pistol like a tennis racket, two fluid swings that left Sal Cantu howling into his hands, curled up and bleeding on the porch. Mark saw Larry shift from side to side, but his uncle didn't say anything, just watched. Mark didn't look him in the eye.

"You've got a dangerous impression of things," Mark told Cantu, who was writhing in pain, blood running between his fingers. "You think you know why we came here, and what we want, and what we left behind. You don't know any of those things."

Cantu still had his hands up to his face, his fingertips looking as if they'd been dipped in red ink, but over them, his dark eyes were focused. He was listening.

"Allow me to introduce myself," Mark said, kneeling down, "so you don't have to suffer the pain of your misconceptions any longer. I'm Markus Novak, and I'm not here because of anything that happened with my uncle or my mother or any of the people you consider relevant in this situation. That's important for you to understand. I'm here for something very different, all right? And I don't have time to waste."

Cantu breathed through his mouth and stared at Mark and didn't speak. Mark looked at him for a moment and said, "You're going to test my seriousness here, aren't you?" He shook his head. "That's a poor play."

Mark stood up and holstered the gun and extended his hand to his uncle without looking at him. He kept his eyes on Sal Cantu.

"Let me borrow that slapjack."

Larry didn't hesitate. The weighted leather socked into Mark's palm. He grasped it, stepped back, and took a couple of short practice swings, testing the feel. It was perfect; heavy enough but balanced and flexible. A craftsman's answer to brass knuckles. Mark ran his thumb along the worn leather and advanced toward the bleeding man on the porch floor.

Sal Cantu watched him come and said, "I'll tell you where to go, but you'll get more than what you're ready for. With Pate, you'd better believe that."

"Sure. Where is he?"

"There's a warehouse in Byron, maybe a mile out of town north on Route 5, toward the oil field. A big prefab deal with an eight-foot fence around it. Looks empty." He was speaking to Larry now.

"But it's not empty," Larry said. "He's there? Pate himself?"

"He's there."

"It's a long drive if he isn't."

"Guess you'll have to trust me."

"Guess so," Larry said, and then he reached behind him and withdrew the length of paracord he'd stuck in his pocket. He tossed it to Mark. "Hands and feet."

Mark caught the cord, tossed the slapjack back to his uncle, and knelt to tie Cantu's hands.

"Hey," Sal said. "The fuck you think you're going to do? I just told you—"

"When we find Pate, someone will find you," Larry said. "Until we do, you'll join the missing. Consider that, and consider if you want to give different directions."

"Nobody's tying me. I gave you what you needed, damn it." Cantu struggled upright.

"Glad to hear it," Larry said, and then he stepped forward and swung the slapjack again, and this time he had more than his wrist behind it. The lead-laced leather cracked off the back of Sal Cantu's skull, and the big man dropped to the porch floor. Mark stared as blood dripped down the unconscious man's face. Larry put the slapjack back in his pocket and looked at Mark with challenging eyes.

"You forget how to work a knot?"

Mark bound Sal's hands and feet while Larry opened the cabin door. Then they hauled him inside. Larry found a dishrag, shoved it into Cantu's mouth, and said, "Tie that in there good too. If he wants to breathe, he's got a nose."

"You believe those directions he gave are worth a damn?" Mark asked.

"Oh, I'm sure they're worth something," Larry said. "That boy isn't the sort to send you on a wild-goose chase. He's the sort to send you into a hornet's nest."

47

The recruitment of Doug Oriel had been Janell's primary assignment in Florida. His combination of military-grade demolition skills and full-blown conspiracy-theorist paranoia was enticing to Eli, but his network of like-minded souls was even more intriguing. The problem with Doug was that he had a deep-seated distrust of the Internet, which meant Eli's standard recruiting tactics were ineffective. Thus the decision to approach him in person.

For nine months, Janell had devoted herself to the coddling of this oversize child. In the miles since they'd left Ardachu's house, she realized that it had all been a waste.

He didn't speak for nearly two hours, and when he did, it was to demand that she drop him off at a bus station.

"A bus station," she said. "That's your idea of where you should go now? Only a few hundred miles from being a part of this, you want to stop and get on a bus?"

"Yes. I don't want any part of this. Not anymore. Not with you."

She gripped the wheel tighter. "You are not going to a bus station. We are going to finish the journey."

"You can do what you want. I won't be along for the ride."

In the hours of silence, he'd managed to locate some confidence to fill in the places where before shock and horror had existed. He was sitting taller, his shoulders back and his big chest filling. Trying to make himself larger, the thing they told you to do if you stumbled across a mountain lion in the woods.

She wanted to laugh.

"No bus station," she said. "You want out, you can pick your place on our route, but I'm not changing course."

But she knew she'd have to.

The group Eli was gathering all believed a narrative of non-violence. That was the great irony of the first strike force—they were mostly peaceful by nature, shepherded together by their opposition to oil drilling, fracking, big business, and pollution, all the tedious minutiae of those who believed the earth was worth saving. Janell's understanding was that, with the notable exception of bodyguards recruited from some meth runners, the tribes, as Eli called them, would recoil at the idea of murder.

Now she was driving Doug and his new story to their doorstep. That could not happen. It would be safer to take him to the bus station as he wished than to deliver him to anyone whose resolve could shatter.

She hated to lose him, though. Through Doug, they had reached dozens of potential players. To a man, they feared the government, believed in shadow conspiracies, and were firmly convinced that the U.S. military was looking for any excuse to claim first the guns and then the freedoms of Americans. Doug had facilitated contact with three different militia groups, an arm of the Ku Klux Klan, and a team of Texas preppers who were better armed than most third-world militaries.

All this energy expended preparing for a nonexistent war, and a single dead man had brought Doug to his knees.

"There are casualties in any worthy mission," she said. "You've always known this."

He shook his head. "This is exactly what the police want us to do. They won't even have to lie about us now. You've made it the truth."

She fought for patience, for the right words. There was no time to waste finding the right words, though. Recruiting days were done. They were in action now, and she had neither the time nor the energy to return to the wars of rhetoric.

"You understand that's all a lie, don't you?" she said.

"What is?"

"Every word we've ever said. Every…single…word."

She looked away from the road, at his face, and he blinked at her, utterly oblivious, and her frustration swelled to something deeper and darker.

"We find people of value," she said, speaking like a teacher addressing a young child, "and we determine what story they need to hear. It's the story that they're already telling themselves, don't you see? It's the nightmare they believe in. Once you understand that nightmare, you join them in it. Their fear becomes your fear. It's all a shared experience then. And once you have that, once they feel that is the truth, all the way down to their core, then your coping strategy becomes theirs. It's a natural progression. This is the power of the shared narrative. Of the echo chamber. Do you follow that? Can you comprehend what I'm saying?"

He stared at her, his broad face showing all the intellect of a steer who has reached the end of the slaughterhouse chute without realizing where he's been led.

"Infrastructure," he said stupidly. "That's all that needs to be hit. A man like the one in that house, he might have believed exactly what we believe. You don't know. You didn't bother to ask, you just cut his throat."

She took a deep, patient breath. Said, "Let's try this once more. Everything you have heard me say is a lie. Take your time. I'll give you a few seconds to figure it out."

"I don't know what in the hell has gotten into you," he said. "You're out of your mind. You're right—I don't believe a word you've said. Not anymore. Pull over. I'd rather walk to prison than ride another mile with you."

She remembered nine months ago, when they'd arrived in Cassadaga, how quickly she'd been able to convince him that he needed to stay away from television and computers. They were the most common tools of brainwashing, she'd explained, and then she'd given him a book about neurolinguistic programming. It had been, admittedly, a risky joke to play, because if he paid any attention to the book at all, he might have had some questions about her, but instead he'd swallowed the story whole. Why? Because it was what he had already suspected. Already feared.

Everyone wanted to believe he or she was the prophet of truth, and when that truth was rooted in fear, the desire was even stronger. Every human response was stronger when it came from a place of fear.

Now the source of Doug's fear had shifted.

"Pull over," he repeated.

They were driving through prairie country, flat and desolate and entirely empty. She slowed the Yukon and pulled off the road and bounced over the shoulder and onto the grass beyond. She was reaching for the gearshift when she saw the gun in his hand.

"On second thought," he said, "you'll do the walking."

She looked at the gun, not his eyes, while she nodded. Then she moved the gearshift into park, let her foot off the brake, and said, "I'm taking the phones and radios. You clearly won't have a need for them, and when you're caught, I'm not letting you get caught with those."

"You can have your phones. Just get out."

"Such a waste of potential," she said.

"Get out."

She opened the door and stepped out onto the road. The sun put a haze over the asphalt, but the day wasn't warm. Spring in the high plains, a climate of confusion.

As she walked toward the tailgate, Doug shifted awkwardly. He wanted to just slide from the passenger seat to the driver's, but he was too big and clumsy for that. She had the tailgate up when he opened the passenger door and stepped out onto the crunching, brittle grass.

On top of the radio bags was the 12-gauge shotgun she'd stolen from Gregory Ardachu's cabinet. It was loaded with double-aught shells. When she stepped back from the Yukon, he was blank-faced, the pistol at the side of his leg pointed to the ground.

She'd endured this for nine months. It ended in a tenth of a second.

The sound of the 12-gauge echoed across the plains, then faded into their vast spaces. Doug Oriel's body fell in the dirt beside the Yukon, taking the bottom of his head down with it. The top had been separated from it, and now the remains settled in the grass in a red mist. A bad shot, too high.

But in the end, effective.

She walked to the body and looked down. Only one of his eyes remained, and it was staring into the dust, looking away from her. She sighed and shook her head. Eli had harbored high hopes for Doug and wanted to meet him in person. He'd be disappointed by this result, but he would understand. Doug had lost track of his narrative, and once that happened, he was not only of limited value but high risk.

As a dead man, though, he had renewed potential. She would see to it that he fulfilled his own prophecy.

It seemed he deserved at least that much for his service.

She put the shotgun back in the Yukon, closed first the tailgate and then the passenger door, and got behind the wheel, alone.

48

I t took Mark and his uncle nearly an hour to reach Byron, and during the drive neither of them said much. Mark was thinking of the way Sal Cantu had smiled when he'd looked at Larry and said, *You actually think your sister matters?* It reminded him of the amusement Janell Cole had shown over the idea that Mark believed Lauren mattered. Yet Lauren had known the phrase *rise the dark,* which mattered to all of them, and certainly mattered to Lynn Deschaine and Homeland Security. How had Lauren heard of it? He was beginning to wish they'd gotten in a few more questions before Larry had knocked the man out.

"This would be the place," Larry said, slowing. "The warehouse Cantu described. That's it, right?"

Calling it a warehouse was lipstick on a pig—the place was just an oversize old prefabricated barn in a gravel parking lot surrounded by a high fence and a gate with a keypad. There were no vehicles in the lot, and the property looked beyond empty. Desolate.

Larry was pulling in when Mark felt the sensation that had come over him in Cassadaga—that soft, rubber-band sound, and suddenly he was tense, hand drifting toward his gun.

"Drive past."

Larry obliged without comment, cruising down the lonely road for another mile, until the barn was out of sight and they were facing a sign for the Byron oil field, which loomed just to the north.

"Okay, chief," Larry said, pulling onto the shoulder and turning off the car, "what's the master plan?"

"We go back on foot. It's so damned empty that they're going to hear anybody in a truck, particularly this abomination of an exhaust system."

Larry looked wounded. "I had Blue tuned up not five years ago!"

"There's only so much a mortician can do to improve a situation, Uncle."

"It was a mechanic."

"Uh-huh. Regardless, I'd like to go in quietly. It's not much of a walk."

"It's a damned empty one, though. A truck pulled up outside of that place looks like it belongs, maybe. Left here? It's abandoned. It draws the eye. If anyone *is* in the place, they'll see us coming ten minutes before we get there instead of thirty seconds. And if anything goes wrong, we've got a mile of empty highway to come back up, with nowhere to hide."

He pointed at the surrounding countryside, bleak and barren, looking more like West Texas than Wyoming. There was no snow here; the earth was dry and fissured, like the palm of an old man's hand. Until the Pryor Mountains rose up in the north, red-baked and uninspiring, there was no shelter. Fleeing on foot would mean covering a long stretch of open land dotted with scrub pines and brush. Larry was right—if it came to that, they'd wish the truck were a hell of a lot closer.

"All right," Mark said. "Just make it fast. This wreck sounds like a steam locomotive."

"Don't you listen to him, Blue. Don't you listen." Larry started the engine. The exhaust fired like a cannon volley, and then they were in motion. Mark's mouth was dry, and the strange, echoing pops were back in his skull. He was aware of a single bead of sweat trickling down his spine.

What's the matter with you, Markus? It's an empty pole barn, nothing more. What in the hell is the matter with you?

He'd felt this way before; that was the problem. His body had trapped the memory of the house in Cassadaga and was throwing it back at his mind.

But why? The house in Cassadaga was straight out of Edgar Allan Poe. This is an empty barn in wide-open country. There's no similarity.

Still, the feeling was there.

Where's that strange boy when I need him? Or, better yet, Walter, the dead man who apparently took a shine to me. I could use his advice right now. Tell me, Walt, what's the issue up ahead?

Mark forced a smile as the fenced-in barn came back into sight, looking as if it had been abandoned for months. Beyond the fence was sun-and-wind-blasted soil with a few thatches of brush clinging to whatever groundwater there was to be found.

"I'll drive right up to the gate and we'll climb again," Larry said. "Ain't no point in jacking with that security box."

The box he'd referenced was a curved metal pole with a keypad. High-tech for an isolated barn. A deep ditch ran between the road and the fence, ready to drain runoff and snowmelt out of the mountains, and you had to cross a massive cattle-guard grate to get across that and onto the last thirty feet of dusty drive. Larry was scanning the property, searching for watchers, and Mark knew he should be doing the same, but for some reason he was fixated on that cattle guard. It looked new, the stainless-steel gleaming in the sun, high angled pieces that rose on each side, allowing for heavy equipment to lower the grating into place easily. Cattle guards were common in this part of the world, so why this one held Mark's eye made no sense, and yet he couldn't look away from it, and the echoing, popping noise in his head was back and louder, closer to the surface.

You've seen it before.

Of course he had. He'd seen a million of them, old and rusted and dusty, while this one was new.

It shouldn't be new, nothing else here is new—

There was nothing strange about it, nothing threatening; it was a straightforward device for livestock and drainage and—

You've seen it before!

The voice in Mark's head didn't seem to be his own, and the light reflecting off that polished, clean steel pierced his brain like an ice pick through the eye and he was just about to look away when a memory finally broke the surface like a drowning man fighting a riptide.

The basement in Cassadaga. The trap on the table. It was a model. It was a scale model and that means this one, at full size, is—

"Uncle, hang on," Mark said, and Larry glanced at him but kept driving. As the front wheels bounced off the gravel road and onto the cattle guard, Mark grabbed his uncle by the back of his neck and jerked him down, away from the windshield and the window, pressing their faces together and slamming their heads against the gearshift. For one blissful instant, a tenth of a second, he thought, *I was wrong, and I am going to look like a fool.*

Then the truck rocked like it had taken a direct hit from a howitzer, and glass exploded all around them.

Just like the tiny one. That was a model for this. Turning a standard bit of equipment into a bear trap. That is what they were working on.

Larry was struggling against him, swearing and fumbling for his gun. Mark held him down for a few seconds, but there were no more impacts, so he released him and they both rose shakily to look at the damage.

The windshield was spiderwebbed with fractures, and all of the windows had blown out. Larry's cheeks and arms were laced with small cuts, and Mark's showed the same damage. As they looked at each other and then the truck, Larry whispered, "Mother of God, what is that?"

He was looking at the doors. Pieces of metal each as big as a man's fist but filed down into shark's teeth had punctured the doors, slamming shut on the truck with such incredible force that they'd bitten clean through. The doors themselves had buckled inward, and on a newer vehicle, a smaller one with less solid metal in the frame, the damage would have been even worse. A compact car would have been crushed. In another car, the airbags would have deployed, but Blue had come off the line long before airbags. Mark twisted in his seat and opened the latch on the bedcover window.

"We gotta get out."

He wormed through the narrow opening and fell into the corrugated bed, landing hard, bits of glass biting into his hands, and again he thought of Cassadaga, of his crawl out of the basement while the house had burned around him.

He climbed across the truck bed, noticing for the first time that Larry had a trio of long guns—two rifles and a shotgun—hidden under a roll of old carpet, and he found the latch to the tailgate and opened that and pushed out, stumbling into the dusty road, shedding pebbled glass and drops of blood. He turned back and saw Larry following suit, swinging down to the road.

"You okay?" Mark asked.

"Fine. Thanks to you, that is. If you hadn't pulled me in like that, that fucking thing would have taken my head off. Damn sure it would have broken my arms and ribs, probably my leg. How in the *hell* did you see that coming?"

"Walter," Mark murmured.

"Who?"

"Nothing. I saw a version of it in Florida, and I nearly lost my hand to that one. It was so small I didn't understand what it was a model of. I finally recognized the shape. Almost too late."

"Just in time, that's for sure." Larry stepped away, looking at his beloved truck from the side. The hood and the cab were demolished, smashed and ravaged by those massive steel teeth that had been welded onto the angled side of the cattle guard. The design could not have been simpler—it was an old-school trap, springs responding to pressure, but Lord, they were powerful springs.

Why use springs, though? Mark wondered. An explosive and a pressure sensor could have incinerated the truck and killed them both in the time it took to blink. The technique employed here was far more labor-intensive, resulting in far less damage. It was a step backward in the art of war.

It fits Pate's preaching, Mark realized. Pate needed to sell the idea of the dangerous world of modern technology. He would, therefore, go to war with old weapons, or at least old theories.

"Look what they did to Blue," Larry said. The look on his face made any expression he had shown at Sal Cantu's seem positively kind. "Do you have any idea how many miles I've covered behind the wheel of that—"

The gunfire that interrupted him was a sustained burst of shots, rapid and fired from a semiautomatic. The bullets lit up the truck, taking out what was left of the windshield and pocking the hood like hail. The shooter wasn't armed with a large magazine, apparently, because he ran out of ammo almost as soon as Mark and Larry managed to react, and they were pressed against the back bumper, guns drawn, during the brief respite where one magazine was dropped and another inserted. Then a second burst fired. More glass and metal flew, but the bullets weren't penetrating, and many of them were sparking off the steel cattle guard.

Mark dropped to the gravel and rolled sideways as Larry hissed, "Markus, don't go out there!"

Mark had his gun raised but wasn't about to return fire with the .38. That was like bringing sparklers to a fireworks show. He just wanted to see where the shooter was.

He wasn't hard to locate—there was a pedestrian door on the east-facing side of the building, toward the front gate, and a man stood in front of it with a rifle, probably an AR-15, at his shoulder, spraying bullets at the truck.

Mark ducked down and said, "What kind of rifle do you have back there?"

"A thirty-aught-six and a three-hundred Win Mag."

"Give me the three-hundred and I'll own this guy."

"I'll do the shooting." Larry rose high enough to fumble the folded carpet out, then dropped with a shout when another burst of gunfire rattled the truck.

"You hit?"

"No, but it was closer than I'd like."

Mark pressed up against the rear passenger-side tire, holding the .38 and feeling impotent. He was a fine pistol shot, but the distance rendered that meaningless.

"I think he's shot himself out of bullets," Mark said. "Hurry!"

Larry grabbed for the rifle and instead caught the roll of carpet and dragged the whole mess out, flopping it into the gravel. The shooter took a few steps farther from the building, as if considering coming all the way out, then stopped, and Mark caught his breath.

Garland Webb.

"It's him," Mark said, though his uncle had no idea who he was talking about. "He's here." He swung around the truck, rose to his knees, and shot the cylinder on the .38 empty. None of the bullets came close, and Garland Webb turned and fled into the shadows of the building.

"*Shit!*" Mark looked at Larry, still fumbling through the rolled-up carpet for the right rifle case, and shouted, "Give me your pistol!"

"Pistol, hell! We've got to make up the distance!"

"Give me the pistol!"

Larry looked up at him in shock, saw Mark's face, and handed over the gun. It was a Colt .45. Mark checked the load and took off at a sprint while his uncle screamed at him to stop. If Webb had more ammunition or another weapon, it was a suicide run, but Mark couldn't think clearly enough to care. Webb was there, and Mark had a gun in hand.

He'd waited two agonizing years for this moment.

He ran down the ditch and scrambled up the other side and then hit the fence and climbed. There was barbed wire along the top, and he felt it shred his stomach as he flipped over and then landed in the gravel on the other side, but he didn't pause, just stumbled forward and then ran hard once he had his balance, praying that Webb would show himself again, step out of the darkness and into the daylight. Into shooting range. For too long, he'd been hidden just like this— behind high fences and thick walls, locked inside dark, inaccessible rooms.

Now, though, he was right there.

Mark was halfway to the building when he heard an engine start. He pulled up short. Then he realized that the engine was coming from behind the building, and he began to run for the closest corner of the barn. He was halfway there when a truck came into view from the opposite side, a white Silverado with mud spattered along the side. Instead of driving toward the gate, it angled across the empty parking lot and toward the fence, gathering speed. Mark took two shots at a run—foolish, wasting bullets—and then forced himself to stop and take careful aim, going for the tires. He squeezed off the rest of the rounds in the gun, hitting the tailgate but never the tires. Meanwhile the truck was still accelerating, heading right for the fence. On the other side of the chain link, the land was rough but flat enough for driving, and the road was only a hundred yards away.

"Damn it, Larry, *shoot! Shoot him!*"

But no gunfire came from his uncle, and the Silverado hit the fence at fifty miles per hour at least. It tore through the chain link as if it were so much twine; the engine howled and the truck fishtailed and bounced over a short clump of brush, down into the ditch, and then up onto the road. The tires burned rubber, smoke rose from the pavement, and the truck was gone.

Mark dropped to his knees in the parking lot. His chest was heaving, and he could not take his eyes off the spot where the truck had just been.

Where Garland Webb had just been.

Had him. He was here, and so was I, with a gun in my hand. Finally.

He felt so tired, so beaten, that it took two tries for him to rise to his feet. By then, Larry had reached him and was in midsentence as well as midstride.

"…stupidest stunt I've ever seen! If he'd had another clip you'd be splattered over this parking lot like roadkill! Running into the wide-damn-open with nothing but a pistol, and you—"

"*Why didn't you shoot?*" Mark screamed. "You had a three-hundred Mag and you couldn't get off a *single shot!*"

"I don't drive around with that thing loaded up and ready to fire from the hip, Markus! If you hadn't run up there like a damned kamikaze pilot, I'd have been ready to pick him off no matter how he came out."

They stood there and stared at each other, both of them glaring and breathing hard, and then Mark turned away and said, *"Stupid son of a bitch!"* He was talking to himself, not his uncle. Larry was right; if Mark hadn't forced the issue, there would have been enough time to load and scope in, and then no matter how Webb chose to leave, it would have ended with a squeeze of the trigger.

It would have ended.

Mark reached into his pocket and closed his hand over Lauren's old dive permit. There was blood on his hand from either the glass or the fence, and he could feel it oozing between his fingers.

"I'm sorry," he said.

"You should be, acting that damn foolish," Larry said, unaware that Mark hadn't been apologizing to him.

"That was him," he said. "Uncle, that was the man."

"I got that impression, son. Tell you something else—I know whose truck he was driving."

Mark turned to him. "What?"

Larry's face, speckled with fresh cuts leaking blood, was taut with anger. This time, though, it didn't seem to be directed at Mark.

"That Silverado belongs to Scotty Shields."

"The hunting guide? I thought you said he was in Alaska?"

"He did say it. But he wouldn't leave that truck behind. Not by choice."

For a moment Mark was silent. Then he said, "Let's see what he left in there."

They crossed the parking lot and approached the open side door from which Webb had emerged. Even though it seemed unlikely there was anyone still inside, Mark lifted a finger, asking Larry to wait. Mark had made enough foolish mistakes in this place. He motioned to the doorway and then back to himself, indicating that he was going through first, and Larry nodded and stepped to the side, ready to provide covering fire. Mark went in low so Larry could shoot over him if needed.

Nothing but silence and darkness greeted him. The inside of the barn smelled of rust and something with an acidic tang that Mark couldn't place. He turned sideways and checked both sides of the door and found the light switches.

"I don't want to turn these on," he whispered.

"Hell, son, ain't nobody here but us and the rats. Light the place up."

Mark glanced into the expansive dark, clenched his teeth, and hit the lights.

The fluorescents had that little hitch, the half-second pause before full glow, and by the time the barn was illuminated Mark had placed the smell—there were pallets of fertilizer stacked around the room. A fine explosive material. Along the far wall were more grates for the cattle guards, loose pieces of steel, and a pair of commercial-grade welders. Quite the workshop.

What was most troubling about the place, though, was how empty it was. Mark didn't think it was a case of slow stockpiling. It looked more like they'd been taking supplies out. Fresh tire tracks lined the floor, and a Bobcat with a front loader was parked near the huge barn doors on the opposite side, where the Silverado had evidently been. It looked like they'd been loading.

"They're getting ready," he said softly.

He walked to the big double doors and pushed them open in a shriek of rusted metal. More tire tracks here, and they were wider than the pickup Garland Webb had been driving. A flatbed, probably.

Larry followed him outside. Neither of them spoke for a moment. The wind blew gravel dust into the air, and it stuck to the blood on Mark's face.

"You know where to find Scott Shields if he really is still around here?"

"Yes."

Mark looked up the road where Garland Webb had vanished. Everything was completely silent again, as if the crush of steel and exchange of gunfire had never happened at all. No car had passed. The countryside spread out vast and empty, the sun high.

"How far is Shields's place from here?" Mark asked.

"Not very, but it'll take a long time walking."

"I guess we'll need a car, then."

"I haven't forgotten how to acquire one when necessary."

They walked back to the truck. Larry handed Mark the two rifles without comment, and then he took the shotgun and his duffel bag. He gave his truck one last sorrowful look but didn't say a word.

They set off together down the dusty road.

49

Eli drove to Red Lodge after the morning council. The tribes were in motion, Jay Baldwin was behaving, and Garland Webb was in position to deal with Markus Novak if he actually appeared on the trail. Eli thought that unlikely, but it was good to have safeguards. For Garland's sake, he hoped Novak actually made it through.

His only concern—that news of her son's arrival might unsettle Violet and throw off the morning's rituals—had not developed. Overall, there was nothing in the warm, sun-splashed morning that suggested harm, and there were only a few remaining tasks. He wished that Janell had arrived, but he was not worried by her absence. If there was anyone among them who could be trusted to handle a crisis, it was Janell.

He stopped at a café in Red Lodge that offered Wi-Fi, ordered a coffee, and set up in a back booth where prying eyes didn't reach. He had a backpack with four tablets and five smartphones, and he had nine messages to send. The first, a text message to Jay Baldwin:

> You are sick today. Call in early, Jay—it's the courteous thing to do. And prepare your barehanding gear. Don't forget the hot stick! Talk soon.

That done, he turned off the phone that had sent the message, withdrew a tablet, and set to work composing a longer, more emotional note. This one was his pet project, the most difficult of all the recruitment efforts, because he'd had to pose as the neophyte in need of convincing rather than the messenger. If the plan was effective, though, the rewards would be enormous.

Using an application called an Android emulator to mask his location and make it look as if he were posting from Seattle, he logged on to a locked social network. There his name was Fasiel, and he was a twenty-seven-year-old Web developer who had converted to Islam twenty months earlier. He had posted references to the vulnerability of Seattle's electrical grid time and again, urging his brothers to take action. The level of trust in Fasiel seemed minimal, although he was subject to recruiting efforts—Eli's post office box in Seattle, which was checked by one of the heavily armed men who had arrived this morning to provide security support at Wardenclyffe, had received everything from gift certificates to Islamic bookstores to a box of chocolates.

Now on to the most important messages, which Eli would write essentially in nine different languages. Each extremist group had a unique jargon with a shared constant—they all appropriated certain words, terms, or ideas that made them feel authentic. In the echo chambers of this online world, where people parroted one another and an original idea was not only discouraged but feared, it did not take long to learn how to join in the chorus.

My brothers, Fasiel wrote,

> By dawn tomorrow you will be aware of a great action, praise be to Allah, the most merciful and most beneficent. The American crusaders will be struck by the Sword of Allah deep in their hearts, and it will cast terror across the Western lands, and from nation to nation his power will be known. I caution you that the truth will not be told, and I suspect you will hear nothing but lies from the infidels, who will not wish to admit they could be so humbled by soldiers of the Caliphate. The crusaders will deny that they have been struck within their own fortresses and across the oceans, struck deep within their own homeland. When the news reaches you, the Americans will surely say that this strike at their hearts

was made by a group of their own kuffar, their own clueless kind, and not by those who, Allah willing, will soon join you in Dabiq. Do not let the lies hide the truth, brothers. You will know of what I speak when you see the news, you will know immediately, and you must claim the work as that of the Caliphate, for I may perish in the fight and for the cause, dying without fear, dying with the promise of the Prophet, blessings and peace be upon him. Please do not delay in this: let the infidels know that it was the Caliphate's sword that found their heart. This is just the beginning, as we know, and a warning for those who wish to take heed.

He posted the message, refreshed the page to be certain it was visible, and then he turned off the tablet, took it into the restroom, cracked the screen against the toilet tank, and let it soak in the sink until any hope of saving the device was gone. He left it in the trash and returned to his booth.

"More coffee?" The waitress was a redhead with blue eyes. Eli smiled at her.

"Absolutely. It's a beautiful day, don't you think?"

"A *gorgeous* day. Hope you'll get outside to enjoy it."

"Oh, yes. Trust me, I intend to enjoy the day."

When she was gone, he withdrew another tablet, powered it up, and went to a site called Sons of Freedom. There, under the identity of a forty-four-year-old gun expert and motorcycle mechanic named Joe Walden, he issued his next warning.

You all know I've got a connection who is BIG-TIME with military intel. I know I've got haters and doubters about that, but you're about to see the proof, and it's fucking scary if it's true. Those army boys are scrambling today to shut down some sort of MAJOR towel-head action. I got the warning. If all of you who call me a liar and say I'm full of shit are right, then nothing will happen, and I'll come back on here and admit it myself. But, boys? It's going down tonight. Don't know what, where, or when, but I got a feeling it's going to be big-league shit, and I don't mind telling you I'm fucking scared. I am sharing this so you all are prepared and because I love all you who are ready to fight for what is right. This shit is Islamic Jihad, ISIS or al-Qaeda or something just like them, and here's what I've been told, by a guy who'd be in Leavenworth in ten minutes if anyone knew he'd whispered a word to me: When it goes down, our fucking joke of a president is going to say that it wasn't anybody from the Middle East. He'll say it was AMERICAN BOYS. That's the truth. Or at least what I was told. Like I said, I'd rather be wrong than right, because if I'm right? Americans will be blamed for MUSLIM TERRORISTS. We are at fucking WAR then, you understand? So if something goes down tonight, and you hear it was anybody but the towel-heads, it's time to wake up and DO SOMETHING. War is coming. It's here. And I for one am not going down listening to a bunch of lies from pussy politicians who get backdoor deals from terrorist oil money. God bless you all.

Eli finished the note, read it again, and couldn't keep the smile off his face. The language was just right. He'd seeded the clouds of fear on each side, and when the news broke, the clouds would burst.

"You *are* enjoying the day!"

The waitress was back, wearing a big dumb grin. "I can see your smile from all the way across the room, mister. Nice to see a happy face."

"What's not to be happy about?" Eli said as he pushed Send. "It's a special day."

50

Janell used the satellite radio, their desperate-measures-only means of communication, from where she was parked behind an abandoned barn nine miles north of Doug Oriel's body. Eli answered quickly but his voice was soft and she wondered if Violet Novak was nearby. The thought of that trite, ignorant woman enraged her. She understood Eli's double life intellectually, but not emotionally. She hoped that her existence with Doug had troubled him in the same way.

"I'm en route but delayed," she said, and then she explained the situation in the simplest terms possible: Doug had threatened the cause; died for the cause. The rest was irrelevant.

He listened without interrupting. For a man of such power and command, he was always a patient listener. Today, though, the silence scared her. Not because she was afraid of him—theirs was a relationship that transcended fear, mocked fear—but because she knew the disappointment he was feeling.

"I was relying on his skill and his devices," he said at last. "Counting on them."

She winced. "I know. Do you think I don't understand that? I've been apart from you for *nine months* to ensure that we would have him. If there had been another option, any other, I would have taken it. There wasn't."

The silence went on even longer this time, and then he said, "I've never liked my contingency. It's been tried before, and without much success."

"But you have it. We've got to try it now. We must."

"Yes." He sighed. "Much pressure rides on the shoulders of my man Jay."

"Will he perform?"

"He's a motivated man."

"That's not an answer."

"Because there's no certainty. But Jay is no different than any other recruit. When faced with his worst fears, he will discover he is capable of more than he realized."

This was, of course, Eli's entire worldview—and their earliest bond, dating back to their first conversation in Rotterdam, when they'd shared a dark amusement over a world that promised progress born from hope but acted, again and again, out of fear. It was not an untested theory, and the years had validated it repeatedly. Still, she was uneasy. She knew nothing of Jay Baldwin.

"I'm sorry it's come to this."

"Sorrow rarely advances a cause," he said. "Proper action, however, always will. So let's look at the energy of this situation and determine how to mobilize it. There's a way to capitalize. There always is."

He explained the potential he saw, and as she listened to his instructions, she couldn't keep herself from smiling. It was brilliant, so perfect that it felt as if it had to have been planned, and to know that he had made this adjustment so swiftly, turning crisis into opportunity, was the ultimate illustration of what separated him from the common man.

"What the morning calls for," he said, "are as many Paul Revere riders as possible. They'll be ignored today, but by tonight? By tomorrow? They'll be forever remembered."

"I understand. I'll make sure the message goes out."

"Good. Doug will serve his purpose, as you say."

"Serve it better dead than alive. What about Markus Novak?"

"If he appears, he'll be killed by Garland."

Good news, but still she felt cheated. Novak belonged to her. Both Novaks, in fact.

"Everything is accelerated now," he said. "I can't delay. You know I would if that was possible, but at this point...we'd risk too much."

"I understand," she said, but a part of her died with the acceptance.

All of their time apart had been predicated on this day together. "I wanted to be there for the morning. I tried everything to be there."

His voice was tender when he spoke again, because he understood what it meant to her. "Dawn was trivial; dusk is critical. Join me then. We'll watch the world go dark together, and then we'll leave together."

Together. The word made her flush with anticipation.

"Give me the location," she said. "I won't be delayed again."

He told her which phone to power up and promised that GPS coordinates would be sent to it. From her current position, he estimated it would be most of a day's drive.

"Can you be there by sundown without taking risks?"

"Yes."

"Good. Approach from the south. You'll see me. We'll watch the train go through, and then we'll leave."

"Together," she said.

"Together," he echoed.

She shut her eyes. It had been years since she'd wept, but at that moment, she was close.

51

As Jay read the text message, the dread that had lived in the pit of his stomach since the day he'd come home to find Eli Pate sitting at his kitchen table bloomed into a cold wellspring that spread through his veins and filled his body.

This is the shutdown, he realized. *The time has come.*

He called his dispatcher and informed her that he was going to be out for the day, that he was feeling ill.

"You sure don't sound good, Jay."

He hadn't been trying to fake any symptoms, but his voice couldn't sound like that of a well man.

"No," he said. "No, I'm not doing too good at all."

"Stay home and get healthy, then."

"I'm working on it."

He hung up. The sun had risen bright and brilliant and he watched it and thought that the storm that had blown in the day before he met Eli Pate, when he and Sabrina had counted the blinking lights, waiting to see if Jay would be called out, seemed a thousand years ago. A different man had left the house on the day of the storm, and that man would never be seen again.

Jay already understood that.

He walked into the garage and to the cabinet that held his barehanding equipment, relics of a lost life. He couldn't climb anymore. That was what Pate didn't understand. He'd picked the wrong guy. He'd picked a fraud. Jay hadn't worked in the flash zone since Tim's funeral.

The hot suit, or Faraday suit, allowed the lineman to contact the equipment directly, instead of having to use a properly charged pole or some other technique. The current would pass through the suit and continue down the lines with none of the deadly disruptions in voltage. When you came into contact, you'd carry a half a million volts all around your body. It was an experience unlike any other in the world, and Jay had always felt strangely spiritual during those times, the way others might in a temple.

That was before he'd climbed up to retrieve his brother-in-law's corpse.

The suit—socks, trousers, jacket with hood, gloves—was made of a blend of flame-resistant Nomex and a microscopic stainless-steel fiber. In the 1830s, when Michael Faraday began the research that led to this suit, in a world that hadn't yet seen a lightbulb, he determined that he could coat a room with metal foil and stand within it, unharmed, as the electricity flowed. Linemen who did barehanding work referred to putting on the suit as "becoming metal." When Jay was encased in the suit, the voltage would pass through the steel mesh, meaning that Jay would energize to the same level as the lines.

He packed the suit in the backseat of the truck, then returned to the cabinet for his hot stick and the accessory bag, which was loaded with fuse pullers and wrench heads and shepherd's hooks, all the things that had once been the tools of his trade. He packed the cutting stick too. Jay assumed that Pate intended him to go up there and cut a live line. It was a terrible plan. The system monitors would know the instant it happened, and a crew would be sent to fix it. That crew would work fast. Power wouldn't be lost for long.

He took the hot stick, which was a long fiberglass pole filled with a special foam that allowed the lineman to reach out and contact the current. Distance was critical—the telescoping rod could elongate to ten feet, and Jay would want every bit of that. If you weren't working from a bucket truck or a helicopter, something allowing a lineman to be safely energized without having a contact to the ground, you'd vaporize if you entered the flash zone.

The flash zone was actually an insulation zone. High-voltage lines were exposed, cooled by the air and wind, which meant that the air and wind also carried some current, always affected by humidity. The higher the voltage, the larger the flash zone could become. With lines at five hundred thousand volts, Jay would never get close before the current discovered him and decided to use his body as a convenient means of doing the only thing it cared about—returning to the earth. With lines at lower voltage, the Faraday suit would protect him, but at half a million?

They'd have to identify him by his boots.

He put the hot stick and tool bag in the truck and then paused to handle the Nomex and steel-mesh suit, thinking of all the times he'd worked in it while the current crawled over him like a swarm of insects. Dangerous, yes, but he'd worked with poise and confidence. Until the day he saw Tim's face, or what had remained of it.

Jay dropped the suit, stumbled to the garage-floor drain, and vomited.

Eli Pate arrived two hours later, walking casually up the street from downtown Red Lodge. If he was concerned about watchers or a trap, he didn't show it. He looked every bit as calm as he had when Jay found him at the kitchen table.

"How are you feeling, Jay?" he said when the door was open. "Calm, cool, and collected? I hope so. It's a big day."

"Do I get to see her?"

Eli Pate smiled warmly as he shook his head. "Not just yet. Now, we've got plenty of catching up to do, I know, but let's stay in motion while we do it. You'll drive, per the norm. I'm more of the shotgun type of guy, you know?"

Jay said, "What do you actually want? What in the hell do you think this is going to accomplish? You might take the power out. They'll put it back on. And for what?"

Pate's smile didn't waver. "I'm the ultimate theorist, Jay. In a nation where people love to say that all they have to fear is fear itself, they have created quite fertile ground for terror. I'll take the power out and they'll put it back on, you say, simple as that. I'm not so sure I agree. When people are faced with events they can't understand, they rush for a narrative that explains it. Rush right past the truth. When the lights go out? I'm interested in seeing what stories come out of the darkness, my friend."

52

The engine sounds had come and gone again, but they hadn't returned, and it did not take long before Lynn Deschaine began to muse on the possibility of escape.

"How is the fence electrified? There's no way they have power lines out here. I don't hear generators running."

"A windmill. Violet is very proud of it."

"You're serious?"

Sabrina nodded. Her swollen nose prevented her from breathing except through her mouth, which left her throat dry and cracked, so even talking hurt.

"So if we stopped it from turning, we would cut off the power?"

Sabrina shook her head. "I doubt that. The windmill would feed batteries, I think. That way the current can be stored and controlled. Actually, that's not right. The current is always alive. The only thing that can be stored is power."

Lynn said, "Okay, I'll confess—I'm stone-stupid when it comes to electricity. I bought another charger for my phone once before I realized I'd accidentally turned off the power strip the original was plugged into. If a fuse blows, I'm calling an electrician. Who would probably tell me it isn't actually a fuse. This is the bad side of apartment living, I guess. I've always had the maintenance guys, right? I've never had to pause to learn. But there has to be another way to shut off the power to that fence without going right to the batteries or the circuit breaker or whatever."

"I don't think so."

"Sure there is. Did your husband ever talk about his work?"

"Of course."

"Okay. He's the guy who turns the power back on. So...why does it go off?"

"Jay does high-voltage repair. I don't think it's the same thing as this."

"Here they've got a power source, and they've got current traveling through wires. Isn't it basically a microcosm of what he does?"

Sabrina nodded slowly. It should be. Whether the power came from a nuclear plant or a windmill or a battery, the idea was the same—generation, transmission, distribution. Lynn's question was a good one: *Why does it go off?*

"Weather, usually," Sabrina said to herself.

"What?"

"I'm thinking of the causes of the outages. Weather. Limbs fall on lines, or trees knock them down completely, or there are what Jay calls the squirrel suicide bombers."

"Pardon?"

"Rodents making contact with a live wire. They'll get fried, and if the shock doesn't blow them clear and they get stuck in the equipment, it creates a fault."

"Why?"

"Because the system is set up to protect itself. Just like a fuse or a circuit breaker. If it encounters something that could create a larger problem, it shuts down. A breaker trips, a fuse blows, whatever. You ever notice how your lights blink sometimes before they go out completely?"

"Yes."

"That's the system trying to clear the fault. It will try two times. If you get two hard blinks, the next one won't be a blink. The next one is a shutdown, and it will be out for a while, because now they've got to send a crew out to fix it."

She was remembering their first home together, a crappy rental in Billings, Jay explaining this as they lay in bed. That was the first time he'd talked about the squirrel suicide bombers, tickling her neck, making a stupid squirrel sound that had made her laugh.

Lynn said, "See? You do understand it."

She supposed she did. At least the basics, at least a little more than most.

"So how do we create a fault that actually lasts?" Lynn asked. "One that doesn't immediately come back on or that can be fixed by flipping a breaker?"

Sabrina took a deep breath, tried to put herself back in that house in Billings. What caused outages beyond equipment failure? Animals, storms, limbs.

"Maybe we could throw a limb up on the fence?"

"Did you see any limbs out there?"

"No." Sabrina also wasn't sure that the system wouldn't just blow the limb clear, achieving nothing. The fault had to be one that lasted. What was bad, beyond equipment failure? Or, maybe a better question, what *caused* equipment failure?

She closed her eyes, remembering that warm, wonderful night in their first home together, Jay's fingertip tracing over her skin as he talked.

If two energized lines touch, say good night for a while. The system does not like that.

Okay. Line-to-line contact. But how did you make one of those copper wires touch another without getting shocked yourself? She hadn't seen any insulated electrician's gloves lying around. Again, the idea of throwing something onto the wires was possible, but whatever you threw would have to bridge the lines *and* be conductive, able to transmit electricity between the two. Water or a piece of metal or...

Sabrina lifted her left hand, her shackles jingling.

"How long is this chain?"

"What?"

"Three feet, maybe?"

"At least. Could be four. Long enough to let us stretch out and lie down. At least three."

Sabrina nodded. She mimed a tossing motion with her right hand, like pitching horseshoes.

She said, "I think I could do it."

"Do *what*?"

"Use our shackles to kill that fence. The live wires are bare, not insulated. They aren't spaced that far apart either. If I could toss these up there and get them to hook, we'd have line-to-line contact. That'll make things go dark in a hurry."

Lynn was watching her with fascination. "You're sure?"

"Positive."

"And you think you could make that toss? Because I doubt we'd have much time, and if it goes wrong, I don't want you electrocuting yourself."

"I don't want that either." She mimed the toss once more, then nodded. "I could do it. Tailgating experience."

"Pardon?"

"Horseshoes, beanbag toss, even darts. I always won those. I'm a tailgating champ." She had started to laugh, and not in a healthy way.

"This won't be a game," Lynn said, staring at Sabrina as if her sanity were slipping away. That was probably what it looked like, Sabrina realized, yet she couldn't stop laughing. Tailgating. That had been her life once, and not that long ago. Montana Grizzlies home games, loud music, beer in red Solo cups—that had been real? It couldn't have been real. She'd been born in shackles, hadn't she?

Lynn said, "You need to—" but Sabrina cut her off.

"It won't be a game," she said. The tears that had come to her eyes with the laughter were leaking down her cheeks now, and the laugh was gone. "I'll make it. If I get a chance, then I will make it. I can only control the second part."

"It would be best to do it in the dark, I think. When they'd have more trouble finding us."

"Yes."

"But we might not get to call that shot. They've got big plans for the day."

"It seems that way."

"So…are we agreed? Next time out, we try this?"

Sabrina's throat tightened and her stomach growled around cold acid. She couldn't conjure so much as a smile, let alone the wild laughter she'd just displayed. Her tears cooled and dried on her cheeks.

"Next time out," she said. It was supposed to be firm; it came out in a whisper.

"All right. We'll have to deal with Violet in here, though. She's taking us to the bathroom one at a time and locking doors behind her. Any attempt to come back will slow us down too much. When this happens, it has to happen fast."

"Right." Sabrina worked her tongue around her mouth, which had gone very dry.

"I'll take Violet, and I'll trust you with the fence. Sound right?" Lynn asked.

Sabrina just nodded. The thought of the attempt had stolen her voice. She was thinking of the chicken with the ruptured eye.

There are only two relevant parties now, Eli Pate had told her. *People and power. Who has power, and who deserves it.*

53

They stole an F-150 from the parking lot of a bar on the outskirts of Byron. The windows were open a crack, leaving it easy to get into, but it had been near the side of the building, not thirty feet from the door, and Mark was reluctant to try it.

"Somebody in there hears something, we're going to end up with a shitstorm on our hands, Uncle. And this is Wyoming—ten-to-one odds that everybody inside that place is packing."

"You're probably right," Larry said. "So I'd suggest we hurry with it."

It took Larry less than three minutes, and he didn't make much of a sound until the engine turned over.

"Do I want to ask why you're in such good practice?" Mark said.

"Just get in the damn truck. Remember, I was asleep in my own bed when you showed up this morning."

This morning. It seemed impossible that this was still the same day.

Mark climbed in the passenger seat, and they drove away from the bar and toward town.

"Pretty nice ride," Larry said. He had the window down and his arm resting on the door, relaxed as could be, no indication that he'd just stolen the truck.

"Isn't it neat how these modern ones can shift gears all by themselves?" Mark said. "I've heard the brakes even work without a rosary."

"You were more respectful when you were a kid."

They drove west, out of town. Mark was thinking of Lauren and Sabrina Baldwin, of Jay asking him what he'd have done for a second chance, when Larry threw the truck into a hard left turn.

"Whoa, here we go," Larry called. They'd been traveling at a good speed, and the truck fishtailed briefly but Larry straightened it out and they bounced along a gravel road that led away from the highway and toward the Shoshone River. A few miles later, the road curled out of the gulch and toward the river and Mark saw an RV parked beside a copse of scrub pines. It was a large, expensive model, at least forty feet long, black and gold, though the paint was covered by a thick layer of dust.

"Is that Scott Shields's?" Mark asked.

"Yes."

"Doesn't seem like he made it to Alaska."

"Nope." Larry cut the engine, and Mark saw that his gun was already in his hand. "And that gives me more than a few questions for him."

They got out of the truck. The sun was high in a cloudless sky and between that and the lingering dust from the truck's rattling ride, the place felt desertlike despite the pines. There were still patches of snow in all directions and yet the day had been sunburn-bright and plenty warm. Springtime in the Rockies.

Everything was still as a portrait. Mark could hear Larry's breathing. He stood stock-still, like a dog smelling the air, hackles up.

"There's a bad feel here," Larry said, and then he walked up to the door and knocked. "Scotty? Scotty?"

No answer. Also no vehicle beside the motor home, although hard-packed ruts made it clear that there was usually a truck there. Mark was just about to ask where Shields might be found in town when he saw the blood.

"Uncle."

Larry turned to him, and Mark pointed. Neither of them said a word as they followed the blood trail. It led from the tire tracks all the way to the front door.

Larry took his ball cap off, pushed his long hair back over his ears, put the cap back on, and bent the bill. He was bowstring-tense.

"Give me cover just in case," he said.

"No. I'll go in first," Mark said, but Larry ignored him and walked to the RV with a brisk stride. Mark was expecting him to at least try the door. Instead, he simply raised his boot and kicked it. The door held for the first kick and snapped open on the second, and Larry reeled back like he'd taken gunfire. Mark was just behind him in a shooter's stance, but he couldn't see anything.

"What's wrong?" he said a second before the answer arrived to Mark on the windless air.

The smell of death wafted out, pungent and nauseating. Larry gagged and spit into the dirt.

"Hang on," Larry said. He went to the truck and found two rags and splashed a small amount of motor oil on them. He brought the rags back along with two pairs of weathered canvas work gloves. His eyes were grim. "Let's have a look," he said, and then he put the gloves on and held the oil-soaked rag to his nose.

Mark followed. Mark took the gloves and the rag, and they walked through the dust and up the steps of the RV. Even against the oil, the smell was strong.

The steps led into a small living-room area with a built-in sofa, empty. To the right of that was a booth and a table, also empty, and then the driver's cab. The inside of the RV had the feel of the *Mary Celeste,* an abandoned ghost ship.

Except for that smell, and the streaks of blood along the floor.

Mark followed the streaks to an accordion door like those in airplane bathrooms. The door folded inward, and now the smell's source had shape. There was a dead man sprawled on the bed.

Mark couldn't see evidence of a killing wound until he took one step closer to the body, his stomach roiling, and saw a neat hole where each of the dead man's eyes belonged. Mark could look straight down through tunnels of black blood that carved through the brain and out of the skull and into the mattress below. Twin shots in the eyes. A .22, probably, held right up against the eye sockets.

"This is him?" Mark said. "Scott Shields?"

"That's him. Let's get out of here."

Larry stumbled away from the bedroom and out of the RV and

there were retching sounds from outside. Mark lingered inside, looking down into those empty eyes. Then he backed out of the bedroom, closed the door on the corpse of Scott Shields, and left the RV. The main door would no longer latch. Tonight, if the body wasn't moved, the animals that had been kept at bay would finally have a chance to feast.

Larry was all the way back by the truck, braced against the hood, spitting into the dirt. Mark walked up beside him and looked down the empty road. This time of year, caught between snowmobiling season and fishing season, there wouldn't have been many people passing by the RV.

"Who told you he was in Alaska?" Mark said.

"*He* did. He said he was headed out."

"So was he stopped from leaving, or was he lying to you?"

Larry frowned. "Scotty was a straight shooter with me."

"Did he know what happened when you tried to get Mom away from Pate?"

"Yeah, he knew."

"All right. Would he have lied to you to keep you out of the fire?"

"You're thinking that he wasn't through with Pate?"

"I'm asking."

Mark glanced back at the RV. "Strange place to leave him. That body could have been scattered all over these mountains by coyotes and bears by now."

"Pate left him there for a reason."

"What do you think that is?"

Larry turned and looked Mark squarely in the face. "So we could see the bones of those who came before us," he said.

For a moment neither of them spoke. A haze of dust rose in the distance, back toward the main road, but then it passed as the vehicle vanished in another direction. Mark checked his cell phone. He had a faint signal. They were standing at a murder scene and he had a cell signal. You called it in, that's what you did. That was the right thing, the only thing.

He pocketed the phone.

"We could go back to Cantu and try again," Mark said. "Let him know that we were unimpressed."

"You're unimpressed?" Larry said, wide-eyed.

"That we were not helped, at least. We're no closer to Pate."

"Cantu isn't going to talk much more than he already has."

"Not even with encouragement?"

"If you're prepared to go back there and take a hammer to the man's fingers and toes, pliers to his teeth, a drill bit to his kneecaps, he might talk. *Might*. Otherwise, he's said all he intends to say. My gut tells me that whatever fear we put into Sal won't be greater than the fear that already lives in him courtesy of Eli Pate."

Mark looked away, back at the RV. He was silent for a few seconds, then said, "What's this guy's role? Shields. He got crossways with Pate and he got killed, that's clear enough. But what was Pate's problem with him?"

"Your mother."

"What does Mom have that Pate could benefit from—and I don't need to hear any remarks about the obvious. Cantu himself said that didn't matter to Pate."

"Son, your mother doesn't have *anything*. Never did. You know that. She doesn't have a dime to her name."

Mark pointed at the RV where the dead man lay. "But he did."

"Scott had some money, sure, but not *that* much. Not killing money."

"Uncle, you know better than me that to the wrong man at the wrong time, ten damn dollars can turn into killing money."

"Not to Pate. He's just not that sort, not impulsive. If Eli killed Scotty, it wasn't a cash grab—and by the time this happened, Scotty wouldn't have had any cash left to grab, anyhow. What he did have he'd put into the hunting camp. And even that was risky. I knew that from the start. All he had was the land—no lodge, no equipment; hell, no good way to get there, even."

"The property is that hard to access?"

"Bet your ass it's hard to access. ATV or a horse. Maybe a tricked-out Jeep. Scotty was going to run horses for the hunting trips, the way he had up in Alaska."

"And Pate knew this place."

"Yeah."

"And now your friend Shields is dead, but it's a surprise to you."

"Only a surprise because—"

"You weren't looking for him," Mark finished. "He saw to that. We could consider that a coincidence, I suppose."

"But you don't believe it."

"I think it's a stretch."

Larry shook his head but didn't say anything. He was unconvinced, but he was also wondering now.

"When you talked to Shields and Pate," Mark said, "did they ever mention the word *Wardenclyffe* to you?"

Larry frowned. "No. What's that mean?"

"I think it's a place. I know people were looking for it."

"Never heard of it."

Mark looked again from Larry over to the RV, then up at saw-toothed mountaintops. The sun was angling down, unfiltered by cloud, burning the snowcap off the peaks.

"How far away is the hunting camp?"

"The drive isn't all that bad, but it's hiking once you get there, and there's nothing up there but woods and rocks and wind."

"When was the last time you saw the place?"

"Maybe seven months back."

"Okay. So who knows what's out at this rough property now? Pate has to be somewhere, Uncle. And he's not alone anymore. He's off the grid, and he needs to be hidden. The land sounds pretty good for hiding."

"It's surely that," Larry admitted.

"I want to take a look," Mark said. "If Pate's not impulsive, as you say, then he killed Shields with a purpose. Maybe the purpose was to keep him away from his own land."

Larry gestured at the RV. "What about this?"

"He's sat this long. He can sit longer. Same goes for Sal, in my opinion."

A ghost of a smile crossed Larry's face. "Yes."

They got into the truck and Larry fired up the engine. The smile was gone and his eyes were sorrowful as he studied the RV before putting the truck in gear.

"He was a good man," Larry said, "and he was a hard man. That's what worries me, Markus. Scott Shields was nobody's pushover. When you see a hard man left like that..."

He didn't finish, and he didn't need to. He'd already said it before, when he'd finished vomiting out the smell of his dead friend into the dust.

The bones of those who came before us.

54

S he sent the e-mails from the parking lot of a fast-food restaurant at an interstate stop in southern Wyoming. She hated not to be in motion, but Doug Oriel had some heavy lifting left to do.

Wording was key, and it took her a while to get it just right. She read it five times through, tweaking here and there, before she finally sent the message. Then she copied the text, pasted it into a fresh message, and sent it again. There were nine groups in all, ranging in size from five members to twenty-seven, reaching a total of more than two hundred heavily armed and deeply paranoid white men scattered across four states. Most were in Florida and Georgia, but there was a Texas contingent as well.

The note needed to convey the proper emotion, so she kept it terse, as close to panicked as possible.

Have any of you heard from Doug? I received a short phone call from him late in the afternoon. Police raided his house in Florida two days ago. All of his guns are gone. Confiscated. The house itself was burned. This was in Cassadaga. He told me the police will claim he murdered a woman there. He said he would not be surprised if he is implicated in another crime for every day that he stays free. He's afraid they have all of his contacts under surveillance. That is why I am warning you. I'm destroying this computer as soon as I send this message. You should do the same. Doug believes there is something big coming. I don't know what. He was scared, and not making much sense. Has anyone heard anything? Rumors, threats? I am afraid to be online, afraid that they will track me, if they aren't already. There is no news about him yet, but the house fire is real. Just search for Cassadaga and fire. You'll see it. There is also NO MENTION OF ANY GUNS BEING CONFISCATED. So they are already lying. I don't know what to do, but I won't use a computer or a phone. Not after what he told me. I don't know if he is still free or if they have him. I don't know what the "something big" means. I don't know ANYTHING except that the police have decided to move against Doug and when this ends he will be in prison for a crime he didn't commit and we all may be next. Everyone do what you feel is best . . . but be prepared for the worst. Doug thought he was, and look what happened to him.

I will contact you all when I feel it is safe. I have no idea when that will be. If you don't hear from me again, you can guess what happened.

PREPARE FOR THE WORST!!!

She hated exclamation marks but thought they served a critical purpose here. The message had a certain tripping rhythm, a stumbling hysteria, and she knew it would be effective. She'd met most of the men in these groups over her nine months with Doug, and they were almost always wild-eyed with burgeoning panic and twisting theories, even on a calm day. After this message, there would certainly be a blood-pressure spike. And then the grid would go down in the West, and they would remember the message, the vague warning of something big coming, and of government lies. From there . . .

Time would tell.

And she was running out of it if she wanted to join Eli by dusk.

55

Twenty-nine miles outside of Chill River, Eli Pate told Jay to turn off the highway.

They were in a basin, with mountains in the rearview mirror and empty big-sky country ahead. Foothills snaked up to the east, Jay saw out his window. Power lines traced the low points, carefully laid in the places of easiest access, even if that was a bit of a joke—there was no *easy* access to the lines in Montana in the wrong kind of weather, and when you needed to get to them, it was usually the wrong kind of weather.

"We wait here?" Jay said. It was a desolate spot but they were far from the lines and he could see no purpose for this location other than its isolation.

"No, no. I want you to watch something."

Pate reached into the backpack that rested between his feet and brought out a pair of binoculars. Zeiss, high-end. He lifted them to his eyes with one hand, the other still on the gun, finger still on the trigger. Jay followed the angle of the binoculars. There was a road far to the northeast, nearly out of sight to the naked eye. Beyond that, the countryside was empty. There was nothing to see, and yet Pate said, "Tremendous," and lowered the binoculars and passed them to Jay. "All yours, my friend. The show belongs to you."

"What am I looking at?"

"I'd recommend you watch the access road directly in front of you."

Jay lifted the binoculars and adjusted the focus. He finally found a single fir, neatly cut, leaning on the power lines at a forty-five-degree angle. It was just as they'd had in the Beartooths on the day all this had started, only down here there was no blizzard to contend with.

Jay thought, *It will take the boys all of ten minutes to clear that shit.*
"Cute work," he said.

"Keep watching," Pate said.

Jay kept watching. Nothing happened. His hands and eyes tired from the effort and he was about to ask just what in the hell he was supposed to see when dust appeared to the west. An oncoming vehicle. A few seconds later, it was close enough for him to identify: a bucket truck.

He'll lose his good humor when he sees them at work, Jay thought. *They'll have it fixed in less time than it took him to cut the tree down.*

The truck lumbered on down the road, the cloud of dust gathering in its wake like a storm. There was a dip where the road met a small runoff stream, but the water was low and there was a grate to make vehicle crossings easier. The truck would be able to get close to the tree, and the crew would make fast work of it.

He was about to say as much when the truck's front wheels made contact with the grate, and then it exploded.

Jay didn't immediately understand what had transpired. One instant the truck had been rumbling along and the next it was a mangled mess of broken metal and glass, and the cattle guard itself seemed to be inside out.

"What did you do!" Jay shouted, and Eli Pate laughed, low and soft and extremely pleased.

"I should have kept the glasses. You got all the fun. A good show, it seems?"

Jay had actually moved the binoculars away, but now he lifted them again and, in horror, panned the landscape until he located the truck.

"You planted a bomb for them," he said. His voice was hollow. All of him was.

"Not at all. Take a closer look, Jay. That is simple technology at its finest. Trapped energy. That is all we did. We coiled the energy that the world is filled with, and we let it speak for itself."

Through the lens, Jay could see what was left of the truck—the front and back ends were intact but it was crushed in the middle as if pinched between a giant's thumb and index finger. One man struggled to crawl out of the passenger window. His blood ran down the remnants of the door panel and joined a pool of steaming fluids dripping out of the engine. He was fighting past something that at first appeared to be a part of the wreckage, but then Jay saw that it wasn't a piece of the truck but rather the steep, angled sides of the grate. They had snapped shut on the truck like a wolf's jaws.

"Why?" Jay said. "For the love of God, what is the point of this?"

"Not the love of God, Jay. The absence of one. Absence of both love and God, actually. I hate to shatter any illusions you might have previously held, but the world you occupy is a cold one, and no one listens. No one cares."

He sounded restful, an old man on a porch chair, close to dozing off.

"You had questioned the thoroughness of my approach. You don't need to tell me that; I've seen it on your face from the start. So let's discuss it now. I'd appreciate your review. Your beloved bride will *certainly* appreciate your review. Understand?"

Jay held the binoculars half raised, staring at the carnage in the distance. Without the zoom, it looked like nothing more than a dust cloud.

"Within the next few hours," Eli Pate said, "a number of utility trucks are going to meet with problems in very desolate locations. I expect that will create a strain on manpower, not to mention equipment. But your kind is used to crisis. They will respond. While they deal with these problems, my own crews will reassemble elsewhere. They're equipped with grid maps and a fine understanding of the most remote areas on the system. They could continue to cut trees and create faults, of course, but that is so frivolous, child's play. What they will do instead is wait for you. Because when you take down the transmission lines from Chill River, what will happen?"

"A massive outage," Jay said. His voice sounded disembodied.

"Exactly. And think about all the lines out there that will suddenly be dead, harmless. Now imagine what fast work one could make with chain saws on the actual utility poles themselves. Without any risk from the current, I think they can bring down *many* lines in a hurry. And my understanding is that your sophisticated computer monitors won't know where this is happening, because the system monitors depend on the current to identify the problems. But there will be no current, and therefore they will be blind. Am I correct so far?"

He was correct. He was also brilliant. Taking the transmission lines out would cause a massive problem, but it would be temporary. If he had teams working with chain saws in the mountains, though, taking down line after line, and then transmission was reenergized with no idea of all the faults that awaited... Jay could picture the grid map on his office wall, and he thought, *Good night, Seattle. Good night, Portland.*

"I'm no fool," Eli Pate said. "I know that they'll send for help and that they'll get those transmission lines back up. But with all those unknown faults scattered about the mountains, what will happen when they reenergize the transmission lines, Jay?"

"The system will try to shift loads. Frantically. And by doing that, it will create more problems. Cascading outages. You'll lose cities. You'll lose states, maybe."

He sounded like a man beneath an interrogation lamp, admitting what he didn't want to admit.

"That," Eli Pate said, "was always my idea. And I'm going to share a little secret, Jay. This is only the start. But I'll be true to my word. If you take out those transmission lines, you will live to see your wife again. That doesn't bother me in the least. In fact, I rather look forward to the media broadcasts of your account of your time with me. It will be fun to watch. Except..." He snapped his fingers. "Damn. It will be awfully hard to find a functioning television in this part of the country. Alas, the price of success."

Jay lifted the binoculars to his eyes again and saw the man who'd climbed free was looking back inside the truck, trying to help the others. Another survivor reached for help from inside the ruins of the truck, reached for the man who'd already escaped.

The bloody arm he extended no longer had a hand.

56

The route Larry took away from the corpse of Scott Shields led them back through and toward the Bighorn Mountains.

"Fastest way would be up and over," he said, "but the pass is still closed with snow at the top. We gotta head south, go through Greybull. The property is private land that abuts the national forest. It's basically cut off from everywhere in the winter and not much easier to access in the summer. You could develop it, I suppose, but it's expensive to build out there. I can't even imagine a figure on utilities. Just to run electric would be plenty of work, and plenty of dollars. But it was good empty land. You know I've always liked good empty land."

He was too chatty, considering what they'd come from and where they were bound, but Mark understood it, remembered it. Larry had always talked more when he didn't want to dwell on reality.

"I'm sorry," Mark said.

"What?" Larry looked genuinely confused.

"I'm sorry that I showed up on your doorstep this morning. Why are you even doing this? You've committed enough crimes today to put yourself in lockup for a long while, Uncle. Why?"

Larry frowned, glanced at him. "You said they murdered your wife, Markus."

"You didn't even know her."

"You're still family."

"Not the kind who has been any help to you."

Larry's eyes were back on the road. "That's not how I look at it, son. You were brought up wrong. I had a part in that, I know."

"You had the good part. You tried to balance Mom."

"Hell, I didn't provide any balance. We were just different kinds of messes, my sister and me. Our brother too. Ronny and Violet and me, well, we stuck together better than most, I suppose, but I don't think we would have if it hadn't been for you. What you needed, none of us knew how to give. But we got something from trying. You'll never understand that." He gave a bitter bark of a laugh. "You know I look back on when you were nothing but a baby, back before you could so much as stand without help, and I think that's why I got clean. Because you needed me. Needed us. But my definition of *clean* would be most men's filthy. All the same... I think I got closer than I would have been because of you, Markus. Maybe even stayed alive because of you. I was in a bad way when your mother had you, and when Isaac skipped, what I wanted to do was kill the son of a bitch, but that wasn't an option. Why? Because you needed your ass wiped. And so I stayed and tried to help. And trying to help was good for me."

Mark said, "Isaac?"

"Shit. It's been so damn long, I guess I slipped," Larry said. He was casual, as if giving a name to an unknown father were a small thing. "He might not even have been the boy. I hate to put it that blunt for you, but that's the way it was. He was the most likely candidate, I guess you'd say. He was leading the polls."

"You knew him."

"Mostly what I knew was that he'd skipped out when he knew your mother was... well, in her condition."

"Pregnant," Mark said. "That was her condition. He knew it when he left?"

Larry's face twisted. "Shit, son, I don't rightly recall how it went or how it didn't. I'm not saying you didn't get shortchanged by not having a father around, but you didn't lose anything by missing out on *that* guy. He was the type who attracted your mother, full of bullshit tales that she wanted to believe."

"What kind of tales?"

"He was a psychic," Larry said with mock seriousness. He looked at Mark for camaraderie in the ridicule, but Mark was thinking of the boy from Cassadaga telling him he belonged in the camp, and the best he could manage was a wry smile.

"For a psychic," Larry said, "he sure was surprised by that pregnancy test."

Mark exhaled and turned toward the open window so the wind blew harder into his face, making him squint.

Larry glanced at him and said, "I don't mean to go on about that. None of it matters. Not him, not even your mother. You got out from under it, from under all of us, and you did damn well for yourself. I'm proud to know it."

Mark thought of his condo the way it had once looked, bright and shining, thought of Lauren and her new Infiniti and her law-school degree, and he thought of his own job. He had done well for himself. That was not a lie. And yet, by the end of today, he might be handcuffed beside a stolen truck and headed to a remote jail in the Rockies.

"You said it right earlier, Uncle."

"Pardon?"

"Every man has a different definition of *clean*," Mark said. "And I've found it's tough to hold your anchor on that one. Even when you think you've got it...there's something you haven't counted on blowing toward you in the wind. Always. And when it gets there? Well, you might find your position sliding then. You might find it sliding fast."

Larry didn't answer. For several miles neither of them spoke. They passed through Greybull and headed east, chasing those mountains, which grew larger and taller and starker with each passing mile.

"I'm sorry that wind blew you back here," Larry said finally. "But we'll find the son of a bitch you need, and we'll get him to answer for your wife's murder."

"Sure we will."

"She was something special, wasn't she?" Larry said. "I can feel it. Hell, I just know that. From the way you...I just know it, that's all."

"Yes," Mark said, rubbing the old dive permit between his thumb and index finger. "She was something special."

The engine's throaty growl labored, rising to a whine as the road steepened on its climb into the mountains, and Mark found that it was hard for him to hold Lauren's face in his mind. She seemed very far away.

57

The place Pate led him to was down a dirt lane through rugged prairie land, fifteen miles away from the nearest town and twenty from the Chill River power plant.

It was, unfortunately, the perfect choice. The transmission lines were equipped with motion-activated cameras in the ranges close to the power plant and the substations, but this stretch in the middle distance was a floater—the kind of stretch that was far too common in the country. Critical infrastructure, absolutely, but monitored? Not exactly.

"Before we get out of the truck," Pate said, "let's take a bird's-eye view of the area, shall we? What do you see, Jay?"

What Jay saw was simple—a cut between mountains that provided access for all things human, all things that the natural countryside rejected. Cars, trains, electricity.

"Speak," Pate said.

"I see transmission lines. And mountains." The mountains were so massive that they threw off distance assessment. They seemed much closer than they were.

"Come on, Jay. You've got to see more than that."

"Prairie. Trees. Train tracks."

"Have you heard of Jason Woodring?" Pate asked.

Jay shook his head.

"He's in prison now. A lone wolf, and an unsuccessful one. But what he did was quite fascinating. He looked at the intrusions on the land and decided to use one to help destroy the other."

Jay saw it then and was surprised he hadn't recognized it earlier—the human path west had been hard earned, ripped from rugged lands, and the various stages of progress followed the same path. First the rock had been removed for train tracks, then roads had been paved. Then power lines erected. Then cell towers. In inhospitable country, everyone tried to make use of the same access points.

"You want to use a train," he said.

Pate laughed. "Very good! But I don't want to use just *any* train. I want to use a coal train. The very one that feeds the plant that feeds those lines. I doubt anyone will appreciate the wit in that, but, nevertheless, I try."

He leaned forward, holding the gun in his left hand while he pointed with his right.

"There are four reels of aircraft cable hidden in those trees. Stainless-steel cable that will hold at least ten thousand pounds, and there's several hundred feet of it. Anchor rings are bored into the trunks. The cables need to run from those anchor points up to the towers. They can't make contact with the tracks themselves; that will trigger an alarm. You will secure them to the towers. Do you follow?"

Jay did. He also knew it wouldn't work. Pate had underestimated the strength of the towers. They would not come down. The cables would snap long before the towers moved.

Pate said, "Now I'm going to make a confession, Jay. These cables were a contingency, not the prime option. Your original task was to climb up there and install plastic explosives on the insulators. The towers never needed to come down. It was, if I do say so myself, a far superior vision, more sophisticated. But not all things today have gone according to plan. You know how that feels, don't you? The way you can open the door and find unanticipated trouble? That's where I am. So we come to the contingency, and to a critical juncture for your bride. This approach with the cables is not one in which I have a high degree of confidence, but for Sabrina to see tomorrow's sunrise, it will need to work."

"No," Jay said. "No, that's not fair, because it won't work. I can't fix that."

"Not fair? Come on. You're past issues of fairness. It's time to think of solutions. Why won't it work?"

"The towers are too strong. They're not going to come down."

"I'll let you in on a secret. Do you know how that steel is held together?"

"By bolts."

"Exactly! I was delighted with that discovery. They reminded me of an Erector set I stole when I was a boy. Such clean and classic work. I learned from models, Jay. I still do. But back to the point—these are strong towers because the steel is joined by the bolts. However, when you get closer, you're going to notice something. Many of those bolts are missing. My goodness, they do not come out easily! But it can be done. And it already has been done."

Jay's throat constricted. All of his confidence that the cables would snap and the train would carry on was gone now. Yes, they would snap, but first, they would tug. And if the structures were already primed to tumble...

It might work.

"I don't travel without a backup plan," Pate said cheerfully. "So my thought is, if you get high enough, Jay, it's a different scenario, don't you think?"

It certainly was.

"You're going to need to get very high," Pate said. "Otherwise the leverage won't be enough, and those towers will stand firm when the train goes by. That was Jason Woodring's problem. He ran just one cable, and it was too weak, and he only went about twenty-five feet up the tower. Now he sits in prison, and the tower never came down. But if he'd gotten higher and worked with better equipment and more cables? Different story. As I say, it's worked with my models. Many tests. Simple yet effective."

Jay saw his brother-in-law's face again. Tim had been a jovial guy, usually smiling, his eyes always seeming to laugh at a joke that hadn't been told yet. At the end, though, he'd had no eyes at all.

"If I climb too high, I'll carry those cables into the flash zone," he said. "That's the problem. If I get too high, I'll die because the air it-self is electrified up there."

"I understand. It's a dangerous world up there. Why do you think we stopped with the bolts below? It requires a high level of education and skill to maneuver around a half a million volts. That's where you come in. Others have tried to take these towers down, and they're all in prison cells. Why? Because they thought like men with boots on the ground. They needed to think like birds. Birds can sit on a live wire and survive. You know who else can do that?" Pate smiled and pointed at him. "*You* can."

"I don't climb anymore," Jay said. He could remember that smoke rising from Tim's open mouth, as if a cigarette were burning some-where inside him. His insides were gone, boiled away by his own blood. That had been on a sixty-nine kV line. A fraction of the power Jay was staring at now.

"That's going to cause some trouble for Sabrina."

The highest Jay had made it up a tower after Tim was killed was seventy feet. He'd frozen there, then finally climbed back down while his crew found other places to look, either down at their boots or off into the horizon. Later, there was no ridicule, no taunting. Just soft-spoken, kind remarks, pats on the shoulder, nobody making eye contact. It was only three weeks after Tim's funeral, and everyone said it was natural, bound to happen, he just needed a little more time. But they all knew he was done, knew it probably before he'd admitted it to himself. Certainly before he'd told Sabrina that he was looking at the foreman's job in Red Lodge because he didn't want to put her through the stress of worrying about him.

You coward.

Of all the sins he'd committed in his life, that was the worst. Claim-ing her as the reason, unable to admit his own weakness, his own terror. She would have let him continue the work for as long as he'd wished. She was stronger than him.

"The options at this point are very few, I'm afraid," Eli Pate said.

Jay said, "It's not possible."

"It's that sort of thinking that ails the world. I'm not interested in notions of impossibility. You climb or Sabrina dies. Now, as you are well aware, you could climb and die. But she's not involved then. It's your choice, Jay. Do you put her life at risk today or not?"

Jay said, "I can do it." He wasn't speaking to Pate. He was speaking to himself. And he knew he was lying.

58

It was well into the afternoon before anyone returned to the cabin, and when someone did, it was Violet, and she was alone. She carried the small solar lantern, which cast a dim glow. Sabrina waited for her to begin preparing food or ask if they needed to use the outhouse. Instead, she brought the lantern directly to Lynn and stopped a few feet away from her, staring down.

"You should not lie," she said.

"I haven't."

"Yes, you have. My son is not with you. That's not possible. That is a lie designed to distract me from my purpose."

"You know that he's here," Lynn said. "It wasn't a coincidence that he walked out of a motel room at three in the morning. He's his mother's son. Tell me this—did he help kill his own wife? Did she try to stop you; did she know too much?"

Violet gave a small shake of her head, but it didn't appear to be a denial of the statement so much as a desire to push it aside.

"I can't hear stories like this," she said. "Not today. Of all days, not today."

Lynn looked confused. "What's the point of the game?" she said. "Why are you pretending? We both know the truth. I came here with him, and he set me up. I know it, and you know it."

Sabrina didn't think Lynn sounded entirely confident about that. The words said one thing, her tone another.

"If this is real," Violet said, "tell me something about him. Something that all your data theft and eavesdropping wouldn't provide. You aren't able to do that, are you?"

Lynn glanced at Sabrina. Lynn's face was still perplexed, but she also seemed to want to rise to the challenge.

"He's your son," she said. "I don't know anything about him that you don't."

"Exactly." Violet stepped back, pleased. She ran her palms over her jeans like she was dusting herself off, then turned and stepped toward the door, but she wavered like a drunk trying to walk a straight line. She was halfway across the room when Lynn spoke.

"He still listens to the chant music."

Sabrina had no idea what she was talking about, but Violet looked like she'd touched that electrified fence.

"I think he hates that he loves it," Lynn said, "because it reminds him of you. Of a place called Medicine Wheel? Does that mean something to you?"

A tremor worked through Violet's face. She didn't speak. Lynn let the silence build, and Sabrina felt an excruciating need to break it, to shout at both of them. Very slowly, the older woman turned to Lynn.

"What does he think happened to his wife?" she asked.

Lynn hesitated. "What he tells people is that Garland Webb killed her."

Violet returned, the lantern bobbing in her hand, tossing light. She moved in a rush, dropping to her knees at Lynn's side.

"Garland is only a *suspect,* a product of lies. They moved her body, *your* people did, all a lie, all to stop us. You know that, all of your people trade in lies, imprison innocents over lies, go to war over lies, build empires over lies! She was never in Cassadaga!"

Lynn's voice was a half whisper when she said, "I've seen the photos, Violet. She died in a ditch in Cassadaga. Her blood was fresh and her car engine was warm. Nobody moved her there."

"That is *exactly* what Eli told me you would say!"

"That's because Eli is shithouse crazy."

"Don't you say that!" Violet leaned closer, her eyes wild and glittering in the light, her finger extended, pointing in Lynn's face. "What he hears from the earth is the truth, and I will not be told—"

Lynn Deschaine moved in a blur of speed so fast Sabrina didn't even see her first strike, only the result—Violet's head snapping upward, whiplashed by a blow under the chin. The second strike was a kick that caught her on the side of the head and knocked her into the wall.

She was unconscious when she fell.

"Got a little too close, bitch," Lynn Deschaine said. Then she reached for Violet with her free hand, only to be brought up short by her chain. She turned to Sabrina.

"Help!"

Sabrina was staring at her in shock. When they had discussed their plan of escape, Lynn had made no mention of what was now obvious—she was trained in some kind of martial arts.

And she was *very* fast.

"Keys!" Lynn hissed. "Get her damn keys!"

Sabrina finally went into motion, stretching out to grab Violet's arm. She tugged her forward and Violet moaned softly but didn't move. Lynn saw the keys in her hip pocket, pulled them free, fumbled at the cuff around her wrist, and promptly dropped the keys. Before Sabrina could reach for them, they were in Lynn's hand, and Lynn had her cuff off, and then, in another blur of speed, she rolled Violet over and fastened it to her wrist and clamped the cuff shut.

That fast, the captor had become the captive.

"Hold still," Lynn said, and then she unlocked Sabrina's cuff and removed first the end in the bolt in the wall, then the one around her wrist.

They were free.

"My God," Sabrina said. "How did you do that?"

"I just needed to get her close, but I wasn't sure how. I guess Mark works well for that." She paused. "I don't know what to believe about him. Not anymore." Then she shook her head, got to her feet, and helped Sabrina to hers. When they were standing, she didn't loosen her grip on Sabrina's arm, but tightened it to a nearly painful level. Her eyes seared into Sabrina's.

"Are you ready?"

Sabrina could only nod.

Lynn handed her the cuffs. "Then let's get out of here."

As Violet moaned behind them, they went to the door. Lynn found the right key without difficulty, ratcheted the dead bolts back. She hesitated then, the first and only hesitation she'd shown in the astounding sequence; she'd been so competent, so confident. Now she looked unsure, and Sabrina understood why—everything beyond the door was unknown.

"Straight to the fence," Lynn said. "Run straight and run fast. Then when it comes to the fence…"

She looked over her shoulder, and Sabrina nodded. The cuff that had become so familiar around her wrist felt strange in her palm.

"I'll take care of the fence," she said. Her voice was confident. Her heart wasn't.

Lynn's chest rose and fell with a deep breath. "Okay. Once we're over the fence, just run like hell. We'll try to stay together, but…if there's shooting, then we'll separate."

If there's shooting. Sabrina felt bile rise in her throat and swallowed it down.

"Okay," she said.

Lynn squeezed her arm again, then pulled the door open.

Sabrina was ready for anything—guards, gunfire, Eli Pate looming in the doorway. Instead, there was only a wide-open expanse leading down to the fence. No one was in sight.

"Run," Lynn whispered.

Sabrina ran. The stiff and wooden muscles didn't slow her. Pure terror overpowered the aches, driving her forward. If anything, she felt *too* fast, as if her speed would send her tumbling down the hill. She reached the fence several strides ahead of Lynn and pulled up short—*just* short, almost colliding with it.

The electrified hum was louder here. She stared at those exposed copper wires, remembering the explosive impact of her first attempt. Beside her, Lynn was breathing heavily but didn't speak.

The copper strands were held in place by brackets that protruded maybe two inches away from the fence, providing a small gap that would allow the cuffs to hook and hold. It was not much space. But it could be enough, if her toss was accurate.

Two live wires, Sabrina. Bridge them with a conductor and you will cause a fault. It will work, it will work, it will work.

And make that toss count.

Sabrina adjusted the handcuffs so she was holding them spread as wide as the chain would allow. It was long enough. If she hit it right, it was long enough to bridge the two lines. Just a matter of—

Lynn said, "He sees us. He's coming."

Sabrina looked back and saw Garland Webb behind the cabin, in the direction of the pole yard. He started running.

"Hurry!" Lynn said.

Sabrina turned back, and though hurrying certainly sounded good, she knew she would get only one chance and couldn't rush it. She mimed the toss, like a practice swing, gauging the weight of the cuffs and envisioning how they would fall.

Please God, please God, please God...

She repeated the exact same motion, but this time, at the top of her extension, she released the cuffs. They flew up, arced down, and the top cuff collided with the top copper wire and whipped around it in a flare of sparks.

Not enough. It wrapped too tight and now it will not be long enough to—

When the bottom cuff swung back and made contact with the lower wire, sparks weren't all that came—there was a loud, clear *boom* somewhere behind them, and then the hum was gone.

It worked. Holy shit, it worked.

Lynn said, "Is it safe?"

Sabrina reached out with a shaking hand and touched the copper.

Nothing. Just cool, harmless metal.

"It's safe."

"Then let's go!"

Lynn began to climb to Sabrina's left—she was *so* fast, scrambling to the top in a blink, while Sabrina's right foot slipped as she struggled to get past the dangling handcuff. There were three strands of barbed wire at the top of the fence, but Lynn swung her leg over them without hesitation. Sabrina could see that the wire had raked her badly, but Lynn didn't show any reaction. She paused at the top. She was looking behind Sabrina and could see what Sabrina could not.

She screamed, *"Hurry!"*

Sabrina *was* hurrying, but when she reached the top of the fence she couldn't immediately ascertain how Lynn had swung over the barbed wire so easily. It was angled in, and just to get a grip seemed impossible, as if it would require holding the actual barbs for support. Then she saw that there was a post just a few feet to her left. Lynn must have used that.

Sabrina struggled sideways, reached with her left hand, and had just wrapped it around the post when Lynn screamed again, no words this time, just a *scream,* and then a hand closed around Sabrina's ankle.

She thought, *I just need to hold on to the fence,* but in the instant that she tried to tug her captured foot free, she was jerked down in a single motion, whipped backward with tremendous power. She not only felt her ribs break when she hit the ground but heard them, and then Garland Webb was looming above her, his face furious, his fist balled. The fence rattled and Sabrina saw that Lynn was actually trying to climb back down.

"No!" Sabrina rasped. *"Ruuun!"*

She saw Lynn hesitate, and then Garland Webb's massive fist hammered down and she saw nothing at all.

Part Four

THE FLASH ZONE

59

The territory where Larry drove them was a rugged stretch along the southern face of the Bighorns, not far from the Cloud Peak range, not all that far from Medicine Wheel.

They'd climbed steadily on the rural roads outside of Greybull, and the prairies and plateaus of Lovell and Byron were forgotten—this was mountain country, and it hadn't heard any rumors of spring yet. Splashes of scattered snow gradually turned into snowbanks lining the road. They were deep in the woods and the country was just as desolate as Larry had promised, but it was also not empty. They had seen countless tracks on their way in. ATVs, mostly. One set of truck tires.

Eventually, Larry left the road entirely, putting the truck in four-wheel drive and navigating a boulder-strewn path that had Mark's back aching and his teeth clacking. They followed this for a mile that felt like fifty, and then Larry almost hung up the truck. He put it into four-low and the tires roared ruts into the snow, the truck leaning at a precarious angle before it finally found purchase and kicked them loose. From there, the ride was too rough for talking. The only words spoken came from Larry after they had clipped one snow-covered rock with enough force to bounce them both into the air: "Glad the fella we stole this from had a skid plate."

Larry stopped when the boulder-strewn path turned to sheer slope and they saw the white Silverado in front of them.

"Well, now," Larry said softly. "You got some special instincts, Markus."

His gun was already in his hand.

They got out of the truck quickly and quietly, staying low as they advanced to the Silverado. It was empty, and when Mark touched the hood, it was cold against his palm. The woods were silent except for the soft sounds of a stream a hundred yards away. The steep slope ahead of them was laced with even more tracks.

"A lot of traffic going up there today," Mark said.

Larry squinted at the summit. "Are my eyes playing tricks on me, or are those telephone poles?"

Mark shaded his eyes and stared for a few seconds before he said, "Those sure as hell look like poles."

"If anybody up there has a scope..."

"Yeah. Let's get into the trees in a hurry."

There weren't many trees to speak of. The closest was a cluster of three dead lodgepole pines that had lost their branches and pointed upslope like waiting missiles.

Mark returned to the truck for Larry's rifle and then ran in a crouch into the trees, where Larry had already taken up position at the base of a towering fir. Mark sighted on the summit. The telephone poles came into stark relief immediately—they were outfitted with transformers and insulators, but no lines.

"This would be the place," Mark said.

"Pass it here and let me look."

Mark lowered the rifle and extended it to Larry reluctantly. Without the scope, he felt clueless as to what was going on up above, and exposed.

Here on the side of the slope, sheltered only by the fir and a small rise that had a higher snowbank than the surrounding ground, they would be easy targets for someone firing on them from above, and going in any direction required side-hilling, moving across the steep grade and over the snow. The change in altitude created a remarkable change in environment; the hot dusty road and glaring sun where Mark had traded fire with Garland Webb seemed as far away as Cassadaga now. The snow also meant that they'd be leaving obvious tracks.

It was quiet on the hillside, the sounds of the stream farther away, but everything seemed intensified somehow, from those soft water noises to the feel of the breeze and the smell of the snow. Mark's hands were cold and numb, and even the tingle in his flesh felt stronger than it should have. All of his senses seemed unusually sensitive, sharp.

"We could work up that gulch," he said, blowing on his hands. "Getting there, we'd be pretty exposed, but once we're in it, we'll have protection. Looks like it leads all the way up, almost."

Larry had just returned his attention to the scope when a scream came from up above. It wasn't loud; it was so faint, in fact, that both of them looked at each other with a question, as if needing confirmation. Then another came, and while it was still soft, there was no mistaking it.

"We're either too late," Larry said, "or just in time."

He returned the rifle to his shoulder and lowered his eye to the scope. Mark ached for it, their only set of eyes here.

After a few seconds of silence, Larry said, "There's a woman up there, and she's running like hell."

"Anyone behind her?"

"Not that I see, but the way she's moving, she expects there is."

"Which way is she headed?"

"Toward the gulch. Maybe two hundred yards away. Shit, she just fell."

"I need to see her," Mark said, crawling closer. "I need to see if I know her."

Larry didn't want to turn over their only pair of eyes any more than Mark had, but he gave up the rifle. Mark put his eye to the scope but couldn't find the woman.

"Two hundred yards to our left?"

"About. There's a swale in the trees. She's trying to work her way down it."

Mark found the swale and panned up and down it but saw nothing and was about to ask for more guidance when he caught a flash of motion. He moved the scope back toward it and caught the woman in the crosshairs.

It was Lynn Deschaine, and up on the summit, two men had emerged in pursuit of her.

60

Putting on the Faraday suit had once felt like putting on a knight's armor. Now it felt like putting his head in a noose.

Jay had climbed towers more times than he could count. Even his worst nightmares about what could go wrong on them hadn't involved a train pulling them down with live lines sparking the whole way, but now it was his job to make that happen.

"Have you ever considered how fascinating electricity's desire is?" Pate asked as Jay dressed. "We force it up on those lines, but what does *it* want to do? What *will* it do if given an instant's chance? Go to ground. Return to the land."

Jay didn't answer. He was fastening the grounding strap that connected his pants to his jacket to prevent any separation of the suit. Even something that small could be the difference between coming down alive or smoking.

Pate handed Jay a radio. "You'll be operating on my frequency now." Then he pulled a pair of canvas gloves from his hip pocket, put them on, and grabbed the free end of one of the spools of stainless-steel cable.

"Time to climb, Jay. Be safe up there. There's a lot riding on it."

With Pate paying out the cable behind him, Jay walked to the base of the massive steel tower.

One hundred and ten volts could kill a man if he made a mistake. The lines above Jay carried more than four thousand times that much electricity. He would never have free-climbed in a situation like this—there'd be a bucket truck, extra safety equipment, a full team. Sometimes there'd even be a helicopter. At the very least, there'd be a rope system.

Today, he free-climbed, pulling the aircraft cable behind him. He'd fastened the end of it to his hot stick and used a piece of hot rope to fashion a sort of sling so the hot stick rode against his back and allowed him to have both hands free. Almost immediately, not even ten feet off the ground, his legs began to shake and his pores opened, his skin slick with sweat against the Faraday suit.

At least it was steel. Tim had died on a pole, not a tower, and the tower felt more stable, certainly. The latticed steel towers were built in a way that made climbing both simple and dangerously inviting. Early in his career, he'd responded to a call-out on a steel tower. A kid had climbed up to the first arm to sit and drink beer. They'd found several empties resting peacefully, and the kid's charred corpse blown eighty feet away. The prevailing theory was that he'd sat in safety for long enough that he grew comfortable and his bladder grew full, and then he'd gone to take a leak, unaware that he was near the flash zone. He'd been electrocuted with his own piss.

That was on a solid tower. As Jay climbed this one, dragging behind him the cable that was to be used as a snare wire for a train, he could see where the enormous bolts had been removed. Eli Pate was right—it was clean and classic technology, and it was also simple technology. Over the years, security experts had become increasingly concerned about possible cyber attacks on the grid. Jay was aware of high-dollar and high-tech efforts to enhance the computer security on every level.

He doubted that any of those security experts had ever looked at the towers, studied the individual bolts, and considered a child's Erector set.

The idea that it would be such antiquated and simple thinking that brought down a system of ever increasing sophistication suited Pate's cruel amusement perfectly. While the grid experts rushed to write new code and produce dazzling layers of encryption and firewalls, Eli Pate had picked up a wrench.

There was a horrifying genius to thinking small.

This explains his boots, Jay realized. Pate wore those battered but expensive boots that didn't contain a trace of metal, and Jay hadn't understood why before, but now he did—Pate had gone up on the towers at least far enough to weaken them, and he'd been cautious, as he was about everything. Pragmatic. He had worn the right gear and he had not gone up high enough to risk encountering the current.

For that, he'd selected Jay.

Initially, Jay tried to count the number of missing bolts and analyze their leverage points as he climbed. That soon increased his fear, though, so he stopped. Even under the circumstances, he still felt the stomach-clenching sense of awe that the towers provided. He'd always thought it was different in Montana, where the big sky was so damn vast that the transmission structures seemed almost laughable, the notion that they powered this territory nearly impossible to believe because they looked so flimsy, almost foolish, set against the Rocky Mountains. In cities where skyscrapers dominated the landscape, maybe a lineman could feel like he really ran the show. In the Rockies, though, Jay always had the sense that he was just part of the team that kept a long con game in play. Whenever nature wanted to bring things to a stop, she did so swiftly.

On the day he'd made his last climb, he'd stopped at seventy feet. Today, the first panic attack hit him at forty.

As his pulse accelerated and his lungs clenched, he made the worst choice possible and tried to hurry, as if speed were the answer to overcoming panic. The clumsy suit was not built for hurrying, and he missed the handhold he was reaching for by an inch, not even making contact, his body swinging toward open air.

He didn't fall, didn't even come close. Even though he was well balanced, the anticipation of solid contact that was met by nothing but the wind made the world reel, and he threw his arms around the angled upright brace and clung to it like a drunk slow-dancing.

He was facing east, and the late-day sun reflected off the steel and seemed to give the towers added depth, turning them from latticed interruptions of the horizon into a long, shimmering gray tunnel. He closed his eyes, hissing in short, fast breaths as the horizon swam around him. Certain that he was going to faint, he sat awkwardly on the crossbar—fell, really, landing on it with enough impact to jar his spine.

Memory overrode emotion. Enough experience was still trapped in his brain to shout instructions at him, and as the world whirled from gray toward black, he wrapped his legs around the crossbar and circled his elbow tight around the end of a bolt that Pate hadn't removed. He was now as close to self-arrested as he could be without a rope or harness. Then he leaned forward, the way his grandfather had taught him, a lesson from the days when these towers had been going up and before the Faraday suit was in use. His grandfather always advised placing your forehead against the steel, convinced that having the cold stability of it so close to the brain made a difference. Today, Jay couldn't feel it against his skin, but still it saved him. He was aware first of the solid metal against his head, then of the size of the bolt under his elbow, and then, slowly, the overall balance of it all. He was not falling, was not even sliding. He opened his eyes.

The first time Jay had experienced nerves on a tower, Tim had been with him. Jay thought he was faking his way along well enough, determined that nobody would smell his fear, when Tim said, "The tower holds you up, bud, not the other way around. Stop squeezing her so tight."

He tried to remember that now. *The tower holds you up, bud, not the other way around.* Slowly, he relaxed his muscles. He forced himself to concentrate on nothing but the steel, to think of how strong it was, how sturdy, all the conditions it weathered easily and without fail.

To not think about all those missing bolts at the key leverage points.

When his breathing slowed, he willed himself to conjure an image to replace Tim's face. He thought of Sabrina on the video, Sabrina with the cuff on her wrist. That was why he had to climb. It would be better to die here than not to climb.

Once you get in motion, stay in motion, he instructed himself. *If you're moving, you can't lock up. The longer you stay still, the harder it becomes to get going again.* He reached up, grasped the next bar of steel with his right hand, and took a step. His whole body shook, and he wondered if Pate could tell how he was struggling, if he understood yet that he'd picked the wrong man for the job.

Keep climbing.

Sixty feet, seventy, eighty, sure the whole time that he was going to faint and fall. Even continuing the climb offered little reassurance—the real danger waited not below but above, the corona effect crackling like laughter as the lines watched him climb.

Tim had no eyes, no face. Just those curled black ribbons of flesh, like charcoal shavings...

He climbed on. Inside the suit he was soaked with a thin cold sweat. Above him the lines hissed and spit with their distinct, menacing sound, the air alive with current that would sweep through his suit. The sensation was like a thousand ants crawling over his skin, a swarm of strange tingling. He gritted his teeth. The Faraday suit kept you alive in the current, but it didn't make you comfortable. All that voltage crawled over your skin, a feeling that was both unpleasant and exhausting.

At the top of the arm, the insulators hung pointed toward the earth. They were made of a series of porcelain disks, each disk designed to support a designated voltage, the sum of the parts great enough to handle the massive voltage load of the transmission lines. He stopped fifteen feet below them, thought, *I made it,* and then made the mistake of looking up and out, following the path of the lines into the distance. The lines spread out over the landscape like fine black threads, every bit as intricate and delicate as a spiderweb, except that these threads were actually the veins of a nation.

And you're about to pull them down.

This time he nearly *did* faint. The immovable mountains seemed to slide closer to him and then fall away, and he was aware of how radiantly blue the sky was as it spun over him and then swam into a gray haze as his muscles went liquid and he shut his eyes and regripped the steel, no longer believing it would hold him up.

Then the radio came to life.

"Is that high enough for our task, Jay?"

Jay opened his eyes, taking care to look only at his hands and not the open expanse around him. He held tight to the tower with his right hand while he removed the radio from his pocket with his left. The simple performance of a minor physical task made the dizziness dissipate.

"Any higher and you risk turning this cable into an energized conductor," Jay said. "That would be worse for you than me."

It would, in fact, kill Pate instantly. As appealing as that idea was, one of Jay's priorities had to be keeping Pate alive. Whoever else was listening on this radio, waiting on his command, knew where Sabrina was and knew the arrangement—if the power died, she lived. To kill Pate would be to kill Sabrina.

"I appreciate your concern, but that would be very bad for your bride as well," Pate said, confirming Jay's thoughts. "I think our leverage point is fine. Secure the cable and come down for the next. You'll need to start climbing faster."

Jay pocketed the radio, swung the hot stick from over his shoulder, and wrapped the cable three times around the steel arm. He kept his focus tight on his hands, tried not to think about the sky or the mountains or the broad sweep of the lines across the land. Looking at the horizon was a mistake he couldn't make again, and looking up at the crackling lines might be even worse.

The hot stick, which could telescope up to ten feet but was collapsed to five, was outfitted with a crimping head, one of the dozens of tools you could attach to it. Once the cable was looped around the steel, Jay twisted the free end around the line that led back down to the fir trees and used the crimper to bind them tight. The result was a taut, secured cable between the top of the tower on the north side of the tracks and the trees on the south side. It crossed the railroad tracks at chest-level. Even if the engineer saw the cables in the darkness, he wouldn't be able to stop before he made contact with them. With that much power dragging them forward, the cables wouldn't need to hold long either. They'd just need to tug. Mass and momentum would handle the rest.

"One line set," Pate said. "Five to go."

Five more climbs.

Jay closed his eyes, took a deep breath, and started back down.

Pate's voice came over the radio again, but this time he wasn't speaking to Jay. It was a message for the unknown parties who waited out in the mountains, chain saws in hand.

"Stand at the ready," he said. "We are under way at ground zero."

He'd never sounded happier.

61

Janell had the GPS coordinates programmed, and the Yukon that smelled of wet dog fur was purring down the highway, the cruise control locked in at three miles over the limit. Excruciatingly slow, but necessary. She couldn't afford any more delays; the sequencing of time and miles was already too tight, but if she managed to keep it at this pace, she would beat the sunset.

That would be enough. To be there when the world went dark would be enough. Her head ached and the road swam in front of her eyes until she blinked hard and shook herself awake. She couldn't remember when she'd last slept. It felt like the endless road had been all she'd known for weeks now. Cassadaga seemed as far away as Rotterdam.

It was such a large country, and nothing connected it on a drive this long but the ribbons of highway and the power lines. The land blended subtly, and you were well into new terrain when you realized just how astonishingly different it was from the place you'd last been. She'd started among orange trees and humid breezes, and now there was snow on mountains that looked so far removed from that place that it seemed to be another country entirely.

Once it had been.

Maybe it should have stayed that way.

She considered turning on the radio and listening to the news reports, curious about any theories that had surfaced regarding the sad fate of Deputy Terrell and whether they'd identified Doug's corpse yet, but decided she didn't want the distraction. Not now, when she was so close.

The GPS told her she was only thirty-three minutes out. The sun was harsh and slanted in the driver's window, as if it didn't want to give up the day without a fight, but it would soon be down, and when she reached Eli, she doubted there would be more than a pale pink glow left.

That seemed perfect.

There was a handheld radio resting on the console, turned on, waiting for his voice. When it came, the joy she felt made her move her foot to the brake pedal, as if she might not be able to drive and handle the euphoria simultaneously. She wanted to pick up the radio and speak back, to rejoice with him, but he was clearly giving instructions to someone. The returning voice was unknown to her, but it seemed he was the climber, and he was at work.

The radio fell silent for a few seconds, and then Eli's voice came again.

"Stand at the ready. We are under way at ground zero."

Alone in a dead man's car, Janell began to laugh.

62

"You changed the rules, little bitch. You're going to wish you hadn't."

The voice was the first thing Sabrina was aware of. A man's voice, but high and lilting, positively giddy. A stream of repetitive chatter.

"A silly mistake, little bitch. Garland had to play by the rules unless you changed them, and now you have. If you don't listen to the rules, why should Garland? He shouldn't!"

Sabrina kept her eyes squeezed shut. Maybe if she just stayed like this, eyes closed and body limp, he would grow tired and leave. Like playing dead during a grizzly bear mauling.

"Little bitch? Wake up, little bitch."

It was hard to keep her body limp and her breathing shallow, though, because pain was an issue. Her head ached from his punch, but her shoulder joints held the worst pain, the tendons stretched and screaming. There was tension around her wrists too. He'd bound her against something that held her in the air. Gravity was her enemy, making the pain worse by the second, and she was desperate to lessen the pressure on her wrists and shoulders.

But then he'll know. Just stay like you are, and he'll get tired, and then—

When he slapped her, she gasped and opened her eyes despite herself. She saw him then, directly in front of her, his mouth twisted into a grin, his eyes hungry.

"Good morning, little bitch! I *thought* you were awake. You've been trying to hide from Garland, haven't you?"

Sabrina gasped with pain and began to scramble with her heels, searching for any way to reduce the pressure in her shoulders. She finally found purchase, but it was soft and yielding, and it wasn't until she'd pushed high enough to alleviate the pain that she looked down to see what her situation was.

He had overturned a bed, and it was resting on an angle against the wall and Sabrina's arms were tied above it, ropes running from her wrists up to the exposed wall studs high above her. She was upstairs in the cabin, it seemed. There were lights and radios and electronics scattered all around, along with rows of cots, five or six at least. There was a window up here, and it wasn't covered—daylight streamed in, and she could see down to the fence.

Garland Webb followed her gaze and shook his head.

"Don't waste your hope on her. She is miles from help, and two men are right behind her. She will be back soon, and she will be punished too. Those are the rules. I'm only allowed to punish those who break them."

He smiled.

"You broke them."

He reached out and touched Sabrina's chin with his index finger, laughed when she recoiled, and then traced a line down her throat and chest, between her breasts and down her stomach. She tried to kick him but missed and succeeded only in knocking the upended bed down farther so that she fell and the ropes sent waves of pain through her arms and shoulders. She screamed and Garland Webb laughed as he caught her legs easily, unbothered by her kicks, and stepped between them, his face almost level with her own.

"Fighters are good," he said. "Fighters are better."

She turned her head in disgust, and when she did she saw the staircase to her right, and saw Violet standing there, halfway up, hidden in the shadows. For an instant, they locked eyes, and then Violet looked away.

"No!" Sabrina shouted. "Help me!"

Violet didn't look up, but Garland turned and saw her.

"Get out of here."

Violet didn't move. Her head was still down, and Sabrina could see that her lips were moving, but no words were coming. It was as if she were whispering to herself. No—chanting. Sabrina could hear the faint sounds now.

Garland Webb released Sabrina's legs and stepped toward the stairs, saying, "I should have left you chained, you stupid slut." He had taken only two steps when a radio in the room crackled to life.

"We have armed visitors at Wardenclyffe," a male voice said.

Webb pulled up short, pivoted his head toward the window, and stared out. Sabrina managed to get her heels braced on the bed frame again, leaning her head back with relief when the screaming tension in her shoulders and wrists ebbed.

Webb crossed the room to a long table, picked up a radio, and walked to the window. He'd put the radio to his lips but hadn't spoken when another voice came on, and this one Sabrina recognized— Eli Pate.

"Come again?"

"Two armed visitors at Wardenclyffe. Don't look like police. But the woman is running toward them."

"Where is Garland?"

Webb pressed a button on the side of the radio. "Right here. With the other one. Baldwin. She is secured."

Violet's head was bobbing gently, the soft chants still coming from her barely moving lips, her eyes closed. For a few seconds that was the only sound, and then Pate spoke again.

"Can you take the others out?"

The unknown male voice said, "Affirmative."

"Then do so."

"Ten-four."

Garland Webb said, "I'm coming down," and then clipped the radio to his belt. He turned from the window to face Sabrina. "I'll be back, little bitch. We'll have our time together."

He moved across the room to the top of the stairs. Violet was still chanting, eyes still closed.

"Get out of my way," Webb said, starting down the steps.

Violet opened her eyes, lifted a pistol, and pulled the trigger.

There was a soft pop, a hiss of air, and then a hideous blend of gasp and scream as Garland Webb reached for his throat and the dart that was embedded just below his Adam's apple.

63

When he saw Lynn, Mark dropped the rifle and picked up the .38. His uncle watched with curiosity.

"You know her?"

"Yes. She's the one I came here with, the one looking for Pate."

Larry reached out and grabbed Mark's arm as he turned to run. "Don't set off like a damned fool again."

"There are men right behind her!"

"Thank the good Lord for a scoped rifle, then," Larry said.

"We aren't shooting anybody unless we have to."

"You didn't have that problem earlier today." Larry picked up the rifle and leaned forward, burrowing himself into the snow and assuming a sniper's position on his belly. "Might as well back them off a touch, wouldn't you say?"

Mark looked at him and then up the slope helplessly. He wasn't going to cover the ground to Lynn uphill faster than those two would do it going downhill, but he didn't want to start a firefight either. Not as exposed as they were here.

"Markus, they are closing on her fast," Larry said.

"Back them off, then."

Larry went silent and enough seconds passed that Mark thought he hadn't heard the instruction. Then his uncle squeezed off four shots in succession, fluid as a firing machine, racking the bolt and squeezing the trigger, racking the bolt and squeezing the trigger, no change at all in his expression or posture.

"Well," he said, "they didn't care for that much."

"You hit them?"

"Of course not; I wasn't trying to hit them. They both dropped and went for cover. I can see one of them. The other one made it down in the rocks, out of sight."

"Where is Lynn?"

"She stopped running too. She's hiding in that gulch. I wish she'd been smart enough to keep running. This was buying her good lead time."

"She probably thinks any shooting is hostile fire." Mark looked at the gulch, two hundred yards away over open hillside. It was a ribbon of shadow in the gathering dusk. Once he got there, he'd feel safe enough.

But he had to get there.

"Shit," Larry said. "They've got radios. That means they've got friends."

"I'm going for her," Mark said. "When I start running, put up some cover fire. Shoot to wound if you can. You don't need a murder charge."

Larry was feeding fresh cartridges into the rifle. "I'd say we're past the point of worrying about our booking sheets."

He was probably right.

Larry said, "When you get to her, head straight down the gulch instead of coming back across the hill. I can hold them off, and you'll have better cover. You get to the bottom, where that stream is, just run like hell for the truck. I can keep them occupied long enough for you to make the truck."

"How do *you* intend to get back across?"

"Creatively." Larry didn't look away from the scope. "If you're going to move, now's the time. They're getting themselves collected up there."

"All right." Mark put one hand in the snow, bracing himself on the steep slope, and said, "I'll run with your first shot."

There was a two-second pause, and then Larry opened fire again, this time sending the bullets into the trees, blowing chunks of bark and branch loose.

Mark put his head down and ran.

The first bullet into the ground beside him barely registered. It was nothing more than a puff in the snow. The second passed close to his skull, and he ducked involuntarily and promptly lost his balance and slipped, landing hard and painfully on his right side, but fortuitously also, because more bullets stitched the air above him. Larry returned fire, shooting faster now, connecting with rocks near the summit, and when the bullets aimed at Mark ceased, he stumbled to his feet and charged on, crossing the last fifty yards without taking fire.

At the edge of the gulch he slowed, but just then a new bullet separated the branch of a fir tree from its trunk only a few feet above his head, and he jumped into the boulder-lined gulch without further hesitation.

The drop wasn't much, ten feet at most, but he landed in the loose rocks and fell backward. In another few weeks the fall might have ended disastrously, because massive rocks waited to catch his head, but today there was still enough snow to cushion the impact. It hammered the breath from his lungs, but it didn't crack his skull. For a moment he lay there and fought for air, listening to the popping barrage of the gunfire from the summit—an AR-15 or AK-47—and the responding booms from his uncle's Winchester. He hadn't asked Larry how many rounds he had. He'd told Larry not to shoot to kill, but if his supply went low, he'd have to start making the shots count.

Mark got to his feet and scrambled up the gulch, holding the .38 in his right hand and using his left for balance. He was prepared for gunfire, but none came. Above him, all had gone silent. He was alone in the gulch, scrambling through the shadows, the sun below the mountain, the evening sky lit pink. He'd gone about a hundred feet and was breathing hard, the altitude taking its toll, when the gulch made a sharp bend to the left that was partially blocked by the massive root ball of an overturned fir. He hurried around it, the gun held down along his leg, not in firing position, when he thought he heard a whisper of motion and slowed by a half step. As a result, the softball-size rock that Lynn Deschaine slammed at his face missed by inches.

Her momentum carried her past him, into the tree roots, as he raised the .38 and almost fired. He'd partially depressed the trigger before he registered her long dark hair, a stark splash against the snow where she'd fallen.

"Lynn!"

She slipped and fell as she tried to rise and turn and finally ended up on her back, facing him, stunned. She was breathing too hard to speak. Mark looked from her to the chunk of rock she'd swung at him when she'd sprung from her hiding spot. She would have neatly crushed his skull if she'd made contact.

"Let's go," he said, reaching to help her.

She kicked him in the throat.

He was unprepared for it, and it was a hell of a blow. His breath split into agonized trapped halves between brain and chest and he stumbled and fell to one knee as she rose and chopped at his wrist and knocked the .38 loose. It bounced into the rocks and he watched her go after it without attempting to stop her, frozen by pain and shock.

She was three feet from the gun when a shot rang out and fragments of rock exploded just inches from the revolver.

Larry.

"He won't miss next time," Mark rasped. The effort of speaking raised specks of light in his vision. He sat down and rubbed his throat. Lynn was motionless down in the rocks, torn between reaching for the gun and believing his words. She looked back at him warily, like a trapped animal.

"Are you with them? Did you know?" She was panting, fearful but fierce, and he knew that if she reached the gun she meant to use it. "You left the motel and they appeared. That's a *coincidence?*"

He thought of his own outrage, standing in her motel room discovering the undisclosed connection to his family, finding the Homeland Security ID, and he realized for the first time that his own sense of betrayal had to be nothing compared to hers when she'd awoken to find him gone and attackers at the door.

"I don't know that I even believe in that word anymore, but I didn't set you up."

She breathed hard, watching him and trying to decide. He knew that Larry was watching her with a finger on the trigger.

Mark said, "Go straight down to the bottom of the gulch, and you'll find a truck. Take it and go. You're in the crosshairs of a scope, but he's a friendly shooter to you. For now."

Her distrust began to waver. She stared into the trees. "Who are you here with?"

"My uncle."

She turned back to him. "You're telling the truth?"

"I'm telling the truth. I came to help you, and to kill Garland Webb. That's all. I left the motel room because I was thinking about my wife. When I came back, you were gone. And I...and I found my way here."

She rose unsteadily, her chest heaving. Strands of hair caught in her mouth, and she wiped them aside. "I'm not going without her."

"Without who?"

"Sabrina Baldwin."

Mark looked up at the summit. It was backlit with that beautiful sunset, but below, everything was giving way to the encroaching darkness. They were out of sight of the shooters above for now, but he expected the shooters were in motion and that they knew the terrain. Time was short. If they were going down, it had to be in a hurry.

But he remembered Jay Baldwin's face. *What would you do to get your wife back?*

"She's up there?" Mark asked.

"Yes." Lynn took a deep breath, eyes on him, and added: "She's with Garland Webb. And your mother."

64

The dart, as Sabrina knew from experience, carried a fast-acting tranquilizer. She hadn't even had time to ask *Why?* before the blackness overtook her. Garland Webb had time to say "You stupid bitch" before his legs went liquid beneath him and he tumbled down the stairs, but he was large and strong and he caught Violet by her hair as he fell. She vanished from sight with him.

Sabrina, still bound to the wall, screamed.

No one answered.

As the silence settled and she realized she was alone without either immediate threat or immediate rescue, she tried to figure out some means of escape. Nothing. With or without Garland Webb, she would remain here.

Something moved on the stairs. A thump and a drag. Sabrina twisted her head toward the steps and stared into the shadows. *Thump, drag. Thump, drag.*

Someone was climbing the stairs.

Coming back for her.

She was braced for the sight of Garland Webb when Violet appeared halfway up the steps.

"Help," Sabrina said. "Please, help me."

Violet came up the stairs slowly, still holding the pistol, dragging her left foot behind her. It hung awkwardly, the ankle or lower leg broken, but she kept approaching with patient steps. She looked at Sabrina's knots quizzically before giving up and going to the woodstove across the room. There she set the pistol down and picked up a hatchet. She tested the blade's edge with her thumb.

"That woman wasn't lying about my son, was she?"

Sabrina didn't answer. She wasn't sure what would help more now—the truth, which was clearly a torment for Violet, or the lie that she wanted to hear.

"I know that she wasn't lying," Violet said before Sabrina got a word out. "And if Markus is here, he's here for the truth. He's special. In ways he doesn't know. Which means that I ..." She fell silent, and her eyes filled with tears. "Look at you. Oh my God, just look at you. What I've allowed. Embraced."

"Help me, and we will leave together. I promise."

Violet shook her head.

"I can't leave. My fate has called me here. You were brought against your will, and there is no other way to look at that, is there? And yet I tried to find one. Because the goals are good, they're *critical*. Someone has to speak for the earth. It's past time for that. But all of this ..." She shook her head again. "This isn't the way Eli promised it would go. It's nothing like he promised. I wanted to believe in him, but the morning council was wrong. He was false. I've always put my faith in the wrong places, but only while searching for the right one. No one would believe that."

Outside there was gunfire, sharp, cracking shots. Sabrina jerked at the sound and almost lost her balance atop the precariously leaning bed frame.

"Please cut me down. Please!"

"I let him change her fate too," she said. "Lauren's. My own daughter-in-law. Think about that. I allowed it to happen to her."

She pushed her thumb against the blade. A bright bead of blood appeared and Sabrina winced at the sight, but Violet seemed unmoved.

Another fusillade of shots echoed outside. Sharp, high pops interspersed with low, echoing booms. Violet moved the hatchet away from her thumb and stared at the blood as it dripped down her arm.

"I never heard what happened," she said. "They never told me, but I didn't try to find out either. I probably didn't want to see. That's the problem for me. I want the truth but I never see it."

She sighed and lowered her hand, showering the floorboards with speckles of blood.

"I just hope she told him the things I'd asked her to tell him," she said. "I'd hoped she would be the one to convince him to believe."

There was a long silence, and then Violet lunged forward, swinging the hatchet high over her head and then whistling the blade down. It cleaved through the rope on Sabrina's left side and drove into the wall, and she swung free, knocking the bed frame away. For an instant she was hanging only by her right side, but Violet wrenched the hatchet out of the wall and swung it once more, cutting the second rope. Sabrina fell to the floor, and Violet left the hatchet in the wall this time and reached down to help her up. Her left hand was hot with blood.

"Can you walk?" Violet said.

"I think so." Sabrina was struggling to her feet when she saw the bloody hole in Violet's stomach for the first time. It was a deep puncture, and the blood that filled it was bright red and flowing fast.

"My God...what happened?"

"Garland's knife." She said it simply but sadly. "Go on now, dear. And be careful."

"Both of us."

"No."

"Violet...*yes!* When he wakes up, he is going to kill you."

"Perhaps. But this is my fate, dear. I've been on a long, strange road to get here. I can't leave. I think you can, though. I think you should."

Sabrina didn't pause to argue. Outside the gunfire had begun again, and she didn't know how long Garland Webb would remain unconscious.

"Thank you," she said.

Violet nodded and said, "Yes, dear," for the last time as Sabrina went to the stairs. She stepped over Garland Webb's inert form. He was facedown, the dart no longer in his throat but trapped in his massive fingers.

At the bottom of the steps she turned back, prepared to ask Violet to join her, but she was nowhere to be seen.

65

J ay had completed a second climb, secured another cable, and was
on his way back up with a third when he heard the first creak from
the steel.

It wasn't a menacing sound, not like the corona discharge. Inside
his hooded suit, it sounded muffled and almost friendly, a low moan
with a high, whining finish, like the yawn of a sleeping dog.

Then the tower began to move.

At first, the sensation was so subtle that he almost didn't believe it.
Chalked it up to dizziness again; the world had been reeling around
him plenty up here.

The dog's yawn turned into a scream then, the shriek of torquing
metal, and Jay had a tenth of a second to think, *Oh shit, it's real*, before
the angled upright closest to the tracks tried to pull apart from the
rest of the tower.

It was the highest spot Pate had reached to remove bolts. Jay saw
the brace shifting as he began to fall, watched it lean from sky to earth
like a palm tree in gale-force winds, and then he lost his footing and
plummeted down.

He hit the steel before the air, landing on his chest on the crossbar
he'd been standing on an instant earlier, a feeling like catching a pull
hitter's bat at the end of his swing.

The pain saved him. Pain powered instinct that his brain hadn't
been able to conjure earlier, and he reached for his chest as his feet
swung free. The steel crossbar was between his hand and his chest.
He hooked it with his left arm and caught himself with a jarring impact, the crossbar pinned under his armpit. Beneath him he saw his

booted feet kicking impotently at the air, searching for nonexistent purchase, and the distant ground below.

His aching arm was squeezed tight as a python around the steel, so tight that it pressed into the meat of his biceps like a dull knife.

Right arm, right arm, right arm! he thought frantically, but when he swung to grab with his right, it forced his left loose, and for a moment he was sliding again. Then his right hand clamped over the crosspiece and held.

Beneath him, the tower groaned again as the wind freshened and the loose brace, which had to weigh several thousand pounds, strained to adhere to gravity's demands.

The overhead lines didn't let it. They'd given all the slack they intended to give, and now the loose brace was held up by their strength.

Jay took three quick but deep breaths, then heaved himself upward, like a man trying to pull himself out of the water and over the stern of a boat. He got his chest onto the crossbar and then wrapped his arms around it and clasped his left wrist with his right hand.

The tower holds you up, bud, not the other way around. Stop squeezing her so tight.

He laid the side of his face against the steel and gasped in air, blinking sweat out of his eyes. His chest and arm ached and he felt a strange pressure along his spine and thought, *I've broken my back,* before he realized that it was the hot stick, still slung in place over his shoulder and still attached to the cable Pate had anchored below.

When the voice came over the radio, he thought the sound was from the tower again, and he tightened his grasp, ready for the inevitable fall. Even after he realized the source of the sound, it took him a few seconds to process the words.

"Don't look like police. But the woman is running toward them."

Jay lifted his head. The tower didn't shift; the steel was solid again beneath him. Only seconds ago it had occupied his every emotion. Now the radio summoned them elsewhere.

The woman? Were they talking about Sabrina? But then the update came from a man named Garland: "Right here. With the other one. Baldwin. She is secured."

A hundred feet below, Eli Pate lowered the radio and shouted to Jay in a calm, cold voice.

"You just heard the man! Sabrina is in capable hands! Time to get up, Jay! Back on your feet!"

Jay pushed up slowly but didn't rise to his feet. He shifted into a sitting position astride the crossbar, his feet dangling free, and adjusted the hot stick. The ground cable was still secure, unbothered by the excitement. Jay wasn't even sure if Pate had been aware of it or if he'd been distracted by the men on the radio. Did anyone have any idea how close it had been?

Doesn't matter. You're alive. Sabrina may not be for long. Get the hell up.

Baldwin, they'd said. *She is secured.*

Secured by this man Garland. Jay's instinct said it was terrible, but the other woman, the unknown woman, was on the run between groups of armed men, and Pate had instructed his men to take out the others, the armed intruders. That meant that the woman who was not *secured* was in a lot more danger than the one who was.

Didn't it?

He inched out on along the crossbar until he reached the upright. Then he got both hands around it and pulled cautiously to his feet. The tower didn't shift, which shouldn't have been a surprise. Jay's weight was insignificant when dispersed amid all that steel. The loose brace had hopefully shifted as much as it could, or would, unless it had some powerful help.

As if in answer, a new sound joined the mix, far off but audible.

A train whistle.

There was the help. Hustling westward, unaware of the trap, and guaranteed to pull down the towers. Jay began to climb again, into the darkening sky. He was vaguely aware that on his next trip he would need a light. He was vaguely aware of the pain in his chest and arm. He was only vaguely aware of anything.

He'd just gotten high enough to swing the hot stick free, ready to crimp the second cable into place, when the radio came to life again, the same voice as before but sounding anything but composed now.

"We are taking heavy fire!"

Pate said, "Then return it," cool and indifferent. Jay wondered if the men on the other end were Pate's followers or if they were more like Jay, pulled in against their will.

"Garland, report, please," Pate said.

The radio was silent. A few seconds passed. Pate said, "Garland?"

Again there was only silence from the radio, and, all around Jay, the humming chorus of five hundred thousand volts.

"Get to work, Jay!" Pate shouted, and for the first time his voice had lost its detached cool.

Jay looped the cable. He had the hot stick in hand, ready to crimp the cable, when his radio chirped.

"We have a runner. The second woman is out. Both women are out!"

A hundred feet in the air, Jay froze and stared down at Eli Pate, who held the radio to his lips but didn't key the mike.

For once, something had silenced him.

66

Mark and Lynn were still in the gulch when Larry ran to join them. Mark's tracks had disappeared as the sun descended, a fringe line of blackness that kept working higher up the mountain.

Larry gave no warning he was coming. Mark and Lynn heard the sound when he was almost on them. He made it across the steep pitch without a fall, better than Mark, and used a tree to aid his drop into the gulch, landing on his feet, rifle at waist-level, pointed at Lynn.

"That didn't look like a real warm reunion you all had. How's your throat?"

Mark said, "Mom's up there. With Garland Webb."

"Violet is up there?"

"Yes."

Larry looked up the slope. He was quiet for a moment, then said, "We wait long, and we'll be pinned down here."

"How many left for the Winchester?" Mark said.

"Four."

"Shit."

"Yup."

"Any more rounds in the truck?"

"No."

"How many for the handgun?"

"Two handguns, two clips each."

"Give one to her."

Larry looked at Lynn and hesitated, but she extended her hand and made a *gimme* gesture, curling her fingers in toward her palm. He drew a Ruger semiautomatic from his pocket and gave it to her.

When she closed her hand around the gun, she looked at Mark. He turned his palms up. "Got enough trust yet? I'm the only one without a weapon. You want to kill me and figure out you were wrong later, there's nothing stopping you."

She knelt, picked up the .38, and passed it to him.

"Thank you," he said. "Now tell me what I'm running into up there."

"A high fence that may or may not be electrified at the moment. A cabin. I don't know if they took her back there. I don't even know if…if she's alive. They got her as she was going over the fence. She shut it down long enough for me to get over, but they got her."

"How many are there?"

"Four. Three men and your mother."

Larry swore under his breath and spit into the snow, then scrambled to the high side of the gulch and peered up at the shrinking pool of sunlight where the telephone poles stood.

"You take her down to the truck. I'll go see about your mother."

I'll go see about your mother. How many times had Mark heard that? In the past, it had meant that they were going to pull her out of some bar or flophouse or con's bedroom. Now it meant that Larry intended to head up the gulch alone toward three armed men.

"Not happening, Uncle," Mark said. He gestured to Lynn. "We've got to take her down."

"You're not taking *her* anywhere," Lynn snapped. "Until I know what happened to Sabrina, I am not leaving."

"That's a stupid choice," Mark said. "We need to leave and call for help."

He was watching the ground shadows seep down the mountainside, deepening the darkness. Any chance of reaching the truck depended on moving now, while enough visibility remained to get down the gulch in relative quiet. They were outgunned above, and if their trek was pinpointed by clattering stumbles over rocks and snapped branches underfoot, they'd be shredded.

"She'll die in that time," Lynn said. "Once they know we're gone, they'll kill her."

"I've got no interest in leaving my sister up there either," Larry said. He turned back to them when he said it, so he was facing away from the woods when the shadowed slope gave birth to something bright and white. A man dressed in white camouflage like a 10th Mountain Division soldier spun around a tree not twenty feet from them and lifted his rifle.

Mark saw it all with strange clarity, a neat, clean line: Larry, the lip of the gulch, a downed tree, a shooter. The tableau was stamped into his memory instantly and forever.

The shot he fired, though, he would never remember.

He wasn't aware of it until the man dropped, shooting as he fell, peppering a line of bullets into the sky, ripping apart pine boughs that fell with a peaceful whisper. Larry and Lynn both hit the ground, but Mark just stood there, the .38 still extended.

"*Son of a bitch!*" Larry scrambled up and stared at Mark. "You put him down?"

"Yes."

"Lord, son, you must've fired faster than you saw him. Who taught you that?"

Mark looked at the gun as it if were unfamiliar. He had never been the best shot. Not the worst, but certainly not the best. Both of his uncles had been better. So had his wife.

"I guess it was Ronny," he said.

Before his uncle could answer, they were interrupted by the crackle of a radio and a voice. It was coming from the dead man's belt, but his body muffled the words.

Mark said, "Cover me, will you? I want to get a look at him."

Larry snapped at him to stay down, but Mark climbed over the lip of the gulch. He glanced back once and saw Larry standing waist-deep in the gulch, braced against the earth, panning the gloaming forest with the scope.

"You see the other one?" Mark asked.

"No, but hurry up."

Mark crawled to the dead man and saw a face he didn't know. Not

Garland Webb. That was a shame. Lord, was that a shame. If it had been Garland Webb, he could have gone on back down the gulch and out to the truck and driven out of here.

No, you couldn't.

The voice made Mark jerk, because for an instant it seemed to come from the dead man himself. Just a trick of the mind. Adrenaline was cooking in Mark's veins now, and if he wasn't careful it would overrun him. You had to stay cool under fire, and he was doing anything but that. Not only his focus was slipping; his whole damn mind seemed to be.

He took the dead man's rifle, then rolled him over. As he did so, he heard the voice again.

You'll die here. All of you.

Again Mark jerked back.

"What the hell's the matter?" Larry whispered behind him.

Mark didn't know how to answer. Adrenaline, that was all. You felt crazy things in crazy moments, and this moment was about as crazy as they got.

He grabbed the dead man's radio in a hurry, tugged it free, and then crawled back to the gulch with the radio and the rifle, heading right toward Larry, who was still scouring the trees through his scope, finger on the trigger. He wasn't all the way back when the radio came to life in his hand, and this time he could hear it clearly:

"We have a runner! The second woman is out!"

Lynn jumped to her feet. "Sabrina!" she called. More of a shout than Mark would have liked, but even as she said it, she moved sideways and deeper into the gulch, wisely anticipating that she'd risked giving up their position. No shots came, but an answer did, a woman's voice shouting without Lynn's restraint. *"Lynn! Lynn, where are you!"*

Mark turned and started to tell Lynn not to answer, that shouts would get them killed, but Larry's shot silenced them all. Lynn took a stumbling step back, Mark stopped crawling, and Sabrina Baldwin's shouts ended. For a few seconds, the forest was absolutely still.

Then Larry lowered the rifle.

"Had to take it. She wasn't even into the trees yet, and he'd stopped to fire. With that AR spitting bullets, he was going to kill her fast."

Mark stared up at the pink-tinted peak where Larry had fired, and though he couldn't see anything, he could hear something now. Someone was crashing clumsily through the woods. He scrambled to the base of a tree and lifted his revolver, but Larry didn't move at all, just stood with the rifle lowered and waited on whoever was running out of the daylight and into the darkness.

A minute later, they saw her—a woman, slipping and stumbling down the slope, falling every few feet but bouncing up so fast it all seemed part of the plan.

"Sabrina!" Lynn climbed out of the gulch and ran toward the other woman and Mark made no move to stop her. Instead, he looked at his uncle.

"We've got two. Lynn said there were three men."

"That's all that have been shooting, at least. I've found four people with the scope since we got here. Two are here, and two are dead."

Lynn Deschaine and Sabrina Baldwin met halfway up the slope. Sabrina fell into Lynn's arms, and Lynn tugged her down immediately, pulling her to the ground and guiding her behind a fallen tree. Mark watched them and wondered what horrors they had shared and how they'd managed to get loose in a place like this.

"Nice shooting, Uncle," he said.

"Shit, son, that was target practice. You were the one who went Wild Bill Hickok."

It wasn't much of an exaggeration. The bullet had punched through the other man's heart before Mark knew what had happened.

For some reason, that bothered him.

He wiped sweat from his face and said, "Lynn? Let's get the hell out of here."

Lynn got to her feet and helped Sabrina Baldwin to hers and they came down the side of the mountain together, arm in arm, as if neither of them wanted to risk letting go again.

"You okay?" Mark asked the new woman. Sabrina Baldwin was shaking, but she nodded.

"We need to get out of here," Mark said. "Is there anyone left to stop us?"

"I don't think so," Sabrina said. "Not if we hurry. He'll be down for a while longer."

"Who will be?"

"One of the men who works for Eli. Garland Webb."

"Garland Webb," Mark echoed. His voice had the same flat crack as Larry's killing shot.

She looked at him with wide eyes. "You're him," she said. "You're the one. Novak."

"Yes."

"Violet...I think she's your mother? Violet shot him with a dart."

Lynn said, *"What?* She did?" and she seemed stunned when Sabrina Baldwin nodded.

"She saved me," Sabrina said.

"Where are all the ATV riders?" Larry asked. "We saw plenty of tracks coming in."

"I don't know. There was a large group this morning, but they left. If they come back, though..."

Lynn said, "She's right—we need to get out of here fast. There are enough of them that we'll be outnumbered, badly."

Sabrina said, "My husband...do you know anything?"

"He was alive," Mark said. "And I gave him his chance to play it the way he wanted. He didn't want to risk doing anything that might threaten you."

He thought about that and then looked at the radio in his hand and said, "You know, I just might be able to get a report on Jay."

He put the dead man's radio to his lips. Keyed the mike and heard static.

"Hello, gentlemen," he said. His heart thundered but his voice was steady. "This is Markus Novak, reporting in from Wardenclyffe. I've come to see Garland Webb. We are long overdue."

67

"This is Markus Novak, reporting in from Wardenclyffe. I've come to see Garland Webb. We are long overdue."

At the top of the tower, hot stick in hand, Jay heard Novak's voice and thought: *He made it. The crazy bastard actually made it to them.*

Then he thought: *He'd better not ruin it.*

He reached for the radio and spoke before anyone else had responded.

"Novak, this is Jay Baldwin, where is my wife, have you seen my wife?"

Down below, Eli Pate screamed at Jay to shut up, but Novak's voice returned on the radio immediately.

"Jay, she is safe and well. Repeat, she is safe and well."

Jay sagged back against the transmission tower. He was not aware of the pulsing, swarming current, his own fatigue, the heights, or even his own tears.

She is safe and well.

Eli Pate's voice came over the radio next. Calm, no trace of the shouting he'd done down below. "Mr. Novak. What a surprise. It will be good to meet you one of these days, but I'm going to suggest you leave the property immediately. It will not end well for you there. That is a promise."

A long pause, then Novak: "I'm going to assume I'm hearing from the great Eli Pate himself?"

"The same," Pate said. "You are no doubt proud of your achievements right now. Hold on to that feeling for as many minutes as you can. I assure you, they won't be plentiful."

Safe and well. Sabrina was safe and well. Jay looked at the radio as if he wanted to embrace it, and then he heard Pate come back with an addendum.

"All listening must understand that this changes nothing. The plan is in motion. Wardenclyffe has not been compromised. I am on scene right now, and we are nine minutes to shutdown."

He had to be talking about the train. Jay had nine minutes to get off the tower before it came down and brought a half a million volts with it.

"Do you hear that, Novak?" Pate said over the radio. "Please don't believe that you are a concern to me."

As Pate talked, he walked. Up from the trees and onto the tracks, standing between the strung cables that would be invisible to the engineer until too late. Novak had stopped responding, and all of Pate's attention was on this place, wherever it was.

None of it was on Jay.

Safe and well. Repeat, she is safe and well.

Jay looked down at Pate and thought: *You have no more leverage, asshole. You have no more power.*

Except for the gun. By the time Jay came down, that gun would matter. And if he didn't come down to face the gun, he'd be perched up here when the train roared through. One way or another, he was coming down soon, and he'd rather take his chances with the pistol than the five hundred thousand volts. One was likely to kill him; the other was certain to.

It was then, watching Pate stand with the gun in his left hand and the radio in his right, demanding a response from Novak that did not come, that Jay allowed himself, for the first time, to look up at those killing lines overhead.

He was fifteen feet away from turning his cold steel cable into a live wire.

And Eli Pate, a hundred feet below, was standing on metal train tracks.

68

The GPS said that Janell was seven minutes out.

It seemed impossible that so much could go so wrong in seven minutes, but it was happening.

"This is Markus Novak, reporting in from Wardenclyffe."

Hate for him rose through her like a fever, and her hands were so tight on the wheel that her wrists ached. She looked at the radio but did not reach for it. Eli was still in command, and she was only seven minutes away.

She'd join him, at least. No matter what else happened today, they would escape together. The way it had always been. Together, they would regroup and adjust. Together, they would set it all right.

69

The hot stick could be telescoped to ten feet. The flash zone, depending on conditions, could reach beyond that in the world of a half a million volts.

But it shouldn't. Not today. The air was dry and the sun had baked it all afternoon. There was no rain or snow, no high humidity, none of the things that should extend that flash zone beyond ten feet. With the hot stick, Jay should be able to extend that cable high enough to make it live and kill Eli Pate in a literal flash.

What he had to figure out first was how to do it without killing himself too. The Faraday suit was not enough protection, not when he was standing on a steel pole. In an energized bucket or helicopter, he could do it, but not reaching out from the steel tower. Jay would turn into Tim's corpse in a blink. Worse than Tim's corpse, actually. With this voltage, he'd vaporize. There'd be nothing left of him but boots and smoke.

Just climb down. Take your chances with the gun.

But the memory of Sabrina in chains was back with him, and the image was wider now. It included the blinking lights Jay had watched from bed with his wife, that first warning that the madness of Eli Pate was coming his way; it included the phone in Pate's hand as he sat in Jay's kitchen, sipping his coffee and holding Jay's world under his thumb.

I'm not a kind man, he had said.

No. He was not. And he'd held too much power over Jay for too long, and held it through the force of fear. What was left to fear now was no longer up to Pate. It was up to Jay.

Jay looked down, confirmed that Pate was still in the same position, on the tracks and between the cables, no more than a foot from the cable Jay currently had wrapped around the head of his hot stick, and then he took a few steps higher, edging toward the flash zone.

All it would take was contact. That was just how damn powerful the current up here was; the briefest touch between the world above and the world below would create an epic collision, sending a blast of current strong enough to power a city down that cable in the blink of an eye. Eli Pate had not been wrong about one thing: all that the electricity on these lines wanted to do was return to the earth.

To make it happen, Jay was going to have to let go of the tower completely. He'd need his left hand to free enough slack in the cable to throw the hot stick, and his right hand to toss it. He'd need to be strong with it too, because if he threw it short and the cable swung back into the tower...

Well, if that happened, at least he wouldn't know it. Speed was the only blessing in a death on the high lines. You wouldn't have time to recognize the mistake that killed you.

He held his hot stick in his right hand. Then, six months after he'd frozen seventy feet in the air and known that his climbing days were done, Jay Baldwin removed his left hand from the tower and stood hands-free one hundred and five feet above the ground.

You're going to have to hurry, because if he sees you, he'll understand. And you're going to have to be strong. You'll have to get the legs into it.

He'd have to, in short, make an upward lunge out and away from a tower that had already tried to buck him off like an angry horse and manage not to fall off it.

Just climb down.

No. No, that was not an option. Sabrina had seen to that. She had gotten away somehow, and that was all that had ever mattered. He thought of Novak's voice on the radio and remembered the look in his eyes back when he could have removed all hope from Jay and chose not to. He'd given Jay time, and Sabrina had escaped on her own.

Eli Pate was not allowed to do the same.

Jay balanced the hot stick in his right hand like a javelin and pulled up slack cable with his left. He counted its length as he reeled it up—two feet, four, six, eight, ten. Ten would do it.

The train whistle rose loud and shrill from the east, and Jay glanced toward it and then down at Pate. Pate did just the same, looking first east, then up at Jay, as if remembering, finally, that he was still up there, the bird on a wire.

When he saw the way Jay was standing, he seemed to understand immediately. Eli must have realized that he'd committed the cardinal sin of high-voltage work: he'd allowed his mind to go elsewhere.

As Eli Pate tried to run off the tracks, he backed into one of his own cables, stumbled, and fell. Jay looked away and pivoted his body to the right, winding up for the toss. The hot stick's awkward length nearly kept the momentum going, though, almost spun him right off the tower, but old instincts saved him, and he slid his foot as he turned, muscle memory protecting his balance up on the high steel. He reversed the turn then, whirling back to the left, and released the hot stick and its trailing cable. The cable rustled over his Faraday suit, and he thought, *Dead, you are dead now*, but then the cable pulled free, away from him and the tower as it followed the hot stick toward the power lines.

It never reached them. The throw was short by two feet.

That was still enough.

The electricity-filled air around the lines, crackling with corona discharge, smelled the first, faint chance to return to the earth, and leaped at it. A brilliant cobalt-blue arc flash ripped through the air, found the stainless-steel cable, and rode it home.

Jay heard the explosion below but never saw it. It was over that fast. The hot stick was falling then, out of the flash zone, already turned back into a dead tool carrying a dead line.

He wrapped both hands around the steel tower and looked down at the place where Eli Pate had last stood.

He couldn't see anything but smoke.

70

When the last radio exchange was finished, Mark stood in the cold breeze and looked up through the dark trees to the place where the faintest traces of crimson light lingered at the summit. Then he turned back to Lynn.

"You know you've got to get her out of here," he said. "That's the first thing. Everything else is secondary. She's innocent. You've got to get her to help."

Lynn nodded but didn't speak. She was staring at Mark with soft eyes. This was not the feral woman who'd tried to kill him in the gulch but the one whose face had hovered so close to his in the dark motel room in what seemed like another lifetime.

"Don't go up there," she said. "We'll call the police. They'll handle him."

"When he wakes up," Mark said, "I want mine to be the first face he sees."

Lynn started to speak, stopped, and finally settled on "Don't take chances that you don't need to."

"Right."

"There will be other times to get him. Other places. Better places."

Mark nodded. Lynn tugged Sabrina forward, and they were walking down the slope in the twilight when Mark and his uncle began to climb toward the last patch of daylight on a mountain summit drowning in darkness.

The sun was completely gone when they reached the top. They watched the headlights of the stolen truck Lynn was driving crawl over the rock-riddled path toward the road, toward safety.

Mark had no flashlight, but he'd found the body of the man Larry had shot and taken his rifle, an AR-15 with a flashlight mounted on the barrel. Mark panned the area inside the fence with light before he entered. He saw no movement. The gate stood ajar, and beyond it were a cabin and an outhouse and a bizarre collection of utility poles. Shadows everywhere. Everything still and silent.

"Stay here and cover me," he said, and he took Larry's silence as assent and stepped through the fence.

"Garland," he called. "Where are you? I've come a long way. It's time to talk."

Silence.

He advanced through the strange compound and was closing on the cabin when a voice came from behind him.

"Markus."

He whipped around, rifle elevated, finger on the trigger, and saw that he was aiming the gun at his mother.

She sat on the ground with her back against the fence, wearing jeans and a flannel shirt that was too large for her, making her look small inside of it. There was blood on her hand, and two streaks of it on her face, one beneath each eye, like war paint. Her eyes were wet and shimmering as she squinted into the glare.

Mark said, "Where is Garland Webb?"

"Inside. Unconscious."

"Take me to him."

"Markus..."

"Take me to him."

She sighed. "He's at the bottom of the steps."

Mark turned from her and advanced toward the cabin, and there he saw Garland Webb collapsed at the base of the wooden stairs. Webb's eyes were only partially closed, but he didn't react to the light. He didn't move at all.

Just shoot him, Mark thought, *just put a line of bullets in him from head to toe, and then get the hell out of here.*

But...no. It couldn't go like that. Not without Webb being awake and understanding who had come for him.

And why.

Mark knelt and removed the paracord that was still in his back pocket, the remnants of his work on Salvador Cantu, and used it to tie Garland Webb's hands around the bottom banister. Before he was done he heard footsteps and his uncle said, "Just me, stand down."

Mark returned to his work securing Webb. Satisfied, he picked up the rifle and stepped back. He was still looking at Webb when he heard Larry whisper, "Good Lord, Violet, what happened to you?"

Mark turned and saw Larry kneeling beside her.

"Markus, she's bleeding out."

Only when Mark went closer did he see the dark wound in his mother's stomach. She'd covered it with her hands before, but now Larry had pulled them aside and the damage was evident. Larry unbuttoned his shirt and folded it and pressed it gently to her belly, murmuring reassuringly. Her eyes were fixed on Mark.

"Markus," she said, her voice filled with both wonder and sorrow. "Look at you."

Mark couldn't find any words.

She said, "I'm so sorry about Lauren. I didn't know." Her voice quavered and tears shone in her eyes. "They never told me. I didn't know."

"Violet, stop talking," Larry said. "You're going to need to be still."

The blood had already soaked through his shirt. She tried to push him aside.

"I need to speak to my son."

Larry rocked back on his heels and looked down at his bloody hands, then up at Mark. His eyes said all Mark needed to know about the wound.

"I'm so sorry," his mother said. "I know she was lovely. In the—"

"Stop."

"—letters she was always so kind, so generous, and—"

Mark said "Stop" again before her words registered. Then: "What did you just say? In what letters?"

"I wrote to her. I knew you wouldn't answer. But there were things I needed to tell her. Things you wouldn't be willing to hear."

Mark knelt beside her, close enough that she reached for him but not quite close enough that she could make contact.

"She wrote the words *rise the dark* in a notebook. Did you tell her that?"

"Of course. I needed to warn you that the darkness was coming. Eli wouldn't have allowed it, but…you're my son. I had to warn my son. And tell her the things you don't know. About your gifts."

"Oh Lord…"

"You must have your father's gifts, because they were in the blood, passed from generation to generation. That's why I tried to encourage your contact with the spiritual world, took you to places like Medicine Wheel, because I knew—"

"Stop, please."

"—that you had rare gifts. I didn't know how to call them forward, what it would take. He wouldn't explain that…he didn't like to talk about it. He could sense death coming, though, he could and his father could and his grandfather and grandfathers even beyond him. I know that smoke is part of it. And voices. There will be smoke and there will be voices. Premonitions. That's in you, so I hope you can—"

"*Stop!*"

Larry lifted a warning hand. "For God's sake, son, she's dying! She doesn't know what she's saying."

Her eyes flicked to Larry and back to Mark. "I do," she said. "I know this. It is one of the few things I know for sure. I've always struggled with the truth."

Mark gave a harsh bark of a laugh at that.

"Markus," she said, "the things I did, things I told people, they weren't all lies. You need to—" She choked and fresh blood poured from her stomach. Larry swore and reapplied pressure. She closed her hands over his. "It wasn't all a lie. You're special. Once I had you, I had traces of it. Glimpses. But not like what's in you."

"Rest," Larry said. "Please, just rest." His voice was ragged.

She ignored him, straining to speak, blood in her mouth now. "I had to write to Lauren because I wanted you to know…about your father. You'd fled from me before I was willing to share it. His name was Wagner. Isaac Wagner. He was from Maine. A town called Camden."

She was struggling so hard to get the words out that Mark felt obligated to respond, even if this was just more of her madness.

"Camden," he said. "Okay. Thank you."

She seemed pleased to hear him say it, but when she tried to speak again, no words came. Just blood. Her eyes dulled, and when Larry gripped her shoulder she showed no reaction. She was still looking at Mark but couldn't seem to see him.

He didn't intend to reach for her. It was like the shot he'd made down in the gulch, an involuntary action, recognized only after it was done. But when he closed his hand around hers, her eyes brightened.

"I love you," she whispered. "Always. You were the reason for all of it. I had to find ways to provide for you."

There were so many terrible memories associated with his mother, but the terrible memory that came for him then wasn't one of her. It was of Lauren, his last moments with her, his last words. *Don't embarrass me with this shit.*

Mark said, "I love you too."

Did you hear that, Lauren? You deserved those words. Deserved so much more than them, deserved so much more than me. You were the light. The only one I had. I'm sorry. But I'm learning. I will be a better man because of you. I promise.

When he squeezed his mother's hand, she squeezed back, but her eyes were dull again.

Larry said, "Come back, Violet, come back."

She wasn't coming back. Mark felt her grip slacken, and he was about to withdraw his hand when she spoke.

"Don't kill him," she said.

He stared into her eyes, which looked absolutely lifeless. "I have to."

"No, you don't. Lauren doesn't need that. And she doesn't want that."

"You have no idea what she wants," Mark said.

"What the hell are you saying?" Larry asked.

"She doesn't know. Nobody can," Mark said to his uncle.

"Doesn't know what?"

"You heard her. Telling me that Lauren wouldn't want me to kill him."

His uncle reached out and grabbed his shoulder and shook him. When he did it, Mark's hand was pulled away from his mother's, and there was a fragile static jolt and then stillness. Mark blinked and looked at her face—dead; she was unquestionably dead.

"She's gone," Larry said. "She's been gone. What in the hell is the matter with you?"

Mark sat back on his heels. She was gone. He wiped at his eyes again, as if to clear something from them, and then turned to Garland Webb. He was motionless at the base of the steps.

Mark got slowly to his feet. He'd never felt less steady. Well, in Siesta Key, maybe. After the sheriff's deputy gave him the news. Maybe then.

He said, "You need to get out of here, Larry."

"I'm taking her."

"No. She'll slow you down."

Larry's voice was firm. "I'm not leaving her in this place. I'll set her somewhere clean. Not here."

Mark didn't argue. Didn't speak at all, in fact, while Larry gathered his mother's body gently into his arms and stood. She looked so small.

"She's my sister, son," Larry said. "I've not left her behind yet."

His uncle left without another word, carrying her body through the high fence and out to the world beyond. Then it was just Mark and Garland Webb.

71

Got him. The realization filled him with wonder rather than triumph. Pate had seemed untouchable since that first sighting in Jay's house, his implacable calm evidence of something he'd understood from the start—he would survive. He would win.

The train whistle shrilled, low and mournful, and Jay looked east and saw the oncoming lights and then looked south to the silhouette of his truck, to the trees where Pate had anchored all the cables for the trap.

Jay wouldn't have enough time to detach them from the towers. No chance. But he also didn't need to. Not anymore, not with Pate and the gun gone. If Jay could cut the cables at their anchor point and haul them across the tracks and over to the north side, he could just watch the train roar by, the engineer oblivious to the near disaster.

There was enough time left for that. The train was coming fast, but Jay could climb down faster. The fear was gone now and the old faith was back. He knew the steel better than most men knew their front steps.

Sabrina was safe, Jay was alone, and Eli Pate was not going to win any part of this day.

72

Mark found an ancient kerosene lamp in the cabin that cast a faint, flickering circle of light where he sat waiting for Garland Webb to regain consciousness. Inside the circle, it felt as if the world had condensed—or collapsed—and this place was all there was to it. The massive western sky, blanketed with stars, hung so close it seemed to be within reach, but the mountains had vanished in the blackness and all that remained was the circle of lantern light that contained Markus Novak and Garland Webb.

There was nothing else.

And yet they were not alone.

Lauren was between them. Mark understood that. She was somewhere in that light between him and this other man, and his always-receding memories of her felt closer, fresher, sharper.

More painful.

His mother's last words, the imagined words, the impossible words, would also not recede.

Lauren doesn't need that. And she doesn't want that.

He knew that it was true. Lauren had seen many horrors and studied countless more, yet her opposition to capital punishment had never wavered. Not for a second.

But still he could not leave.

He had to know how it had come to pass. How his wife and his mother, two people who had never met and who were separated by thousands of miles and many years, had come to die at the same man's hand.

Mark wished he could believe in coincidence. He had never liked that notion before, but now he wanted to wrap it around himself to keep the other possibilities at bay.

He couldn't, though. Not here in the mountains of his youth.

Garland Webb stirred a little and moaned. He was slumped over, held partially upright by the post Mark had tied him to, and Mark reached out and jabbed his belly with the muzzle of the rifle. Webb grunted and his eyes fluttered open. He looked directly at Mark, and then closed his eyes again. This happened several times before he registered Mark, and then he tried to rise. The knots caught him.

Mark said, "You know who I am?"

He was still foggy with the drugs, but he shook his head.

"Think about it," Mark said.

Garland Webb blinked at him, wet his lips, then stared at the ground as comprehension returned. Mark could see a change in his face.

"Novak." He slurred the name.

"Good. We were going to wait until you had it. I'm glad you're finally there."

Webb looked away from Mark, scanning in other directions.

"There's nobody else," Mark said. "You are alone."

When Webb's attention returned to Mark, there was hate in his eyes, and Mark was pleased by that.

"You told your cell mate that you murdered my wife. Bragged about it." Mark had a tremor near his left eye, but his hand was steady on the rifle. "What we need to determine is whether you told that man the truth."

Garland Webb smiled.

Mark's hand moved toward the trigger of the AR-15 almost involuntarily. He considered things for a moment, then set the rifle aside entirely and took the revolver from his jacket pocket.

"This is a Smith and Wesson thirty-eight. I think you're familiar with them."

Webb didn't say anything. He kept smiling.

"Why don't you tell me what you told the other man, Garland."

Webb did not slur when he said, "Go ahead and use the gun."

Mark shook his head. "I don't intend to use the gun. I would like you to talk."

"You think that will help you? Why? How would it help you?"

"I need to know if you killed her."

"Yes."

Holding off on the kill shot was incredibly hard. Mark gripped the .38 so tightly his hand ached.

"You've been told the truth all along," Webb said. "You're just missing one thing. Why she wanted to go to Cassadaga. You don't understand that, do you?"

Mark cocked his head. The reason had been clear. Dixie Witte was the reason. The case had been bound for Mark's desk when Lauren intercepted it and told Jeff London she'd take it because Mark wouldn't believe the psychic was credible.

"Why was she in Cassadaga?"

"Looking for your family."

Mark stared at him for a few seconds and then shook his head. "No. She wasn't, and she wouldn't have been. Try again."

"She was," Webb said simply. "You can deny it if you'd like, but I've never feared truth. I embrace it."

"Not in the courtroom."

"The courtroom is not my truth."

"Lauren knew nothing about my family other than that I wanted no part of them," Mark said. "And she sure as hell wouldn't have consulted a psychic to find them."

"Correct. She didn't want a psychic. She wanted a town."

Mark felt cold, remembering that house in Cassadaga, the fevered sickness of the place, its dark allure.

"Why would she want a town?"

"Because your mother had written her a letter about it." Webb was enjoying himself now. Enjoying Mark's face, whatever reactions he was seeing there. "Your mother is the reason any of us went to Cassadaga." His laugh ended in a cough. "Maybe that's not right. Maybe your father is the reason. He convinced her it was a special place. She convinced Eli. It suited him. He liked the energy there. For a while, that was going to be Wardenclyffe. Until your wife came, with the letter from your mother."

"She came for a case. I know that. I was part of it."

But he could see the possibility of truth here. A wider truth than what he'd known before. Fuller, like a sunrise revealing a world that was different than the one you'd imagined in the night.

Garland Webb spoke with mocking patience, as if talking to a dullard. "That case was the *excuse*. She really had questions about your family. Didn't you wonder why she stayed in town after she was done with Dixie Witte?"

Everyone had wondered. The car being on Kicklighter Road never made sense. Unless she had a second goal in town. A secret goal.

"Are you ready to laugh?" Garland Webb said. "Here's the best joke you'll ever hear, Novak. Your mother told your wife that when the dark rose, you two should go to Cassadaga for protection. I took that letter. It was the only thing I took. Feel better now? All the answers—do they help?"

His laughter was rich and delighted. Mark slapped the side of his face with the gun barrel. As soon as he'd done it, he felt rage thundering in his blood and he wanted to swing again and again, until Webb's face was nothing but a memory, the remains nothing but blood and bone fragments. He stilled himself with an effort. Webb grinned, forcing blood from his lacerated lips.

"It's about trust. You and your wife kept so many secrets from each other." He made a tsking sound. The blood bubbled on his lips when he did it. "No trust."

Lauren had knocked on the wrong door, and she had given her name. Mark's name. The one that she'd taken as her own, along with all that came with it. She had been killed for this. Because she had joined her name with his, and his past had infected her like a cancer.

Mark shook his head. "No. That is not why she died. That is not enough."

"But it's true."

"Why kill her?" Mark said.

Webb's indifference vanished and his face turned graveyard serious, almost innocent.

"Eli told me to."

Garland had done what he'd been told. How would that play in court? What deals would he be offered for testimony about Pate?

"If you're going to kill me," Garland Webb said, "let's move it along. I don't fear it. I welcome it. Death for a cause isn't death at all."

"You'll be a martyr, that's what you think?"

"I'll have died for a purpose. Not like your wife."

Mark grazed the trigger. He could feel his heartbeat in his fingertip where it touched the metal. A pulse like thunder, telling him to just end it. Lauren's memory urged him otherwise.

Evidence. Find the evidence that shows the truth. A bad detective builds a case, his wife would say, *a good one finds the truth.*

"How did you get her out of the car?" he said.

Webb seemed to consider not answering or perhaps telling a lie, but in the end he smiled again and said, "I called for help. I waved at her and shouted for help. She stopped right away. Got out of the car. Didn't even close the door. And I pointed into the woods and I said, 'She's drowning.' That's all I said, just those two words. I just needed to get her away from the road, but she *ran* away from it."

Lauren had stopped her car because of either trust or threat, the police had surmised, detectives torn between opposite theories. For the first time, Mark had heard an explanation that fit Lauren's character: she had been trying to help.

His mouth was dry and his head ached. He could picture the pearl-white Infiniti on the side of the road, door standing open. Could picture the way Lauren would have run. Without hesitation, without questioning.

She's drowning.

Yes, she would have run fast. She would have run right down that dark path.

His hands were shaking. Webb saw it and his smiled widened.

"Look at you," he said. "Just *look* at you."

Shoot him, Mark thought. *Kneecaps first, then testicles. Then find a knife and cut the flesh from him in strips. Skin him alive and leave him for the wolves.*

He worked saliva back into his mouth and said, "I will have to prove this, you understand? I don't think this confession will hold up in court. Not under your current circumstances. I suspect a judge would consider this unfair duress."

"You can't prove it," Webb said. "So you'll have to use that gun."

Mark shook his head. "Not an option."

"You are a very weak man."

"Maybe."

"Weaker than your wife."

"Absolutely. I always knew that."

Webb laughed again. His face looked bright in the lantern light. The sound of his laugh traveled through Mark's nerves like an electric charge. *You're making the wrong choice,* he thought. *It's like you told Jeff—who's to say what she thought in the last seconds of her life? Who's to know that her heart didn't change then?*

"You don't get to keep taking things from her," Mark said. "Lauren was so much more than I deserved. And she wanted to keep me clean. She died trying to do that." His voice had the sound of a wood rasp. "You don't get to take that from her. This would be an execution, and she did not believe in execution. She believed in hope. Lived for it. You live for fear. You don't get to beat her. You don't get to win."

"I've already won."

"I don't think so. You're going to prison. And who knows, maybe Innocence Incorporated will take your case. But I'll be working on the other side of it. You're going to stay in prison this time, Garland. God help me, I will see to that."

"She would have been ashamed of you. You're nothing like her. She had the kind of fight I enjoy. I wish I'd had more time with her. It just wasn't the right day for that. But when she saw the gun, her eyes, oh, they were wonderful."

Mark's finger slipped back onto the trigger. The gun shook in his hand.

"Most times, I see fear," Garland Webb said. "But with your wife? She was *angry*. When she understood what was about to happen? She wasn't afraid of me, she was *angry* with me, and she looked beautiful. You know the look I'm talking about. The two of you would have had fights, arguments. Then you made up, I'm sure. I bet that was fun. How could it not have been with her?"

"Shut the fuck up."

"You wanted talk! So I'm talking. And, yes, you know the look I'm describing. How the anger can actually be sexy. She radiated sex in that last moment."

"Shut the—"

"No, it's important for you to know the way she looked at the end! I want to complete the picture for you. All those hours you must have imagined it! What you're probably missing is the anger, and the sex. You imagined fear, imagined terror, but you were wrong. Trust me, after she saw the gun, she was something beyond gorgeous. I had to shoot her in a hurry, because time was an issue. I think she felt my hands on her, though. Yes, I would say the last thing she ever felt was my hands on—"

The bullet split the center of his forehead. His eyes went wide and his jaw slackened and his tongue fell forward a half a second before his head did. Bright blood streamed from his skull.

Mark looked at his own hand and back at Webb, and for a moment he was truly and deeply confused. Then he heard footsteps and turned to see his uncle.

Larry walked up beside him and came to a stop. He was crying without making a sound. He looked at Webb and spit on him, and then opened the cylinder of the revolver in his hand, shook the used cartridge out, and offered it to Mark.

"I couldn't let you listen to any more of that," Larry said hoarsely.

"I know what you were trying to do, and it was the right thing. But I couldn't let it go on."

Mark turned the bullet casing over in his fingers and watched Garland Webb's blood soak into the earth.

Larry said, "I didn't know your wife, Markus. I wish I had. But what you said, about how she died trying to keep you clean? I believe that. It's far too late in this life for me to ever get clean, but I can still help her with you. I just did."

Mark got slowly to his feet. He stepped over to Garland Webb's body and used the toe of his boot to roll the dead man's head to the side. The lifeless, empty eyes stared back. Mark spent a long time looking into them. Memorizing them. He knew that he would need the memory for many days to come.

For the rest of his life.

"She wouldn't have wanted it," he said. "But it should have been me who did it. It *had* to be me."

"Nothing has to be," Larry said.

"She wouldn't have wanted it," Mark said again.

"I'm sure I would've loved your wife. But I don't think I would've agreed with her on some of the finer points." Larry studied Garland Webb's corpse. "There may come a day, I suppose, when we'll know. If there's a God, Markus, I'll be curious what he thinks of this one."

Mark watched Garland Webb bleed out and half of him wished he'd fired the shot and another half wished it hadn't been fired at all. When he turned from the corpse and looked away from the circle of light, he was aware of the vastness of the night as if it were a new player in the scene. A cold wind was blowing out of the north, rustling the pines below them. Far off down the mountain, the blackness was broken by flashers.

Police en route.

"They're coming," Mark said.

"Yes."

Mark knelt and untied Garland Webb's hands, then slid the AR-15 over with his foot until the rifle and the body rested together. Larry watched in silence, understanding.

"Hell of a defensive shot I made," Larry said.

"You saved me with it," Mark said. "There's no lie in that."

Mark lingered with Webb's corpse for a moment, looking into those eyes. Then he turned away.

"Where is Mom?"

"She has the view." Larry pointed up the slope, to the high rocks above the plateau. It couldn't have been an easy climb.

"I'm sorry," Mark said. "I forced things in that direction, just by coming here."

Larry shook his head. "I'd rather have her there than here. That's the truth. And I don't think she was leaving this place on her own."

They walked away together, through the high fence and down the rocky slope toward the distant flashing lights below.

73

The radio had been silent for the last five minutes of the drive, but when Janell pulled onto the narrow lane that ran parallel to the railroad tracks and the power lines she saw a truck parked off the road, in the trees, and knew that it had to be him.

The relief she felt then made her eyes sting, and she blinked back the approaching tears. He had no use for tears, and after so long a wait, she didn't want to disappoint him when she finally arrived.

A train whistle shrilled to the east, and she realized, with a delirious joy, that she would be with him for the moment. When it all began, when the darkness rose, they would be together.

Just as it had always been planned and promised, in a place years and an ocean away from this spot in the mountains.

She drove as far as she could on the road and then left it, following the tracks in the grass that led to the truck, bouncing over the uneven terrain. The headlights captured a glint above the train tracks, and she braked hard and stared.

The cables were in place. Novak hadn't disrupted anything.

She slammed the gearshift into park, opened the door, and took off running toward the truck. Her eyes were focused on the truck and the tracks, and she never saw the thing that tripped her. One minute she was running, the next she was down, landing hard, a jarring impact that stole her breath. She rolled over and looked back to see what had caught her feet.

It took her a few seconds to understand that the twisted, blackened thing in the grass had once been human.

"No," she said, her voice clear and reasonable. It was not him. It absolutely could not be him. It was the climber, Jay, the last recruit, the one who'd be blamed for so much in short order, the man whose name the world would learn. The trusted worker who'd killed his wife and then turned on his country.

"Eli?" She sat up and looked into the darkness as she called for him. When he answered, all would be well.

It was silent until the mournful train whistle sounded again. The approaching train made the ground tremble.

She knew she should look at the terrible corpse again, look closely, but she couldn't bring herself to turn.

Not him. No, no, no, it is not him.

The voice came from the outer dark north of the train tracks.

"He took my wife."

She looked in the direction of the sound, but she couldn't see the man. He spoke again.

"He thought I couldn't do anything about it. He was wrong."

The lights of the oncoming train appeared, and in the increasing glow she could finally see the man. He was climbing down the tower.

She forced herself to look back at the body. At Eli.

The tears started then. Silently. She had not wept since she was a little girl.

Approach from the south, he'd said. *You'll see me. We'll watch the train go through, and then we'll leave....Together.*

The climber reached the base of the tower and came on, walking awkwardly, stiff as a spaceman in his strange suit. He took clumsy, stumbling steps toward the tracks. It was impossible that a man such as this could have killed Eli.

The climber said, "If you want to run, I'd start now. I'm coming over to cut those cables down, and I've got a gun."

The vibrations in the earth were stronger, the light from the train harsher. The moment almost at hand.

She got to her feet, stepped carefully around Eli's body, and ran to the stolen Yukon. Opened the tailgate and pulled out the shotgun and racked a shell into the chamber. Then she walked back toward the train tracks, the shotgun braced against her body.

When the man who'd come off the tower stopped on the north side of the tracks, she knew that he'd been lying. He had no gun.

"If you want to run," she said, "I'd start now."

He hesitated. She saw him turn and look to the north, to the place where distance and darkness would hide him if he ran.

Then he said, "It's been too long of a day for that," and started forward again.

She fired from the waist. The first blast of double-aught rattled into the gravel and sparked off the metal rails and he tripped and wavered but did not drop, stumbling on over the tracks as she levered another shell into the chamber and fired again.

This time he fell. His heavy boots caught the lip of the second rail and he didn't even get his hands out in front of him. He fell onto the embankment and slid down it, one gloved hand outstretched toward the grove of fir trees on the other side of the tracks. The cold wind rose with the sound of the train whistle, and the trees shifted gently and the earth shuddered beneath Janell's feet.

She wanted to go to him. Wanted to feel his pulse. She had the thought, brief and bold as a flash of lightning, that he would have a very strong pulse and that she would need that in days to come.

There was no time, though. The train was too close and there were more important tasks for her. The one thing she could not grant them was Eli's body.

It was crucial that they wonder and rush for explanations. Rush right past the truth.

74

J ay could taste blood in his mouth and he thought that there should be pain, but he couldn't feel it. Could feel nothing but the tremble of the earth, constant now, like a drumroll of the gods. He felt that and waited for the pain and when he could not find it he thought, *Of course, the Faraday suit.*

Saved again. The suit had kept the current at bay. Not at bay, exactly, that wasn't right. The suit had energized him. He had become the current, safe within it.

But it wasn't electricity. It was a gun.

Maybe. It seemed there had been a gun. Still, the suit made sense to him. You had to trust it, that was the first lesson. Because if you had no faith that you were protected, if you could not believe that there was a shield between you and the ground, you would make a mistake. Your last moment was promised then.

The earth trembled and rolled. He thought that he had forgotten something, failed to achieve something, but for the life of him he could not recall what it was. He'd been going somewhere, reaching out, a plan in mind, a goal. He was not supposed to be down on the ground.

Sabrina.

For a horrified moment, he was overwhelmed by the fear that Sabrina was not safe. But then voices whispered, hers blended with another's, a man's voice.

She is safe and well.

Yes, she was. Jay knew this. It was all that had mattered, up there on the steel.

I climbed, he wanted to tell her, *in the end I climbed,* and he knew that couldn't be the truth because in the end he'd found himself here on the ground, but it was hard to remember how that had come to pass, and the climb was vivid; the climb was victory.

He thought it strange to end in darkness. He had been sure that it would end with light, had always understood that, and for six long months he had even seen it—this life would end with a flash. Seen and gone, spectacular for the last moment.

He had known this and yet somehow he was down here on the ground and in the dark and in his own blood.

Then out of the trembling earth came a light. Brightening rapidly, like a dimmer switch being dialed all the way up, the thrum of the earth intensifying in proportion to the light. The sound was just like an oncoming train, but his mind called up a memory to make sense of what he could no longer parse in his pain-addled mind, a memory drawn from so many nights in so many storms, a knowledge of exactly what that combination of power and light meant: the system was back online.

The job was done.

The spectacular flash, when it came, was all that he had known it would be.

75

Mark was in custody when he learned the transmission lines had gone down. A tower carrying a half a million volts that fed the West was pulled down by a train that had then derailed and wiped out a second tower, and a third.

The first interrogations took place in a dimly lit police station. They were running on backup generators, and the overhead fluorescents were more than the generators could handle.

The detectives who asked the first questions about Eli Pate asked them from out of the shadows.

The investigators lost interest in Garland Webb's death quickly. Garland Webb they understood—or thought they understood. What they cared about was Wardenclyffe. How it had come to exist, who had been there, and who might still be alive. Garland Webb was not in that mix.

Neither was Jay Baldwin.

They'd found his body in the train wreckage. When they told Mark that, all he could see was Baldwin's anguished face in the darkness outside of his home, imploring Mark for one chance, for just a little more time.

And if you had the chance to go back and save her? If you could have made a deal to keep from losing her? What would you have been willing to do?

Mark had been answering questions for hours by then, and the detectives seemed to accept his exhaustion when he lowered his forehead to the tabletop and closed his eyes.

76

The body count was high, but it did not include Eli Pate.

In official statements, law enforcement suggested that his corpse had been destroyed in the carnage of the train derailment. That was not the news a terrified American public wanted to hear. They wanted the body.

They wanted proof.

Nearly a million people in the West were without power. What Pate had succeeded in—wiping out a transmission line that fed areas from Montana all the way to the Pacific and taking down another 107 poles once the lines were dead—was an unprecedented act of domestic terrorism, and the only good news was that the law enforcement agencies who wanted to talk to Mark were not the kind who cared about a stolen pickup truck or an assault on a thug like Salvador Cantu.

Or even the bullet in Garland Webb's forehead.

They wore assorted badges—FBI, Secret Service, military intelligence—and their questions often overlapped, but the focus was the same: How had Pate achieved it, and who from his group remained?

Mark couldn't help much, and neither could his uncle, but the questions kept coming, and the new faces kept appearing. The only information Mark gleaned from the process was a sense of why his mother had mattered so much to Pate. She was a recruiter, assembling the followers who bought into Pate's philosophy that the world needed a wake-up call.

This was the story the investigators understood and the story that meshed with what Mark had seen and heard firsthand.

It did not mesh with the public narrative. Already reports were coming in saying the attack had been engineered by a right-wing militia based out of Texas, though on social media, ISIS proudly and repeatedly claimed credit and promised that it was just the first strike.

"It's tense out there," one of the FBI agents admitted to Mark. "We've got to prove this shit fast, and the explanation needs to be ironclad."

Mark had been through two full days of interviews—a generous word; the more accurate one was *interrogations*—before he was given the chance to meet with Sabrina Baldwin. Even then the environment was bad, a conference room in the courthouse in Billings, and one that he was certain was bugged.

She didn't get many words out before the tears came. Mark held her hand, a hand that felt too hot, her heartbeat a steady throb against his palm, and he watched her cry and he thought: *This is the other road.*

Anything, he had told Jay, had told Jeff, had told whoever dared to ask and many who did not. That was what he would have done to keep Lauren from Cassadaga if he'd had the chance. Absolutely anything, including trading places with her. Of course he would have done that.

Now he watched Sabrina cry and felt her pulse beat against his hand and thought of the anger that could overtake him so often, a survivor's anger, the loneliness of the lost, and he said, "Jay was not selfish."

She lifted her head and stared at him with shimmering but outraged eyes.

"What are you talking about?" she said. "Not selfish? Of course he wasn't. It's not as if he had a choice."

Mark could see him again in the shadowed yard in Red Lodge. Could hear him begging for the choice. He wondered how it had gone for Jay up there on the tower with the train coming on, what other choices he'd made and why he'd made them. But he only nodded, because that was the right thing to do.

"He was a hero," Sabrina Baldwin said. "That's the only word."

"Yes," Mark said. He touched Lauren's dive permit briefly. "Yes, he was. And yes, it is."

77

It wasn't until the third day that Mark was allowed to see Lynn Deschaine. He'd been moved to a hotel in Billings that still had power. It was called the Northern, and it was a fine hotel if you didn't mind the police watch outside your bedroom door. His uncle wasn't as fortunate. Larry was still in a Wyoming jail, and by then it had become clear that the authorities intended to keep him there to ensure Mark's full and continued cooperation.

Lynn came by in the evening, wearing her badge for the first time.

"Are you ready to get out of here?" she said.

He was struck by how good she looked, how confident. She didn't have the shell-shocked expression of Sabrina. Only if she let her eyes linger on his could he see the imprint of Eli Pate and Garland Webb.

"You kidding? I didn't want to show up in the first place. But I don't think they're quite done with me."

"They're not, but they'll let you leave Montana, at least. You'll even be allowed to travel with me, if you're willing to try that again."

He was sitting in a chair beside a window that looked out on the refineries and railroads of Billings, and she was leaning against the wall. Loose, confident. Until her eyes lingered on his.

"Where would we be headed?" he asked.

"Virginia."

"There are some serious agencies headquartered in Virginia. The Pinkertons aren't one of them."

"I'm sorry," she said. "That was my cover story. It was all I had clearance to—"

"Of course. I'm sure I'll hear plenty of explanations in Virginia as to why nobody from your agency ever bothered to consult with the homicide detectives on my wife's case. But I'm not leaving without my uncle."

"You're going to have to."

Mark shook his head. "After what he did for me, Lynn? I'll sit in a cell if I need to, but he's not taking the fall for anything that happened."

"If you care so much about him, then you *definitely* want to go to Virginia. That's the only way I can speed things along, Mark. Help me, and I can help him. I was able to negotiate you out of here, but they'll spend a little longer with him, just because they don't need him to move forward."

"I don't see the difference between Larry and me in all this."

"He never met Janell Cole. That's one difference."

"She hasn't surfaced yet?"

Lynn shook her head. "And we want her. Badly."

"Badly enough to make a deal for my uncle?"

"They want the right fish, Mark. Not the other ones who got caught in the nets."

He hoped she was right. The idea of sitting down with anyone in Langley or Quantico wasn't appealing, but it was also the very least he owed Larry.

"What we need are people who can explain Eli Pate to us," Lynn said. "Where this attack started and where it ends."

"You seemed to know plenty about Eli, and Janell. Or was the story from Amsterdam all bullshit?"

"That was true," she said. "It's the first time he came on the international radar. He was in the Netherlands studying, and so was she, and he was arrested but she wasn't. When he walked out of prison after years of bizarre and intensive research, he seemed to fall off the map, but he clearly found his way back to her."

"Bizarre and intensive research?"

"He went into prison immersed in the work of Nikola Tesla. He emerged with several hundred pages of writings about the Kennedy assassination, 9/11, and Charles Manson. It seems he decided to reverse-engineer things—where Tesla wondered how the world might look with electricity, Pate became curious how it might look without it. The only constant presence in his life seems to be Janell Cole."

"I don't know how I'm supposed to help," Mark said. "Despite what you might believe, you really did hear all I know about Janell."

"All I'm asking for is your cooperation."

"And I ask the same for my uncle."

"You'll get it. The faster we get to Virginia, the faster I can get him out of jail."

He took a deep breath. "When do we leave?"

"Tomorrow at one," she said. "Police escort to the airport, but we get to fly all by ourselves."

"Hey, that'll be fun." He remembered the way she'd slept on his shoulder on the flight out. It felt like something from another life, the way Lauren did now. He looked away from her and out the window at the refineries. Her reflection was ghosted across the glass.

"I don't know if it matters to you, but I'd asked for clearance to talk more honestly with you the night it all happened," she said. "I trusted you by then."

He let a few seconds pass, and when he spoke, he was still facing the window. "Clearance," he said. "Sure."

"You're right to be angry with me. I lied to you. For whatever it's worth, I also thought you might be lying to me. Especially after you were right there with me, and then gone in the middle of the night, and they came to the door."

"I don't blame you a bit. Let's call it the cost of business, right? Neither of us trades much in trust."

"I disagree."

He looked back at her. Her confidence was wavering. Her posture hadn't changed, but something in her face had.

"What you don't know," she said carefully, "is the way I actually felt that night. And sometime, I'd like to tell you. If you want to listen."

He leaned forward, braced his elbows on his knees, and held her eyes. She didn't look away. At length, he nodded and said, "Down the road, if it works out, we could go somewhere by the water and have a couple drinks. We could talk there, the way we did the first time. But a little differently."

"I hope it works out," she said softly. "Somewhere down the road, as you say."

She seemed to want to say more, but didn't.

Mark rose. "Hell, it was my fault, anyhow."

"How's that?"

"I should have known you were full of shit. You're not a good enough detective to work with the Pinkertons. But for the government...that seems right."

A ghost of a smile crossed her face. "I'm building my résumé for the Pinkertons."

78

It had been five days on the road and she had slept only three hours per day. Speed was critical, because they had to travel a great distance, and as panic gripped the nation and rumors of new attacks spread, roadblocks went up in unpredictable locations.

Police were everywhere. Police, and the military. In Missouri, a militia group had taken control of a national forest campground, and a standoff with the FBI was building. In Kentucky, seven were killed in an attack on an army base. In New Hampshire, a husband and wife drove a van loaded with explosives into the statehouse and blew themselves up, wounding a dozen. For every incident there were a hundred threats; for every threat, a thousand rumors. Worldwide, terrorism alerts were raised to their highest levels, and police presence increased around the globe. More than twenty groups had claimed a role in the attack on the American electrical grid; a dozen more had been accused.

The fear virus was flowering, and if Eli had been alive to see it, he'd have reveled in the moment.

She avoided the interstates, sticking to back roads and using her map of the electrical grid as much as her GPS, because she knew the areas where they would be hearing the worst of the rumors. She was disappointed in the lack of action but held out hope. The seeds of fear had been planted and carefully tended and soon they would flourish.

In occasional breaks, she sent e-mails and posted on forums and social networks and then destroyed the devices, leaving a trail of shattered iPads and cell phones from west to east.

It was important that people heard from Eli. Important that they understood all the news they were being offered was a lie.

The only truth ever spoken had been between Eli and Janell.

Approach from the south. You'll see me. We'll watch the train go through, and then we'll leave.... Together.

And so they had.

While she drove, she talked, and took comfort in his presence. The smell of charred flesh, so repellent when she had gathered him into her arms in the sparking blue flashes and orange flames, had become tolerable by the time she reached the Mississippi, and it was almost comforting when she drove through New Hampshire.

On the morning of the sixth day she sat alone on the rocks, the mountains at her back, and watched the sun rise over the North Atlantic. Somewhere out across that water, over some three thousand miles of open sea, the harbor town of Rotterdam was already awake, the day well under way.

That was where she had met him. So long ago.

The memory brought tears to her eyes for the first time since she'd understood that the corpse at her feet was his, and she allowed them to flow. She cried into the rocks as the sea crashed and threw foam at her feet, and when the sun was fully risen and there was a golden glow across the water, she was done and she knew that she would not cry again.

Ever.

She looked at that shimmering golden line between sun and land, splashed over the sea like the careless paintbrush stroke of the gods, and she thought that it must lead back to the place where all of this had begun, to that crowded, sweaty pub with the cloying smell of fish, to a man whose eyes held all the secrets of the world.

Dead now. Burned alive.

This is Markus Novak.... We are long overdue.

She supposed the man named Jay Baldwin was to blame, but by now she'd learned enough from the radio to tell her that Sabrina Baldwin had escaped before Jay found his courage, and while the media was giving Sabrina and the agent named Lynn Deschaine credit for their survival, Janell could not be so gracious. What she remembered was that first message on the radio, the first slip on what soon revealed itself as pure black ice.

Each time she tried to accept that this was the way of the world and not her responsibility, she remembered Novak standing above her behind his harsh beam of light, her knives just out of reach, and then she heard his voice over the radio.

We are long overdue.

Yes. Already, she could agree with that sentiment. Already, it had been too long for them.

And his mother. The news reported her death, and it was probably true, which meant only that Janell had lost another chance, because Violet Novak deserved to die at her hand. She had lost Eli because of a woman who could not be trusted. He'd stayed in the West with her because she could not be trusted, and he had died because of that.

The sun had warmed the rock beneath her by the time the tide was high enough to put the small boat in. She carried what was left of the greatest man she'd ever known, what was left of the only true love she would ever have in this life, as delicately as possible. He was wrapped in a blanket, but the smell was still heavy, even against the ocean wind.

She wanted to go slowly, to linger with him, but she knew the risks. If his body was found, the questioning of the truth would cease.

That could not be allowed.

She motored out into the sea, enjoying the strength of the slapping waves, knowing how he had always loved listening to the immensity of the sea, a sound that told of its astonishing depths and promised its unfathomable power. Dormant power now, but it would rise again. It always did. And the fools who didn't listen to its promises would perish, and then they would settle back into their ways, only to be shocked when it rose once more. Year after year, civilization after civilization.

Always surprised by the power of the world.

She followed the golden light out, out, out. As far toward Rotterdam as was possible in such a small craft and with so much work yet to do.

She killed the engine and took a moment alone with the sounds of the sea.

Then she spoke.

"Your energy lives," she said. "You know that, right? You can feel it? In all of this?"

The waves crested and fell, crested and fell.

"They can't kill your energy," she said. "Can't trap it, can't guide it. They've merely released it from its latest form. So it takes a new form, resurrected and refocused, but still in motion. Onward it goes. You know this."

Spray soaked her, and the taste of the salt on her lips was perfect.

"And so I follow it still," she said. "Lead on. Always."

She gathered his blanketed remains gently, lifted him above the bow, and eased him into the water. The sea accepted him gratefully, and why not? Power understood power.

She watched as he sank slowly, watched until the blue-gray water had hidden any trace of him, and then she started the motor, turned the boat, and piloted it west, toward the rocky Maine coast, with the sun of the new day warming her back.

79

Mark and Lynn were at the airport by eleven in the morning for their flight to Virginia. Billings International—all four gates of it. The only restaurant in the airport was outside of the security gates. Once you were inside, there was a food counter that looked like it belonged in a bowling alley, but they served booze along with the hot dogs and nachos. The television was tuned to the news. A retired FBI agent was expressing his concern that so many groups were claiming the attack on the western electrical grid. A middle-aged couple was watching, and arguing. The husband thought it was ISIS, no matter what the government said. His wife didn't believe the government would lie about it. What was to gain?

Panic, he said. If the United States admits they hit us right in the heart of the country, it will be panic, and the stock market will collapse. That's all that really matters to anyone—the money.

She said she didn't think it was ISIS. If it was anyone foreign, it was the Chinese.

Mark closed his eyes. He was sitting in a chair with his hand in his pocket, touching the dive permit the police had returned to him and wishing for the spent bullet casing that they had not, when Lynn appeared with two bottles in hand. Moose Drool.

Mark grinned and straightened in the chair. "Montana's finest tempts you even this early in the day, eh?"

"Something *that* delicious? Obviously." She handed him one of the bottles and sat down beside him. "Cheers to a flight out of here."

They clinked bottles and drank and she made a sour face. "I have to admit I preferred the Rainier."

"Never admit that."

They finished the beers and then moved to their gate, pausing to check the flight-status monitors. Everything was on time. They were routing through Minneapolis. When Mark looked at the alphabetical destination list, his eye caught on one just below Minneapolis—Portland, ME—and his mother's voice returned to him.

His name was Wagner. Isaac Wagner. He was from Maine.

It doesn't matter, Mark thought. *I didn't have a father; I had a donor. His name and his history do not mean a thing. Not after all these years.* He turned away from the monitors and took a seat at the gate, leaned back, and closed his eyes. Lynn sat beside him, close enough that they touched slightly. Just a graze. The contact felt good in the way he didn't want it to, but it also felt comfortable. Hell, *he* felt comfortable. He'd slept no more than three hours at a stretch for at least six days now, and the weight of it was pressing on him. It was warm in the airport, and his eyelids were heavy. He felt himself beginning to doze, barely aware of the conversation around him and of the announcement that boarding for Detroit had begun, and he opened his eyes lazily, a sleeping cat's blink, checking on the surroundings before checking back out, and one of the passengers boarding for Detroit turned and looked in his direction, and while Mark watched, the stranger's eyes filled with whirls of smoke.

He sat bolt upright, moving so fast that Lynn gave a little shout. The stranger boarding for Detroit gave him a curious look too—from behind blue eyes. There was nothing abnormal about him at all. The smoke was gone. No, the smoke had never been there.

Obviously.

Of course it hadn't.

Lynn put her hand on his leg. "You okay?"

"Yeah. I just started to…have a nightmare, I guess. I expect I'll have a few of them from this place. A few more of them, that is."

"Trust me, I know," Lynn said. "I've woken up in cold sweats every night, feeling like the handcuff is still on my wrist."

He nodded and leaned back in the chair, but she didn't move her hand, and he was grateful for that.

My mother, he thought. *What a gem. My last words with her, and they give me nightmares. Couldn't have gone any other way with her, though. Whatever parting shot she offered, it was bound to mess with my head.*

He closed his eyes again, tried to find sleep again, but it was harder now. His mind was too active, bouncing from image to image, memory to memory.

There will be smoke, she'd said. *There will be smoke and there will be voices. Premonitions.*

It wasn't all a lie.

Even his uncle had heard that much. But for days now, Mark's thoughts had returned, time and again, to the impossible words he'd *thought* he'd heard. First from the man he'd killed on his way up the mountain, then from his mother after she was dead. He wanted to dismiss them but they continued to surface, just as the last words of Ridley Barnes had taunted him for months. *She doesn't want you yet.* Then came his mother's words, unheard by his uncle but so clear to Mark, so real. *She doesn't want that.*

Stress. It was stress and adrenaline and fatigue. The mind did funny things under great stress—this was well understood, researched, documented. It required no questioning.

Beside him, Lynn said, "Are you kidding me?"

He opened his eyes and followed her pointing finger to the monitor above their gate—the status had changed from ON TIME to DELAYED. The revised time was an hour later. Still enough leeway for their connection, but it would be tight.

"Beautiful," he said. "Want another beer?"

"Might as well."

Thirty minutes later, a crowd began to gather around the main status monitors. Nobody looked happy, and most of them were putting cell phones to their ears. Mark raised an eyebrow and Lynn frowned and they walked over to see what the situation was.

A third of the board had gone red with canceled flights. As they watched, several others went red. The screen looked more like a stock-market index than a flight-status monitor now, one city name after another ticking into the red.

"Unbelievable," Lynn said. "Let's go see what the deal is. Maybe we can reroute."

Mark followed her, but he was a step behind. He was a little dizzy suddenly, and there was the faint popping sound in his head, the one that had been blissfully missing for the past few days. By the time he caught up to her, Lynn was in midsentence with the gate agent, asking what the options were.

"I'm afraid it's unlikely you'll make it there today. Anything on the East Coast is a mess."

"Storms are that bad?"

"It's not weather. It's more outages."

Lynn's face drained of color.

"Ma'am? We can try to rebook you, I'm just saying that all connections are—"

Lynn turned from the gate agent before she could finish, stepping aside as the next flier pushed forward to ask the same question about rebooking. As the rest of the travelers at the gate began to rise from their seats and form into a disgruntled, muttering line and cell phones were put to ears all around them, everyone dialing the help numbers or travel agents who they believed could set this right, neither Mark nor Lynn spoke. They just looked at each other. They were alone amid the bustle, the only travelers not concerned only with scheduling.

He said, "It's a small airport. They're going to run out of rental cars fast."

Lynn nodded. "Let's get one."

Mark shouldered his backpack and they walked away from the gate together as the loudspeaker came on and a voice filled the room.

"Ladies and gentlemen, please bear with us here—there seems to be some trouble on the Eastern Seaboard..."

ACKNOWLEDGMENTS

First, foremost, and forever—thanks to Christine, who not only improves the books but somehow endures me while I write them.

I've had the enormous good fortune of patient and helpful early readers, and to the people who are willing to give of their own time and energy, I can't offer enough gratitude. But I can name you here!

Tom Bernardo, Stewart O'Nan, and Bob Hammel have hung in there with me through many drafts on many books, and their guidance and encouragement are always critical. John Houghton also brought a wonderful eye and a lot of passion to these pages, for no apparent reason other than his abundance of kindness. And I really can't say enough about the insight, questions, and patient discussions that Pete Yonkman provided. It's a better book because of him, and I also had more fun with it than I would have. Deepest thanks, Pete.

A few professionals played a role too. Namely, Joshua Kendall, who is a remarkable and tireless editor. If he has a point of fatigue, I haven't found it yet. It is a privilege to work with you, Josh.

Richard Pine's guidance and enthusiasm steers the ship on good days and bad. In fact, Richard doesn't really allow bad days. Much appreciated. Gideon Pine might not know yet how much he helps. Angela Cheng-Caplan better know how much she helps by now. Same for Lawrence Rose.

ACKNOWLEDGMENTS

Amanda Craft and Lacy Nowling help me to exist in the social media world. I'm grateful for their enthusiasm and work.

The teams at Little, Brown and Company and Hachette Book Group are consistently fantastic: Michael Pietsch, Reagan Arthur, Sabrina Callahan, Nicole Dewey, Heather Fain, Craig Young, Terry Adams, Garrett McGrath, and so many more.

Tracy Roe's copyedits save me time and again. Parse on, Tracy! Parse on.

Anything I got right about high-voltage work is thanks to Jim Staats and Jim Koryta. Anything I got wrong is my own fault.

The people of Cassadaga, Florida, couldn't have been better to me, and the same goes once again for the people of Cooke City and Silver Gate, Montana. Particular thanks to Doug and Cathy Pate, Bill and Carol Oriel, and Michael and Rita Hefron, as well as Troy "the Storechief" Wilson.

Most important, thanks to the booksellers, librarians, and all readers.

ABOUT THE AUTHOR

Michael Koryta is the *New York Times* bestselling author of twelve novels, most recently *Last Words*. His previous novels—including *The Prophet, The Ridge,* and *So Cold the River*—were *New York Times* Notable Books and national bestsellers and have been nominated for numerous awards. A former private investigator and newspaper reporter, Koryta graduated from Indiana University with a degree in criminal justice. He lives in Bloomington, Indiana.